Cast-Iro

Dominic Kearney

"Gripping, gritty and ultra-realistic. It's great – give it a go." - **Kevin Sampson, author of *Awaydays*, *Stars are Stars*, *Powder*, *The Killing Pool*.**

"Well-written, meticulously researched, gripping" - **Liverpool Echo**

"On the surface, the story of murder and betrayal and corruption, but its themes run much, much deeper. This is a powerful and gripping novel. I recommend this book, without reservation!" - **MJ Hyland, award-winning author of *How the Light Gets In*, *Carry Me Down*, *This is How*.**

"The novel is also a love-note, and perhaps a battle-cry, to Liverpool. Kearney treasures the detail with which he lays bare his city's streets, neatly traversing between the wealthy and the deprived, conjuring the fierce collective pride and desperation of a city in transition. A compelling debut." - **Sophie Scott, e-thriller.com's Thriller of the Month, February 2013**

"This is a hugely enjoyable book and an impressive debut novel." - **Liverpool-Noise**

About the author
Dominic Kearney was born in Liverpool in 1963. He studied English Literature at the University of Newcastle upon Tyne and taught English in Bristol and Manchester. In 2012, he moved to Derry, where he lives with his wife and brother. He writes regularly for the Irish News and Culture Northern Ireland, and is an arts reviewer for BBC Radio Ulster and BBC Radio Foyle.
Copyright ©Dominic Kearney 2012 2016
All rights reserved

Contact details:
kearney4@gmail.com
T @KearneyDominic
Facebook Dominic Kearney

The early hours of Saturday 8 December 2007
They burned the woman, before which they broke her. They smashed fingers and tore skin. Grey bones broke through brittle, creased skin as they smashed her face and teeth and jagged into her eyes, nose and cheeks.
Petrol soaked the cheap clothes, splashed onto the rubble around her. The first match extinguished as it arced to the body. The second caught the petrol, and flames leapt orange into the black, flashing vivid the faces of the four men. Then the flames fell back, a blue orange glow haloing the body, feeling into flesh, eating into flesh.
One man turned away, pressed a handkerchief into his face. Another man gripped his shoulders, tore the handkerchief from his grasp. "Breathe it in," he told him. "It binds us." And the stench filled their nostrils and mouths and wrapped into their hair and clothes.
At first they'd been tentative, timid. The broken bricks picked from the builders' rubble strewn all around had made no impression on the woman's face and hands.
Whispered disputes and hissed commands.
"No. Why should I? He did it. He can sort it. Leave me out of it."
"D'you not think they can trace you? Her fingernails? They can find us. They find me, yours'll be the first name I tell them." One man taking charge. One man the foreman. His gut churned at what he was doing. At the same time though, a spark of opportunity.
One of the men sitting stupidly next to the body. His legs apart, his overcoat open, his shirt hastily tucked back into his trousers. Another man dragging him to his feet, pushing the fragment of concrete into his hand, making him be the first to hit the woman. Another stumbling over the rubble to see what was taking them so long, shouting for answers then seeing the girl lying there and still not knowing what was happening. The blows became harder. Frenzied finally. Her skull was

smashed, teeth splintered, eyes pierced, hair matted with blood on the bricks, skin on the fingers ripped and torn. Apart from the driver they'd all taken turns on the woman. And then the third man had cried out and the other two had come running. The woman was lying on the ground. Her short skirt was hitched up around her waist. Her stockings had snagged and laddered and her knickers were caught round her right ankle, from where she'd stepped out of one leg. She wasn't moving.

Gasps for breath in the freezing air. Drink and bile forced back down the throat. Petrol splashed over the body. Then cheap clothes crackling in the flames. Flesh singed and black and burning and melting.

Back to the car. Silence at first, each man seeing and hearing and smelling and tasting his own version of the same film.

"For Jesus' sake speed up, will you?" the man in the passenger seat said. "We're bound to get stopped crawling like this."

The driver gripped the wheel as tightly as he could to stop his hands from shaking. But the trembling simply spread through his arms and up into his teeth and down his body and into his legs. He could barely press down on the pedal, but he did as he was told and brought the car up to 30. The two men in the back said nothing.

"Remember what I said," the man in the front said. "Get rid of the stuff in the bag."

"What should I do with it?" the driver asked.

"Think for yourself for once in your life, will you? Throw it in the river or something."

"Now?" the driver said.

"Not now. Can you not see how many people are around? Tomorrow will do. But just make sure you do it."

"Why do I have to get rid of the things?" the driver asked.

"Because we're the four fucking musketeers, aren't we?" the man to his left said. "All for one and all that shite."

One by one the driver dropped the men off, and then went home himself.

Chapter One

Sunday 9 December

Rachel Jack slowed the car to a halt by the pavement. The snow new on the road slewed the car slightly as she touched the brake. She hated driving in the snow and was too alive to the chance of ice and the car getting out of control. It was late too, just gone eleven, and the darkness made things worse to her. But this was work and that gave her a sense of purpose, like playing a part in a play or a game. That was why she felt nearly calm about this meeting.

Turn right opposite the entrance to the golf club: those were the instructions. The short road led to an oval roundabout, a large one, with big, imposing detached houses on the outer ring looking in. She'd driven round the roundabout and left it on the short road, back the way she'd come, facing the golf club entrance. All she'd have to do was get back in the car, turn left and she'd be on the road back towards Liverpool. The golf club was Royal Birkdale. It was world famous, she knew that. They held the Open there. The area was just Birkdale, although she'd once been told by a taxi driver that a lot of the residents liked the Royal, and would get into the cab and ask for Royal Birkdale, when they didn't mean the golf club but just some address in the area. She smiled as she remembered this. It was exactly what her mother would have done.

Rachel turned off the engine. The interior light came on in her car. She took her handbag from the passenger seat and pulled out the letter. She'd received it three days ago and must have looked at it 30 times. It was from Franny Sweeney. She knew who he was, of course. There couldn't have been many people in Liverpool who didn't. Gang boss, drug dealer, pimp, extortionist, brute, murderer. Had only been in prison once, though, and that was more than 15 years ago, when he was 19, for football hooliganism. The letter had been sent to her at her home address, not the newspaper office. That scared her but at the same time she knew it was meant to. She even tried to kid herself into appreciating it as a nice touch, subtle.

She looked at the letter without reading it. She knew what it said and she knew the address. She folded it, put it back into the envelope, put the envelope back into her bag and got out of the car. She stepped carefully through the snow but there was no need. It had started just over an hour ago and she was the first to walk on it, her tyre tracks the only sign of any car on the road.

The house was number nine. A brick wall about seven feet high ran along the border of the house. At each end of the wall was a heavy iron gate, for cars. Next to the left gate there was the smaller entrance for people on foot to use. There was a buzzer and a letter box alongside the gate. She pressed the buzzer and a voice over the entrance intercom said "Name?" and she said "Rachel Jack. I…" and was about to say she had an appointment to meet Franny Sweeney but the intercom switched off so the last word just hung there. There was a buzz and she pushed at the door and it opened. The drive arced from one heavy iron gate to another, past the double front door in the centre of the house.

The outside of the house was glowing with Christmas lights, along the eaves and around every window frame and around the double front door. On the roof a neon Santa Claus was slowing his six reindeer to a halt by the chimney. Two elves stood guard either side of the front door, which was opened as Rachel approached.

The doorman was in a tracksuit and trainers. He was about six feet tall and thickset and his eyes were feral. His hair was black and short and heavily gelled and he was wearing three sovereign rings on each hand. It was like a wardrobe assistant had dressed him for the part but that didn't make Rachel any less intimidated even though she tried not to show it.

"What'll it be?" she asked him. "*Silent Night* or *Once in Royal David's City*?" The false pitch in her voice was loud to her own ears but the doorman didn't react at all. He just pulled the door open further so she could step into the hall. More decorations. Streamers down one wall held columns of cards. A tree towered up into the well space next to the stairs. It was a real tree but it was hard to see any green for all the tinsel and baubles and decorations. Maybe three dozen presents, wrapped and finished with bows, were on the floor at the base of the tree. Tinsel had been wound round the banisters right the way up and along the landing rail.
Five doors led off the hall. They were all closed. From behind one came the sound of flushing, then the door opened and out came Franny Sweeney. Slim, medium build, brown hair, jeans, slippers, and sweat-shirt. Around 35 years old. Only the eyes showed him to be anything other than an ordinary young man who'd achieved a fair bit of success quite early in his life. The eyes were green and simply said don't cross me, whoever you are, and Rachel could tell they'd been looked into by kids at school who thought they might be tough and teachers who thought they could control him and policemen and truant officers and cellmates and rival gangsters and by one or two neighbours who came close to complaining that the flashing Santa on the roof was keeping them awake. With one or two exceptions the eyes had won each argument before it had really started and Franny Sweeney had won the rest.
Now he was closing the bathroom door behind him and looking at her.
"Someone likes Christmas," she said.
"My wife would tell you she does it for the kids, but it's really for her," he replied. "It's all I can do to make her wait until the start of December before the decorations go up. She just loves everything about Christmas. Don't you?"
"I'm Jewish," she said. "We don't do Christmas."

"You don't even get presents?" He seemed genuinely concerned.

"That would be a little unorthodox." Trying to sound tough.

"Still," Sweeney said, "peace and goodwill to all men, though. You can't argue with that."

"And women, I hope. Don't forget us."

"Oh no, never." Sweeney hadn't moved from the bathroom door. Now he came towards Rachel. "I was forgetting my manners, however. I'm sorry I didn't come to the door myself. Let's introduce ourselves properly. You're Rachel Jack of the *Liverpool Morning Mail* and I'm Franny Sweeney." He held out his hand for Rachel to shake.

"I know who you are," she said. She didn't take his hand. Sweeney's voice showed mock hurt. "What? You're not going to shake my hand? Are you wondering how many men I've killed with it?"

"No," Rachel replied. "I'm worried you didn't wash it before you came out of the toilet."

Sweeney smiled. "What am I meant to say now?" he asked. "That I like a woman with spirit? That I admire the fact you're not scared?"

"Don't worry," Rachel said. "I'm not stupid. I'm scared enough."

"Well don't be. I'm hardly likely to invite you to my house and then hurt you, am I? And don't imagine I lack all social graces simply because I'm a psychopath. Come on. Shake. Let's be civilised." Rachel took his hand and was surprised to feel it so small and soft. "There," Sweeney said. "That wasn't so bad, was it?"

Rachel let go of his hand. "I heard you say in court last month that you were a simple businessman. Now you tell me you're a psychopath. Which is it?"

"If I'm being honest," said Sweeney, "a bit of both. It pays to diversify. But you must know that, Rachel. You've been on the paper a few years now and you grew up in Liverpool.

You've heard of me you said, and you know my reputation. Look, why don't we stop playing these roles and just talk? I won't be the nasty gangster and you can stop being the tough hack. You don't have the eyes for it, anyway."

Rachel was relieved. She was scared and nervous and drained and the authority she felt inside herself as a reporter on the job was starting to fray. "What do you want?" The words were blunt and again she heard the pitch of her voice, this time showing her fear and tiredness. She looked at Sweeney hoping he hadn't heard it too but when she saw him smile she knew he had.

"Let's go through here," he said, pointing to a door on the far side of the hall. "We can't stand here all night. What kind of a host would that make me?"

Sweeney opened the door and motioned Rachel through into a large room that had been converted into a home gym. There was a running machine, a cross-trainer, a rowing machine, free weights, a chest press, a punch bag. On one of the walls in front of the running machine was a flat screen television. Rachel saw a sound system and saw also the room had been extended out into the back garden with floor-to-ceiling windows separating the room from the blackness and the snow outside. Sweeney pointed to what looked like a huge bath at the side of the room.

"What d'you reckon?" he asked her.

"What is it, a Jacuzzi?" she said.

"It's a wave pool," he said. "It creates a current you have to swim against. Swimming's the best exercise you can do – strength, suppleness, stamina. I do an hour a day in here. The weights are for the lads. They like to have big muscles." He turned round to the man who'd opened the door for Rachel, who'd followed them into the gym. "What is it you lot say?" he asked him.

"Buff," the doorman replied.

"Yeah, that's it," said Sweeney. "They like to look buff."

"Don't you?" Rachel asked him.

"You don't need big muscles for what I do, Rachel," he said. "Just nerve." His tone was light, matter-of-fact. He wasn't trying to impress or scare her at all. He knew he didn't need to try.

"It's getting late, Mr Sweeney," Rachel said. "What is it you want to see me about?"

"I read a piece you wrote about me, about my trial," Sweeney said. "When they threw the case out of court. It was good. I liked what you said about the police messing it all up. You said they turned the whole thing into a joke."

"They did. They didn't keep tabs on the evidence. There was no way they could have won that case." She took a deep breath. "You did it, though. You did kill that man."

Sweeney's reaction was one of mild irritation. He rolled his eyes and said, "I know that. You've no need to tell me. Look, you're missing the point. The coppers screwed it up and they knew that before the trial even started. So they tried something else. Crowley got up in court and lied. He swore on the Bible and then lied through his teeth. Just to get me."

"Crowley?" Rachel said. "The Assistant Chief Constable? He lied in court?"

"There. I knew it. Everyone loves Vincent Crowley, don't they? He's never out of the papers, never stops giving speeches. Travels the world, doesn't he? Always on the lookout for new ways of solving crime." Sweeney paused. "Your rag's turning into his personal fanzine. Well, he's not so clean."

"Can you prove he lied?"

"Make a nice story, wouldn't it? But no. I can't. I know it, though."

"So what's this all about?"

"1998, the crime figures for Keighley. Remember them?" Sweeney asked her.

Rachel hesitated. She hated not knowing something and hated

admitting not knowing something even more. "Go on," she said.

Sweeney smiled. It seemed to Rachel he was always smiling. "You can admit you don't know something," he said. "It's not a crime, you know."

"Just tell me," she said.

"Don't be so tense," Sweeney said. "Maybe you should have a swim. Relax you."

"Sorry. This whole situation…" Rachel stopped herself before she started confiding in the gangster in front of her. "Please. I don't know anything about the 1999 crime figures for Keighley."

Sweeney corrected her. "'98. And don't apologise. I'm surprised, though. A rising star like you…They were impressive, very much so. They attracted a lot of attention. And some say they got Crowley his promotion."

"What do you mean?"

"You really should do more research," Sweeney said. "Crowley was high up in the Keighley force. On the fast track. Like yourself in many ways." Rachel stared at him. "You're highly regarded, Rachel," Sweeney said. "And not just by me. Lot of people say you're ready for a move up onto one of the nationals. And I know you fancy the idea yourself." He paused. Rachel wanted to say something but the words didn't come. "I do my research, Rachel Alice Jack. I don't invite just anyone into my house."

Rachel forced herself to recover the poise she'd felt when she'd first walked up the drive, an age ago now. She wasn't used to feeling like this, to having her reactions shifted and manoeuvred so easily. Especially not when she was working, when her job gave her an assurance she didn't always have at other times. "What is it you're telling me?" she asked.

"You go and speak to a friend of mine," said Sweeney. "Name's Billy Jackson. He's in Strangeways. You should be able to catch him any time. He's in most nights. But don't leave it too long. He's out in six weeks."

"What will he tell me?"

"Now, then. You'll just have to ask him, won't you?" Sweeney looked at her and smiled. "Now, if you don't mind, it's time for my swim."

"What?" said Rachel. "Oh, yes, of course. I'll be going."

"Unless…You can always join me if you like."

"I can't swim," she lied.

"And there was me thinking reporters liked going against the tide."

Rachel was struck by a sudden thought. "Why me?" she blurted out. "What is it you want from me?"

Sweeney's voice was calm, and that's what Rachel found most chilling. "Just do your job, that's all. Expect a visiting order to arrive in the next day or two." He nodded to the doorman, who touched Rachel on the arm, making it clear it was time to leave.

Rachel didn't move. "Allen," she said. "The editor, Hugh Allen. He and Crowley are close. He'll never print anything against him."

Sweeney shrugged and smiled. "You do your job right and he won't have any choice. That's why I'm doing it this way. It'll be sweeter to watch his very own fanzine bringing him down." Still Rachel didn't move, even though the doorman was trying to steer her to the door. "You didn't answer my question," she said. "You didn't say why me."

"I have an eye for talent," Sweeney replied. "I like to nurture it. Makes me feel I'm putting something back into the community." He chuckled.

"And what if I let you down?"

Sweeney's smile left his eyes. "You don't have that choice," he said, and Rachel felt herself gripped by a chill that would stay with her.

She let herself be pushed gently on her way. As she reached the front door, Sweeney called after her. "It's seven, by the way," he said.

Rachel turned round. Sweeney had taken his sweatshirt off and Rachel could see his chest was firm and his stomach was flat. Nothing ostentatious, he was no gym monster, just a lean, fit, quick, dangerous man. "Seven what?"

"Men I've killed with these hands," Sweeney said. "I've ordered the death of more, of course, but it's seven personally."

"Including the one Crowley lied in court about?"

Sweeney grinned and rolled his eyes again. "You're right. Eight. Mind like a sieve. Happy Holidays."

Outside, she walked to her car. Instead of getting in, though, she walked straight past it and over the Liverpool Road to the entrance to Royal Birkdale. There were no gates or fences, just a road wide enough for two cars, and the land undulated low and sandy and gentle out over the course to the beach and the Irish Sea. The snow had stopped but the wind knifed into her eyes and face. When she turned back to the direction she'd come from she couldn't see Sweeney's house but she could still sense the glow of the neon Santa in the black sky.

Rachel was 27 years old. A reporter with a big future they all told her. This was proof of that, she thought, this might be a real chance to make a name for herself. She was clever, confident and impatient for success, but panic and fear had always run parallel with that impatience. When she was a girl, she regularly became so nervous before school that she would be sick. Same at University, same in this job. Once done, that was it, she was fine. She wouldn't try and take the day off, she wouldn't avoid work. She was secure and sure of herself, and even when she was rightly nervous, as she had been in the gangster's house, she could draw strength from her intelligence and from the job she was doing. In some ways she felt the job gave her a sort of invulnerability, so she could cope with people and situations that she would have struggled with in other circumstances. But still she would be sick, always just before the working day started, in the ladies' toilets at the *Mail*'s offices. She was used to it now and thought little of it. It was a habit, like some people need a cigarette or a coffee first thing in the morning before they could function.

Now, calmly, detached really, she knelt down on the sharp grasses at the edge of the course and vomited. Still kneeling, she realised this was the wrong way round, she should have been sick before meeting Sweeney. Then she understood it simply meant there was worse to come. She retched again. Then she stood up, wiped her mouth, went back to her car and drove back to Liverpool and the house in Childwall where she still lived with her parents.

Chapter Two

Tuesday 11 December
LIVERPOOL MORNING MAIL, Front Page
CITY GEARED FOR CULTURE LAUNCH
Everything is in place for Liverpool's reign as Europe's Capital City of Culture next year, organisers promised yesterday. With only weeks to go before the launch of the year of events, fears that the city was not ready have been quashed.
"The next fortnight cannot go quickly enough," said Howard Searle, head of Culture 08, the organisation responsible for the success of the year. "We're itching for the whole thing to start. This will be better than any other city's time as Capital of Culture and we're ready for the world to see the best that Liverpool has to offer."
The opening ceremony will be held on the steps of St George's Hall on New Year's Eve, with a fireworks display beginning at the stroke of midnight. From then on, events will be held in venues throughout the city, including concerts, festivals, poetry readings and theatrical productions. Many of the city's leading performers will be returning to Liverpool to perform. An extra million tourists are expected to visit, boosting the city's coffers.
By a Liverpool Morning Mail Staff Reporter.

The offices of the *Liverpool Morning Mail* were open plan. There were partition walls, screening off groups of desks, but the partitions were low and easy to look or speak over. Recently, one of the marketing managers had tried to introduce hot-desking, where the employees would take a different desk each day, would work wherever they found themselves, but the idea hadn't caught on. Everyone liked their own space, their own routine, and people liked to personalise their spaces – photographs of children, husbands, wives, football pennants, cartoons torn from magazines and pinned on the partition walls.

Susan Clarke always went to the same desk. It was tucked away in a corner, unusual because it was one of the few desks in the office that stood alone. Susan sat there now, facing a wall, with another wall to her left and a partition wall to her right. Apart from her computer and a telephone, the desk was bare: no photographs, no personal items, no post-it notes stuck to the side of the computer screen, not even a coffee cup. She sensed the deputy news editor making his way across the office and she knew he was coming to speak to her. She didn't know what he was going to say but she knew it would be a complaint, another little thing she'd messed up.

She started going through the motions, knowing the deputy news editor would soon be standing behind her. She switched the computer screen on, took her notebook out of her bag, placed it on her desk, opened and closed a drawer, picked up the phone and held the receiver between her shoulder and cheek. She flicked through the notebook, pretending to look for a number.

A copy of yesterday's paper was slammed down onto her desk. The deputy news editor, Trevor Bassett, had finally reached her. A stupid, little nobody, Susan thought, a talentless little creep who couldn't find a story, couldn't write one, probably couldn't even read one. He was waiting for her to turn around, so she didn't. She let him stand there, snorting his breaths out, ready with the tirade of words that he'd been practising in the walk from his desk, just like all the others, a buffoon who thought shouting, swearing, bullying and misogyny were the keys to a successful career in journalism.

"Are you going to do me the favour of turning round to look at me?" He spoke in snarl that was weak but was the best he could do. Susan didn't move. Her head hurt with a low pain that was with her as often as not these days and her skin felt dry and tight and brittle. She sometimes felt she was on the verge of screaming or crying but always managed to keep from doing so, just, at least until she got home.

Bassett gripped the back of her swivel chair and spun her round to face him. He put his hands on the armrests and leant down into Susan's face. Susan felt detached, certainly felt no fear of this man pushing his face into hers.

"Do you know how I've just spent the last 15 minutes?" His teeth were gritted and he'd lowered his voice to a violent whisper. Susan wondered what he wanted her to feel and say. She felt detached, almost like she was watching the scene play out from the other side of the room, with the sound turned down.

She said, "Not brushing your teeth." Her voice was toneless, mechanical, no intonation, just the words.

Bassett kept his face close to hers but pointed with his right hand to the paper he'd slammed onto the desk. The *Mail* was a tabloid. This one had been folded open to a page near the middle and then folded again crossways. The crease through the middle had been laid sharp. Bassett had slid his fingers and thumb over it again and again. Susan saw this when she leaned her head left to see what Bassett had pointed at. The sharp crease is to show the strength of his anger, she thought. Then it struck her, when Bassett didn't speak, just kept on pointing, that he didn't know what to say next. She realised he hadn't planned to spin her chair round and it had thrown him, leaving him to try and ad lib.

"Could you get your face away from my face?" Susan said. "Could you stand up, please?" Even to her own ears, her voice sounded strange, the phrasing odd, the intonation robotic almost.

Bassett stood up, slowly. He kept pointing to the paper. Susan looked at it more closely now and saw a picture of two schoolgirls in sports kit, holding a trophy between them. They were grinning broadly. Beneath the picture was a caption and then a short piece beneath that, four paragraphs, no more.

"I've just spent the last 15 minutes on the phone with her mother," Bassett said. "I'm a busy man. I don't have time to waste like that."

"Which one?" Susan asked. When Bassett looked at her puzzled, she said, "Which girl's mother was on the phone? The girl on the left or the girl on the right? As we're looking at it, I mean." Then she added, "I know you're busy, Gordon. You're deputy news editor."

"Yes, I am," Bassett said. "And it doesn't matter which girl. What matters is you couldn't get the name right. It's Keeley, not Kylie. A simple four par filler and you couldn't get the bloody name right. I don't know why we keep you on. And don't tell me about brushing my teeth. Your breath stinks. You smell like a brewery."

"You should have said that earlier, when I made my comment," Susan said. "Now it doesn't have any real impact." Her words were combative, goading, but, again, there was no tone. No sneer, no aggression. She felt like she was listening to herself reading the words aloud, just going through the motions and struggling to change.

"I do know why we keep you on," said Bassett. "It's pity."

"Have you just remembered that or finally worked it out?" Susan asked. "A minute ago you said you didn't know why." When she spoke again it was the first time that morning there was any emotion in her voice, and she no longer felt like she was listening to herself speaking out loud. "Anyway, pity'll do." She pushed her chair back against the wall. "I'm sorry about getting the name wrong. Do you want me to ring the mother back?"

"Don't bother." Bassett's voice still held the spit and snarl. "You can do this instead." He handed Susan a slip of paper with an address written on it. "They found the body of a whore down near the river behind the Northern Warehouse. You know, where that new hotel's going to be? Go and cover it."

"How do you know she was a prostitute?" Susan asked.
"She just is, alright? And don't go on a crusade about it. Keep it short. It'll probably be tucked away on page nine."
"Why?" Susan asked. "It might be a murder."
"Then it'll definitely be page nine. Even sitting hidden away over here, you should know how the boss feels about this capital city of culture business. He's not going to let anything get in the paper that might make Liverpool look bad. Not without a fight, anyway, not for some whore, and certainly not for some whore found on the site of a big new development."
"Why do you keep using that word?" Susan asked. "Why not say prostitute, if you've got to call her anything?"
"Don't tell me how to speak," Bassett said. "Just get down there. You're only doing this because everyone else is busy. And your boyfriend said to send you."
Susan began to speak. "My boyf…" Then she stopped herself. She stood up, picked up her notebook, bag and coat and walked away from Bassett and her desk.
She walked into the ladies' toilets and stood in front of one of the mirrors. Her face was lined, her hair was flecked with grey and badly needed a cut, her clothes were dull, plain. Still and silent she started to cry and simply watched the tears come down her face, arms hanging loose at her sides.
Her boyfriend. He meant Dalton. Gerry Dalton, assistant editor of the paper. He'd been the last of her flings, the one that had pushed the patience of her ex-husband too far, or his family anyway. Peter had always needed someone else to make him reach a decision. That was five years ago now, when she was 41.
She looked at the face staring back at her and thought about those five years. Gerry Dalton had been the sports editor back then, and she'd been in charge of the features page. He had risen up the ladder while she fell like a stone. She'd been a golden girl who'd known only success as a news reporter and who turned the features pages into the envy of every

provincial paper in the country and more than a few nationals too. She'd had no time for soft stories, articles about creative decorating or the ramblings of some superannuated hack harking back to the time when coppers clipped you round the ear and everyone left their back doors open. She set up a special team of reporters and oversaw hard-hitting, in-depth investigations into everything a city like Liverpool had to offer – gang violence, drug abuse, misuse of council power, the selling-off of school playing fields, prostitution, the growing gun culture.

And she'd had fun too. Too much fun. She'd drunk too much and stayed up too late and went out too often and didn't let a little thing like a husband stop her from seeing other men if she wanted to; didn't let a little thing like a son stop her either. But everything stopped when the divorce proceedings started, a day or two after her husband, Peter O'Hare, arrived back at their house to find her in bed with Gerry Dalton, her son Michael asleep in his bedroom along the landing.

She tried and failed to stop herself from thinking about the divorce and the custody case, when the judge took no more than five minutes to decide that Michael should stay with his father, and she shut from her mind the faces of Peter's family taking up so many rows in the courtroom. The O'Hares, a big Liverpool Irish family, all ranged against her, their faces smug and full of contempt. They'd even enlisted their parish priest to join the fight against her and she'd had nobody on her side. Her mother was dead, her father refused to make the journey up to Liverpool from Hampshire, her brother had stayed in Hong Kong, hadn't even telephoned to see if she was okay. No, the O'Hares won that day in court, as they'd been planning to win all along, from the moment Peter had first taken her to visit them. Susan was all wrong. She was too old, too clever, she wasn't from Liverpool, she had no Irish blood in her. She wasn't even a Catholic. Not that that had stopped Eugene, Peter's father, from making a pass at her one

Christmas though. "What's the matter, Susan, love? From what I hear, you're not that fussy."

It was all her fault, she knew that. There was no-one to blame but herself. And now here she was, 46 years old, with a job she was always a couple of mistakes away from losing, a son she hardly ever saw, and a drink problem she refused to admit to. She wiped away the tears and ran the cold tap, splashing handfuls of water onto her face again and again. She wasn't wearing make-up so there was none to smudge. As she did so, she heard retching from behind a cubicle door, then a spit. Then the toilet flushed and the bolt was pulled back and Rachel Jack came out of the cubicle. Slim and just under 5'4, her hair was jet black and cut short, boyishly, which only served to emphasise how pretty she was. Flecks of sick clung to the corners of her mouth.

Rachel looked at Susan's reflection in the mirror and briefly held her stare then, embarrassed, went to a basin and began to wash her hands, head down. Susan, despite the fact she'd just been standing there crying, felt no embarrassment.

Susan looked at her watch; it was just after 9.30. "Bit late for you," she said.

"I don't know what you're talking about," Rachel said.

"It's gone half nine," Susan said. "You normally finish throwing up at least an hour before now."

"How do you know about that?" Rachel snapped. "And what are you doing? Got a flask in here?"

"Why would I keep a flask in here?" Susan said. "Wouldn't it make more sense to keep it in my handbag? Besides, I don't drink nearly as much as people seem to think. And never in work. If you're going to insult me, you really should do your research."

Susan's words echoed what Sweeney had said to her the other night and made Rachel look up sharply from the basin. "What do you mean by that?" she said. "What made you say that?" She heard her own voice and realised she was almost shouting.

She felt brittle and jumpy, with no control over her words or her reactions.

"What's got into you?" Susan asked. "What do you mean what made me say that?"

"Forget it."

"Look," said Susan, "I'm sorry if I upset you. What I said about you being sick came out wrong. What I should have said was…"

Rachel interrupted her. "Drop it! You're a has-been, some old soak who…" The words stopped as she heard what she was saying. Her next words lacked all energy or conviction. "Just leave me alone. Understand?"

"I understand." Susan dried her face with a paper towel, picked up her bag and left the room.

Alone, Rachel slammed the hand-drier with the heel of her hand. She fought to calm her breathing and control the tremor of her muscles. Like Susan, she had no idea where that outburst had just come from.

Chapter Three

The *Mail* offices were on the edge of the city centre, just across the dock road from the River Mersey. The Northern Warehouse was less than half a mile away, up the river and on the other side of the road. Susan decided to walk. It would keep her out of the office for longer and it was a good day to be outside anyway. The sky was bright and clear and blue and the air was cold and fresh. Susan was glad of the icy wind that whipped in over the water. It sparked again in her the intermittent desire to take hold of herself and start living better. She hated that her mouth and skin were always dry and her head was always fuzzy and clouded. She never quite had a hangover, no splitting headaches or nausea, but a bottle of wine a night kept her on the verge all the time and made sure that body and mind were always a little lank and dull, and she'd started to notice a slight shake in her left hand when she held a cigarette to her lips.

No, she'd start to do things differently. She'd eat, what was it, five portions of fruit and vegetables a day. She'd at least cut back on the cigarettes and she'd carry a bottle of water round with her. Everyone else was doing it, sipping regularly, going to the water cooler in the office. And she'd moisturise too; she was 46 but looked 10 or 12 years older. Then she remembered how she'd said the same things to herself yesterday and the day before and last week and last month and last year. But she'd do it soon – maybe tomorrow, maybe if someone just gave her a nudge, a human touch. She crossed the dock road and walked down to the railings by the river. She'd give it a minute or two before heading for the warehouse.

Construction work was going on all over the city centre and the sky was full of cranes. Some sites were being cleared for new developments, while in other cases facades were being kept intact as the interiors were gutted and boxed. Investment was flooding into Liverpool as it hadn't done for years and the *Mail* was gleefully reporting it all. Every day the front page heralded some new scheme or other and the inside pages were full of artists' impressions and architects' visions. Setbacks, like hold-ups to the proposed tram scheme, were tucked away deep inside the paper or became the focus of yet another *Mail* crusade to force action from those holding the purse strings in central government. And always grinning out from some picture or other, surrounded by city councillors, dignitaries, civic leaders, development agency bosses and general movers and shakers, was Hugh Allen, editor of the *Liverpool Morning Mail* and champion of all things Merseyside. When the announcement was made that Liverpool would be the European Capital of Culture in 2008, Allen had greedily grabbed the glory, as if it had been down to him and him alone. Of course, he'd made sure Gerry Dalton's byline was at the bottom of any articles giving him the credit, but Susan knew Allen had written them himself.

Susan looked around at the road junction near where she was standing. To her left ran the dock road, past the Pier Head and the Liver Building and the Albert Dock. Behind her was the business district – Business Quarter, Susan remembered it was called now, one of about five or six quarters the city was divided into – between the *Mail* building and the new Radisson Hotel and Beetham Tower, whose flats for sale filled the *Mail*'s property pages. Head right across Scotland Road, you reached Everton and Anfield and Kensington, areas of the city that remained poor and squalid, as yet untouched by new investment, on neither the Beatles tours nor the City of Culture map.

She set off away from the city towards the Northern Warehouse, along the dock road, the river to her left. Money was creeping up this stretch of the river, but it was still at best dilapidated. She walked past shabby buildings, low and ordinary, whose use was uncertain and temporary. There was a transport café and a derelict pub that still announced Irish theme night every Friday.

All these buildings would go, Susan knew. They were too shabby and dull to exist in the new Liverpool. Planners were itching to get to work on them, to create concert venues, office blocks, skyscrapers full of open-plan apartments for cool young professionals who wanted views over the Mersey to the Wirral and the Welsh hills. The idea was to create a new waterfront for the 21st Century, from the mouth of the Mersey south all the way to Garston and Speke, that would match the best developments in the world – Bilbao, Shanghai, New York even. Nothing would stop the development. There was plenty of work still to do, but they had a good start. The Albert Dock, the Liver Building, the structure that housed the Mersey Tunnel's ventilation shaft, all wonderful buildings, all overlooked by the two cathedrals that stood on top of the hill at the other side of the city centre. And Susan couldn't argue with it; it was all good for the city. It was just that she couldn't feel a part of it, either. She was too old and too worn down by life. She shrugged off these thoughts as she got nearer to the Northern Warehouse. She spent too much time alone with her thoughts and the consequences of all her mistakes and bad decisions.

The Northern Warehouse was one of the later additions to the riverside. Built in the 1920s, its architecture was severe and utilitarian, with vast high walls unbroken by any design feature or decoration. Smaller than the Albert Dock warehouses further down the river, it was still substantial, if deliberately less grand than its Victorian counterpart. It was in fact two buildings, separated by an alleyway at ground level, but joined higher up by a series of enclosed walkways.

It was in this alleyway between the two halves of the warehouse that the body had been found. By the time Susan arrived, the body had been taken away. All the photographs needed by the scene of crime officers had been taken and the only sign that anything had happened were the two officers clearing police tape from the entrance to the alley.

"Is this where she was found?" she asked one of them, nodding towards the alley.

"That's right," came the reply.

"Anything you can tell me?" she asked, showing her press badge.

"You'll have to ask at the station. DI Nolan's in charge of the case."

"Susan?" She turned at the sound of the voice from behind her, knowing exactly who she'd see.

"Peter? What are you doing here?" Her ex-husband, Peter O'Hare.

"I'm working on this site," he said.

"Me too," Susan replied. Then she added, "You look well. Really well." He did too. He was 42, four years younger than her, but he looked no more than 35. His hair was thick and blond with no signs of grey. Tall and slim, his face seemed more boyish than she remembered. It had been over a year since she'd seen him in the flesh. On the increasingly sporadic occasions she could bring herself to see the son they'd had together, Peter's father or mother or one of his sisters would bring him Michael round to meet her.

"You too," he said, softly, trying to mean it.

"Liar. I look bloody awful. Divorce suits you better."

Peter smiled. "You've said that every time we've met since it happened."

"Well, I wouldn't want to disappoint you." She paused, feeling awkward, and looked around at the alley, then back at Peter. "I'm here about the murder."

Neither Peter nor Susan had noticed the man approaching from the main road, and they both jumped slightly when they heard him shout. "No one said anything about a murder." His voice dropped a little when he reached Peter. "No one said anything about a murder," he repeated, looking straight at

Susan. "It's just a dead woman, a dead whore."
"Hello Eugene," said Susan. Susan had always been amazed at how perfectly Eugene O'Hare, her former father-in-law, fitted the stereotypical description of the owner of a building firm. Shorter than his son, at about 5'10", Eugene O'Hare was red-haired and pale, apart from the blood vessels burst by too many pints and too many shorts. He was fat, but his broad frame carried it well, increasing his sense of power and strength. His arms and shoulders were muscular, straining the seams of his camel-hair overcoat, and his hands were big and calloused. He was a mean man, cruel and quick with his fists, and he always said he'd do anything for his family, that they were the only ones that mattered. To be fair to him, Susan thought, that was true. He might not show it the way she wanted, but he loved his grandson especially. He'd come to Liverpool in the 1960s from Ireland, bringing his wife, Imelda, with him. She'd raised the children while he built up the business, starting as a labourer then setting up on his own. Susan sometimes wondered if his Irish accent was even stronger now than when he'd first arrived in Britain.

"What do you want?" Eugene O'Hare's voice rasped as he spoke. He'd walked quickly down from his car, speeding up when he recognised Susan. He lit a cigarette as he struggled to get his breathing even again. "You're not bothering my son again, are you?"

"Dad," Peter began.

"It's okay, Peter," said Susan. "I don't know what you mean by 'again' Eugene, but I don't suppose it matters. I'm here because of the body that was found."

"Just some tart," said Eugene. "She'll have taken an overdose or something."

"The police said she'd been beaten and burned, Dad," said Peter. "So that does make it murder, Eugene," said Susan.
"Well, then," Eugene said, "who cares, eh? Just some tart."
"Everyone's so sure she was a prostitute," said Susan.

"What else would she be, eh? Down here?"

"Why are you so bothered anyway?" Susan asked Eugene.

"Who said I'm bothered?" he asked back. Susan said nothing. Peter spoke next.

"We're working on this site," he said.

"Yeah, I know," replied Susan. "You told me. What is it, you doing a bit of design work and Eugene's hoping to pick up a bit of business as well?"

"No, I mean…"

"We own it," said Eugene.

"What?" said Susan.

"I said we own it. I put together a consortium and we bought the warehouse and now we're going to develop it. Peter, show her your card." Peter reached into his jacket for his wallet. He pulled out a business card and handed it to Susan.

"'O'Hare Design and Construction'," she read out loud.

"Me and Peter," Eugene said. "He does the design. I do the construction."

"Yes," said Susan. "I worked that one out. Quite a step. And this is your first job, the Northern Warehouse? Not starting small, are you?"

"What's the point?" Eugene asked. "This city's changing and there's plenty going on. Why shouldn't we have a slice of it?"

"No reason," Susan said. "So what's the plan for this place, Peter?"

"Do you not read your own paper, woman?" snarled Eugene. "It was on Saturday's front page. Go and see for yourself. We're busy." He pushed Peter away from Susan and the mouth of the alley, down the road towards a site hut near the waterfront. Eugene himself lingered. When he reckoned Peter was out of earshot, he turned on Susan. "Now you listen to me, you nosy little bitch," he said. "I'm glad they've not sent a proper reporter but I'll tell you just in case you're thinking of trying to make a big splash with this. A whore's dead and I'm sorry enough but at bottom I don't care. No investigation is going to halt work on this site. So why don't you go and find some pub to crawl into and forget you were ever a real reporter, eh? Or else I'll make trouble for you." He pulled a ten pound note from his pocket and stuffed it down the front of her shirt. "Have a couple on me." He turned and followed Peter to the site hut.

Susan was left stunned, with no time to react and no idea how to. She felt the note inside her shirt, against her skin, and left it there. She took one last look at the alleyway where the body had been found, then headed unsteadily back up to the main road, the card Peter had given her folded in her hand. Recovering slightly, she unfolded the card and on it wrote the name of the alleyway and the policeman's name, Nolan.

She stopped at the transport café on the way back to the office. She wanted simply to sit by herself, to sit and think and work out what she was feeling. She ordered tea and toast and chose a table by the window. The only other customer was a pensioner who was smoking a roll-up cigarette and reading every word on every page of the *Daily Mirror*, making the minutes go by before the next stop on his daily routine.

Susan ignored the toast. She'd had no intention of eating it even as she'd ordered it. She lit her own cigarette and took a sip of the tea, too hot, too strong, not enough milk. She thought about Eugene. The way he'd reacted was typical of him. Violent, threatening, angry but calm at the same time. He could go from one extreme to another and back again and leave everyone else wondering what had hit them. Even so, it had taken her by surprise. It couldn't simply be due to her turning up. This development of his must be a huge risk, she reckoned, betting everything on the turn of one card.

The waitress came from behind the counter and gave the old man the breakfast he'd ordered. As she returned he called to her.

"Eh love, did you cook this egg? It's still movin'!" he said.
"Lerrus know if it starts cluckin'," she told him. He laughed

and started eating.

Susan looked over at him, tucking into his food, smiling still, devouring every piece on his plate and every word in his paper. He probably came here every day, she reckoned, always with a crack for the waitress, always waiting for her response. Going through the motions, following certain routines. Susan knew they weren't all that different, except her life lacked the laughter. She would return to work and mechanically fill the screen in front of her with words and paragraphs that would then be cut and squeezed into some empty space in tomorrow's paper. At 5.30 she would leave work and go back to her flat, jammed into the eaves of a Georgian house in what was now called Liverpool's cultural quarter. She would go out to the corner shop and buy bread and eggs and maybe a tin of beans and then she would go home and wait for the clock to reach nine, when she'd run a bath and open the bottle. If she started drinking any earlier she'd be too tempted to finish the bottle and would need to open another one to keep her going until it was time for bed. She'd have the bath and drink the wine and listen to music and read and try to take in *Newsnight* or hope for a good film on television and then she would go to bed and lie awake, drained but unable to sleep, until at some point she'd drift off and then the alarm would go off and the next day would start.

She felt knocked about. That was it. Knocked about and bruised by so many tiny events in her life; it was just that today had been worse than normal. First that cocky idiot in the office, hissing his boorish threats at her. Then Rachel Jack, suddenly launching a completely unprovoked attack on her in the ladies' toilets. Then Eugene added his boot. And of course meeting Peter. It wasn't by any means the first time she'd seen him since the divorce, although the occasions had been kept to a minimum by the agency of family members who beavered away on his behalf. There was just something different about this time. She didn't love him anymore, of course, had only ever really loved him briefly, if she was being honest. He was kind and thoughtful, malleable, eager to please, worthy. Never as bright as her. Not just in intelligence but personality too; he never sparkled like she once did.

She felt in her pocket for the folded business card, took it out, unfolded it and lay it on the table.

"'O'Hare Design and Construction'." She felt briefly self-conscious as she realised she'd said the words out loud, but neither the old man nor the girl behind the counter seemed to have heard her.

Five years on, she thought. Look at him and look at me. He's still a young man, with a fine young son and an exciting new business. I'm five years older and an old woman with no-one and next to nothing. I feel sorry for myself and I can't stop it. And then Eugene's words came back to her. Not the threats this time, but what he said when she took the card. "He does the design. I do the construction." Susan wondered what she did. Maybe I stop going through the motions, she said to herself. Maybe I stand up to Eugene this time, show him he can't order everyone around. She stood up, put the card back in her pocket and walked out of the café.

Rachel Jack had spent most of the morning distracted from her work, constantly watching out for Susan's return. When she finally came back, Rachel crossed the office, reaching Susan's desk just as the older woman hung her coat on the back of the chair. She waited for Susan to speak, but she simply sat down, switched her computer on and picked up the phone, ignoring Rachel's presence completely.

Awkwardly, abruptly, Rachel reached out and took hold of Susan's wrist, preventing her from bringing the phone up to her ear. She gripped Susan's hand more tightly than she'd intended. It was like Eugene's threats hit Susan all over again. She dropped the phone and swivelled her chair slightly, towards Rachel. As she did so, she turned her arm round, forcing Rachel to release her grip, then grabbed hold of Rachel's hand and twisted it violently. Rachel was pulled down so her elbow hit the desk and her face was level with Susan's.

"Listen, you little bitch," Susan hissed. "If you think I'm going to put up with the likes of you and that creep Bassett treating me like dirt, then you're wrong. And if you ever touch me again I'll break your arm." She kept hold of Rachel's hand, almost unable to release it, and was suddenly breathing deeply, the anger and speed having shocked her and driven the air from her lungs.

She forced herself to let go. Her breathing was still ragged, her mouth wide open as she forced air in and out, her skin clammy with a smearing of sweat. Rachel had stood up, but Susan was unaware of this, unaware of anything but her breathing and the suddenness of her rage.

"You've hurt me," Rachel said. She was bemused, amazed at the other woman's furious reaction. "There's a mark on my arm."

"I'm sorry," Susan said. Her tone was mechanical, the expected response. Not that she didn't care, but her emotions hadn't yet engaged with what she'd done. At the moment she was able simply to say the right thing; saying it with conviction would have to wait.

In the same way, Rachel said, "That's okay." They both felt awkward now, unsure how to react to what had just happened, how to leave the situation naturally and neatly. Rachel said, "I've got to…" and made to walk away.

Before she could finish what she was going to say, Susan said, without looking up, "Yeah. I need to…I've got to phone…" Rachel went back to her own desk, numb from the incident. Susan likewise went through the rest of the day at arm's length from her tasks, her mind detached, again as if she was observing herself as a stranger from a distance. She made her calls and found that the body had been discovered by Peter, first thing that morning. It had been there around 48 hours, since early Saturday morning. Heavy rain on Sunday had removed any evidence that might have been available to the police. It was a brutal killing, the woman battered with a heavy object then set alight. Police were unable to identify the body. The woman had not been carrying any cards or driving licence, nothing with her name on. Police doubted they had been taken from her as she was still carrying around £80 in cash on her. There was no sign of a mobile phone. She was believed to be about 40 years old. Police were appealing for witnesses or anyone with a female relative or friend or neighbour who had just gone missing. Police believed the woman to be a prostitute.

Once she'd made the calls and looked at her notes, however, she realised she had a choice. Respond to Eugene's threats and follow Bassett's instructions, or do the right thing, maybe with a bit of mischief thrown in. She went for the latter. The MP for the area where the murder had taken place was a new man, Labour, in his late thirties, desperate for a reputation as a firebrand and troublemaker. She called him. A few choice questions and she put the phone down. Before she wrote the story she checked the council website and found the plans to Eugene's dream building on the planning department page. She smiled as she recognised the name of the officer in charge of granting planning permission. She decided to make that call later, after she'd filed her story.

A local MP has reacted angrily to a police decision to shut down a murder scene only hours after the body of a woman was found beaten and burned earlier today…
The words flowed. Just like old times, Susan thought. She knew Bassett would hit the roof but if she picked her sub-editor carefully then enough of her story might just squeeze through.

She sent it through with a mixture of pride and defiance. She knew it should make a front-page splash. A brutal murder, lack of police diligence, an outraged MP; it had plenty going for it. She knew it wouldn't get anywhere close to page one, though. Still, she'd done the right thing by herself, not to mention the victim. And Eugene would be rattled. He'd be even more rattled if she could get the planning officer on side.

Chapter Four

That evening, as she was leaving the office, Susan found a copy of Saturday's paper, the one Eugene O'Hare had mentioned. She walked to her spot in the underground car park reading, looking at the photograph on the front page, her ex-husband and former father-in-law standing proudly behind a scale model of their vision for the Northern Warehouse. The article spoke of grand plans – two boutique hotels, flats, office space, a gym, a cinema – and there was a lengthy extract from a speech given Connor O'Brien, the leader of the city council, at the party the night before which launched the project. The speech lauded Susan's ex-father-in-law. A man of vision and determination, a man of risk and enterprise.
She didn't see Rachel Jack standing by her car, and was startled when she spoke.
"Susan," Rachel said.
Susan stopped in her tracks, four yards or so from where Rachel was. "What is it?" Susan asked. "What do you want?"
Rachel's tone was soft and friendly, conciliatory. "I want to apologise. For earlier, for both times earlier. I shouldn't have said what I did in the toilets, and I shouldn't have…well, you know, that business by your desk."
"Thanks," Susan replied. "I'm sorry too, about grabbing you. I don't know what made me do it."
"I also want to talk," Rachel added, her voice now uncertain. She was finding the situation difficult already. It had all gone so smoothly when she'd planned it in her head earlier.
"Talk," Susan said. "To me? You've barely said a word to me since you started here."
"I know," said Rachel. "Look, can we meet later? In a pub, maybe?" She quickly added, "Or a café; we could have a coffee together."
"It's okay," Susan said. "A pub's fine. I'm only a borderline alcoholic." She laughed and Rachel said, "What's funny?"

"I said that to the editor once," Susan said. "He said I should have my passport ready. I can't stand the man, but it was a good line all the same." She looked at Rachel and asked, "Do you know Peter Kavanagh's?"

"Off Catharine Street?" Rachel answered.

"Yes. Seven okay?"

"Seven's fine. I'll see you then. And thanks." Then Rachel moved away, again feeling clumsy, at first moving in the wrong direction towards her own car and then turning round and heading the right way, a comedy moment in the wrong place. Susan watched her go, then got in her car and drove home.

Peter Kavanagh's was a pub not far from where Susan lived. It was tucked away down a narrow road, Little Saint Bride Street, in what was now called Liverpool's Georgian Quarter. The area surrounding it, streets full of tall, reserved Georgian houses, built for Liverpool's early merchants, had until recently been allowed to fall into disrepair. The council had planned in the seventies to demolish the houses, but had run out of money. Now the area was in the last stages of being reclaimed. Developers had bought the grand four storey terraced houses and divided them into flats to suit the demands of the young professionals who wanted to live on the edge of the city centre. Peter Kavanagh's had remained untouched and unchanged while all around it work had gone on. It was a proper pub, slightly cramped, in need of a lick of paint and some re-upholstery, but a warm place, where local amateur musicians would often meet and play together, entertaining both themselves and the locals in for a quiet pint.

Susan lived a few roads away, in Hope Street, between the city's two cathedrals, just down from the Philharmonic Hall. When she first moved in, just after the divorce, she had been impervious to the charms of the area – there were too many other things to occupy her mind. But she had grown to appreciate the place. She liked the mix of young and old. She liked the atmosphere of culture and learning the place possessed. She would often see musicians carrying their instruments, or art students with their portfolios heading to college. She liked seeing the concert-goers on their way to the Philharmonic. Occasionally she would join them. She knew she didn't quite belong with them, knew she was somehow separate from the life of the area, but she was comfortable there now, as near to being at ease with herself as she could ever be.

Susan arrived at the pub about 15 minutes early. She had suggested Peter Kavanagh's because it was the first name that came into her head, but she was glad she'd chosen it. She mostly drank alone, in her flat, but she'd been here a few times over the years and had always liked it. She was pleased to see it hadn't changed, and that the only concession to the approach of Christmas was an advent calendar behind the bar. She ordered a glass of red wine and sat down. She was reminded of her visit to the transport café that morning. Once again she was sitting alone with a drink in front of her. There was no old man with his *Daily Mirror* this time, just a two young men with a girl, all sipping pints, talking and laughing together. They looked like students, Susan thought, although she couldn't say why exactly.

As with that morning, she started to think about herself. It was a problem, she knew. She spent too much time alone and was too self-absorbed. So many things she did were solitary activities – reading, crosswords, watching films – but she couldn't be sure if that was through choice or circumstance. Now she was sitting here waiting for someone to arrive, and what could be more normal to anyone looking in from the outside? Two work colleagues meeting for a drink a week or so before Christmas. And yet she had no idea why she was there or what Rachel would say to her. She felt uneasy, but there was something else. For five years. She had kept life at bay with routine, while gradually slipping down the rungs of the ladder at work. She had coped with each day through a series of mechanical activities, steps she followed to fill in the hours. Her mind had switched off, it had ceased to engage. She had given little or no thought to simple decisions. When she bought food she just filled her basket with essentials. If she shopped for clothes she bought simple, functional items; style wasn't a consideration. Events had left her numb. But now, she felt different. She felt as if she was recovering her senses. She felt excited, almost, simply because someone was reaching out to her. The business that morning with Eugene was having a similar effect. He'd challenged her, and for the first time in years, she found herself taking a step forward, instead of back. The feelings were just faint stirrings, fragile things which would maybe wither and die at the first knock or exposure. But there was something to hold onto, possibly the hope she'd wished for earlier in the day.

She had known she would arrive early but couldn't stay in the flat, had nothing to occupy the spare minutes. And she had brought with her the paper from Saturday, the one she'd picked up as she left the office. Maybe that was something, she thought, maybe a sign of something good. I didn't just bring it to make myself look occupied; maybe it was because I was curious.

"Saturday's paper?" Rachel had arrived and, for the second time that day, was standing next to where Susan was sitting without her realising it. "Catching up on old news?"

Susan looked up and found herself smiling at the young woman next to her. She looked at her properly and saw her thick, dark hair and green eyes and strong, attractive features. And her smile, relaxed and relieved at the same time. Rachel was dressed for the cold – duffle coat, scarf, woollen gloves. As she unwrapped herself, she nodded at Susan's glass and asked, "Do you fancy another, or are you okay with that?"

"I'm fine thanks," Susan replied. She stood up. "You sit

down," she told Rachel. "I'll get this one."

"Great," said Rachel. "I saw they've got a bottle of Bushmills behind the bar. I'll have a glass of that, please. With just a drop of water."

When Susan returned from the bar she gave Rachel her drink and sat down. Rachel took a sip and made a face to show how good it was. The two women sat facing each other, suddenly awkward, both of them feeling like they were on a first date. Susan opted for small talk.

"Find the place alright?"

"No problem," Rachel said. "My Dad gave me a lift. Said he didn't want me drinking and driving." She paused, then added, "I live with my parents still. Haven't got round to moving out yet, I suppose. In Childwall."

Susan said, "I used to live in Childwall. With him." And she pointed to Peter's picture on the front of the paper.

Rachel looked at where she was pointing. "Oh," she said. "He's your…"

"He's my ex-husband. Peter," Susan said. Her finger moved to the man next to Peter. "And that's my ex-father-in-law, Eugene. Peter and Eugene O'Hare."

"O'Hare Design and Construction," Rachel said.

"You've heard of them?" Susan asked quickly.

"No," Rachel replied. "I just read there, the caption."

Susan said, "Oh. Yes, of course."

"A few other faces are familiar. Look," Rachel said, and she pointed to the picture. There were ten people in all in the frame, among them councillors and representatives of the various development agencies overseeing Liverpool's regeneration. Rachel ignored them and pointed out three others, one by one. "There's Allen, our esteemed editor. And Gerry Dalton's in there, stuck on the end, nearly out of the picture." She laughed and then stopped, remembering what she knew of Susan and Gerry Dalton's history. "I'm sorry," she began. "I didn't mean…"

"It's okay," Susan said. "It was ages ago. Doesn't matter now."

"There's another one I know," Rachel said, tapping her finger on the face of Vincent Crowley.

Susan looked at the face. "Crowley," she said. "Top Cop."

"Yes," said Rachel. She frowned and took another sip of her drink. This time she grimaced as the liquid burned down her throat.

"What about him?" Susan asked. When Rachel didn't reply, Susan took a deep breath and said, "Look. Rachel. What are we doing here? Why did you want to see me? This morning you called me a has-been, you practically screamed at me. Then later I nearly broke your wrist and now we're sitting having a quiet drink like it's the most normal thing in the world." She paused and looked down at her drink. "Look," she said again. "I don't know…I don't understand what's happening to me today." Her voice trailed away. She took a cigarette from the packet on the table.

The two women sat in silence for a moment, before Rachel said, her head now bowed again, "I'm the same. I mean I'm the same as you said. I don't understand what's happening to me either." She raised her head and pushed her hand through her hair. "I'm sick every morning."

"I know," Susan said. "I set my watch by it." They both smiled.

"I've always been like that," said Rachel. "Even at school. My parents used to want to keep me off but I always wanted to go in. Funny role-reversal."

"It's nerves," said Susan.

"I suppose so," said Rachel. "It's funny though. I never really feel nervous even. No butterflies, nothing like that. I don't snap at anyone." Susan grinned at her. "Yeah, I know," Rachel responded to the smile. "I snapped at you. But…That's part of it, you see. Nothing's ever bothered me. At school, at university. I could always do the work. Exams were just things I passed. I could never understand the other girls, cramming, panicking. And work, well, it's the same. I can do the job. I've always known that. And after a year or so more here then I'll move into television."

"You've got it all planned out," Susan said.

"Yes," replied Rachel. "I suppose so."

"Nothing ever throws you?"

"A little, I suppose. I'm not explaining myself well, am I? Sometimes, now, since I started working on the paper, well, it's like I'm playing a part."

"How do you mean?" Susan asked. "Like an actor?"

"Yes," Rachel said. "You know. You see all these films with reporters in them, flashing their press passes, meeting deadlines…"

"Holding the front page."

Rachel smiled. "Yes. That's it. Holding the front page. I guess I've been like that. The job, being a reporter. It's like it's shielded me. I can do things, handle situations because it's my job. It's not just Rachel Jack, it's Rachel Jack…"

"Ace reporter," Susan said, finishing Rachel's sentence.

"Something like that," Rachel said. "The point is I've breezed through. It's like nothing could touch me. And I've just assumed that it'll always be the same. I'll be covering wars or floods or whatever."

"I don't understand," said Susan. "What's happened? What has this got to do with being sick every morning?"

"It was always something I did. Like I said, I never felt nervous. I'd just throw up, then come back as if nothing had happened. Because nothing had happened. It was just like going to the toilet, or getting a coffee. But this past day or so, it's not been like that. I've been nervous, scared. I've been sick more often and it's not made anything better. And then this morning, shouting at you. It's like there's no shield anymore."

"So what's different?" Susan asked.

From her bag Rachel took the letter she'd received from Franny Sweeney. She pushed it across the table to Susan. "This," she said.

Susan read the letter. Like Rachel, she recognised the name straight away.

"Jesus," she said. "Franny Sweeney. I can see what's different. Did you go?"

Rachel nodded. "Sunday night. Like it said."

"And what did he say?"

"He said I should go and see someone called Billy Jackson," Rachel replied. "He's in Strangeways, a few weeks to go."

"Why did he say that?"

"Because of him." Rachel pointed to the paper. "Crowley. Franny Sweeney hates Crowley. Says he lied at his trial."

"The one which was thrown out of court?" Susan said.

"That's right," Rachel replied. "He was up for murder. Said he did it as well."

"Well," said Susan. "It wouldn't be his first."

"No," said Rachel. "He said that too."

"Have you seen Allen about this?" Susan asked. "Or mentioned it to anyone else?"

"No. You're the first person I've shown it to."

"Good. Not good that I'm the only one. Just good you've not let anyone else see it, especially Allen."

"Why?" Rachel was curious. "I'm know you said you don't like Allen, but…"

"It's not that," Susan said. "Look at the picture again. Crowley and Allen are standing side by side. Allen's not going to sanction anything that puts his mate in a bad light."

"But, surely," Rachel protested. "If it's a good story…" She stopped as she saw Susan begin to smile. When she spoke next she struggled to hide her indignation. "You're going to tell me I'm being naïve."

"No," said Susan. "Not at all. It's just that…Look, you're right. It sounds like it might be a good story. Even a terrific

41

one. But do you really think that's what Allen is interested in? He thinks of the *Mail* as the city's in-house magazine. Don't worry. I made the same mistake this morning."

"How do you mean?" Rachel asked.

"A woman found murdered," Susan said. "Down by the river. That kid Bassett sent me to it. Told me to keep it short, no drama. Bad news comes in brief fillers in the *Mail* these days, and starts on page nine."

"And Allen's said this?"

"Not to me. Doesn't talk to me anymore. But, like Bassett said, nothing gets in the paper that might stain the reputation of the fair city of Liverpool." She took a drink of her wine. "And this would, or sounds like it would, anyway. Top Cop lies in court to secure a conviction. It looked bad enough when the case was chucked out."

"He printed that."

"Couldn't avoid it, could he?" Susan said. "I'm surprised that piece of yours got in under the radar, though." Rachel looked up from her drink, surprised. "What?" said Susan. "Shocked I read the paper? I do sometimes, you know."

"No, it's not that," Rachel said. "It's just that Franny Sweeney mentioned that piece. Said he liked it, which was why he got in touch with me."

"You should be flattered."

Rachel tried to smile. "Yeah, I suppose so."

The two women were quiet for a while, each feeling slightly ill at ease, each drinking a little too quickly, trying to look occupied. The pub was starting to fill up. Regulars, mostly, locals not interested in the trendier bars that littered the city now, wanting to avoid the Christmas party groups that would be staggering from drink to drink. All they were after was a couple of pints and a laugh and a joke with a few friendly faces.

"It's a nice place this," Rachel said eventually. "The people here seem…well, they don't seem your usual types."

"This is the Cultural Quarter, remember," said Susan. "Or the Georgian Quarter. Maybe both. These are your usual types round here. Lecturers, students, artists, musicians, writers. Or at least they'd like to be. Nice crowd, though."

They were both being polite and they both knew it. Susan felt they'd run out of things to say and could sense her old routine returning to draw her back in. She hadn't known what to expect from this invitation and it seemed to her that, if Rachel had wanted something from her, she had now changed her mind. Rachel, though, was summoning up the courage to say something.

"Gerry Dalton," she blurted out.

Susan was instantly on her guard. "What about him?"

"I'm sorry," said Rachel. "But…Look, I know there's a history there…"

Susan stood up. Rachel thought she was going to leave and reached out to lay her hand on Susan's arm. She stopped short as they both remembered what had happened earlier that day.

"Don't…" began Rachel.

"I'm going to the bar," said Susan. "You just work out what it is you want to say and then say it."

When Susan came back from the bar, Rachel was sitting upright in her seat. She took her drink from Susan and straight away took a sip. She grimaced slightly as the whiskey burned sweetly down her throat. Looking straight ahead, avoiding Susan's eyes, she said, "About Gerry. Look, what you said before about Allen. Well, why doesn't Gerry say anything? I mean, you know him. Maybe if I went to him with this Franny Sweeney business…"

"Gerry Dalton's weak," said Susan, her voice soft and gentle.

"But, you don't seem the type who'd…"

"Go for weak men?" Susan asked.

Rachel looked at her and nodded. "Yes," she said. "From what I've heard about you."

"Well, what you've heard is probably all true," said Susan,

"so I won't ask you to repeat it. But all the men I went for were weak. My husband, Gerry Dalton, all the others. And now? Well, now it's me who's weak."

"But he seems so…" Rachel struggled for the right word, anxious to be both accurate and not to give offence. "So passive. In editorial meetings he barely says a word. Except to agree."

"Well," said Susan, "he could never stand up to anyone. Certainly not to his wife. And certainly not to Allen. That's one of the reasons he became deputy editor. But he's changed. From what I hear, I mean. We keep our distance. I heard someone say he seems to be shrinking." She paused. "Oh, I don't know. I can't really talk about changing for the worse."

"Was there ever any chance of you and he ever?"

"What?" Susan said. "Getting married? God no! I wouldn't have wanted to, for one thing. Gerry was just a fling for me. I mean I liked him, but it was never serious. And anyway, once I was divorced, well, he kept away from me. Maybe he was terrified his wife would find out. It's funny, I don't know if she ever did find out. The whole office knew, of course, but Gerry's wife was never one for any of the parties there used to be. I don't think Gerry ever was, really, to be honest. And now, well, now I don't know. I'm never invited to them myself anymore."

"You're not missing much," said Rachel. "And Gerry only seems to be there to ferry Allen around."

"He's too good just to be Allen's poodle," said Susan. "But he'll never say no to him."

Once again, quiet settled on the two women. They sipped their drinks, taking in the growing bustle around them and reflecting on the conversation they'd just shared.

"This is nice," said Susan. "I don't really get out much. It's good to be in a place surrounded by people." She looked at her watch and saw it was after nine.

"I'm sorry," said Rachel. "Do you need to go?"
"No, no," Susan said. "It's not that. I was just thinking…normally this time of night I'd be…well, I've just got into such a routine. You can become scared to break it. Doing the same things every day can keep life at bay. You wouldn't know. You're too young."

Rachel laughed. "You know my routine," she said. "Part of it, anyway. Get up, come to work, be sick." Now she looked at her watch. "Now then, let me see. Nine fifteen on a Tuesday night. I'd be at home, with Mum and Dad. We'd have eaten, done the washing up. We'd be in the lounge. Mum would be doing a crossword or reading some thriller or other. Dad and I would be playing chess or maybe doing a jigsaw. There'd be music on. Classical maybe, if Mum's got to the record player first. More likely jazz. Dad loves Art Blakey. Always says if he'd not married Mum he'd have gone to New York, scratched a living playing tenor saxophone in one smoky dive or another. Not that he can play, mind, but that doesn't stop him saying so."

Susan laughed. "Sounds idyllic."

"Yes," said Rachel, solemnly. "Yes, it is. It's very…safe."

"So why are you here, sitting in a pub with me?" Susan asked.

"Because I don't feel safe anymore."

"Sweeney? Because that letter was sent to your home address?"

"Oh," said Rachel. "You noticed that, did you?"

"Not quite a has-been, you see."

"I never said you…oh, yes, I did, didn't I? I'm so sorry."

"Forget about it," Susan told her. "But is that why you're worried?"

"No, not really," said Rachel. "I mean, it's not good, but I know why he did it. Wanted me to know he knew where I lived. Not a specific threat, but just to let me know how things stood between us, how he was more powerful. But casual with it."

"So what is it then?"

"I think it's because suddenly things feel unfamiliar," Rachel said. "Like you said before, maybe. You realise you've been keeping life at bay, then something gets through the defences. I told you before I always felt I could cope. Now I'm not sure I can."

"So why tell me?" Susan asked. "I mean I'm flattered. But, well, what is it you want from me?"

"Help, I guess," Rachel told her.

"And what makes you think I can help you? There must be plenty of people on the paper who you could go to. Certainly most of the men there would be more than happy to help, even if it did mean getting a bit close to Franny Sweeney."

"No," said Rachel. "I wouldn't trust any of them. Ask for help and they'd use it somehow, or they'd charge me for it, make me pay somehow. You…you seem different."

"Maybe I look like I don't care anymore. I wouldn't ask anything from you because I don't care enough to want anything. Is that it?"

"Maybe," admitted Rachel.

"Well, at least you're honest," said Susan.

"Look, I didn't think about it," said Rachel. "I didn't go through a list of everyone in the office and come out with your name. I just saw you. In the bathroom, when you'd been crying, and you were just standing there. You just looked like you'd come out the other side. Am I making any sense?"

"Yes," said Susan. "Yes, you are. So," she continued, "I'll help if I can. But I'm not special, you know. I'm as scared and shaky as anyone."

"Thanks," said Rachel. "It'll be nice to have someone's hand to hold."

"Okay," Susan told her. "Although if it's Saturday it might be a problem. I have to be somewhere for three."

"Oh," said Rachel brightly. "Something special planned?"

Susan face clouded. "My son," she said. "Michael. He's playing rugby for his school. I try to get along and watch."
"I didn't realise," Rachel said. "That you had a son, I mean. Did you have to get a baby-sitter for tonight?"
"No," Susan said. "He lives with his father." She took a sip of her drink and then said, "Look, getting back to Sweeney. I'll do what I can to help but I don't know how much good I'll be. I will say this, though. Be careful. He's a mad bastard and he's done plenty of bad things. The murders are the tip of the iceberg."
"This isn't making me feel better, you know?" said Rachel.
Susan leant towards her. "I'm not trying to make you feel better. I'm trying to make you scared. No matter what he says, if he's asked you for something he'll want it, and if he doesn't get it…"
The women parted soon afterwards. Rachel rang her father to come and get her, as she'd promised she would. Susan met him briefly and turned down his offer of a lift back to her flat. She lived only a few minutes' walk from the pub. On her way back she noticed there were more people out than usual. Christmas, she thought. Only a few weeks away; everybody in the party mood. Her mood was different too. She felt lighter, more determined, energised by the night out with Rachel and by all the things they'd talked about and she realised that she couldn't remember the last time she'd been out and talked to anyone. It felt good.

Chapter Five

Back at her flat, instead of having another glass of wine, Susan made herself a coffee and took it into the spare room. This was where Michael was supposed to stay whenever he spent the night with her, but, somehow, in the five years she'd been divorced, that had never happened. She rarely went in the room now, using it to store things she wasn't sure if she should throw away or not. The child's desk was littered in old envelopes filled with bills and bank statements. The single bed was unmade and the bare mattress was covered in boxes and files she'd told herself she might one day need.

Susan put her coffee on the desk and knelt by the bed. She forced from her mind an unwanted image of Michael doing the same thing by his own bed at his father's house, kneeling down to say his prayers before going to sleep. She opened one of the boxes and started to go through it. By the time she found what she was looking for, in the second box, her coffee was cold and the bed was covered in scraps from her past life – notepads, ashtrays, empty photograph frames, old letters and postcards. She hadn't realised she'd kept so much, but then she remembered that the boxes had simply been dumped in here by her ex-father-in-law and one of Peter's brothers not long after she'd moved out. They'd gone through the house she and Peter had lived in and just swept any evidence of her into some old cardboard boxes collected from the supermarket. Then they'd driven round to the flat and dumped the boxes one by one into any available space.

The memory threatened her sense of purpose and tempted her to finish the half a bottle of wine she knew was still in the kitchen, but she fought the temptation and the threat to her mood and went back into the living room with the notebook she'd found and the cup of cold coffee.

It wasn't so much a living room as a kitchen-diner. The companies who'd renovated these houses had not shown the same concern for the interiors as they had for the facades. The elegant, spacious rooms had been replaced by chipboard walls and room dividers as every spare inch of the houses had been used to squeeze as many flats as possible into the available space. She could see the top of the Roman Catholic Cathedral and could look down on the glow of the city from her skylight windows. She was used now to living beneath the sloping roof, accustomed to the slight sense of being pressed down. She switched on the music centre without bothering to check what CD was in the tray. As she crossed to the kitchen area to put the kettle on again, she recognised the lightness of the opening notes of Ravel's *Tombeau de Couperin*. The melody skipped through the room, a Summer dance in contrast to the cold darkness of the December night outside.

Susan leant on the kitchen counter and flicked through the old notebook. She had filled pages with dense shorthand and she wondered now at the drive and energy of the woman who'd packed so many pages and filed so many stories. She stopped at the page she was looking for, containing the name and number of a policeman she hadn't spoken to for over three years. She just hoped he hadn't moved on.

She made the coffee and took it to the couch and sat down. It was just after 10. She thought about reading but decided instead simply to sip her drink and listen to the music, to concentrate on the melodies and themes being played out, rather than just use it as background noise for a novel. Later, when the music was finished, she rinsed out her cup, brushed her teeth and went to bed, no swaying, no stumbling, no promises that tomorrow she wouldn't drink so much.

Chapter Six

Wednesday 12 December
LIVERPOOL MORNING MAIL, P9
WOMAN'S BODY FOUND
The body of a woman was found in the early hours of yesterday morning at the site of one of Liverpool's latest city centre developments. The woman, whose identity is not yet known, had been beaten and then set alight. Her body was found by Peter O'Hare, of O'Hare Design and Construction, developers of the Northern Warehouse site on Little Porter Street where the body was found.
A Police spokesman refused to speculate on the motive for the killing and said investigations were ongoing. The MP for the area, Gordon Fowler, expressed concern that the scene of the crime had been opened up for construction work to begin again so soon after the body had been discovered. "Vital clues could be lost," he claimed. "I will be contacting the police to get guarantees that mistakes have not been made."
By Susan Clarke.

Susan was at her desk an hour earlier than usual. She picked up a copy of the *Mail* and found her story of the murdered prostitute hidden away on page 9, as Bassett had promised, and cut to shreds, as she'd expected. She felt her new, positive mood to be fragile, but was pleased to find it strong enough to remain unaffected by this. And there were some positives. Butchered though it had been, enough of the original was there to make a few waves in Eugene's pool. The company name was included, and the fact that the warehouse was under development. And when Gordon Fowler MP read what he'd said, he'd feel duty-bound to follow it up.
She heard shouting coming from the landing by the lifts. She recognised the voice. It could only be one man.

"Allen! Allen! Where the fuck are you?"

Eugene O'Hare had read Susan's story.

As he stormed through into the office, his big right fist crushing a copy of the paper, Susan stood up. She wanted him to see her. He did. He stopped and glared and said, "I'll deal with you next. First I want to see that bastard editor of yours." At this, Hugh Allen's door opened, and Eugene stalked across and into his office.

Inside, Allen was standing looking out of his window, his back to the room. Eugene slammed the paper down on the desk.

"Have you seen this?" he yelled.

Allen took his time turning round. "Of course I've seen it. It's my paper isn't it?"

"Then why the fuck did you let it in?"

Allen sat down. "Stop shouting," he told Eugene. Looking him in the eye he went on, "And give the hard man act a rest, eh? Everyone else might shit themselves when you come the muscle but it doesn't work with me. I've known your sort since I was a kid, and I stopped being bothered since about the same time."

Eugene began to speak, then changed his mind. He started pacing backwards and forwards across the room. Finally he said, "Do you know how much this could cost me?"

"Me too, remember."

Eugene stopped pacing and faced Allen. "Yeah," he said. "But not as much as me. Everything I've got's in this."

Allen shrugged. "Greatest risk, greatest gain. Look," he went on. "There's been a murder. We don't get so many in this city that we can ignore a few. So what if it was mentioned in the paper?"

"My company was mentioned too. And my son's name. Nothing can stop this development. There can't be any hold-ups, no calls from the bank wanting to know what's going on. No reporter sticking her nose in."

"There won't be any hold-ups. No-one's going to get fussed about this. Tomorrow's fish and chip paper, remember? And Susan Clarke won't bother any longer. She'll have crawled back under her stone by this afternoon."

"No hold-ups?" Eugene repeated. "Then why did I have some prick of an MP on my phone last thing yesterday. And that's not all. Get that bitch in here now."

Allen looked puzzled. Though he was tempted to tell Eugene to stick to bossing his own men around, he buzzed his secretary and told her he wanted to see Susan Clarke right away.

Susan walked straight into the office without knocking. She had a fair idea what to expect, and she was determined to face down any assault. Allen sat behind his desk. He leant forward, his forearms heavy on the desk top. Susan was struck by the similarity between the two men. Allen didn't carry his fat so well, but it wasn't just the height and build. They both had the same mean look in their eyes. Neither man would put anyone before him.

Susan ignored Eugene. "You wanted to see me, Hugh," she said.

"He wanted to see you," he replied and he nodded towards Eugene. "It's about the story you wrote. You know Mr O'Hare, don't you?"

She wouldn't let herself be drawn into the question. "What's the problem, Hugh? And why am I being summoned to your office to see a member of the public?"

Eugene stepped towards her. His fists were balled up and his eyes were livid. "You cheeky drunken bitch," he hissed.

Still Susan ignored him. "What's the problem with the story, Hugh?"

Allen squirmed. He knew he was on poor ground. But then he wasn't going to let a member of his staff challenge him either. "It was insensitively written," he said.

"From whose point of view?" she replied. "The dead

woman's? The one who was beaten and set on fire?"

"Don't get smart Susan," Allen warned. "You deliberately set out to provoke. The city of Liverpool is in the midst of full-scale regeneration. Investment is pouring in…"

"And so we just ignore murders?" she said. "Is that it? Or only the murders that happen on a redevelopment site?"

"I told you not to get smart," Allen said. "Calling the MP, badgering the police. You wrote it like a personal issue. You deliberately tried to halt work on the site and so threaten its completion." He looked away. "That could put jobs at risk, as well as lose a lot of money for people."

"People like who?" Susan asked. "Merchant bankers?"

Eugene spoke. "Not just bankers. Ordinary folk who've put a few bob in."

She looked at Eugene for the first time since coming in the room. "Ordinary people? You're joking, aren't you? How many ordinary people invest money in hotels?"

"Local businessmen," Eugene said. Now he looked at Allen. "Important people in the community."

Susan laughed. "You've got money in this, haven't you, Hugh?" she said. "That's why I'm here. Not just your mate I've upset, is it? Worried about a few of your bob going down the drain?"

"That's enough!" Allen shouted, pushing himself to his feet. "From now on you keep clear of this story, do you hear? No gnawing at it, no shit stirring. Stick to caption writing. I'll get someone I trust to write it, if anything more needs doing. Someone sober."

"And while you're here," Eugene said, "can you explain why I got a call from the planning office this morning? Why some dozy little nobody wants to come and inspect the site? Check I've not gone a foot beyond what the proposals said?"

"Now how on earth would I know anything about that, Eugene?" Susan said. "I'm just some drunk who's only good for writing captions, aren't I?" She turned to Allen. "Is that all, Hugh?" And without waiting for an answer, she turned and headed for the door. As she began to open it, Eugene stepped behind her and pushed it shut with an easy press of one thick, fat hand. Susan tried to pull it open but Eugene held it closed. He smiled at her, then suddenly stepped back and let her out.

When she'd gone, Eugene said to Allen, "I've got too much money in this and so have you. Any delay adds to the cost and the bank won't give a shit about shutting it down. You put the brakes on that bitch, do you hear? Or we'll find out for sure if you've really met the likes of me before."

At her desk, Susan took the old notebook out of her bag, found the number and dialled it. Allen might have taken her off the story, but she was too fired up to take any notice. The call was answered on the fifth ring, another target probably missed by a force committed to serving the public fast.

"Sergeant Nulty, please," Susan said, hopefully.

"We've an Inspector Nulty," replied the receptionist.

"That'll be him," Susan replied.

"Putting you through now."

The call was transferred before Susan had a chance to say thank you. This time the phone was picked up before the second ring was complete.

"Nulty." The voice was just as Susan remembered it, thick Scouse.

"Brian?" Susan said. "Brian, I don't know if you remember me. This is…"

"Fuckin' hell, girl. Susan Clarke," Nulty said.

Susan was amazed. "Yes," she said. "How on earth did you remember? It's been over three years."

Brian laughed. "You've lost a year, love. It's more like four. I take it from tha' you're still drinkin'?"

"Well, yes," Susan admitted. She loved hearing his voice again. He spoke quickly but every sound was relished and every word enjoyed. He had the patter alright and though

Susan hated it in others she loved it in Brian Nulty because he was a hard, tough, warm, honest man who'd never let a friend down.

"Ah, it's no wonder I'm a detective is i'?" Nulty said.

"Anyway, good for you. It's the only way to avoid a 'angover. I've gorra confession though. I'm sittin' 'ere with the *Mail* open at page 9," he said. "I left me magnifyin' glass at 'ome with me deerstalker and meerschaum pipe. If I only 'ad it with me, I'd be able to read the story. I did manage to make out your name, though, so it was in me mind when I heard your voice."

"And there was me thinking I was unforgettable," Susan said. "Congratulations, by the way."

"Wha' for?" asked Nulty.

"Your promotion," she said. "Inspector Nulty now, the receptionist told me."

"Well, gee, tanks. They're making me commissioner next. I'm gonna get me own bat signal an' everythin'."

Susan laughed. "Look, sorry about the story. It should have featured more prominently, but…"

"Don't apologise," said Nulty. "Not your doin', I know. Bit of publicity wouldn't hurt, though, but why should a murder take precedence over…" He paused, turning the paper in front of him over to the front page and putting on a reading voice. "Over another delay to the city's proposed tram scheme?"

"It's a bit embarrassing," Susan admitted.

"You never know, though. It might be a serial killer. 'e'd put i' on the front page then," Nulty said.

"Only if the murder scenes go onto a Capital of Culture tour," said Susan.

"Maybe the killer beat the girl to death with a city of culture club."

"What?" asked Susan.

"Culture club," repeated Nulty. "That's more than a joke, Clarkey. That's comedy gold."

"Oh," Susan said, suddenly getting it. "Yes, well, I'll take your word for it." She paused. "Look, Brian," she began again. "I'm sorry, is it okay to ask you a few questions about the death?"

"Course," Nulty replied. "Not much to tell you, though. And remember, I'm not in charge. I'm just stickin' me nose in 'cos she was a prostitute. One of my girls." Nulty worked in Vice.

"You're sure she was a prostitute?"

"Looks like i', Clarkey," Brian said. "Where she was found, what she had on, the approximate age, the dyed hair." He sounded embarrassed now. "Look. We're making assumptions, I know tha', but, well. She looked like a prostitute. The Doc said she'd had sex at least once that in the previous 24 hours. A condom was used. No-one's reported anyone missing," he added. "And it's been four days now."

"Any name yet?" Susan asked.

"No name, no mobile phone, no purse, no nothin'."

"Beaten to death with a brick," said Susan. "Hands smashed to pulp. Arms outstretched like a crucifixion. Does that mean anything?"

"Don't know, to be honest," Nulty admitted. "It might do if there's another. But, for now, well…We're not going to jump the gun at all. First thing we need to do is find who she was. And warn the other girls on the street."

"Have you started that yet?"

"Oh yeah. Dead right," Nulty said. "I 'ad some men out last night. Just on me own say-so, like. No-one 'ere's jumping through any 'oops about i'."

"Someone called Nolan's in charge," Susan said. "Is that right?"

"Yeah," Nulty said. "Fuckin' waste of space."

"Are you going out again?" Susan asked.

"Tonight. I'll be doing it meself," Nulty told her. "Fancy taggin' along?"

"I was just about to ask. Would that be okay?"

"Yeah, course it would. Be like the old days," Nulty said. Susan swivelled in her chair. She looked back across the office and saw Rachel standing talking to one of the photographers. "Mind if I bring a friend?" she asked Nulty. He laughed. "You got yourself a date Clarkey?" He didn't wait for an answer. "Be my guest. More the merrier."

They arranged to meet and said their goodbyes. Susan put the phone down and went over to Rachel. As she made her way across the office, she was aware of a sense of renewed energy and confidence. The doubt and fear and self-consciousness that had dogged her for so long were ebbing away. Slowly, certainly, and liable to turn back at any time, but there was something happening which was giving her hope for the first time in years.

Rachel was sitting on the edge of her desk, her back to Susan. Bassett was with her, and another man too, Pete Lee, a chief sub on the news desk. She was looking over some sheets of paper, listening while the two men talked and laughed.

When Bassett saw Susan approach, he stopped laughing and sneered at her. "How come you're in here so early?" he said. "Get drunk and put the clock forward by mistake last night?" He waited for the others to laugh, but Rachel just kept reading and Lee could manage no more than an embarrassed flicker of his mouth.

"No," Susan said. She looked Bassett in the eye. "Do people do that kind of thing often?"

"What are you doing over here, anyway?" Bassett said. "Come to see what real reporters look like?" Again he glanced at Lee and then looked at Rachel for a reaction, but again they gave him nothing.

Susan was determined not to rise to any bait, not to enter into any mindless exchange with Bassett. She would simply answer his sneering questions as if they were genuine requests for information.

"No," she said. "I just wanted a word with Rachel." Her

confidence, so secure just moments ago, was fading, and she felt like a schoolgirl ready to give up her dinner money to the class bullies. She willed herself greater strength, but none was coming.

"And what makes you think she wants to talk to you?" Susan couldn't believe this skinny, sweaty, stupid oaf, with his fat tie knot and cheap suit and gelled hair thought it was okay to talk her in this way and could still less believe that she was just standing there letting him.

"I'm sorry," she began. "I just…"

Rachel could stand the discomfort no longer. She stood up quickly and pushed the papers she'd been trying to read at Pete Lee, who took them and went back to his desk, grateful for a chance to get away. Without looking at Susan, she said, "I'll see you back at your desk in a minute." Susan knew she'd been dismissed. Without a word, she simply turned and went back to her place in the corner, fighting away tears of impotent anger, all energy and confidence flicked away contemptuously by the callous spite of Trevor Bassett and by Rachel's apparent indifference. Susan felt small and stupid and at prey to forces inside her that she couldn't control.

Rachel, meanwhile, felt a mixture of guilt and tension. She wished she could have just smiled at Susan and spoken normally to her. She didn't care what Bassett thought and she knew Pete Lee had worked at the *Mail* long enough not to be interested in the petty dramas the office threw up each and every day. Somehow, though, things were different today. Susan was now someone she'd connected with, someone she needed and wanted to work with. A week ago, Rachel would barely have registered her existence.

Similarly, a week ago, Trevor Bassett was a harmless nonentity of limited ability who was currently her senior but who she'd soon blithely overtake as her career developed. He was someone who'd hint at asking her out without ever quite doing so, who'd suggest she might like to come along with him and a few others for a quick drink after work. She'd smile and ask where and say she'd see how she was fixed without any intention of ever turning up. A week ago, Rachel had known where she stood and where everyone else stood in relation to her. Now, though, things had changed, and now the simple fact of two particular work colleagues standing either side of her had made her uncomfortable, awkward and rude. It was as if they were from completely different areas of her life and she couldn't stand them meeting, not with her in the middle.

She sat down at her desk and began moving the cursor around the computer screen with her mouse. She willed Bassett to go away, but he stayed where he was. Worse, he sat down on the edge of her desk and looked like he was settling in.

"What's she doing here?" he asked.

"Yeah," Rachel replied.

"I mean, she contributes nothing," he continued. "I know she used to shag Dalton, but that was years ago. Don't tell me he's keeping her on just in case he fancies some more. Don't tell me he's that desperate."

The macho sexism of the newspaper office had always been something Rachel had simply pretended to enjoy, even though it left her cold and feeling naïve. She made another non-committal noise and waited for the inevitable.

"Listen," said Bassett, as he stood up with studied casualness from Rachel's desk. "A few of us are thinking about having a quick drink after work. Thought we'd wander down to the Blue Bar at the Albert Dock. Fancy it?"

"I'll see how I'm fixed," Rachel replied. "Might have to make a dash for it tonight. An old friend's back in the city. Said I might see her."

"Oh, well, bring her too," Trevor said. "'bout half six."

"Okay then," said Rachel. "Maybe see you later then." And thankfully, Trevor moved away, pretending he'd seen someone he needed to catch before they left the office.

Both Rachel and Susan spent the rest of that morning trying to immerse themselves in their work so as to push more pressing concerns out of their minds. Rachel struggled to cope with how unsettled she felt. Even though she knew the cause of it – the letter from and subsequent visit to Franny Sweeney – that didn't help her deal with it any better. She was nervous and on edge, her sense of normality thrown off balance. The visit to see Sweeney had brought her too close to a world which frightened her, revealing her sense of control and purpose to be no more than a veneer barely concealing a scared little girl. The drink with Susan the night before had restored some of that assurance and given her someone willing to hold her hand. And yet now she'd pushed that hand away, barely able to be civil to a woman who was there and happy to help. And why? Because being pleasant to the office has-been would have damaged her image, would have sent Bassett scurrying away to tell his cronies how she and Susan were now best friends? Maybe that was part of it, she told herself, maybe the scared little girl that Sweeney had exposed was also spiteful and immature, too bothered about what others thought of her, too weak to be honest, like the girls at school who'd be nice one minute then blank you the moment someone cooler came along.

Chapter Seven

Returning to her own desk, Susan sat down and went through a pantomime of activity, all the while digging her nails into the palm of her hand to try and force back the tears which were filling her eyes and blurring her vision. She felt tricked by Rachel and cursed herself for allowing it to happen so easily. Last night had invigorated her. She had connected and had felt wanted and, after spending so long using routine to hold at bay loneliness and bitterness and regret, had suddenly and so easily decided she was ready to rejoin the world. She was even going to follow up a story on her own time, something she'd not done in a decade or more. Being sneered at by Bassett would have counted for nothing, if only Rachel had just looked at her when she spoke. But no, she couldn't even manage that and now Susan imagined the pair of them holding back their sniggers while she made her way to her desk, a mess of a woman with bad skin and dowdy clothes and a future a long way behind her.

The hours to lunchtime dragged for Susan, but eventually it came. She'd tried to call Nulty to cancel their meeting but he wasn't available. She'd do it when she came back to the office. Quickly and unobtrusively she picked up her bag and put her coat on and made her way to the stairs, avoiding the crowd gathering at the lift. Soon she was outside in Old Hall Street. The road was crowded with cars, the drivers trying to find some way through the road works and diversions the Council had authorised to make the city centre more accessible. In the meantime, every journey took an extra half hour and bus drivers made up their own routes past the temporary traffic lights and cones and barriers. The council called it the Big Dig, vital if Liverpool was going to be ready for 2008, when the influx of money-laden tourists drawn by the lure of the Capital of Culture tag would swarm the streets and bars and hotels.

Susan was surrounded by progress, some of it being directed by her ex-husband as he rejuvenated his little corner of Liverpool and made his fortune. She wished him well, and felt instantly guilty about the recent phone calls which might have temporarily thwarted that progress. His father might be a pig but Peter was a decent man she'd mistreated and taken for granted. He deserved to do well and, of course, if he did well it could only benefit her son, Michael.

The December clouds had the dirty pinkness that suggested snow and the air had a bite to it which sliced through Susan's light raincoat and made her hurry her pace. There were plenty of places to eat close by the *Mail* building – sandwich shops, pubs, restaurants, coffee shops churning out people so busy they had to take their coffee on the move from paper beakers with plastic lids – but Susan ignored them all, as she always did.

She headed to the same place she always went. She walked in from the bottom of Old Hall Street on the periphery of the city centre towards the heart of the old business district. Here the roads were flanked by buildings which bore testament to the riches of Liverpool's prestigious past, housing shipping magnates and cotton merchants. Now, too many of the facades were crumbling and the offices empty, or occupied by hairdressers or cafés or bars or apartment complexes whose names alone were reminders of their past use – the Exchange Café and Restaurant, Merchants', and Clippers Salon. Susan had read of moves to restore the buildings, but more recently the *Mail* had trumpeted plans for the construction of a new business quarter for the city, with state-of-the-art office suites to meet the demands of the modern business.

She walked along Dale Street and then cut down a flight of steps to the basement of the India Buildings and into the Mercantile Café. The Mercantile was a relic of the past. Not from the glory days of Liverpool, but dating from the 1960s, when the city had been on the downward slide, becoming known only for music and football and strikes, the Mercantile looked like it had been frozen in time. The large floor space was filled with booths, with peeling formica table tops and shiny dark green vinyl seats, yellow foam pushing through the splits. Low veneer walls separated the booths, but customers could still reach over for the salt or ketchup. Along the far wall was the counter, a pile of trays at one end and a register at the other, the two divided by clear plastic hatches which you had to open to reach for the cellophane sandwiches or greying cream cakes or plates of crackers, butter and yellow cheese, each ingredient sealed in its own separate wrapper.

If you wanted anything more than a sandwich, like a warm sausage roll or a poached egg on toast, you had to ask for it. A drink meant tea or coffee or Coke or orange juice and there were only two types of coffee – milky coffee or coffee.

Again Susan ordered food she had no intention of eating and a cup of coffee which came in a Pyrex cup and saucer. She took the coffee and headed for a booth in the far corner. The four other customers also sat alone.

The Mercantile still allowed smoking, so Susan lit a cigarette. Then she simply sat there, with her coffee in front of her and the cigarette burning between her fingers, staring ahead of her, trying to flush all thoughts from her overworked mind. The Mercantile encouraged the empty occupation of time by the solitary – no need for iPods or laptops or mobile phones to give strangers the impression of activity and progress.

Susan briefly glanced up to acknowledge the waitress and then ignored the food. The thought of cutting into the yoke of the egg and watching the yellow ooze over the toast, the thought of cutting a piece and putting it into her mouth and chewing and swallowing repelled her. She would leave the food and just smoke her cigarettes and drink her coffee and retreat. Then her body would make its way back to the office and work, then go home and drink and sleep and get up and do it all again.

"I'm sorry." Susan hadn't noticed that Rachel had come into the café and made her way over to the booth where she was sitting. She hadn't noticed her standing next to her table and didn't connect the sound of the words with the person who spoke them. Now she looked up and clawed her way to the front of her mind and registered Rachel's presence and the meaning of the words she'd said.

Susan's expression was blank as Rachel timidly nodded towards the seat opposite her and then slid in to face her across the formica table. Rachel gave her a tight-lipped, nervous smile and shrugged her shoulders and spread her hands palm up in front of her.

"I'm sorry," Rachel repeated. "I shouldn't have spoken to you like that."

Susan waited, was unsure if she was going to speak at all. Then she said, "You apologised to me yesterday too. Haven't spoken to me for all the time you've worked at the *Mail* and then two apologies."

Rachel shrugged and made to speak but said nothing instead.

"So why did you?" Susan asked, her voice empty of feeling. Rachel looked puzzled. "So why did you speak to me like that?" Susan explained. "If you're sorry about it."

"I felt…" Rachel began. "I felt awkward. With Bassett and Pete Lee there. I just..."

"You're the golden girl and I'm nothing," Susan told her. "You didn't want to be seen speaking to the office joke. No. Worse than the office joke. A ghost. A non-person, someone who counts for so little she's more or less invisible."

"I…I don't know," said Rachel.

"It's okay to talk to me here. Or in a car park or a pub. But nowhere someone from the office might see us. Because then there'd be a conflict, between how things are and how you want people to see you." She took a drag of her cigarette and then continued, all the time her voice devoid of any emotion. "Like at school. Where the misfits are only allowed to consort with the cool kids under certain conditions. Well, I knew I was one of the untouchables, but I never realised a prick like Bassett was a cool kid. Shagging him, are you?"

Rachel looked shocked. "No!" she said. "No, I'm not."

"He wants to, though. Doesn't he?" asked Susan.

"I don't know," said Rachel. Then she said, "Yes. Probably. What does it matter anyway?"

"You're right," said Susan. "It doesn't matter at all."

The two women were quiet for a short while, before Rachel said she was going to get a coffee and asked Susan if she wanted another one, to which Susan said she did.

"I rang Strangeways," she said as she sat back down. "A visiting order had already been arranged. By Sweeney I guess. The appointment's for 10.30 Saturday morning, I'm afraid, but that should give you time to get back for your son. You still interested?"

"Yes," Susan said. "The funny thing is I am. If you want me."

"Of course I do," said Rachel. "Everything I said last night still holds. I need your help. What happened in the office this morning was bad of me, I know. I'm sorry. There, I've said it again. It was stupid and immature of me."

"I'll come," Susan said. Inside she felt restored to some extent. She didn't like the fact, but it was true. She had sometimes wished for a life of unthinking monotony, with no sense of hope or release because those promises were too often empty and just left you feeling worse. But maybe it wasn't what she really wanted. In the space of a day now, she'd been picked up and thrown down and then picked up again and while she resented the lack of control, she was nevertheless reaching out her hand to help raise herself up, even if she suspected that it was only to be dropped again.

"I'll come," she repeated. "But I don't want to feel like this again." She took a piece of paper from her bag and scribbled down her mobile number on it. "Here," she said, passing it to

Rachel. "If you want to avoid talking to..."

"It's not that," Rachel protested, but Susan ploughed on. "If you want to avoid talking to me, use that. Call or text me. Might be better anyway. I don't think anyone in the office is going to encourage us on this story."

Rachel took the number and nodded. "Fine," she said and took a card out of her pocket and handed it to Susan. "All my numbers are on there," she said.

"Everyone's giving me cards these days," said Susan. When Rachel looked puzzled, she said, "Nothing. Doesn't matter."

Rachel made to get up and leave. "I'm not going back to the office," she said. "Otherwise…"

Susan waved her away. "Don't worry. We're undercover now, remember?"

Rachel smiled. "Yes," she said. "But I didn't want you to think…I've got to go and get my Dad a present. It's his birthday soon."

"More Art Blakey CDs?" Susan asked.

"No," Rachel replied, smiling still. "I'd just get him something he's already got. No, a cardigan probably. Something safe."

"Get him a saxophone," Susan suggested.

"God, no. My Mum would kill me."

Susan watched Rachel go, then she thought and suddenly called her back. "You'd better sort another visiting order for me."

"That means ringing Sweeney," Rachel said. She took a deep breath and added, "Okay, no problem."

"And another thing," Susan said. "Are you busy tonight?"

"What…" Rachel began. "I mean…"

"Don't worry," Susan said. "You don't have to give me one of your Bassett evasions. I'm out tonight following up that prostitute story. Thought you might like to come. Be interesting."

"Okay," said Rachel, after a little hesitation. "Yeah, I will."

Susan held up the card Rachel had given her. "I'll text you," she said. "Let you know the details."

Later that day, back at the office, Susan rang the planning office to see if a visit had been made to the Northern Warehouse site. When she'd finished the call, she wrote what she had and passed it to Pete Lee for subbing. She knew it wouldn't get through, and that she'd soon be back in Allen's office, but she didn't care. She smiled at what the planning officer had told her, and reminded herself that, though her ex-husband might be a decent man, his father was still a pig.

Chapter Eight

At just gone 20 past 11 that night, Susan left the bar at the Adelphi Hotel and walked back along Lime Street to the station, where she'd arranged to meet Rachel. She had spent the evening caged inside her flat, wanting a drink but forcing herself not to have one. Too early, but keen to get out, she'd left her flat and started on foot down into the centre of town. Something stopped her as she walked past the Adelphi and she'd gone in and walked straight into the bar. Without thinking, and without even liking whiskey, she'd ordered a glass of Bushmills and sat at the bar and drank it. It was a shabby place, in truth, well past its prime as the best hotel in the city, the place where wealthy travellers stayed before catching one of the ocean liners that used to cruise the Mersey to head for New York or Shanghai or Buenos Aires. The bar had been renamed after a jump at Aintree – Becher's – in some desperate attempt to attract new custom, and posters advertised a cellar disco called Shooter's where you could dance till 2am on Friday and Saturday. The carpet in Becher's was worn and the upholstery of the seats was torn in places. The horse racing prints that hung sadly on the walls spoke of job lots and amateur interior design. Apart from Susan, there were only two other customers, both fat men convinced they looked good in bright block colour shirts hanging untucked over their trousers.

Susan liked the bar. It reminded her of the Mercantile and she imagined herself coming here again. She saw one of the fat men staring at her, wondering if she was a prostitute and then deciding that, even if she was, she was too old. She caught sight of her reflection in the decorated mirror behind the bar, her face looking back at her from beside a horse landing on the far side of a fence. She looked rough, she thought. She needed a haircut and a new coat and that was just for starters. A complete makeover was what she needed, like those offered on TV to housewives who've forgotten they're women. So she'd had another Bushmills and decided if she drank enough of it she could get to like it.

At 11.25 Susan stood at the entrance to Lime Street Station. She felt sick and wished she'd eaten something that day. Her mouth felt sour and her head was slightly clouded. The events of the past day or so would have been considered ordinary to so many others – a woman found dead, a few conversations with a colleague. Yet they had shaken her out of her torpor and started her thinking and talking and reacting again. She'd felt better than she had for years and worse also and had no idea where matters were taking her. Still, she was here now, standing in the freezing cold on a Wednesday night near Christmas, outside Lime Street Station.

Town was fuller than usual, but then that was because Christmas was coming. This part of Liverpool had none of the cosiness or restrained enjoyment of Peter Kavanagh's bar the night before. And none of the grace or elegance either. Above Susan towered the Concourse building, a 1970s eyesore that overpowered the listed status of the railway station and that was now bothering the planners and architects who didn't know what to do with it. The councillors were desperately trying to hide the city's mistakes, like people who stuffed things in drawers and called it cleaning.

Around Susan swarmed people who were out in earnest. They'd come out wanting to get drunk and most of them looked like they'd managed it. Now they wanted their next drink, or their train, or their taxi, or their kebab, or their boyfriend back. Girls who'd looked good a couple of hours ago staggered into the station still with traces of tinsel in their hair, their mascara smudged and their heels buckling. Sharp eyed boys with cropped and gelled hair defied the cold in their short sleeved shirts and stalked around girls too drunk to notice they were there.

Susan stood, a still point in this quiet mayhem, shivering in her thin mac, her gloved hands pushed deep into her pockets. Rachel was late.

Fifteen minutes later Rachel arrived, jumping out of the back of a black cab that was immediately swamped by would-be fares. She was wearing a thick black parka and blue jeans tucked into calf-length leather boots. She also had on a hat and a pair of woollen gloves, in all a sharp contrast both to Susan and all the other women weaving through town.

"Don't tell me," said Susan. "You're sorry."

"My Dad," Rachel explained. "He insisted on bringing me and I insisted on getting a taxi."

"You won in the end, though."

"Just," said Rachel. "You must be freezing."

"Yes," said Susan. "I am." The thought that another glass of whiskey might warm her up flashed through her mind, but she knew instantly that that was an excuse just to have another drink. Alcohol did nothing of the kind. Even a St Bernard knew that. "Did you talk to Sweeney about a VO for me?"

"Left a message with one of his men," Rachel said curtly, trying to push Sweeney out of her mind. She forced herself to sound cheerier. "Our date not here yet?" she asked. Susan shivered a no, and Rachel went on, "Look, on Saturday, I know you want to be back in Liverpool for your son's football match."

"Rugby," Susan corrected.

"What?" said Rachel. "Oh, yeah, sorry. Rugby. But if we're finished at Strangeways in time, we could have a quick look round the shops. Get you a Winter coat. They say it's just going to get colder."

"We'll see," replied Susan, still guarded after the way she'd been treated that morning, but nevertheless pleased by the idea, not least because she was so cold. Rachel was about to say more, but Susan had spotted a car pulling into the station and circling around to pull up next to them. "This is us," she said, nodding her head towards the blue Mondeo. "I hope he's got the heating on."

A man got out of the car and smiled tentatively at the two women.

"Clarkey!" he shouted, then beamed a smile. "How you doing, love?" He beckoned them towards the car, moving to open the back door for them.

Susan was too cold to bother with reunions or introductions. She darted into the car and slid along the back seat. Ignoring everyone else, she sat with her arms folded, her legs clamped together and her eyes shut, waiting for the warmth from the car heater to make its way around and into her. Rachel, too soon out of her taxi and too well-dressed to have felt any cold, got in after Susan. Brian Nulty closed her door, then got into the front passenger seat and closed his own door after him. He turned round in his seat to look at the two women. He smiled at Susan's shivering figure.

"Don't you worry yourself, Susan, girl," he said. "We'll handle the introductions ourselves." Still with her eyes shut, Susan managed to raise two fingers at Nulty, instantly back in the easy relationship she'd had with him in the past. Nulty laughed and sang a burst of '*Like You've Never been Gone*'. He then twisted further round to look at Rachel, directly behind him, awkwardly manoeuvring his right arm round and over his seat.

"Always was a stickler for the social niceties, our Sue. Comes from being born down south," he said. He reached towards Rachel. "Brian Nulty. And 'e's Kevin Monroe," he said, tilting his head towards the driver..

"Rachel Jack," Rachel replied. She took his hand and shook it as best she could. "I work on the *Mail*, with Susan."

"Aye, aye, Kev, lad," Nulty said to the driver. "That's two stars of the print media we're in the midst of. This one covered the Sweeney trial. Pleased to meet you."

Momentarily, Rachel's smile lost its warmth at the mention of the name. "Yes," she said, uneasily, then, recovering, added, "I'm flattered."

Nulty ignored the comment. "What a fuckin' mess that was," he said. "Farce." He looked over at Susan, smiling as he noticed she'd relaxed a little and had opened her eyes. "Better?" he asked.

Susan shivered a nod. "A little. I can almost feel my fingers." She looked at Nulty. He hadn't changed. Still the most unlikely man you could imagine to be involved in vice work. He must be nearly 50, now, she thought, remembering he was a few years older than her when they first met, but full of life and energy, so he could seem years younger. Mischievous eyes twinkled beneath his short-light-brown hair, and he was rarely without a smile. Susan remembered that people constantly misjudged him. One of the nicest men you could meet, dedicated to his family, Brian Nulty cared fiercely about his work and was highly protective of the girls on the street. Anyone who failed to share his high standards, or who dismissed him as a lightweight, would lose one sort of fight or another.

"It's good to see you again, Brian," Susan said. "How's your son?" Nulty's son was maybe a year older than her own boy, born with Down's Syndrome.

"Stephen?" he replied. Immediately his voice became warmer. "He's doing well. Twelve now, goes to a school in Mossley Hill. Just become interested in football, unfortunately. I blame DC Monroe here," he said, nodding towards the man behind the steering wheel. "Taken him to a few Everton games, and now the poor lad's hooked. I mean, it's bad enough the boy's got Down's Syndrome. But Everton as well?"

Monroe couldn't stay quiet any longer. His accent was thicker than Nulty's. "'bout time Steve 'ad some guidance from a decent role model!" He looked over his shoulder at Rachel. "I couldn't stand by any longer, love. Know what I mean?"

Rachel smiled. "I'm afraid I'm not much of a football fan."
Monroe groaned in mock disgust. "That's i'," he said. "I'm stopping the car tight now. Youse can all walk."

"All walk alone, eh, Kev?" asked Nulty.

"That's not even close to bein' funny, Brian," Monroe told his boss. "You've crossed a line there."

"You were a rugby man, weren't you, Brian?" Susan asked.

"Rugby League," Nulty replied, pretending to bridle with indignation. "St Helens. None of your soft, overpaid pretty boy rubbish."

"Don't get him started," Monroe said. "Please. How can a Scouser not like footie? It's not natural."

Nulty ignored Monroe. "Got a daughter now, too," said Nulty. "Lucy. Seven. Anyway, what about your lad? Michael, isn't it?"

Susan's eyes saddened briefly. "He's well," she said softly. "Started senior school a couple of months ago. You'd be pleased. He's started playing rugby for his school."

"League or Union?" Nulty asked brightly.

"Does it matter?" said Monroe.

"You pipe down, you," Nulty told him. "Go on, Sue."

"Oh," said Susan, sheepishly. "Union, I'm afraid."

Nulty sighed. "I might have known," he said. "Still, better than nothin'."

"This is good of you, Brian," Susan said. She didn't want to talk about her son anymore and was anxious to switch the conversation round to the matter in hand. "Still no idea of who the woman was?"

"Nah," Nulty replied. "Nothin's changed since we spoke earlier. No-one's come forward to report anyone missin', so chances are she lived alone. No real contact with neighbours, no friends of any sort. Or, of course, the people who did know her aren't the sort who like chattin' to coppers."

"This is the prostitute whose death you covered?" Rachel asked Susan. Nulty looked around at her, surprised at the question.

"Rachel's not working directly on the story," Susan explained. "Not yet, anyway. She's just here for the experience as much as anything." Then she turned to Rachel. "Yes," she said. "The woman who was found at the Northern Warehouse. Early Tuesday morning."

"Late Monday night," Nulty corrected. "Beaten to death, then beaten some more then set on fire. We don't know much about her and what we do know we can't be sure of. Mid-forties, probably a prostitute, maybe murdered by someone with a religious hang-up."

"How do you mean?" asked Rachel.

DC Monroe replied to this question. "She was laid out with her legs together and her arms outstretched. Like on a cross. Her face was pulped and the skin on her hands and fingers was mashed down to the bone."

"Dear God," said Rachel. "You think maybe the thing with the hands is like a…" She struggled for the word.

"Stigmata," Nulty said. "You never know. But the powers-that-be have decided that we just keep it low-key. Until there's another one. If there's another one. Just a dead prostitute, after all. Come on, Kev," he said to Monroe. "Let's go."

Monroe eased the car left out of the station and onto Skelhorne Street. Within a second or two they were away from the crowds of festive drunks and Christmas lights and signs declaring new investment. The streets they were heading for now had little foot traffic and few cars. The brick and concrete they passed were grimy and uncared for, the backs of buildings not intended to be on view and therefore left ignored.

"We're just going on a trawl round," said Nulty, Monroe keeping the car in second gear, not going over 15 miles per hour. "Warn the girls. Ask if they've noticed anyone missin'."

Monroe crisscrossed the streets between Copperas Hill and London Road. The roads were still and freezing. The shouts and cries of revellers only a few hundred yards away came to Rachel as muffled, threatening, disembodied.

They pulled up next to a girl standing alone on the pavement. She was wearing high-heeled shoes and a short skirt. Her denim jacket was open, showing a crop top revealing the pale flesh of her stomach. The skin on her legs was blotched. Stiff in the cold, she held a cigarette in her right hand, pressed tight to her side with the fingers fanning out slightly. Her hair was lank and dyed black. She approached the car. Rachel guessed she was 30 but knew she could just as easily have been 17 or 18.

"Do we know 'er, Kev?" Nulty asked quietly as the girl leaned in towards the open window. Monroe shook his head. "You must be freezin'," Nulty said to the girl. His voice was tender and considerate.

"You gonna warm me up?" the girl asked. She was resting one hand on the roof of the car and jutting one hip out, trying to look provocative. She just looked awkward. She hadn't noticed the women in the back. "If you want me to do both of yous, 'e'll to wait in the car. Not 'avin' you both gerrout together."

"Sorry, love," said Brian. "That's not why we're 'ere. Police, I'm afraid. I'm Brian Nulty and this is Kevin Monroe."

"Fuck off," the girl said. She made to walk back to her mark but Brian asked her to wait.

"There's been a murder," he said. "We just wanted to let you know. Warn you, like."

The girl was standing up straight now. She flinched a little when she heard the word murder, but quickly restored a look of blank defiance and nonchalance.

"Right," she said. She waited for the car to pull away.

"What's your name?" Brian asked.

She hesitated and then said, "Trish."

"Mind if we get out the car, Trish?" he asked. "Nicer talkin' that way." He handed her his and Monroe's warrant cards. "You check those first. Make sure we're kosher." He waited until she'd looked at them and given them back, even though he knew she didn't really know what to look for. Then he and Monroe got out of the car and stood near her. They leant on the car, giving her space, not crowding her.

"You had this patch long Trish?" Brian asked.

"Few weeks," she replied, guarded.

"Noticed anyone missin'?"

"How d'you mean like?" she asked.

"We don't know who the murdered woman was," Nulty said. "We're tryin' to find out. You might've noticed one of the girls not in her usual place."

"No," she said. "Seen nott'n."

"Okay," Nulty said. "Thanks anyway." He held out his card to the girl, who waited a second or two before taking it. She glanced nervously back over her shoulder as she took it. Behind her, in the shadows, there was a movement. Without needing to be told, Monroe jumped back into the car and drove it round the corner, bumping it up onto the pavement. Nulty followed on foot, sprinting to where he'd seen the movement. By the time he got there, Monroe had pulled the nose of the car tight against the wall, pinning the figure in place. He got out and pushed the man back as he tried to clamber over the bonnet of the Mondeo. Susan got out too, with Rachel following after a moment's hesitation. The two women stood on the far side of the car while Nulty and Monroe had the man trapped, one at the bonnet, the other at the boot.

"Aye, aye, pal," Monroe said. "In a bit of a 'urry, aren't you? If we were the sensitive sort, we might take that a bit personal."

The figure edged away from Monroe, towards the middle of the car, stopping before he got too close to Nulty. It was enough to bring him out of the shadows. He was wearing a sweatshirt with the hood pulled over his head, a donkey jacket over that.

"Take the hood off," ordered Monroe.

"Who the fuck are you?" he demanded.

Nulty smiled. "Lovely," he said. "That's broken the ice. We can start to get to know each other now. Who the fuck would you like us to be?"

The man looked bemused. "You wha'?"

"Who would you like us to be?" echoed Monroe, bringing the man's attention back to him. "We could be part of an East European gang, flooding the streets of Liverpool with young Romanian girls," Monroe said. "But we need to get rid of the local competition first. Start with no-marks like you. Nobody'd miss you."

"The accent gives us away, Kev," Nulty called over to Monroe, leaving the man trapped between them out of the conversation. Nulty went on. "'ow about we're vigilantes? You know, two ordinary men who've been pushed too far. Now we're cleaning up the filth from the streets?"

"Ey Bri, I like tha' you know," Monroe said. "Can we be tha'?" He looked at the man in the hood again. "Is tha' alright with you mate? We're vigilantes. And we're goin' to clean you from the streets."

"Fuck off," the man told him. His voiced lacked conviction. Nulty turned to Susan and Rachel. "There's your Scouse wit for you. It's no wonder we've got a reputation for humorous repartee."

"We're police," said Monroe patiently. "We're not really vigilantes. 'ad you goin' though, didn't we?" He took his warrant card out of his pocket and showed it to the man. "The hood," he said and the man put his hood down. His face was sharp featured and his eyes wary. He wore an earring in his right ear and his hair was cropped close to the scalp.

"One of yours, is she?" asked Monroe, nodding his head back

to the corner where the girl had been standing.

"Don't know what you're talking about," he said.

"What's your name?" Nulty asked.

"John," the man replied.

"Surname?"

"Smith."

"Do you have any identification on you, Mr Smith?" Nulty asked.

"No."

"Would you mind if we searched you?" Rachel was amazed at Nulty's calmness and smiling manner with the man, which threw him off guard completely.

Reluctantly the man took a wallet from his back pocket. He gave it to Nulty, who opened it and pulled out a card.

"Mr Smith," Nulty said. "This card is in the name of Jason Dooley. I'm not sure I understand. Do you not want the people at Blockbuster Video to know your real name?" He took another card out. "This also is in the name of Jason Dooley. If you've just found the wallet and are on the way to a police station to return it, we could give you a lift."

The man stared sullenly at Nulty. Monroe went back to the car and called in the name they'd just been given.

"Mr Dooley," said Nulty. "Would you mind just waitin' 'ere while we check one or two things?" The man said nothing. When Monroe came back, he told Nulty Dooley's last known address and gave him a short list of the petty offences which Dooley had committed.

"Mr Dooley," Nulty said. "It wouldn't at all surprise me if you were acting as pimp to this girl and maybe others too. We regularly patrol this area. If we find you 'angin' around here again, we'll take you in for questionin'. Do you understand?" Dooley snorted derisively at this, then walked away. Monroe was clearly angered, but Nulty showed no reaction at all. The two officers got back into the car; Rachel and Susan followed suit.

"Frustrating," commented Susan.

"Oh yeah. Too right," agreed Nulty. "'e was 'er pimp alright. But she'll never give evidence against him. Even if he beat 'er black and blue, she'd just say 'e didn't mean it and 'e loves 'er really. They always do. Best we can do is let them know we're around."

Monroe pulled the car back onto the road and they resumed their crawl through the back streets. Coal Street, Pudsey Street, up Lord Nelson Street, over Copperas Hill and into Russell Street, creeping round the Royal Mail sorting office and along Hawke Street, behind the Adelphi Hotel. In all they stopped maybe eight or nine women, all different ages and all exactly the same, colourless skin, convulsed with cold, sucking on cigarettes. Some of them wore strings of tinsel and one, Mandy, had a headband from which tinny bells stuck out on elasticated stalks. Susan had seen many girls wearing such things as they weaved their way past her while she was waiting for Rachel. Mandy, numb with cold and drugs, giggled as she said the bells jangled while she bobbed up and down on the punters.

None of the girls was aware of anyone missing and all were going to take their chances if there was a killer on the streets. Up towards the University, meandering their way towards it as if trying to take it by surprise. Then across past the Catholic Cathedral, Paddy's Wigwam, a giant Apollo capsule crashed into the top of Mount Pleasant, along Hope Street, passing Susan's flat, and around the Anglican Cathedral, which loomed into the sky, its red stone thrown into light and shadow by spotlights dotted around its grounds.

They called it a day at 2.30. Rachel and Susan accepted Nulty's invitation to go for a drink at a private members' club on Rodney Street.

"Remember this place?" Nulty asked Susan as Monroe signed the two women in.

"I do, yeah," said Susan. "Although I'm not sure how. I think

I only ever came here when I was blind drunk to start with."
She turned to Rachel, who was looking puzzled. "It used to be the Press Club," she explained. "Before your time. What is it now?"

"The Green Room," Nulty told her. The four of them walked through into a large lounge area with a bar down one side of the room. "They're trying to make it into some sort of gentlemen's club. That's the look they're aiming for, at least." The walls were panelled in dark wood and hung with black and white prints showing scenes of old Liverpool. Around the room were clusters of leather chairs around low tables. Nulty led the way to one such group near the back of the room.

"It's certainly changed," said Susan. "At least I think it has. Like I said, I was never here and sober."

"I've never heard of this place," Rachel said. "I love it."

"You should join," Monroe told her. "The clientele's not up to much, mind. Coppers and journalists mostly." Rachel laughed. "I'll put you for membership, if you like."

"Thanks," Rachel told him. "I'd like that."

Monroe saw some people he knew and excused himself to go over and say hello. Nulty went to the bar, leaving the two women alone.

"Good night?" Susan asked.

"Really good," Rachel said. "Sorry. I don't mean…you know, driving round red light areas trying to identify a dead prostitute. It's been interesting. An eye-opener."

"I know what you mean. It felt good to me too," said Susan. "It's been years since I've done anything like this. Feels almost like the old days."

"No joy though."

"No," Susan agreed. "But it's another story, anyway. Even if it'll just get thrown out."

Nulty came back from the bar with the drinks, signalling to Monroe that his pint was there. He put the tray down on the table. Susan tried not to look too eager for the red wine Brian

had bought her. But at least it was a small one, she told herself, and she wouldn't smoke. She felt she wanted to try, if nothing else. She took the wine and sipped at it. Nulty smiled and sat down. He passed a glass of Bushmills to Rachel.
"You've good taste in whiskey, Rachel, love." He took a sip of his own drink and settled back in his chair, a look of tiredness creeping over his features. Monroe returned and gulped down some beer.
"So," Susan said. "What next, do you reckon?"
Brian sighed. "We'll keep on asking the girls on the streets. 'ope someone'll come forward. Wait for conclusive results from the lab, see if that throws anything up."
"What about the massage parlours?" Susan asked. "Might be worth trying them." Nulty nodded.
"She was found on the streets, though," said Monroe. "There are no parlours nearby. Stands to reason she was on the streets 'erself."
"But think about where she was found," said Susan. "Down some alley way between two halves of a disused warehouse. Not exactly a good patch. No passing trade there."
"That's where she died, Sue," said Nulty, again surprising Rachel by using the shortened version of her name. She didn't think of her as a Sue, had barely thought of her as a Susan until a day or so ago. Susan noted the familiar use of her name as well, and glowed inside. She was being treated like a person again, someone who could contribute. Then again, Brian Nulty had always been like that. Straight as an arrow, open and kind, one of the few men she'd worked with who'd never tried anything on with her and with whom she'd never have tried anything herself. She could have guessed what the answer would have been.
"She wasn't moved there, you mean?" Rachel said.
"No," Nulty said. "Sure of it. If she was taken there, she was alive at the time. But she died in that alleyway."
"Little Porter Street," Susan said. She took another tiny sip of

her wine, trying to make it last, desperate not to be the only one ordering a second drink. She looked around at all the other customers who were smoking and fought her longing for a cigarette.

"The women we saw tonight," Rachel said. "They were all addicts, weren't they?"

"Yeah," Monroe said. "Pretty much. That's the main reason they do it, to get money for drugs. The money they don't 'and over to their pimps, any road."

"Well, was this woman?" Rachel asked.

"No obvious signs," Nulty told her. "No track marks on her arms. There could be something in the bloodstream. As I said, not got the results back."

"But even so," said Susan. "What are they likely to show? Those girls tonight are on heroin. They inject. If the dead woman's shown to have been using weed, well, a habit like that's hardly likely to send her out onto the streets, is it? And she's not going to be a cokehead, is she? That's not the drug of choice for someone like her."

"Don't make too many assumptions, Susan," Brian warned.

Susan nodded. "But you've got to make some assumptions, Brian. Until there's something concrete to go on, at any rate. If we assume she's a prostitute, then we can assume she's more likely to have been a prostitute in a massage parlour."

"Why is that?" Rachel asked.

Nulty smiled. "There's a 'ierarchy in prostitution," he began. "At the bottom are the ones who work on the streets. Addicts, almost exclusively, just tryin' to pay for their 'abits. Controlled by pimps. Not the big gangs you 'ear about, by and large. Small-time crooks, petty criminals who run maybe two or three girls. Sometimes the pimp'll get the girl 'ooked and then put her out to earn 'im some cash and she'll get paid in whatever drug 'e's got 'er into. Often it'll be a boyfriend, who convinces the girl that if she really loves 'im she won't mind going out and earning for him. It's pathetic, truly pathetic." He sipped some more of his whiskey. "Now, above the street girls you 'ave the massage parlours. You should know all about those, seeing 'ow many adverts the *Mail* carries for them every Friday."

"Not really massage parlours then?" asked Rachel.

Nulty smiled. "They will do massages, if that's what they're asked for," he said. "But no, they're brothels, basically. Clean and well-run, mind. Where do you live, Rachel?"

The question took Rachel by surprise. "Childwall," she said. "Menlove Gardens."

"Near the 'alfway 'ouse?" Nulty asked and Rachel nodded. "Well," he continued. "You've got two very nice little parlours within ten minutes' walk of you. One on Taggart Avenue and another on Allerton Road, near the library. Discreet, of course. That part of the city wouldn't stand for anything else. But they're there. Kev and me can show you when we drop you at 'ome."

"You look appalled," Susan said to Rachel.

"I am," she replied.

"You ought to follow your father," Susan said. "Next time he pops out for a paper." Rachel looked indignant and playfully slapped Susan's arm, while Nulty and Monroe laughed.

"They're good, these places, for the most part," Nulty said. "The women who work there are just looking for a few more pounds a week to make ends meet. Hours to suit, letting them pick up the children from school and so on. Regular 'ealth check-ups."

"And," said Susan, "the owners don't take addicts. A lot of these parlours remind you of seaside B&Bs, run by landlady types. I did a story on them years back, a big feature. A real education I got. Plus, I got to know Brian here."

Nulty became serious again. "If she did work in a massage parlour, then what was she doing in Little Porter Street so late on Friday night?"

"Private client?" Rachel suggested. "A married man who took

her there?"

"It's a grim place," Nulty told her. "They could have found somewhere better."

"Do you think he might have taken her there knowing he was going to kill her?" asked Susan.

"Possibly," said Nulty. "We'll start with the parlours tomorrow. Now, if you've finished your drinks, we'll take you 'ome."

It was a short drive from the Green Room to Susan's flat on Hope Street. Nulty walked Susan the few short steps to her door.

"Thanks, Brian," she said. "I mean it. It's been great."

"Looking for prostitutes in the dead hours of the night followed by a glass of cheap wine in a seedy club?" Brian said. "My wife always insists I take her to a nice restaurant."

Susan smiled briefly. "No, really." She paused, could almost feel tears pricking her eyes. "I've not found things easy, not for a long time."

"Get some sleep, Sue. And ring me tomorrow, early evening. I'll 'ave been to a few parlours by then. Might 'ave some news."

Susan went inside. Nulty returned to the car and they set off to take Rachel back to her home in Childwall. Monroe refused to tell her where the massage parlours were near her house; he said she had to guess and then call him and he'd tell her if she was right. Rachel sensed he was flirting with her and, unusually for her, liked the feeling.

By the time she got home it was nearly 4 and she was grateful tomorrow – today – was a day off. Tired, but exhilarated by the evening, she undressed and got into bed. Before turning off the light, she checked her mobile. The message icon was flashing. Deep in her thick winter coat she must have missed the signal, she thought, or wondered if it was Susan sending her a message about the night they'd had together, like two girlfriends comparing notes.

She pressed to read the message and instantly all tiredness left her, leaving only cold and fear in its place.

That second VO means I'm doing you a favour. And that means the rules have changed. What did you think of the Green Room? Night night. FS

She checked the time of the message and saw that it had been sent maybe half an hour earlier, when she'd been in the car with Monroe and Nulty, Susan too, possibly. She wished she'd looked at it then, wished she'd heard the beep of the phone tucked deep inside her coat. She would have been able to tell someone else then, at least she would have had the choice, would have been able to seek reassurance from Susan or the two policemen.

But no, she hadn't heard it. And so she'd read the message here, in her bedroom, sitting up in bed wearing the pyjamas her parents had bought her two birthdays ago, her feet touching the still-warm hot water bottle her mother had put in her bed before she herself went to sleep in a bed in a room just across the hall. This bedroom was a private place. Her life was in here. Her laptop sat on the same desk where she'd studied for her A Levels, there was a chest containing old exercise books and folders from university. There were family photographs on the shelves as well as books she'd bought last week and books she'd had since she was a little girl. Rachel felt exposed and open in a way she couldn't fully explain. It was more than the fact Sweeney had got hold of her mobile number, that he knew she'd been in the Green Room that night. It was like he'd crept up beside her, almost like he was in the bed with her. Stupid to think like that, she told herself. Stupid to let him affect you so much. And what did he mean by the rules have changed, she asked herself. She thought back to their conversation. Just do your job, he'd told her. That was all he wanted. But now? She fought against the feeling that he'd want more, and that he'd take it whenever it suited him.

She got out of bed, put on her dressing gown, took the duvet and went downstairs to lie awake on the couch until her mother came down later that morning to put the kettle on.

Thursday 13 December

LIVERPOOL MORNING MAIL
DEVELOPMENT DELAY RISK TO INVESTORS

Work on one of Liverpool's latest development projects was halted yesterday after a breach of planning regulations.

The Northern Warehouse, a vast site on the banks of the Mersey, just off the dock road, had been earmarked as Liverpool's newest four-star hotel, with local firm O'Hare Design and Construction heading its redevelopment. However, in a routine visit, planning officers noted that construction work currently being carried out had gone over the boundaries set by the accepted application by just over a foot.

An officer in the council planning department said that while a foot might not seem important, it was vital that the integrity both of the planning application and the design were maintained, for the good of the city's heritage.

No-one from O'Hare Design and Construction was available for comment last night, but it is thought that a serious delay may threaten the whole project, resulting in many small investors losing all their money.

By Susan Clarke. Story spiked.

It was just after five in the morning and the sky was still black with night. Apart from the three cars parked side by side the car park was empty. They had arrived one after the other, the last within five minutes of the first. Each car was new, each a shiny executive saloon, expensive, fast and dominant. In each car sat one man. One of them, to the right of the line, got out of his car, pulled his overcoat lapels together, and made his way to the middle car. He climbed into the front passenger seat. The man in the left hand car got into the back seat of the middle car.

"We'll not bother waiting for the other feller," the man in the back said. "Who knows when he'll turn up, if at all."

"He lives closest too," said the man in the passenger seat.

The man in the back spoke again. "So what's all this about? What's so important we have to skulk together at this godless hour like criminals?"

"I thought we should talk," said the driver.

"You did, did you?" asked the man on the back seat. "Well, go on then. What have you got to say?"

The driver hesitated. Now he had been put on the spot, he couldn't think of anything. "What's going on?" he said at last.

The man in the back snorted. "You should know better than either of us," he said.

"The police aren't paying much attention to it," the driver said. "Only a prostitute is the unofficial line. Other enquiries petering out."

"So that's good then," the man in front said.

"But what about the reporter?" said the driver. "Will she keep with it?"

"There's nothing to worry about there," the front seat man said. "She'll give up soon enough. She's lost it. A drunk. Ask anyone."

"But shouldn't we do something about her?" the driver said.

"What do you suggest?" the man the back demanded. "Have her killed? Christ man, we're not the fucking mafia, you know. Have you got a taste for this business? Another body won't be ignored so easily."

"I didn't mean that," said the driver.

"So what then?" said the man in the back. He was staring at the rear view mirror but the driver wouldn't meet his eye.

"I don't know...warn her?" the driver said.

"She might be a drunk but she's not stupid," the man in the back said. "Do you not think warning her off will have just the opposite fucking effect?"

The driver turned round angrily, but his anger was weak.
"I've got a lot to lose..." he began.
The man in the back laughed at him. "We've all got a lot to fucking lose, you idiot. What do you think? You're the only one who'll go down for it? The rest of us will just have our arses smacked. You fucking idiot."
"We can get a message to her somehow," the man in the front said. "So she won't suspect anything."
"Then we've said enough," the man in the back said. He got out, returned to his own car and drove away.
"And if that doesn't work?" the driver said.
"Then you can think of something else," said the man next to him.

Chapter Nine

Rachel's mother cared deeply for her daughter, Rachel knew that. But she also knew that her mother wasn't the type to ask questions. She'd wait until Rachel wanted to tell her something and then listen. So Rachel wasn't surprised when her mother ignored the fact that her daughter was lying on the couch instead of in bed when she came down that morning. She simply asked her if she wanted tea or coffee, then told her she might want to take the duvet back up to her bedroom before her father came down and started pestering her with questions, demanding to know why she was down here when there was a perfectly good bed upstairs, before launching into an interrogation regarding what she did the night before.

Rachel did as her mother suggested. In her room, she looked again at the message from Franny Sweeney. Its effect wasn't as powerful as it had been at four that morning, but it still gave her a tremor of fear and worry. Shrugging it off, she changed into shorts, T-shirt, tracksuit and trainers, determined that her normal routine on her days off, which always started with a trip to the gym, wouldn't be thrown off track.

Returning downstairs, she found her father and mother sitting at the kitchen table. Tea, coffee, milk, cereal, toast, newspapers, everything was as it should be for a retired couple with time to enjoy life and a nice regard for the proper way of doing things. The sight reassured Rachel, made her smile to herself and reminded her why she was happy, for the moment at least, to keep her search for a place of her own to buy at a leisurely browse.

"Good night?" asked her father.

"It was, actually, as it turned out," Rachel replied. She poured herself a cup of coffee and took a banana from the bowl. She tried to sound as if everything was normal. "Just the usual Christmas thing, you know. We kerb-crawled for prostitutes, then ended the night at a drinking den."

"I'm not going to rise to the bait, you know," her father said. "I know you like to tease me."

"But it's true, though, Dad," she protested.

"It sounds very exciting, Rachel," her mother said.

"And safe, too," said Rachel. "I went with another reporter and we were escorted by two policemen." She finished her banana and gulped down the last of her coffee. "Anyway, I'm off to the gym."

"We're going down to Allerton Road for lunch," said her mother. "There's yet another new place opened that we thought we'd try."

"Before you decide to stick with the usual place?"

"Before he decides, you mean," said her mother, indicating her husband, hidden behind a newspaper.

"I'm perfectly willing to try something new," huffed Mr Jack. "So long as it's better than something old."

Rachel and her mother shared a sceptical look, then Rachel said, "Call me and let me know where you're going." She left the table and went out, picking up a gym bag with a change of clothes in it on her way.

In contrast to Rachel, Susan had fallen asleep instantly and then woken three and a half hours later feeling fully refreshed. She showered quickly, dressed and then drove the short journey down to the river, along the dock road and then up into Old Hall Street and the *Mail* offices. Early again, for the second day running, she felt good about things, so much so that she treated herself to a takeaway coffee from one of the nearby cafés, a grande latte they'd called it, which she carried into the office, complete with plastic lid and drinking hole. If it's good enough for the youngsters, she told herself, laughing inside, then it's good enough for me.

At her desk, she wrote a follow-up story on the dead prostitute, detailing the police search for information among the girls on the city's streets, the appeal for anybody with information to come forward, and a quote from Brian Nulty about test results and his intention to continue his investigation in the massage parlours. She even jazzed up the story with the suggestion of a serial killer. She worked smoothly, with a buzz of satisfaction. The only false note came when she rang DI Nolan, the officer in charge of the investigation, who seemed surprised to hear of Vice's involvement in the case, although he quickly put it down to a break in the communications chain. The story written, she sent it through to be subbed, knowing it would be severely cut but not caring, then settled to the usual routine of translating badly written press releases into space fillers for tomorrow's edition.

Less than an hour later, Bassett was at her shoulder.

"What's the point of sending stuff through when you know it's just going to be thrown out?" he demanded.

"It's a good story, Trevor," she replied, her voice confident and assured.

"It's shit," he told her. "No-one cares about this dead whore. I told you that. And what's all this crap about a serial killer?"

"Listen, Trev," she said. "Now that you've learned to read, perhaps the next thing you should think about is learning what a good story looks like. They don't all have to have the words Capital of Culture 2008 in them, you know. Maybe you could think about that next time you're not kissing the boss's arse. Just a thought."

"Fuck off, you drunk."

"And work on the repartee, Oscar."

"Dalton wants to see you," he said. "Remember, your boyfriend?"

"You're running his messages now, are you?" Susan said, standing up and staring straight at him. "Your mother must be so proud."

"My mother's dead," Bassett said, his face twitching with anger.

"Like I care."

For a moment it seemed years had slipped from Bassett's face, leaving the features of a little boy about to crumple into tears. As if pushed, he stumbled back a pace, reaching out to the partition wall to steady himself. Susan advanced on him, pushing her face into his, as he had done to her the day before. "Sorry, Trevor," she sneered. "I forgot. I'm not meant to fight back. I'm just supposed to take whatever you choose to throw at me, aren't I? Not too much fun being on the receiving end, is it, eh?"

She pushed past him, striding towards Dalton's office. She felt good about standing up to Bassett and knew he'd just got what he deserved, but nevertheless regretted what she'd said about his mother. Still, she wasn't going to apologise.

Dalton's office was on the far side of the room to Susan's little corner. Any further away and she would be on a different floor. It was separated from the main office by a glass-panelled wall. The door was wooden with a clear glass window. Outside, at her desk, sat Monica, Dalton's secretary. Next door was the editor's office, the two room divided by a plasterboard wall but with a connecting door.

Susan hesitated a few feet from Dalton's door. It was shut, unusually, and an overcoat on a hanger over the back of the door prevented anyone from seeing in. The window blinds on the inner wall had all been pulled down and closed shut.

"Is he in?" Susan asked Monica. "Trevor Bassett has just said he wants to see me."

"Oh yes," Monica replied. "Not that anyone's seen him."

"Not like him to be hiding," said Susan. "Normally has the blinds up, doesn't he? Like he's on display? Unless it's been longer than I thought since I was on this side of the room."

"It has been a while," said Monica, who had been with the *Mail* for twenty years without, it seemed, looking a day older. "I still miss you not being over here, Sue." Another Sue, another face from the past. "It was never dull when you were near the top of the ladder."

"I was going to say I met a snake and ended up back at the

bottom," Susan replied. "But that wouldn't be entirely honest."

"Oh, say it anyway," Monica said. "You never were entirely honest, after all. That was one the things I liked about you."

Susan smiled. "I'll go straight in. Okay?"

Monica made a sweeping gesture with her arm and Susan walked up to the door, knocked and went into Dalton's office. Gerry Dalton had aged badly since his affair with Susan ended around five years previously. It wasn't simply that he'd put on some weight and lost some hair – he was 50 after all, so it was to be expected. It was more his pallor and demeanour. His shoulders seemed to be permanently slumped and his face looked dry and drained of colour. It seemed to have got worse with each promotion. The stress was bound to take its toll, but his self-esteem had suffered too, as if the closer he got in his work to Allen, the editor, the more his energy and pride was sapped.

In the years they had worked in the same office since their affair, Susan and Dalton had had little to do with each other, had barely spoken to each other. Without trying too hard, they'd by and large managed to avoid coming within 20 feet of each other, and even when some work matter demanded they talk, conversation was brief and eye contact non-existent. So Susan was surprised when Dalton asked to see her and shocked to stand now within a couple of yards of him, scrutinising him, seeing how time and life had affected this man who once had so appealed to her that she'd taken him to her bed. He was always weak, though, she thought, remembering what she'd said to Rachel the other night in the pub. Then she recalled something else she'd said, about not being able to talk about changing for the worse.

Dalton seemed to be preoccupied, unaware almost that Susan had come in. He was sitting at his desk, looking at something on the computer screen to his left, but not really looking, just turned in that direction, his eyes open but not seeing.

"Gerry?" Susan said. He seemed to remember himself and turned to look at her.

"Susan," he replied. She waited for him to go on, but he said no more.

"Bassett said you wanted to see me," she said, trying to prompt him.

"Yes," he said. "Sit down." He nodded his head at one of the chairs on the other side of his desk. "You're looking well." Susan smiled. "That's just the good manners talking," she said. "I'm not, I know. Neither of us is," she added after a pause. He looked sharply at her and she wondered if she'd said too much. Even when they were having an affair, they could never really have been called lovers. She'd seen to that. She had wanted sex, not intimacy. The shared remembered fondness her words suggested had no basis in what had actually gone on between them.

But the sharpness in his eyes didn't transfer to his voice, which stayed dull and tired. He clicked the mouse to bring up a page on his computer screen, looked at it for a short while, then said, "This dead woman story. Doesn't seem to be going anywhere."

Susan shifted in her seat. "I wouldn't say that exactly, Gerry," she said. "I know there's..." He interrupted her.

"There's nothing," he told her. His voice was still dull, but there was more force to it now, some vague, unformed anger there, so it seemed to Susan. "There's no name, no evidence, no leads of any sort. The police aren't even sure she was a prostitute; they're just stumbling round the streets hoping someone'll come forward and confess."

"It's a good story, Gerry. A woman found battered to death, no-one with any idea who she was. It's a real mystery. And it could be a serial killer," she added. "You never know, with that crucifixion business."

"Do me a favour," he said, his tone uglier, leaving Susan unsure where his anger was coming from or why it was directed at her. "There's no serial killer. You know that. You're just jumping on a simple story and trying to blow it all out of proportion."

"You put me on this story, Gerry," Susan said. "Bassett said you told him to give it to me."

"I know, but I didn't…" He stopped.

Susan finished the sentence for him. "You didn't think I'd be bothered making anything of it. Is that it?" Dalton ignored the question. "But even so," she went on, "What difference does that make? I mean, if I'm actually doing my job properly, what's the problem?"

Dalton almost snarled at her. "Stop questioning my decision. I've told you. There's nothing there. Just get back to doing your usual stuff, re-writing press releases and coming in stinking of drink."

She stood up and made to leave. Just as she reached the door, Dalton spoke again. The anger that had shown itself so suddenly just as quickly vanished. "Susan, I'm sorry. Allen says to drop it. He said he's already told you."

"He also said he'd put a proper reporter on it instead of me," Susan said. "So who's that?"

Dalton ignored the question. "Nobody wants to read about things like that," he said. "She was only a hooker. And we don't even know her name."

Susan turned and looked at him. "And what do you say? Do you say drop it too?"

"Yes," he replied, and sat back heavily in his seat. "Close the door behind you."

Chapter Ten

Rachel increased the speed on the treadmill, pushing it up to 11 km per hour. Another fifteen minutes at this speed and then she'd do some weights. It was faster than she normally ran, but she felt comfortable at the new pace. Despite the late night and the lack of sleep – maybe because of it – she felt full of energy. She also felt the need to push herself, to cauterise the fears that Sweeney's text had aroused in her again. She looked at herself running in the mirror right in front of her. Legs pumping and pounding, arms punching space. Her ears were filled with the music from her iPod – Keane, Kaiser Chiefs, Coldplay, Arctic Monkeys, songs she only ever listened to in here or in her car.

She watched the clock on the running machine count down each second of each minute. All thoughts were erased from her mind by the music and the exertion. All thoughts except one. Suddenly, with striking clarity, one thought only remained, one question completely isolated in her brain: *How* had Franny Sweeney got her mobile number? As the question struck her, she stumbled, her foot hitting the side of the machine instead of the belt. She gripped the sidebars with both hands and lifted herself off the track, bringing both feet to rest on the platforms, so she stood astride the whirring track and gasped air into her lungs.

Why hadn't this occurred to her before, she wondered. Then she realised she'd just assumed that Sweeney could just summon up whatever information he wanted, like he had supernatural powers. But no. Of course that couldn't be. Someone had to give him the number. He would have had to go to someone and ask for it, demand it, and that someone would have simply handed it over, because Franny Sweeney doesn't ask twice for anything.

She forced herself back on to the treadmill and completed the time she'd set. She moved on to the weights and strained through every set and every repetition. She was suddenly preoccupied with thoughts of Franny Sweeney again. All the energy she'd felt when she first walked into the gym had dissipated, but she was determined that nothing and no-one would make her change the day she had planned for herself. She wasn't going to let anyone dictate her responses or actions.

Later, showered and dressed, her short hair roughly dried and a few quick touches of make-up applied, she left. The gym was built in a converted aircraft hangar on the site of Liverpool's old airport. The terminus itself had been converted too, into an award-winning hotel, the sleek art deco lines and soft curves of the original building retained and enhanced, and every fitting and every piece of furniture added in keeping with the period. This area, like so many in the city, was changing. New office blocks were being built, urban sculptures were being erected, new money was coming in, but around it still the shabby council estates of Speke crumbled and every now and then the crime for which the estate had been feared intruded on Liverpool's bright new future. Only a year ago, at the new airport just a few minutes' drive away, a man had been murdered by two car thieves who'd jumped into the car while the driver was unloading the boot and reversed him into a wall.

Rachel made her way across the car park and into the hotel. She wanted to sit and have a coffee by herself, before meeting her parents. As she walked, she thought of Susan. She thought of her ex-husband and his plans to convert the warehouse a few miles along the river. And she thought of Allen, the editor of the *Mail*, who'd been so reluctant to put the airport murder on the front page the year before. Liverpool should mean progress and prosperity, he'd said, not crime, not murder.

The hotel café was quiet, just a few couples having a mid-morning coffee. Rachel ordered at the bar, then went to sit at a table by the window. The café was at the back of the hotel and Rachel's table overlooked the old runway. The developers hadn't got around to this part yet, so it remained a wide stretch of cracked concrete with tufts of grass and weeds breaking through the cracks. Beyond the runway was the river, grey brown and murky beneath the grey winter sky, and across the river was the Wirral. Colours bled into each other, muted and dull, all shapes indistinct.

Rachel ignored the small cellophane-wrapped biscuit and the tubes of sugar in the saucer and sat sipping her coffee, staring out across the runway. She admitted to herself that, earlier, her thoughts still panicked, she wondered if Susan had passed on her mobile number to Sweeney. It was possible, of course, if maybe a little unlikely. Someone like Sweeney would be happy enough to cultivate a few tame reporters, but he'd only want to know those who could do him some good, useful ones in a position to pass on information or write favourable stories. Susan didn't come into that category; it was a long time since she'd been in a position of influence.

It struck her she came into that category. Quick and clever and ambitious, with a bright future ahead of her, she fitted the bill. Was she so ready to accuse and judge others on the paper when she had left herself open to accusation? Sweeney had picked her out, had given her the makings of a terrific story. And she'd taken the gift. Couldn't have refused, she told herself, but when he comes asking for something in return? What then? He'd said he wanted nothing, just for her to do her job and follow the leads he'd given her. But now he'd said the rules had changed. Who was to say he wouldn't want more? And say he came to her, asking for a phone number, or an address, what would she do?

She dismissed the thoughts from her head, finished her coffee and left the hotel. Once in her car, she called her mother to find out where her parents were having lunch. She set off to the restaurant, determined that her day off would continue as normal: lunch with her mother and father, then a stroll down Allerton Road, stopping off at all the estate agents, picking up details of flats she might like the look of. She'd see Susan tomorrow, tell her about Sweeney, find out what she thought. She wasn't going to accuse her or insinuate anything; she couldn't face another day of insult and apology and besides, if she was going to make something out of Sweeney's information, she was going to have to trust her.

Chapter Eleven

Saturday Morning 15 December
LIVERPOOL MORNING MAIL
POLICE WARN PROSTITUTES AFTER CITY
CRUCIFIX MURDER
Prostitutes throughout Liverpool have been put on alert since the murder of a woman in the city last week. The police believe the woman, who has still to be identified, was one of the city's sex workers and feel she may have been targeted because of that. Officers from the vice squad have been making the rounds of known red light districts quizzing prostitutes and warning them to be extra-vigilant. The body of the woman was found early last Saturday morning at the Northern Warehouse, site of a massive investment and development scheme run by Liverpool firm O'Hare Design and Construction. The woman's face and hands had been repeatedly battered in what police described as a brutal attack. The body had then been doused in petrol and set alight, making identification from features alone impossible.
The body was found lying face up with legs straight and arms outstretched. Police are keeping an open mind as to whether this suggests the murder may have had a religious dimension.
By Susan Clarke. Story spiked.

They decided to go in Rachel's car, a cream Mini with black trim, because the heater was better than Susan's 10-year-old Rover. At 8.30, Rachel pulled up outside Susan's flat, to find Susan, wearing the same thin raincoat she'd been shivering in a couple of nights before, already waiting on the pavement that was slick with an overnight frost.

"We're going to be really early, you know," Susan said as she got in. "You say the visiting time's half ten?"

"I know, yeah," said Rachel. "But I always prefer to give myself a bit of extra time for a journey. Especially if I've not been to the place before. Not the most confident of drivers, you see, particularly in city centres."

"Well, don't worry about it," Susan told her. "Just think, when you're with CNN or Sky News, reporting live from the streets of Baghdad, you'll have your very own driver."

"Well, right now, the way I'm feeling," Rachel said, "Baghdad seems a very long way away."

"Baghdad is a very long way away," said Susan.

Rachel laughed. "You know what I mean."

Even though Christmas was just over a week away, traffic was light. Rachel quickly skirted the city centre and the Big Dig and headed down Edge Lane and on to the M62.

"What time's kick-off?" Rachel asked. "Your son's game. That's what they call it, right? It's not bully off, or anything?"

"You don't really know much about sport, do you, Rachel?" said Susan.

"I went out with a rower at University," she said. "Wasted too many afternoons standing freezing on a river bank dutifully watching him paddle up and down before I realised he was seeing at least three other girls behind my back. That's about the extent of my sporting knowledge."

"The match starts at 3," said Susan. She looked up at the clear cold sky through the windscreen. "Assuming the pitch thaws, that is. Mind you," she went on, "I don't think that would stop them. It's the type of school where pain and suffering are considered beneficial."

"Catholic, then?" said Rachel.

"Very."

They drove in silence for around 15 minutes before Rachel reached into the compartment in the driver's door and pulled out her mobile phone. One eye on the road and one hand on the steering wheel, she began pressing a couple of buttons.

"Naughty," said Susan. "You shouldn't phone while you're

driving, you know."

Rachel handed the phone to Susan. "Read that," she said. She had retrieved Sweeney's message.

Susan read it. Still staring at it, she asked, "When did you get this?"

"Wednesday night," Rachel replied. "Well, Thursday morning, I guess."

"When we were out with Brian?" said Susan.

"Yes," Rachel said. "I didn't notice it till I got home and was getting ready for bed."

"Are you okay? You should have told me, you know. You could have called me as soon as you'd got it."

"I didn't think," said Rachel. "It scared me. It's stupid, I know, but it felt sort of…as though an intruder..."

"You felt violated," said Susan.

"Yes," Rachel said. "Melodramatic, I suppose."

"No," Susan told her. "I don't blame you. I'd have felt exactly the same. You know that's just what he wants you to feel, though, don't you? He wants you vulnerable. It's not personal. He wants everyone vulnerable. That's how men like Sweeney work. And they're not all crime bosses."

"I heard about what you said to Bassett," Rachel said. "Doesn't sound like you're too vulnerable."

"Little bastard had it coming," Susan said. "Besides, Bassett's not Franny Sweeney. I wouldn't have said that to him."

"No," said Rachel, her voice doubtful and shaky.

"Sorry," Susan said. "That makes it sound like you should be scared of him."

"I am scared of him," Rachel said. "More scared now, since that text." She paused. "I've been thinking…how do you think he got my number?"

"The mobile, you mean?" said Susan. "Don't know. He got your home address, didn't he?"

"Yes, but that's easier to get, isn't it?" said Rachel, her voice now close to snappish, as she tried to keep her concern in

check. "Someone could just follow me, couldn't they?"
"Yes, but," Susan began, sensing Rachel's worry. "Look, no-one will have followed you. We've got access to a database in the office, haven't we? We can just enter a name and in no time find out where they live, who they live with, telephone number. It's easy. And just think how many forms you've filled in where you give contact details. Every time you take out a magazine subscription, every time you buy something from a catalogue or order something from a charity website. It doesn't have to be anything sinister. Your name, age, address, telephone number, likes and dislikes. And selling these lists is big business. Someone like Sweeney, he'll want to know things. Not just about you, Rachel, about all sorts of people. He's clever. He knows that information is power."
Rachel glanced across at Susan quizzically. "Okay," Susan admitted, smiling. "I know that's a cliché. But you know what I mean. And you know I'm right."
"Yes," said Rachel. "I'm being…I don't know. It's thrown me. I started to think someone in the office was, like, a spy or something, passing on things about me to Sweeney. And then that got me thinking that Sweeney's getting his claws into me too. Especially with that about the rules having changed."
"He'll get his claws into you only if you let him," Susan said.
"How do you mean?"
"You're worried he's trying to manipulate you, right?" asked Susan.
"Well, he is, isn't he?" said Rachel. "I mean, look where I am. Driving to Strangeways on a Saturday morning following a story he put me on to. Put me on to because he wants to get at Crowley through me. He's using me."
"So?" said Susan. "What if he is? You might come out the other side of this with a terrific story. And just because he put you on to it doesn't mean you're in his pocket. Look, he's a contact, isn't he? And possibly a bloody good one, too. You might just as well say you're using him."

"Except I don't send him menacing text messages in the early hours of the morning, do I?"

"Well, why don't you?"

Rachel laughed incredulously. "Tell me you're joking, please."

Susan smiled back at Rachel. "Okay, I am joking. Even at my drunkest, I would never do anything like that. But who's to say you couldn't call him back, or text him? Or go back to his house? You'd have to be careful, of course, but why not? Why should you just sit around feeling threatened?"

"Well he's not exactly going to feel threatened by me, is he?" Rachel said. "Even if I turn up there with you."

"What I mean," said Susan, "is like what I said before. Treat him as a contact. Use him. If you want to know something, ask him. You're a good reporter. If this visit today gives you a sniff of something then chase it down. Don't wait for Sweeney to tell you to move. And equally, don't move simply because he tells you."

Rachel mulled this over. Susan was right: why should she let herself be pushed around? But then it was easy to feel confident and assured sitting next to her, driving to Manchester on a December morning in her shiny new Mini. It was tougher when she was alone, sitting up in bed at four in the morning.

They were making good time. Even now, having left the M62 and taken the M602 into Manchester, the traffic was still light. No matter how near it was to Christmas, most people wanted their Saturday lie-in and weren't going to sacrifice a couple of hours' sleep for easy shopping.

Soon the outskirts of Salford rose above the urban motorway, blocked on either side by high brick walls. Past high-rise flats and retail parks full of fast food outlets and DIY stores, they followed the signs for the city centre and Deansgate. Once on Deansgate, the traffic thickened. They crawled between the shops, under Christmas lights strung over the road, shining bright in the dark, grey morning.

"We're going right to the end here," said Susan, "then turning left and up towards the jail."

"You been here before?" asked Rachel.

"A long time ago," said Susan. "Before the riots. I don't think much has changed, though. And it was always a bloody dreadful place to visit. The prison officers here are the worst. Used to be, at any rate. Surly, nasty, curt. Funny, the higher security the prison is, the nicer the screws are." She smiled. "Listen to me. Calling them screws. It's like the old days. When I was a proper reporter."

"Been in many prisons, then?" asked Rachel.

"Only as a visitor," Susan replied. "Here, turn here, then up the hill to the right. As soon as you see a space to park, grab it. We'll not have far to walk."

Rachel followed Susan's instructions. She squeezed the car into a tight space on the steep road close to the prison. Most of the other cars lining the side of the road still bore signs of a heavy overnight frost, causing Rachel to wonder where the owners who had left them overnight lived. The area was mean and grimy. There weren't many houses around, just a few grubby business premises, tool hire shops, a newsagents' with metal grilles over the windows, a yard crammed with vans for hire. It was a world far removed from the glamorous department stores and boutiques just moments away between Cross Street and Deansgate. And over it all loomed Strangeways Prison, redbrick, imposing, malevolent, a Victorian monument to punishment and retribution, its tall tower, like a castle keep, watching over the rest of the building and beyond.

Susan looked at her watch. "What time's visiting?" she asked. "10.30, did you say?" Rachel nodded. "We've got an hour," said Susan.

"Sorry," said Rachel. "What should we do now then?"

Susan looked around her. "We could always hire a van for an

hour," she said. Rachel looked nervous and apologetic.

"Don't worry," Susan told her. "It's fine. There's a bit of a rigmarole to go through anyway. They like to make the visitors suffer here too. Besides, it's quite an education to see all the other visitors going in with you." She hunched her shoulders and rubbed her hands together. "If there's time, though, we'll go shopping later. I don't fancy standing watching an hour of rugby in just this. You promised me a Winter coat, remember?"

"I don't remember saying I'd buy it," Rachel protested.

"Well, we'll discuss that later," said Susan. "Come on, let's get inside."

Chapter Twelve

They walked to the gate in the outer walls, where they showed the guard their visiting orders and some identification and were ushered in. Ahead of them was the entrance to the prison itself. A large glass frontage, like an outer porch, had been built around the main door.

"That must have been added since the riots," Susan said. "Pay an architect thousands to come up with a greenhouse that makes it all soft and modern. It'll be like IKEA inside now, all throw cushions and billy bookcases."

"You're quite the cynical old hack, aren't you?" said Rachel.

"To be honest," said Susan. "I feel great." She stopped halfway across the yard and turned to Rachel. "This is the way it used to be. I can't explain it, really, and I know it's only been a few days. But…anyway, yes, I am a cynical old hack. This is what's in store for you, you know."

They continued to the porch, pulled open the heavy glass doors and went up to the hatch in the wall. Through holes punched in the dirty Perspex screen, a prison officer said, "Name." Then, "Visiting Order." Then, "ID." At each word, Rachel and Susan duly provided the information demanded, after which the officer pressed a buzzer to his left and the two women pushed open the door next to the hatch and went in to the prison.

Just inside the door was a metal detector archway and, next to it, a table behind which stood another prison officer. At his command, first Rachel and then Susan handed over her bag to be searched and then stepped through the detector. Once through, the guard returned the bags and pointed across the reception area to an unmarked door. Rachel hesitated, unsure of what to do. She was about to speak when the guard said curtly, "Wait in there. You'll be called."

The room they went into, like the reception area and every other subsequent space they entered, was uniformly and institutionally cold and designed seemingly to drain the spirit. The walls were plastered and painted straight over in an icy light green paint that looked wet with slight condensation. The floor was covered in chipped and fading red tiles. There was a second door, in the end wall in the corner of the room. Plastic bucket chairs were roughly arranged in rows facing one wall. The door shut heavily behind them, closing out the sounds from the corridor outside, brief shouted commands and the slap of rubber-soled shoes on the floor.

Rachel and Susan headed for the back row and sat in the last two chairs in the line, diagonally across from the door they'd just come through. Even though they were the only two in the room, when they spoke they did so in whispers.

"This is awful," said Rachel.

"It's not meant to be nice," replied Susan. "But I know what you mean. Have you thought about what you're going to ask Billy Jackson?" she asked.

"Not really, to be honest," said Rachel. "I mean, other than mentioning Sweeney to start with. Thought I'd just see where that got us."

"And Crowley, of course," Susan said. "How long has Jackson been inside?"

"Three years," Rachel replied. "He's not got long left, apparently. So Sweeney told me."

"That means Crowley must have met him, or whatever the connection is, before he moved to the Liverpool force."

"Well, we'll find out soon, I suppose."

The door opened again, and from then on it wasn't shut for long. A succession of visitors came in. All women, all ages, mothers, wives, girlfriends, mostly trailing children with them. Rachel and Susan stood out. Even Susan, in her old raincoat, her hair in need of a decent cut and the effects of too much drink and too many cigarettes etched into her face and spattered into her eyes, was marked out as totally different. From the youngest to the oldest, they were grey and lank and exhausted, each with a personal history of bad housing, bad diet, bad education, bad relationships, bad luck. Their clothes were cheap and shabby. In many cases, poorly dyed hair was scraped back over the scalp and fingers were heavy with bulky sovereign rings. On the younger women, thin T-shirts revealed flabby midriffs and polyester trousers clung to fat thighs or else hung off legs too thin. And the children, pushed in prams or forced into chairs or let free to run round the room, were heading to repeat the same cycle, the only difference being that the boys among them would be receiving the visits rather than making them.

"Don't look like that," Susan whispered to Rachel.

"What do you mean?" she asked.

"You look appalled," Susan told her. "You look like you want to run back to Childwall and lock yourself in your room and never come out."

"That's because I do," Rachel said.

"This is work, remember?" Susan said. "Get used to places and people like this. Don't be frightened of them. And think yourself lucky you can run back to Childwall and lock yourself in your room. Besides, listen to them."

"How do you mean?" asked Rachel.

"Their lives are bloody awful, aren't they?" said Susan. "You can tell. But they're here, yes? And they're chatting to each other and helping with each other's kids. It's like there's some bond between them. All in the same boat."

Rachel nodded in reply and smiled, trying to look relaxed. Once the room settled down, the second door was opened. A prison officer, tall and imposing, a blue pullover drawn tightly over a fat stomach, came in. He stood, filling the doorway. Making a show of looking down a list on the clipboard he held, he called, "Monk." A couple of rows in front of Rachel and Susan, a woman stood up. In her early 20s maybe, she wearily gathered together her children and awkwardly manoeuvred a pram to the end of the row and then up to the doorway where the officer stood. He looked down at her, then moved aside and let her through. After a few minutes, this was repeated, until eventually he called out Susan and Rachel's names.

Once through the second door, Rachel and Susan were searched again. A female guard frisked them. They had to take off their shoes and hand them over to be examined. Their mouths were checked, to make sure there was no parcel of drugs in there that could be passed over while kissing a prisoner. They had to hand over their bags, to be kept in a locker until they were due to leave. Finally, a guard stamped the back of each woman's right hand. No mark appeared and when Rachel stared at it, Susan told her, "It shows up under UV, so they can check the same person leaves as went in."

The search over, they moved along the corridor and into another room. Again, the plastered walls were painted in the same sickly, institutional green. This room was bigger than the last one, though. There were maybe 50 tables in the room, each with four chairs round it, two facing two. It was a high room, and along two walls was a raised platform, a dais on which sat a line of prison officers, all watching the different groups intently. At the end wall was a hatch, where a short line of women queued for hot drinks and chocolate bars.

At the door to this room, there was another guard, a replica of the man calling out the names in the previous room. The women handed him their visiting orders and was directed to a table in the centre of the room. There sat Billy Jackson, a red bib over a black sweatshirt and blue jeans.

Rachel and Susan crossed the room to where Jackson was sitting. The prisoners they passed were simply male equivalents of the women who'd come to see them. They ranged in age from late teenagers to men in their 60s. Dressed, like Jackson, in red prison bibs over their own clothes, their faces were pale under the harsh fluorescent lights. The room was full of intense, private conversations.

Prisoner and visitor held hands across the tables, or leant into each other to kiss. Occasionally the atmosphere was broken by shouts of greeting from a prisoner at one table to a visitor at another. They knew each other on the outside as well as the inside, were often from the same estates, and wanted to be remembered to mothers and fathers and brothers and sisters. Jackson looked upset. He was fidgeting at the table, digging a thumbnail into the skin on his other hand, as if trying to claw something out.

"Billy Jackson?" said Rachel.

Jackson nodded. "You Rachel Jack?" he asked. Rachel nodded. "Who's this?" He darted his head towards Susan.

"I'm Susan Clarke," she said. "Shall I get us something from the canteen? What do you fancy, Billy?"

"Tea," he said. "Two sugars. And some chocolate."

Susan nodded. Rachel looked in slight panic at her, but Susan just smiled and said she wouldn't be a minute.

Rachel sat down and looked at Billy Jackson. He was a small man, maybe no bigger than 5'8". He was thin, with brown eyes and a sharp, thin nose. She could tell he was agitated, but his eyes suggested he was a kind man, simply upset by circumstances, and she relaxed a little. Still, she was reluctant to forge ahead and was relieved when Susan came back to the table. She'd bought them each a cup of tea, as well as four bars of chocolate, which she pushed across the table towards Jackson.

"Thanks," he said, and slipped all four into his pocket. They each took sips of their tea, Jackson wary and Rachel feeling almost shy, uncertain of what to do next.

Susan spoke first. She was friendly straight away, her voice full of warmth and confidence.

"Where're you from, Billy?" she asked.

"Yorkshire," he replied.

"Oh, yes?" she said. "Whereabouts?"

"Bradford."

"Not too far from Keighley, is it, Bradford?" said Susan.

"Not far, no," said Billy.

"Would you not have fancied a Yorkshire nick, then?"

"Just sent me here," Billy said. "Not like I could book, is it? Besides…"

"Besides what?" said Susan.

"Nothing."

"Billy," Rachel said. "Ever come across a copper called Crowley?"

"What if I have?" asked Billy.

"It's just that someone told me to have a word with you about him."

"Oh, aye," sneered Billy. "Someone, is it?"

"Franny Sweeney," said Rachel.

"Do you know Sweeney?" asked Susan. There was a sudden commotion behind them. Two prison officers had left the dais and made for a table a couple of rows away. They were dragging a prisoner from his chair and pulling him out of the room, while two more guards took away the woman who had come to visit him. She was crying, while the prisoner kicked and yelled that he'd done nothing. Rachel tried to turn round to see what was going on, but found her chair fastened to the floor. No-one else even looked up.

"Screws have spotted something," Billy said.

"Will there be a lockdown, do you think?" Susan asked him.

"Maybe," he replied. "Doubt it though."

"So. Do you know Franny Sweeney?" Susan asked again.

"Heard of him," Billy told her. "Pad mate's a Scouser. He's told me of him. Friend of yours, is he?"

"Don't know him, Billy," Susan said. "Rachel neither. Like you, though, we've heard of him. How does he know you?"

"Guess," Billy said. "Same way as I know him. Through pad mate."

"You knew we were visiting, didn't you?" Rachel asked.

"Sent you visiting order, didn't I?"

"And who told you to send it?" Rachel said.

"Word came through for me to do it," Billy told her. "Messages get in. One night my pad mate told me. Said Franny Sweeney wanted a favour. Gave me your name, address. Told me you were a reporter. Didn't say she was coming, mind." Again, he nodded across at Susan.

"I'm just a bonus," Susan said, smiling. Then she said, "Sweeney's been matchmaking. Did the same thing to Rachel here. Told her to come and have a chat with you. Said you'd have something to tell us. About a copper called Crowley."

Billy just shrugged and drank some more of his tea.

"What are you in for, Billy?" Rachel asked.

Billy laughed, no humour in the sound. "What aren't I in for you mean?"

"What do you mean by that?" Rachel asked.

"Burglary," he told them. "Just bad luck. Owners came home early and called the coppers. Stupid of me, just thought I'd take the chance. Nothing planned."

"How long did you get?" Susan asked.

"Three years."

Susan looked surprised. "Bit steep, isn't it?"

"Not my first time," Billy told her.

"Was this in Keighley?" Rachel asked.

"Yeah."

"And Crowley arrested you."

"No," he said. "Another fella. Met Crowley a couple of times, though."

"And?"

"And what?" Billy asked in return.

"Why did Sweeney say I should talk to you about Crowley, Billy?" Rachel asked. She was no longer nervous, just frustrated with the situation. She'd just thought Jackson would tell her, straight, whatever it was Sweeney wanted her to know.

"You'll have to ask him, now, won't you?" Billy told her.

"Is there anything we can do to help, Billy?" Susan said. "Anything you need?"

"How do you mean?" he said.

"Look, Billy," said Susan. "We're in the dark. Sweeney said to speak to you about Crowley. Said you'd have something to tell us. But either you've nothing to say or you're not as afraid of Franny Sweeney as he thinks you should be."

"I'm not stupid," said Billy. "Of course I'm afraid of him." Rachel remembered her own words.

"So what then?"

"I want something else," he said. Rachel and Susan looked at him, waiting. Slowly he reached into his pocket. He pulled his hand out and placed it palm flat on the table. He slid his hand over towards them, then lifted it, leaving a photograph face up. Rachel and Susan looked at it. It showed a woman. She was laughing, her face flushed and her mouth open. She had a cigarette in one hand and a glass in the other. Her hair was dyed red, the roots showing black, and she was wearing a tight red dress. She was sitting on a bar stool. Billy was standing next to her.

"She should have been in this past week," Billy said. "Once a month she comes. She never misses. Hasn't for three years, not since I've been inside."

"Have you called her?"

"No answer. But she might have changed her mobile, you see. Always said she was going to. Wanted one you could take pictures with. Fuck knows why, mind. Sorry. Shouldn't swear in front of ladies." The kindness that Rachel had sensed earlier was surfacing. Billy looked like he was going to cry. "She should have been in," he said.

"What's her name?" Rachel asked.

"Margy," Billy said. "Margy Girvan."

"She your wife?" asked Susan.

"Girlfriend." Billy squeezed the word out. "She should have been in."

"And she lives in Bradford?" Rachel asked.

Billy shook his head, forcefully, both to say no and to shake the tears away.

"No," he said. "Met her there, six year ago, but when I came inside she moved back home. Liverpool. Said she wanted to be near her mum. Easier for her get over here and all."

"Are we okay to keep the picture?" Susan asked.

"Aye," said Billy. He reached out and took it. "I'll pass it on when you leave. Make sure you're ready for it. Don't want screws to see."

Susan nodded. "Any address?"

"Belle Vale," he said. "I've never been there. Sounds nice though. Sunnybank Road. Flat 17, River View House. Her mobile number's on the back of the picture. The old one, anyway."

The long and drawn out process of leaving began when the prison officers round the room began shouting that time was up. Susan stood up and shook Billy's hand, then hugged him to her, so he could slip the photograph into her hand and she could slip it inside her coat without anyone seeing.

"Two more VOs this week, mind, Billy," she said to him as they hugged. "And we'll be back next Saturday." She felt him nod his head, then they let go of each other.

The shouts to pack up and leave continued, ignored by most couples who carried on hugging and kissing until officers came round tapping on shoulders. Susan and Rachel left straight away. They quickly collected their shoes and bags, had the stamps on their hands checked and left.

Chapter Thirteen

They didn't speak until they were outside, and then only after taking deep breaths of what they felt was clean fresh air.
"Coffee?" asked Rachel.
Susan nodded. "Yeah. But not around here. Let's drive back into the centre and find somewhere to park."
They found a space in a car park just off Deansgate and made their way into Kendal's. In the upmarket department store, Christmas spending was in full swing. Orange women in tight white tunics who looked young from a distance but older close up sprayed shoppers with scents of citrus and musk and cedar and passion, while their fellow workers offered make-overs to women who'd just spent an hour and a half getting ready.
There was wealth and heat in Kendal's and both Rachel and Susan were struck by the contrast with Strangeways, which they'd left barely 10 minutes before.
They made their way to the café where they each ordered a coffee and a toasted teacake. Neither had said much since leaving the prison. When they sat down at a table near the window, Susan looked around her and asked Rachel, "So, which do you prefer?"
"Here or Strangeways you mean?" Rachel said. "It's a close thing."
"The coffee in Strangeways isn't so good," Susan reminded her.
"Oh well," said Rachel. "That's it then. Got to be Kendal's." She bit into her teacake. "We'll make this quick. Then we can get your coat and get back to Liverpool in time for the game."
"We can go through Belle Vale on the way," Susan said. "Just come off the motorway a couple of junctions earlier."
"See Sunnybank Road you mean?" said Rachel. "I hope he was joking when he said it sounded nice."
"It's not that bad," Susan said. "And remember, he'll be

going there from Strangeways. He won't be expecting too much." She reached into her coat and pulled out the picture Jackson had given her. It was marked with small creases and there were traces of thumb and finger prints, showing Jackson had spent a good deal of time holding it and staring at it.

"He thought a lot of her, didn't he?" said Rachel. "Margy Girvan."

"More than he did of Sweeney, anyway," Susan replied. "He was more bothered about finding her than not doing what he wanted, that's for sure. Poor bastard."

"How do you mean?"

"Well, look at her," said Susan. "What do you think, eh? Suddenly there's no visit, doesn't answer his calls. She's found someone else, hasn't she? That's if she'd not found some new bloke long since, and just kept up the visits as a bit of insurance."

"Poor old Billy," said Rachel. "It'll be back to Bradford for him then. No new start in Sunnybank Road. We'll have to be careful how we tell him, though."

"You're right," agreed Susan. "We still need Billy to tell us about this Crowley business. You finished?" Rachel nodded. "Listen," Susan continued. "It's after twelve now. We could just get straight off."

"Nonsense," said Rachel. "We're getting you a coat. You can't go through Winter in that, not if you're going to be watching rugby matches." She stood up. "Come on. Let's find women's fashions."

The department was crowded and, for the second time that day, Rachel and Susan found themselves surrounded by women of all ages. They were very different from the Strangeways women, however, all well-dressed and well-fed, with clear complexions and manicured nails and carefully arranged hair, leisurely browsing through the clothes on offer, untroubled by price tags or prams or children pulling at the sides. Susan felt awkward and unsure of herself. She made straight for the least fashionable, most functional clothes she could find. Quickly picking a coat out, a shapeless anorak with a hood and too many pockets, she held it up and said to Rachel, "This'll do."

"That?" asked Rachel.

"Yes," said Susan. "What's wrong with it. It's warm and thick and," she looked at the price, "quite cheap."

"You could say the same about Trevor Bassett, but you wouldn't want him wrapped around you," Rachel said.

"Come on, we've got time. Let's have a look round properly." She moved across the store and found a rack of long wool overcoats.

"Now this," she announced, picking one off the rack and holding it up, "is just the thing. Military cut, nice and long, double breasted. What size are you?"

"Fourteen," Susan replied and Rachel picked one out in that size.

"Try it on," she told Susan.

"What colour is that? It's very light."

"It's camel." Rachel took the coat off the hanger and held it up for Susan. Susan reluctantly took her own coat off and put the new one on, immediately wrapping the coat tight around her and tucking her neck into the high collar. "That looks fantastic," said Rachel. "How does it feel?"

Susan smiled shyly. "It feels great. But…"

"But what?" asked Rachel.

"I'm just not sure about the colour. And," she said, checking the price tag, "it's £250."

"But it'll last you a lifetime," said Rachel. She took another coat from the rack. "Here, try this one. A deep chocolate brown."

"Chocolate brown's the new black, isn't it?" asked Susan.

"Well, it's probably the old black, to be honest," said Rachel, as Susan tried it on. "But, once again, it looks great. Come on, you're getting it. No excuses. Take it to the cash register while I just get you a couple of other things."

Ten minutes later, with a hat, scarf and a pair of gloves as well as the coat, Susan and Rachel left Kendal's.

"You'll fit in nicely now at Sunnybank Road," Rachel told her as they headed to the car. "Margy Girvan won't be embarrassed about letting you in."

The pavements were crowded with shoppers, all fighting for space, all increasingly laden with bags. Just as they were approaching the road where the car was parked, a young man running along the pavement towards them knocked into Rachel, sending her staggering into a shop doorway. He didn't stop to see if she'd fallen or not.

"Christmas cheer, eh?" said Rachel. She was grateful still to have her handbag.

Once in the car they crawled along Deansgate, fighting the Christmas traffic. Soon, however, they edged out of the city centre, through Salford and had a clear run back to Liverpool along the M62. The clear sky of the morning had been replaced by thick grey cloud, tinged with a pink that suggested snow might fall anytime soon.

Susan had put her old coat back on. She reached into the pocket and took out the photograph Billy Jackson had given her. Margy and Billy both looked happy with their drinks and their cigarettes and with each other.

"They're glowing," said Susan. Rachel had been concentrating on the road and hadn't noticed Susan looking at the picture. She turned her head slightly and Susan angled the picture so she could glance at it.

"Margy and Billy are glowing," she said again. "The drink, obviously. But there's more to it than that. They're happy together. Friday night in some Bradford pub, a few drinks, a smoke, laughing with friends, joining in with the jukebox. Maybe stop for a takeaway on the way home. You can see why he's more frightened of losing her than he is of Sweeney getting to him."

"He loves her," said Rachel simply. "Does she love him, though?" she added.

Susan put the photograph back into her pocket. "Belle Vale's not out of our way, you know," she said. "Why don't we go that way? Then we can cut through to Queen's Drive and you can drop me at Michael's school. If that's still okay."

"Actually," said Rachel. "I was thinking of staying to watch the game with you. Might be a nice way to spend the afternoon." She had spoken cheerfully, and was surprised not to get an immediate response from Susan. She glanced across at her, suddenly worried she'd upset her. "Do you mind?" she asked.

Susan hesitated, her mind frozen at the prospect of a change to her usual routine. She felt her expression also frozen, trapped in a smile which the humour had left. She stumbled with her words. "No," she said. "Of course you…It's just that…"

"It's okay, you know," said Rachel. "I don't mind. If you'd rather I didn't."

Susan stared out of the window. Either side of the motorway was farmland, the fields moving in gentle curves, the brown earth frozen and hard. The bare branches of a copse they passed clawed against the grey sky.

"It's always been private," Susan said slowly. "Always just me. I don't even stand on the touchline with the other parents. I suppose I don't feel I am one of the other parents." She fidgeted her hands in her lap. "I can't smoke in this shiny car, can I?" she asked.

"If you like," Rachel replied.

"No. Thanks." She paused. "Yes. Come and watch the game with me. I'd like it. It was just a bit strange, you know, when you first said it."

"You sure?" Rachel asked. "I won't set off any alarms, will I? You know, a Jew turning up on Catholic grounds."

"Oh," said Susan. "I know where all the trip wires are and the times of the patrols. You just do exactly as I say."
Rachel smiled. "Right then. A rugby game. Well, well. But first stop Sunnybank Road. There's an A-Z in the glove compartment, if you want to have a look."
She took the next exit off the motorway, lining up for the lights among lorries heading for the M57 and the Bootle docks. Once on the roundabout she took the turn-off for Huyton, then after a mile or so turned left, past Childwall Golf Club and Wheathill Riding School and into Belle Vale.

Chapter Fourteen

The estate had been built in the 1960s, housing people shifted from the city centre. Originally all council housing, a number of the properties were now privately owned, boasting new doors and uPVC windows. A mix of houses, flats and maisonettes, they were all boxes, and looked thin and insubstantial. The verges that sat between the buildings looked like scrub, grass and soil churned up by football games and motorcycle tracks. The Belle Vale shopping centre stood windowless over the main road. The directions Susan gave took them past the medical centre, redbrick and purely functional, sitting squat behind locked and bolted gates, surrounded by fencing topped with coils of jagged steel, like tank traps. They passed a Catholic church to their right, Our Lady of the Assumption, that seemed purpose-built for the aged and poor to huddle in joyless worship.

On Sunnybank Road itself stood a long block of flats five storeys high, brown brick turning grey, the window frames peeled and rotting. On the grass verge opposite was a burnt out car and a kiosk, its iron shutters open for bread and milk and papers and cigarettes.

Rachel slowed the car as they drove down the road. Susan sensed her nervousness.

"Don't worry, Rachel," she said. "When we start looking for Margy Girvan we'll come in my car."

Rachel smiled. "That obvious, is it?"

"I don't blame you," Susan told her. "It's not a fun part of the job. Knocking on doors, asking strangers questions. Not in an area like this, especially. The worst that'll probably happen though is we'll get spat on. Maybe a couple of kids charging us on their bikes." Rachel turned and stared at her, shocked. "I'm joking," said Susan. "Mind you," she added, "I won't be wearing my nice new coat from Kendal's. Come on, let's go and watch some rugby."

Chapter Fifteen

Saturday Afternoon 15 December

St Edward's College was in Sandfield Park, in West Derby. It felt secure and secluded, on a quiet road curving between Queen's Drive and Eton Road, its grounds bordered by trees beyond which had been built a series of exclusive executive homes. A drive swept from one gate round to another, past the long, impressive frontage of the college, long established as the school of choice for the city's clever Catholic sons and, latterly, their daughters too. A swimming pool, a music block, a science building and an athletics track bore testament to the ambitions of the college, as well as the eagerness of its parents to contribute to its academic and sporting achievements.

Susan directed Rachel past the entrance gate and told her to park in one of the executive cul-de-sacs. From there they headed across the road and climbed into the school grounds over a section of the wall that had crumbled low enough to allow access. Susan said nothing, although she was painfully aware of how strange this must have seemed to Rachel. For her part, Rachel stayed silent; she merely followed Susan over the wall and took her place next to her, just inside the tree line. The touchline was about 30 yards from where they stood, side-on to the pitch. It was 2.50, about 10 minutes before the game was due to kick off.

Susan, her old overcoat pulled tightly around her, lit a cigarette. She turned to Rachel as if suddenly remembering she was there, and smiled shyly.

"Pre-match nerves," she said, glancing down at the cigarette burning between her fingers. She paused and then said, "Sorry about that."

"What?" Rachel asked.

"You know," Susan said. "Parking round the corner. Then the assault course coming in. And this. Hiding in the trees."

"Don't be silly," Rachel told her. "I understand."

"It's just that I don't want Michael to see me."

"He'd be embarrassed," said Rachel. "His Mum coming to watch him. He'd love it though, deep down."

"Do you think?"

"I'd bet on it," Rachel said.

"Even though I'm a drunk and a slut?"

"What do you mean?"

"That's what they think I am," said Susan. "Peter's parents." She nodded across to the far touchline, where a small group of spectators was starting to gather. "They're over there. That bastard Eugene O'Hare and that sweet and silent and damning wife of his. St Imelda. Hissing out hate in that bloody lilting Irish brogue of hers. Peter too," she added. "But that's okay. I like Peter."

Rachel looked across to where Susan had indicated. She guessed which ones were the O'Hares. A thick, squat, solid bulk stood on the halfway line, proprietorial, challenging anyone to try and shift him. Next to him was a woman, thin, pinched and frail but tough and mean, Rachel guessed. And a little way down the line, separate from the other two, a tall, slim figure, still and shy. Eugene and Imelda O'Hare and their son, Peter, all here to watch their darling Michael toughen himself up on the rugby field. Rachel felt like a spectator both of the game itself and the private war that ground on between Susan and her former in-laws.

Susan watched silently as the teams jogged out onto the pitch, the boys cold, with the cuffs of their jerseys pulled down over their hands. Her heart tightened in her chest as her eyes immediately found her son, Michael, and she instinctively took a step towards him, aching to call him to her and wrap her arms around him.

"Which one's Michael?" Rachel asked.

"Small," Susan managed to say. "Dirty blond hair. Holding a ball." She pointed to one of the boys in the blue and gold hooped rugby shirts. As they watched, he broke into a run and began passing the ball back and forth to a team mate.

"He's a scrum half," Susan told Rachel.

"A what?" Rachel replied.

"Scrum half," she repeated. "His job is to put the ball into the scrum then get it back and give it to the fly half. He's the link between the forwards and the backs."

Rachel smiled at the heat and pride in Susan's voice. "You know your stuff," she said to Susan.

"When I found out he was in the team, I started reading up on it," said Susan. She was silent for a moment, then when she spoke again her voice had taken on a softer quality. "In case I saw him. So I could tell him."

The game lasted an hour. Rachel froze in the bitter December air, but she saw that Susan didn't feel the cold at all. She was transfixed by the action, her eyes following only her son, wincing as larger boys hurled themselves at him, holding her breath then exhaling in relief when she saw him get to his feet again, unharmed, beaming with pride at a well-executed pass and sharing her boy's dismay when the final whistle blew and his team had lost. For a while he would be inconsolable, his entire world crammed into the game's tiny hour, but then he would be instantly fine again. She just hoped he would be given the chance to express his joy and delight at the game on the way home, have some time with his father listening rapt to Michael's descriptions of the game, maybe stopping at a McDonald's where Peter would treat him to a burger on the way home. For an instant she couldn't help but picture the three of them driving back as a family. She would play the role of disapproving mother, smiling inside as she indulged the naughtiness of her boys as they demanded unhealthy fast food. She forced the image away.

With the game over, Susan suddenly felt the cold. But instead of hurrying back to the car, she simply slumped back against a tree, exhausted by the tension of seeing her son and watching him play. She pressed the back of her head against the bark and felt the pain as it dug into her scalp. Rachel stood by, awkward and uneasy.

"I rang the school," Susan said, her head turned up towards the sky without really seeing anything. "One afternoon a couple of months ago, not long after he started here. It was my day off. I was drunk," she added. "I thought I sounded okay, but then you always do, don't you?" Rachel started to answer but stopped when she realised Susan wasn't really asking. "I probably wouldn't have called otherwise. Anyway, it would have just confirmed what Eugene and Imelda would have told the school. They were patient with me. Got Michael's form tutor on the phone for me." She laughed. "Mr Fitzpatrick. They're all O'This and Fitzthat here. Told me about Michael being on the rugby team, sent me a fixture list. I've not missed a game of his home or away. Mr Fitzpatrick rings me now and then. Lets me know how Michael's doing. Very understanding."

Rachel reached over and touched Susan, gently taking her arm and pulling her away from the tree.

"Come on, Susan," she said softly. "Let's get back to the car and get warmed up. You must be freezing. I know I am, and I've got this thick coat on." Susan did as she was told, appreciating Rachel's kindness and the fact that she'd pretended not to notice her crying a little.

"That was some game, though, wasn't it?" said Rachel, her voice jolly to lift the gloom. "I really enjoyed it."

"Liar," said Susan. "You were frozen solid and didn't have a clue what was going on. But thanks, anyway. Both for saying that and for coming."

Rachel smiled back at Susan, but saw that something had changed. Susan was looking past Rachel, and her eyes showed a mixture of shock and fear. Rachel turned round and saw, leaning casually against her car, Eugene O'Hare. His fat, squat, massy bulk seemed to dwarf the Mini, threatening almost to tip it over on to its side. She looked back at Susan, wanting to know how to react, scared of the situation. Susan had stopped in her tracks, and appeared to be struggling to summon some resolve of her own. She took a step forward, but, as she did so, Rachel realised that she should deal with it. It was her car, after all.

"Hey!" she called to the man, striding across the road purposefully. "What do you think you're playing at? Get away from my car." To Rachel's own ears, her voice sounded thin and weak, unlikely to bother the meekest child, let alone this bruiser.

And that was how it came across to Eugene. As she walked towards him, Susan following more uncertainly behind, Eugene gave her a glance of mild scorn.

"Pipe down," he told Rachel, barely a trace of interest in his voice. "It's your drunken girlfriend I'm here to speak to." He turned to Susan, who had stopped on the road, on the far side of the car to Eugene. "What's going on, Susan dear?" he asked her. "Given up on men, have you? Giving women a try? Well, I can't say I blame you. She's a pretty one, that's for sure. Got the look of a Jew, though. Is that what she is?" He smiled at Susan, a genuine smile, full of delight in the anger he knew he was causing to rise in Rachel.

"What is it you want, Eugene?" Susan said. She turned her head to indicate the houses lining the cul-de-sac. "Come to look at how a building should be made?"

"Oh, very good, Susan. Very good," said Eugene, shaking his head and chuckling. "But I'm not interested in little projects like these any more. I told you, didn't I? Me and the boy are moving in richer circles now. Urban hotels. Very nice. Very swanky."

Susan had managed to control her breathing. The fear was leaving her and she was determined to match Eugene, determined not to take a step backwards. For the second time that afternoon, Rachel found herself a spectator in a contest she didn't really understand.

"At least with these houses you don't find women lying battered to death in the driveways. Not so swanky that, eh?" Susan said.

Eugene smiled again. "Ah, now, love," he said. "You might be surprised where you'd find a dead woman. And remember she was only a whore. A dead whore's not going to stop a project like mine. Nor would a dead drunk," he added. "Found rotting and stinking in a poky flat days after she'd finished her last bottle."

"You're not threatening me, are you, Eugene?" Susan asked. She took a step towards him.

Eugene began to laugh. "No, darling, no," he told her. He raised his arms in mocking surrender and moved back from her advance. "I was just giving you a for instance. But I could see why you might think I was talking about you, certainly. The description does seem to fit, doesn't it?" Now he spread his arms wide, looking generous, conciliatory. "I mean to say," he went on, "That could be you, couldn't it? A dried-up old lush. Dead-end job she can't do properly. Ah, and the tasty little Heebee here isn't going to hang around much longer, is she? The novelty'll wear off for her soon enough, won't it? She'll soon be on her way, hitching up with a nice young fella in a skull cap, bringing more little Jew bastards into the world." He turned to Rachel and smiled. "More Christ-killers, eh, love?" Then added, "No offence."

"You filthy, lousy, ignorant bastard," Rachel said. "How dare…"

"Save it, darling," Eugene told her. "I've been called much worse than anything you can think of by people I actually give a toss about. And don't ask what I dare. Because I might just show you."

"He's not worth it, Rachel," Susan told her.

"She's right, you know," Eugene agreed cordially. "I'm not

worth it." Once again he turned to Susan. "Who might be worth it, I wonder?" he asked. He answered himself. "Michael. Little Michael. He's worth it, isn't he, Susan, love? A bit soft like his father, maybe, but I reckon I can toughen him up a bit. Bring out a little of the hardness you yourself have got, Susan, eh? Then he can join the business and make a real go of it."

For a moment the three of them stood still, a triangular face-off in the middle of a nice suburban road, the Winter darkness descending around them. Then Eugene spoke.

"Well, now," he said. "Talking of Michael. He'll be ready and changed now, I should reckon, and Peter can drive the lot of us home." He took a pair of gloves from his pocket, put them on, then pulled the collar of his coat up around his thick neck, for all the world a man making ready to be on his way after a pleasant chat with friends.

"Is that it?" Susan asked him. "That's all?"

"Well, what more did you expect?" he replied. "I've been seeing you at these games for a while now, and I've kept meaning to pop over and have a little chat, catch up on how things are going." He started to walk away. As he was about to cross the road, he called over his shoulder, "Have a nice Christmas, won't you? Not you though, love," he added, to Rachel.

Susan waited for as long as she could, hoping Eugene would get out of earshot before she showed just how much he had got to her.

"Fuck!" she hissed, her teeth clenched and grinding. "That fucking bastard! Everything spoiled. He can't stand anything not spoiled. The bastard. The fucking shit." She took her cigarettes out of her pocket and lit one, her hands shaking with an impotent anger. Exhaling, she turned to Rachel, "I'm so sorry, Rachel. That was horrible."

Rachel's smile was weak. "I've heard swearing before," she said. Then, as Susan began to speak, she said, "Christ-killers though! Does he actually believe things like that?"

"God knows," said Susan. "Probably. St Imelda does, that's for sure." She mimicked a thin Irish accent. "Do you not think the Pope's a lovely man, now, Susan, dear? I made the mistake of saying I thought the Pope's stance on contraception was responsible for more misery in Africa than any number of dictators. Not the thing to say to a woman with eight children." She and Rachel both laughed.

"Come on," said Rachel. "Let's get in the car, at least." She watched as Susan looked at her cigarette, which still had around half to go. "Just this once," she told Susan, who moved round to open the passenger door and climb in.

As Rachel turned the key in the ignition, her mobile phone beeped.

"It'll be my Dad," she said, digging into an inside pocket to haul the phone out. "He's just learned how to text."

She stared at the message.

"Wants to know what time you'll be in for your tea?" Susan asked.

"It's not him," said Rachel. "Franny Sweeney again." She passed the phone to Susan.

Susan looked at Sweeney's message: '*All ok with Billy boy?*' it read, followed by, '*XXX*'.

Rachel sighed and let her head fall against the steering wheel. "Why can't he leave me alone?" she murmured to herself.

Susan tapped her hand against Rachel's arm. Her voice was stern, purposeful. "Come on," she said. "Let's go and see him. Now. I'm sick of being pushed around by these bastards. Think they're the only ones setting the rules."

"But..." Rachel began. "But...let me just call my parents first. Let them know I won't be back for tea."

Susan started laughing, snorting and guffawing at Rachel, who simply sat there, puzzled, until she heard again what she'd just said and joined in with Susan.

"We're a regular Woodward and Bernstein, aren't we?" said Susan. "Fearlessly chasing a story until our mum calls us in to have our tea and do our homework."

It was almost four when they set off, getting back onto Queen's Drive and heading north. Traffic was light. It would be an hour or so before the roads filled again with cars coming away from the football match at Goodison Park or people returning from their Christmas shopping. Christmas lights glowed in the growing darkness. Soon Rachel and Susan had passed through Bootle and cut down towards Waterloo and Crosby on their way to Birkdale and Franny Sweeney's house.

"How did you feel?" Susan asked. "You know, when Eugene was saying those things?"

Rachel considered the question. "It was…strange, to be honest," she said. "I am Jewish, obviously. Not that we really practise. I think of myself as Jewish. But…well, I sort of don't think of myself as Jewish at the same time. It doesn't define me." She thought some more, trying to work out what her response actually was. "I know I started to react, tried to think of something to call him."

"It's not really worth it with someone like Eugene, I'm afraid," Susan said. "He likes to be in control, likes to upset and manipulate."

"Yes," Rachel replied. "I could see that. Funny, you know. Sweeney made mention of it as well."

"Really?" asked Susan. "When you were over there last?"

"Yes, that's right," Rachel said. "Mind you, I'd mentioned it first. He said something about me having Christmas decorations and I said no, because I'm Jewish. Stupid really. I suppose I was trying to come back with an answer, trying to show I was different or wasn't going to lose in whatever type of exchange we were having. I don't know. I said it, anyway. Then, when I was going, he said something about you people."

"Francis Sweeney," Susan said, lingering over the names.

"He'll be another bloody Irish Catholic, won't he? Like Eugene. Lie, cheat, steal, kill all through the week, then mass on Sunday, say you're sorry. Put plenty in the collection plate. Light a few candles. Then you're clear to go again same as before come Monday morning." She looked out of her window and said, quietly, "Sometimes I hate this bloody city."

"Hey!" said Rachel, laughing. "Watch what you're saying. I'm from this bloody city too, you know."

"Oh, of course, yeah," Susan replied. "I forgot. I guess it's because you don't have much of an accent."

"My parents wouldn't let me," Rachel said. "I had to put one on at school, then sometimes I forgot to stop it when I got home."

Susan pushed down further into the car seat, relaxed in the warmth from the heater and the murmur of the radio, revelling quietly too in the company of the woman next to her, who days earlier had been just another causeless enemy in the offices of the paper.

"When I first came here," she said. "I was just me, Susan Clarke. From a little town in Hampshire. Down South, they say here. That's all. If people wanted to know about me, they could ask me, or listen to what I said. Here though, you can't just be yourself; that's not enough. You've got to be something else as well. And people will fill in blanks from just a couple of questions. Sometimes they don't even need to ask questions. They simply find out what your surname is and that's enough. They'll know what you are. Catholic or Protestant. Then they want to know your school, and your parish, and they'll tell you their parish and how they drink in the parish club every Sunday lunchtime, mixing with their own."

"What if you're Jewish?" asked Rachel.

"They'll know that too," Susan said. "When you tell them you're from Childwall, or where you went to school."

"You really mean all this, don't you?" said Rachel.
"I do, yeah," she replied. "I had it all when I was married to Peter. I was always on the outside. This whole place is different, and not in a good way. At least I don't think in a good way, but people here like it like that." Then she added, "I worry about Michael."
"Being with Peter's family, you mean?"
"Yes," said Susan. "You know what they did, after he was born? Eugene and Imelda registered his birth. They named him. Michael Patrick Francis O'Hare. It's like they stamped him. I wanted to call him Robert. Robert Clarke-O'Hare. But no. They sorted it out while I was still in hospital. And then the christening. They had a child who died young. Eugene and Imelda, I mean. One of Peter's older brothers. He was Michael. They gave my son a dead boy's name. Ah well. No point going on about it now."
"We're nearly there," said Rachel. She drove over the brow of a hill, past Hillside railway station, down past the entrance to Greenside High School and the driveway leading to Royal Birkdale Golf Club. Slowing the car, she turned right into Sweeney's road.
"It's the one with the lights, isn't it?" said Susan, surveying the curve of the large detached houses that swept round the edge of the cul-de-sac.
"How did you guess?" asked Rachel.
"You can take the boy out of Kirkby…" Susan said.

Chapter Sixteen

Rachel took the car round the oval verge and it suddenly struck her that she had no idea what was going to happen next. It had been Susan's idea to come here. Susan was the one who'd reacted this way to Sweeney's text. She was the one who'd felt the anger and the drive; Rachel had merely driven. But Sweeney was hers. She turned the engine off and rested her hands on the steering wheel. Instinctively, she lowered the sun visor and opened the tiny mirror embedded in the padding, just as she always did when she stopped the car, to have a quick check of her hair and make-up, even though it was such a reflex these days that she rarely saw what she was looking at. She sat there, staring straight ahead, her mind suddenly full of an image she'd caught of herself the day before, when she was out with her mother and father. They'd been wandering from estate agent to delicatessen, her parents taking turns to say this place was new or that looks nice or do you fancy that for tea tomorrow. Outside one place, an estate agent's, while her mother gasped at the price of a semi-detached off Rose Lane these days, Rachel had looked up and seen their reflections in the shop window. She looked at herself as a stranger might. There she stood, on this chill Friday afternoon, a pretty young woman, clean and fresh and well-dressed, flanked by her mother and father, snug and secure in their guard. And suddenly, with that picture in her mind, she felt the same fleeting chill and doubt that she'd felt on seeing it the day before. She questioned her situation and her courage, asked herself whether the image she presented to people at work – intelligent, ambitious, in control – was a lie to hide the little girl who still lived with her parents and who hadn't had a relationship since university. She wondered how many people were the same, fighting to show the world only what it wanted to see, rather than what was really there.

"You okay?" Susan's voice seemed to come from a long way

away; Rachel had almost forgotten Susan was there.

"Yes," she replied. "Fine." Rachel let go of the steering wheel and reached for the door handle. Then she stopped. "Actually," she said. "There is something."

"Yes?" said Susan. "What's up?"

"Look," Rachel began, "I know it was your idea to come here, but…"

Susan interrupted her. "It's your story," she said. Rachel smiled, relieved, and Susan carried on. "Just like the dead prostitute is mine. It's no problem. We're helping each other, that's all. Just give me a nudge if I say too much."

"Thanks," Rachel said, pulling the handle towards her and opening the door.

"Nervous?" Susan asked, as they made their way over to number 9. Rachel nodded. It was true, but with her the nerves didn't show themselves as butterflies or churning stomach. Inside she was once again feeling that strange calmness settling over her, the one that had preceded every school day and college day and day at work, the one that told her she would be sick, then told her again simply to carry on. She forced the feeling away.

Susan spoke. "Me too," she said. "More than nervous. This man scares me." They arrived at the gates. Rachel pressed the button on the entrance intercom.

"Think I should have worn my new coat?" Susan asked, which made Rachel laugh.

The smile was still in her voice when someone from inside the house eventually answered, so, when she gave both her name and Susan's, she sounded relaxed, almost distracted from a more important conversation by the voice snapping, "Who is it?"

They waited for nearly three minutes before the gate was buzzed open. "Well," said Rachel. "They obviously weren't expecting us. Perhaps he's not watching my every move, after all."

At the house, the double doors were open for them. There was a different man at the door this time, but he was basically the same thug. He said nothing to the two women, just nodded to a door off the entrance hall. Rachel led the way. She opened the door and she and Susan found themselves in a lounge which stretched from the front to the back of the house.

It was a big room but it had been packed with sofas and armchairs and coffee tables, occasional tables and lamps, and a baby grand piano that sat towards the back of the room, never played and gleaming with polish. A huge artificial tree took up most of the front window, laden with baubles and angels and tinsel, its branches encroaching past the edge of the huge flatscreen television to its left. At the base of the tree was a toy train track, a little locomotive chugging and rattling around the wrapped presents piled on the thick cream carpet. Little Santas sat on the mantelpiece over the flame effect fire. Underneath the piano was a model baby reindeer, plugged in and switched on, its head moving slowly from side to side, the mechanism inside whirring quietly. The piano was laden with posed pictures of Sweeney's wife and three children. Sweeney himself was only in one picture, a large studio shot of the whole family, the edges blurred to give a sense of softness and warmth.

The door closed behind them, leaving Susan and Rachel in there alone together, the unspoken message being to wait until Sweeney was ready to see them. Neither felt inclined to speak, like they were in a library or museum, so they just gazed around the room, sharing looks of amazement and offended taste at the room and its contents.

When one of the women finally did speak, it was Rachel who whispered, "Do you think it's okay to sit down?"

Susan pulled a face and shrugged. "You can, if you like," she whispered back. "I'm frightened to leave a mark on the furniture."

"It's all very cream, isn't it?" said Rachel.

Susan nodded, then moved across to one of the lamps, brushing her hand against the tassels hanging down from the rim of the shade, thick cord threaded through glass beads. When the beads clicked together she quickly pulled her hand away and when she looked across at Rachel the two women stifled giggles like schoolgirls told to wait in the headmistress' office.

When Sweeney finally entered he seemed distracted and unsettled by the unexpected intrusion. Rachel guessed he had been in the shower when the news came they were here. His short hair was wet and as he came in he was straightening the collar of the polo shirt he was wearing. Nevertheless, as he looked first at Rachel and then Susan, his eyes showed a certain charm and amusement.

"My wife won't be happy with you two," he said, catching them both by surprise. "No shoes allowed in the lounge. That's her rule." He looked at his own feet. "Even I've got to put my slippers on. Hell to pay if I don't."

"Want us to take our shoes off?" Rachel asked.

"Yes," replied Sweeney. "If you don't mind. It'll be me who catches it if there's a mark on the carpet." He stood, hands in pockets, waiting as the two women reached down and slipped off their shoes. "They've seen better days, haven't they?" said Sweeney, nodding at the scuffed and worn brown court shoes that Susan held, heels together, in one hand. She looked embarrassed, uncertain how to react. "Sorry," Sweeney said. "Shouldn't make fun of you, not when we haven't even been introduced."

"I'm Susan Clarke," Susan told him. "I work on the *Mail* with Rachel."

"And I'm Franny Sweeney," he replied. "I…" He smiled. "Well, I do lots of things."

Susan and Rachel both felt awkward and outmanoeuvred, both standing in front of Sweeney in their stockinged feet, unsure of whether to simply stand there holding their shoes or put them down and take a seat without first being asked. Sweeney enjoyed the moment and let it linger, before gesturing towards one of the sofas for the women to sit down. He let them continue holding their shoes. Rachel and Susan sat right next to each other, prim on the edge of a sofa, legs together, each holding her shoes placed toes forward on her knees. Sweeney took his place on the sofa opposite them, leaning back into the cushions, arms spread wide behind him, one leg crossed casually over the other.

"Now," he said. "To what do I owe this unexpected pleasure?" Then, waiting until Rachel opened her mouth to speak, "Oh, forgive me. Where are my manners? Can I get either of you a drink?" As he said the last word, he looked knowingly at Susan, who felt herself tense at either Sweeney's knowledge or guesswork. Both women muttered that they were fine. "So then," said Sweeney. "Rachel, you were going to tell me why you'd dropped by."

"Billy Jackson," Rachel said. Sweeney gave her a slight smile and waited for her to add more.

"We saw him this morning," Rachel said, forcing herself to be calmer. "At Strangeways."

"Of course, that was this morning, wasn't it? How was Manchester? Bump into anyone you know?" Sweeney asked. Don't let this thug bully you, Rachel told herself. "You sent me there," she said. "You gave me a tip-off that he might be able to tell me something that would make a good story. And you didn't do that because you wanted to give my career a bit of a push. You've got a grudge against Crowley and you're using me to get back at him. Now that's fine," she went on, relaxed now, enjoying the sound of her voice. "We both get something out of it. But when we turned up there Jackson wouldn't say anything to us. Now we'll see him again, but I don't want to be driving to Manchester just to give the car a run out. If you want something printed out of this, then make sure Jackson's willing to talk. Don't waste our time. And you've had your bit of fun with the sinister texts you've been sending. You got me scared, alright? So you can stop that now."

Without quite knowing what she was doing or why she was doing it, Rachel reached down and put her shoes back on. She stood up, leaving Susan to hurriedly follow suit. Sweeney, meanwhile, stayed on his sofa, leaning back and watching Rachel, a broad grin on his face, as if enjoying the performance. He started laughing, chuckling at what Rachel had said.

"Okay, okay," he said. His eyes were dancing with the fun of it all. "Point taken. I'll pass the word and next time you go to Strangeways you can rest assured Billy Jackson will be more than happy to tell you everything you want to know. And no more texts, I promise. You're right; it was childish of me. I should be above such things." He pushed his hands down on his knees and raised himself up. Rachel and Susan were at the door, Susan holding the handle, ready to open the door and leave. Rachel turned slightly to face Sweeney, upright and defiant, pleased with the way she'd handled things.

Without breaking stride, and with his eyes still twinkling with delight, Sweeney drove his fist hard into the pit of Rachel's stomach. She crumpled, folding like a Jacob's Ladder down onto the floor. Susan froze with shock, her grip involuntarily tightening round the door handle. A quick look from Sweeney, bright eyed and still grinning, told Susan not to move, although she didn't need to be told, couldn't have done so even if she'd wanted to. Sweeney reached down and took a fistful of Rachel's thick dark hair in his hand and pulled her to her feet. Her face was ashen and she tasted bile inching its way up her throat. Pain and shock flooded her brain as she became aware of some thought fighting its way to the surface of her mind. It was a tip from a self-defence course she'd taken at the gym the year before, something about digging the fingers into an attacker's side, which would momentarily make him twist and allow her to grab and bend back the fingers of his hand. She smiled at the nonsense of such a suggestion as her eyes focused on the sympathetic smile on Sweeney's face.

Holding her still by her hair, like a doll, he said, "You shouldn't have put your shoes back on. I told you. If the wife finds out, it's my guts for garters." As he spoke, Susan looked down at her own shoes, which she was still holding. Rachel had jumped up to leave too quickly for her to put them on. Sweeney noticed this and said to Susan, "Get the door, love, would you? She's a bit of a weight, this one."

Susan opened the door and stepped out into the hall. As if he knew what to expect, the man on guard was waiting for Sweeney to hand over Rachel. He took her by the hair too, holding it more lightly than Sweeney had done, as Rachel found the floor with her feet and became more able to hold herself upright. He took her to the front door, which Susan had opened, guided her over the step and let go of her like he was putting a bin bag out for the dustmen. Susan followed, her feet cutting into the gravel while she put her shoes back on.

Sweeney stood just inside the house. He looked like a concerned host saying goodnight to a couple of guests who were a bit worse for wear.

"Make sure she gets home safely," he told Susan. "And tell her not to worry about Billy. I'll sort it. There'll be another visiting order for Tuesday. I'll get one for you too. Good night, then." He closed the door.

Susan managed to get Rachel out of the gate and across the road to the grass verge before she collapsed on the ground and began to vomit. As she did so, it struck Rachel that this was the routine with visits to Sweeney now. First the chat, then she'd leave and be sick. This was different to last time, though. Then it had just been the usual, just caused by nerves, after which she could wipe her mouth and pop in a few breath mints and be fine. This time the heaves wouldn't stop, and her eyes and nose and mouth streamed with tears and vomit and bile. And she shivered too, not only with the cold and the pain and the shock, but with the fear she'd felt at this glimpse into Sweeney's world.

Susan watched as Rachel vomited. She wanted to say something but couldn't find the words. At one point, she reached out her hand and touched Rachel on the shoulder, trying to let her friend know her concern. But the movement felt awkward and unnatural, the gesture of a woman unused to reaching out to comfort others, who had missed the chance to show even her own son how she felt about him. And so Susan simply sat on the kerb, her knees tucked up and her arms wrapped around them, while Rachel, on all fours, spewed and pawed at the ground, finally stopping and letting her head loll forward. A woman walking her dog along the pavement looked at them disgusted, wondering how women could let themselves get into such a state, and in Royal Birkdale too. Susan gave the passing woman a wave, then said to Rachel, "I'm glad we decided it was your story."

Rachel pushed herself up and sat back on her heels. She smiled briefly and weakly at Susan's remark. Saliva and mucus and vomit dribbled from her mouth and nostrils. Tears marked her cheeks, but she wasn't aware of crying. She only felt numb.

"I must look terrible," she said.

"You do," Susan replied. "But, every cloud, eh? You're making me look terrific. Maybe we should go out on the pull tonight. You could be my ugly friend." She passed Rachel some tissues.

Rachel took the tissues and wiped roughly at her mouth and nose and eyes. Then she began to cry properly, wracking sobs, bile again filling her mouth. She started to shake too, so Susan inched towards her on the kerb and put her arms round her and hugged her close.

"Come on, Rachel," she whispered into her ear. She felt uncomfortable and unpractised, but Rachel just returned her hug tightly, with real need, and so Susan relaxed into the closeness. "You cry as much as you like. You've just been punched by one of the North West's nastiest gangsters."
Eventually she stopped and Susan helped her to her feet. They walked together to the car, Susan's right arm wrapped round Rachel's waist, holding her tight through her thick parka, both to comfort her and give her physical support. At the car, Rachel reached into her pocket and gave the keys to Susan. "You drive," she said. "I don't think I could."
"Sure?" Susan asked. Rachel nodded, at which Susan said, "Well, you can drive my Rover some time. Only fair."

Chapter Seventeen

Most of the traffic was heading against them, lines of cars making for Southport, Christmas revellers looking to crawl and trawl and drink and fight through the bars and pubs and clubs of Lord Street, a new favourite destination for people looking for a change from the nightlife on offer in Liverpool. Susan, quickly used to the strange car, took them along the road following the coast, though Crosby and past Litherland and Bootle. Towards Seaforth, as they neared the centre of Liverpool, the character of the road began to change. The houses became fewer but meaner. They passed derelict pubs and run down business premises with flyers tearing from the brickwork and windows and patches of waste ground waiting for permanent redevelopment.
Susan ignored the signs which pointed her round the outskirts of the centre to the east bound M62 and the city's suburbs. Instead she drove over the flyover, lifting them up so she could look quickly across at the sheds and yards of the Seaforth container base and the wind turbines and cranes whose outlines sank into the dark night sky. She slowed as she came down the far side of the flyover. They were yards from where Eugene was planning his break into the city's elite, from where Peter would timidly launch himself as an architect of national note, from where a prostitute whose name was not yet known had been beaten and burned and left in an alley between two ideal opportunities for investment.
Rachel had said nothing for the entire journey. Despite the heater being on full in the car, she had spent much of the time shivering, her head down, taking no notice of where Susan was going or how she was driving her car. Now, slightly recovered, she felt the car slow. She lifted her head to see what was happening and where they were. Recognising the place, she spoke for the first time.
"Let's stop," she said.

"We'll be there soon," Susan replied, softly, as if speaking to a child waking up after a long journey.

"No," Rachel said firmly. "I mean let's stop there. Where you slowed down. Let's go and see it. I want to."

"You sure?" Susan asked. "What about getting you back to your parents?"

"No," said Rachel. "Not yet."

Susan eased the car into the right-hand lane as they went through the lights. At the entrance to the Albert Dock, she swung the Mini round and did a u-turn.

She headed back along the dock road then turned off left, moving closer to the river, and along Waterloo Road. She slowed the car and checked off the little roads they passed on the right – Oil Street, Vandries Street, Vulcan Street. She turned up Porter Street, then brought the car to a halt at the narrow mouth of Little Porter Street, where the dead woman's body had been laid out in cruciform, hands and face pulped and seared.

They got out of the car. The night had darkened and the two warehouse buildings looming either side of the alleyway merely intensified the blackness. Rachel kept a torch in the glove compartment of her car. She took it out and switched it on. The weak beam made little impact on the darkness, but she was able to pick out broken bottles and cracked cobblestones, empty crisp packets and assorted rubbish that had been blown through the alleyway and been caught on loose bricks and cobbles that littered the ground. She offered the torch to Susan, but she didn't take it. She wanted to be caught up in the blackness of the scene.

Susan said. "Not much of a place to die, is it? In all this filth and rubbish." She paused and then said, "Come on, let's go. Want to go back to your house?"

"No," Rachel said. She stood, not moving. "I've just realised why he said it," she said.

"Who?" asked Susan, puzzled. "Realised who said what?"

"Sweeney," Rachel replied. "When we were at his house. He asked how Manchester was, and did I bump into anyone I knew. He meant that man who knocked into me on Deansgate. He was trying to be funny, letting me know it was one of his men."

"No," said Susan. "That was just a coincidence. He couldn't have…" She didn't finish the sentence because she knew Rachel was right.

"Let's go and get a drink," Rachel said.

They left the car outside Susan's flat, then walked down Hope Street and round the corner to the Belvedere, a little pub in a Georgian terrace behind the Philharmonic Hall. The size of the place meant that it felt crowded even though there were only a small number of people in, but Rachel found an unoccupied corner between two groups and she squeezed into the space while Susan went to the bar.

"See all those pints lined up there," Susan said when she came back with her vodka and tonic and Rachel's Bushmills. Rachel nodded. "They're for the brass section of the Phil," she went on. "All ready and waiting for them to pile in during the interval in tonight's concert."

Rachel smiled. The drink burned her stomach, and she suddenly realised she was starving. She and Susan were pressed together in the curve of the leather benches that lined the wall of the pub. "Susan," she said. "Could I sleep at your place tonight, do you think?"

"Won't your parents be worried?" Susan asked.

"No," said Rachel. "I'll ring them. They'll be fine. To be honest, I just don't fancy going back there tonight. What I'd really like is to have something to eat and get drunk."

"Oh, well, I think we can manage that," Susan told her. "Takeaway and a bottle of wine?"

"A couple," said Rachel, and she drained the whiskey in her glass.

They took a Chinese takeaway back to Susan's flat and

ate and drank in silence until Rachel pushed her plate away and relaxed into the sofa.

"What do you make of today?" she asked Susan. "Sweeney and Billy."

"Sweeney's easy," said Susan. "He's a nutter. A psych..." She stopped herself mid-sentence, but she'd already said too much. She knew Rachel was frightened of Sweeney, and had good reason to be. She tried her best to continue as if nothing was wrong. "Billy Jackson, well, I don't know. In love, I guess."

"Didn't seem too scared of Franny Sweeney," Rachel said. "I don't think love would stop me from feeling that."

Susan said nothing.

"We're nowhere, are we?" said Rachel. "I mean, neither of us. Me with Sweeney and Jackson and you with the murdered woman."

"No," Susan admitted. "Maybe tomorrow will bring something."

"Tomorrow?" asked Rachel.

"Looking for Margy Girvan," Susan explained. "Billy Jackson's lost love."

"This wine's affecting my memory," Rachel said and poured herself some more, this time topping up Susan's glass too. "Tell you something you've forgotten," she went on. "Brian Nulty. You said you'd call him, see how his trawl of the massage parlours went."

Susan tutted and rolled her eyes. "Damn!" she said, and looked at her watch. "Too late now. I'll call tomorrow, lunchtime. Let him enjoy some part of his Sunday."

Susan insisted Rachel have her bedroom. Rachel was suddenly too tired to put up much of a fight. When she had shown Rachel the bedroom and bathroom and told her to help herself to her toothbrush, Susan came back into her living room. She cleared away the food and plates, leaving the washing up until morning. The CD had finished, so she switched the television on with the sound turned down low. She lit a cigarette and stared unseeing at the screen, her mind full of images of Michael playing rugby and Eugene's fat and mocking face spoiling yet another fragment of her life.

She thought of Rachel too. Susan was worried about her. Sweeney had hit her hard physically, but he'd started to get into her mind too, which was worse. He was increasing the pressure, and wouldn't stop until he'd got what he wanted, regardless of the effect it might have on Rachel. And Susan couldn't tell what that effect was. She'd expected Rachel to open up, say something about how she was feeling, but she'd said nothing, had bottled it all up. Susan knew she'd have to watch out for her, and also knew she couldn't protect her if Sweeney decided to get really rough.

Without thinking, purely out of habit, she poured herself another glass of wine from the just opened second bottle. After two sips she went to the sink and emptied the glass down the drain. She took a blanket from the airing cupboard, wrapped it round her and fell asleep lying on the sofa, pictures from the television flickering through her eyelids.

She slept well, not waking up once. Neither she nor Rachel had noticed the man in the black Saab who had been waiting outside Susan's flat for them, or that the man had followed them into the pub and to the takeaway and back to Susan's flat. He'd stayed in his car for just over forty minutes and then driven home.

Chapter Eighteen

Sunday Morning 16 December

Susan eased gradually from sleep, refreshed for the first time she could remember. She recalled the events of the day before with a slow smile. Despite the violence and confrontation and frustrations, she felt good about everything that had happened; she could sense herself undergoing some sort of process of renewal and, although a voice at the back of her mind warned her to be cautious, she felt ready to embrace it and enjoy the changes. Better than wallowing in the limbo that had passed for her life since her divorce.

She switched off the television. Dull grey light seeped through the blinds over the windows in the roof. Although the flat was on the top floor, it was nevertheless cold, and Susan kept the blanket wrapped round her as she got up from the couch and made her way over to the kitchen to fill the kettle. She smiled again, when she saw it was 10 o'clock, pleased that she'd enjoyed a lazy Sunday lie-in, pleased also that she was putting two teabags in the pot: simple things that ordinary people do on Sunday mornings, rather than picking up wine bottles from the floor and finding the milk sour and searching through ashtrays for cigarette stubs that still had enough left for a smoke.

The noise of the boiling kettle seemed to pull Rachel out of bed and into the living room. She padded on bare feet over to the kitchen counter. Her eyes were full of sleep still and her face was pale. She pulled at the lapel of the dressing gown she was wearing. "Hope you don't mind. Found it on the back of the door."

"Course not," Susan replied. "I was going to bring you this tea in bed, you know."

"Don't worry," Rachel said. "This is just fine." She settled herself on the sofa, still warm from where Susan had been sleeping, and curled her legs beneath her body.

Heavy pink grey clouds hung over Hope Street as they came out of Susan's building to look for breakfast, threatening the late arrivals for 11 o'clock mass at the Catholic cathedral with snow when they'd finished praying. The streets of Liverpool's Georgian Quarter showed other signs of Sunday life too. Residents were emerging from the houses in search of newspapers and late breakfasts, so when Susan and Rachel arrived at the café they found it crowded with large groups of students squeezed round small tables crammed with coffees and croissants and glasses of orange juice, the place full of laughter and chatter and surfaces littered with Sunday supplements and unwanted business sections.

Susan and Rachel were forced to sit at a table outside on the pavement of Falkner Street, gloved hands cradling their hot chocolates and fingers awkwardly tearing at their Danish pastries. Susan was wearing her new coat.

"How do you feel?" Susan asked Rachel. "After the business with Sweeney."

Rachel sipped her hot chocolate and thought for a moment. She was staring down at the table, her face expressionless, then she put down her cup and looked up at Susan. "Sort of blooded, in a way. You know, like I've been through something and come out the other side. That's what I'm trying to tell myself at least. Scared though. I wouldn't want to go through that again."

"I don't blame you," Susan said. "Sweeney's a mad bastard. You'd be mad too if you weren't scared of him. But it's the job, remember? Keep telling yourself that, too."

"What'll he do next though?" Rachel asked. "What if I can't do what he wants?" Unable to control herself she slammed her cup down into the saucer. "And meanwhile we're sitting here drinking hot fucking chocolate and eating Danish pastries like we haven't a care in the world."

Susan ignored the stares from those around them that Rachel's flaring anger had drawn. She patted Rachel's arm. "Enjoy it," she told Rachel. "If you're going to amount to anything, then get used to coping with the likes of Franny Sweeney. And we're sitting with our hot drinks and pastries because we need to get away from scum like him. Remind ourselves there are plenty of nice things and places in the city."

Rachel bit her lip and said nothing.

Susan drained her cup. "Well," she said. "Let's go and continue your initiation. It's about time you had your car tyres slashed and a few doors slammed in your face."

Rachel stood up. "Billy said she'd moved back to Liverpool," she said. "Near her mother. We could try and find her too, if there's no luck with Margy."

A brief detour to Old Hall Street and the offices of the *Liverpool Morning Mail* produced a list of 38 Girvans in the Liverpool area. Rachel sorted them first according to district, then according to proximity to Sunnybank Road. The closest was three streets away.

They'd gone two miles down Edge Lane before the heater in Susan's Rover had any effect at all. The city was starting the day sluggishly; traffic heading into town was sparse. Susan knew there was little she could say to help and that Rachel would have to cope with her fears alone, so talk in the car was as light as the traffic. Even so, Susan didn't register that the black Saab had followed them all the way from her flat.

The closer they got to Belle Vale, the more the character of the surrounding area changed. Things felt meaner, more guarded, more defensive, and the brilliant white of the sticking snow only served to highlight more clearly the shoddiness of the roads and buildings it was beginning to blanket.

There was no view of any river from River View House, just as Sunnybank Road itself offered no bank likely to catch the sun. The four-storey tenement had been one of the first put up on the new estate when the city planners decided to sweep everyone from the heart of the city to its outskirts. Consequently, it had had longer than most to suffer. The

bricks on the outer wall were cracked and in need of
repointing; window sills were rotted. The meagre garden
squeezed between the building and the pavement was littered
with rubbish and condoms and weeds.

On the pavement, blocking the pathway, three girls in their
early teens were practising dance moves, routines copied from
MTV. They were in school uniform, green tartan skirts, dark
green pullovers with pale green collars visible over the v-
necks. They shared the same hair style, built up on the tops of
the heads, long pony tails down their backs. They sang the
words as they swayed their hips and pointed their hands.
Rachel hesitated as she approached them, feeling a shudder of
fear as old images rushed back into her mind. Girls like these
had been the bane of her life when she was at school, taunting
her shyness with their own confidence and loudness on so
many bus journeys home. The girls stopped as the two
women approached.

"In uniform on a Sunday, girls?" said Susan.

"Special mass," one of the girls replied. Susan smiled as the
girls sullenly moved out of their way and let the women pass.

"Lezzers!" a girl shouted as Susan and Rachel went by. When
they turned, the girls met their looks with their own hard-faced
stares. Then they went back to their dance routine.

The tenement stretched from one end of the road to the other.
The entrance which led to flat 17 was two doors down from
the top of the road. Susan went to buzz for Margy Girvan's
home but the buzzer was broken. She pushed at the front door
and it swung open straight away. The inside of the building
was in no better condition than the outside. The weight of the
nicotine brown paint on the walls was pulling away thin sheets
of plaster here and there. The linoleum was pitted with tiny
craters where people had ground out their cigarettes, and lined
with jagged gashes ready to trip the unwary. Not that there
were too many of those in these flats; people had learned to be
guarded and watchful, eyes sharp with mistrust.

On each floor a door led into a flat either side of the central stairwell. Rachel led the way up. Again she felt inside herself the desire to be sick, to start the day with the familiar routine which cleared the way for work to begin. But she was calm too, and excited, feeling that she was getting closer to the story that Sweeney had promised her.

Rachel stood poised at the door of Flat 17, River View House, warmly dressed in expensive clothes, her hair gleaming, her stomach full of hot chocolate and continental pastry, financially secure and wondering whether to move out of her loving family home and buy a flat with actual views of a river. And on the other side of the door was what? A woman whose face was prematurely lined and blotched with burst blood vessels, whose hair showed grey at the roots and dyed red elsewhere, whose fingers were stained indelibly with a nicotine tan, whose boyfriend sat in prison threatened by the gangster reach of Franny Sweeney?

She knocked, Susan alongside her. They waited, then Rachel knocked again, but no-one came to answer.

"Would have been too easy if she'd been in, wouldn't it?" said Susan. She reached into her pocket and pulled out the photograph Billy Jackson had given her. Turning it over, she tapped in the number on the back into her own mobile phone. "Dead," she said to Rachel. "Let's try across the hall. See if her neighbours know where she is."

When they knocked at number 18, the door was answered by a boy of about 13 holding in his arms another child. This other child must have been around 5 and was too big for the teenager, but they clung to each other as if for support.

"Hi there," Susan said. "My name is Susan and this is Rachel. We're reporters from the local newspaper. What's your name?"

The older boy didn't answer. He just stared at Rachel and Susan as if they were from another planet, then, still staring at them, he called out for his father. His accent scraped against the syllables of the word.

From deeper inside the flat came a shout of "Wha'?" The boy just shouted "Dad!" again, which brought the father to the front door. He was in his late 20s, and was wearing nylon tracksuit bottoms, gleaming white trainers and a crew neck pullover. His hair was heavily gelled and short on top with the sides severely shaved.

"Wha' d'you want?" the father said to Susan and Rachel.

"We're looking for Margy Girvan," said Rachel.

"Who?" the man demanded and Rachel said the name again. The man looked blank. "Never 'eard of 'er," he said. He made to shut the door, but Rachel stepped forward, not quite putting her foot over the entrance, but looking as if she might. In turn, the man shoved his son aside and stepped forward to meet her.

Rachel smiled at him. "We're from the *Morning Mail*," she said. "Margy Girvan lives across the hall here, at number 17. Her boyfriend's asked us to find her for him."

The man looked over to the opposite door, as if checking through images in his mind of the door opening and Margy Girvan appearing, so he could recall the face of the woman Rachel was talking about.

"Not seen 'er," he said.

"Can you remember when you last saw her?" Susan asked.

"No," he said.

The teenage boy spoke up, making his father glare down and behind at him. "Seen since last week," he said. "She looked in on us cos Kyle was sick. We were off school." The father looked at the boy again; this time it was as if he was trying to remember who these two kids were and what their connection with him was.

"What day was that?" asked Rachel.

"You gonna pay 'im for this?" the father wanted to know.

The boy ignored him. "Wednesday," he said.

"And you've not seen her since then?" Susan asked. The boy shook his head. "Well," Susan went on. "Thanks for that. You've been really helpful. What's your name?"
"Danny."
"Danny," Susan repeated. "And this is Kyle. He's lucky to have a nice big brother to look after him."
They went back outside and stood at the entrance to the tenement. Susan lit a cigarette.
"We could stay inside while you have that," Rachel said.
"No," Susan replied. "I want fresh air." She looked down at the cigarette between her fingers and laughed at what she'd said. "Some fresh air, anyway. Do you want to try some more doors here?" she asked.
"No," said Rachel. "Let's knock at that closest address we got for another Girvan. Maybe that's her mother. Should be, don't you reckon?"
"There's a good chance," replied Susan. "If she moved back here to be close to her." She had smoked the cigarette down to the filter. Nipping the burning end between her finger and thumb, she squeezed it out and onto the ground, then put the dead filter back into the packet. "Don't feel like adding to the mess," she explained to Rachel.
Pentland Road was lined either side with red brick 1960s council houses. Some, towards the start of the road, had clearly been bought by the occupants, and now featured incongruous new front doors, leaded windows or porches. Their gardens were tidier in general, and their narrow paths guarded by proud new gates. Number 26 looked abandoned. It stood near the bottom of the road, a cul-de-sac which opened onto a large square of grass. Originally intended as a space for local residents to enjoy a patch of green, it was now bare of grass mostly, almost scorched, no chance of growth. A burnt-out car stood in the centre of the field, while the accumulation of broken bottles and empty beer cans on the fringes of the grass spoke of long nights punctured by

outbursts of drunken teenage intimidation. It was empty now, save for two dogs sniffing round the burnt-out car.

Susan did a u-turn at the end of the road, leaving the car facing out of the road outside number 26, as if ready for a quick getaway.

As with the tenement they'd just left, crushed between the outside wall and the house itself was a tiny garden, now full of dead weeds, dog mess and litter. Susan and Rachel picked their way gingerly up the path to the front door. This was a cheap replacement for the original, or maybe another cheap replacement for the previous temporary one. It was merely thin boards stuck together and painted a rough brown. The Yale lock just about held it in place, but over and under the lock a gentle push made the door give way. Rachel knocked, having taken off her gloves because the chip board felt so damp and soft it was hard to generate any sound with the gloves on. She knocked again, while Susan tried to look in through the closed curtains of the front room.

After a few moments, they heard some movement from inside the flat – a difficult, unsteady shuffling, like someone dragging themselves down the hall.

"Mrs Girvan?" Susan shouted, leaning into the door, her mouth close to where the door met its surround. "Is that you Mrs Girvan?"

A voice called back, "Margy? Is that you girl?" It was a strange voice, a woman's certainly, an old woman's, although there was something girlish about it too, just round the edges, a result of the hope raised by the knock at the door. But there was also a rasp to it, like the words were being gargled up with phlegm.

The voice repeated, "That you Margy?" followed by a series of coughs which bent and twisted the woman's body.

Rachel eased Susan away from the door, taking her place pressed close to the door. "Yes," she called back. "Yes, Mum, it's me."

The woman inside the house was too pleased that her daughter had come round again to be angry that she'd left it so long without even calling on the phone. Her voice was more cheerful as she opened the front door and said, "Forgot your keys?" and stayed brighter to the end of the question even though she realised immediately that neither of the two women on her door step was Margy. A look of instant pain and fear squeezed her face and she tried to push the door back closed. Rachel, however, without moving suddenly or forcefully, held her hand in the swing of the shutting door, easily preventing it closing, the woman's strength sapped by years of wear and that one moment of hopelessness.
The old woman had given up any thought of closing the door even before Rachel put her arm in the way. She stumbled back and to her right, leaning against the hall wall. Despair and aloneness had gripped her and without any notions of pride or pretence she just started crying, sobbing, revealing inside the cracked and beaten adult shell a little girl, frightened and hopeless.

Chapter Nineteen

Rachel stepped into the hall. She hadn't looked at Susan since answering to Margy's name. Susan had patted her on the shoulder when she'd said it, telling her it was the right thing to do, because it made Mrs Girvan open the door, but Rachel had been numbed slightly by her own reply. She would confront it later, but not now, not while this weak, thin, frail woman crumbled before her. The woman – too frail to stagger – had shuffled back and crumpled onto the bottom steps of the hall staircase. Rachel eased towards her and went down on one knee next to her, taking hold of her hand and whispering soothing words. Susan held back, quietly closing the door behind her, examining the hallway while Rachel comforted Mrs Girvan. It felt colder than outside and damp too. The wallpaper bubbled and peeled in places, and where it met both the ceiling and the skirting boards it was trimmed with blotches of grey-black mould. Susan could taste the mould at the back of each breath she took.

The hallway carpet had been measured and cut for a different floor, and left irregular spaces between its roughly hacked edges and the walls. The stairs on which Mrs Girvan sat had no carpet at all, just bare wood boards marked by bent nails. The walls were bare of pictures, the closest thing to a decoration being a crucified Christ nailed into loose plaster just inside the front door.

At the end of the hallway was the kitchen. Susan watched as Rachel eased Mrs Girvan to her feet, then offered to go and make them all a cup of tea. Rachel said that would be lovely and Susan realised they were both speaking in the sing-song voices reserved for people who dealt with either the very young or the very old. Rachel guided Mrs Girvan into the front room; Susan went down the hall and into the kitchen. More damp, more mould, a stronger stench than the hallway. She put the kettle on and looked through the cupboards for tea bags and sugar. She kept her gloves on and was careful her new £250 coat from Kendal's didn't come into contact with any surface, pressing it close to her whenever she reached to open a cupboard door. She found tea bags in a caddy marked Greetings from Scotland; next to it was the sugar, the bag ripped open, the contents crusted and stained brown in places where someone had used the same spoon as they'd used for the tea. As the kettle boiled, Susan noted the walls slick with damp and condensation and the rotting window frames waiting for the council to replace them.

She made just the one cup, checking first to see if Mrs Girvan took sugar. "Yes, please, love. Three," was the reply. Then, briefly, Mrs Girvan seemed to force some jollity into her response, perhaps suddenly feeling the need to set these strangers at ease. "Sweet tooth, you see," she said to Rachel. "My age, it doesn't matter if I put on a couple of pounds." There was no spare flesh on her body.

"You're lucky," Rachel said to her. "I so much as look at a biscuit and I pile the weight on." But the old woman had lost attention, and had subsided back into her world of worry and isolation.

Rachel said nothing until Susan came back into the room with Mrs Girvan's tea. Susan stood by the door, telling herself she wanted to keep out of the way, so as not to intimidate the old woman, but also because she needed cold air from the hallway. While the rest of the house was freezing, the front room was stiflingly hot. A portable gas heater stood in the middle of the wall opposite the door, just where a real fire would have been. It was full on, and felt to Susan and Rachel that it had been that way for days, forcing heat into the room and driving the air out. Mrs Girvan sat on a threadbare armchair close to the heater. Rachel sat to her left, on the matching sofa. Mrs Girvan had turned the television off when they'd come in the room, but she continued to stare at the screen. Susan and Rachel both soon noticed the picture of

Margy on top of the television. It was much the same as the one Jackson had given them – a woman in a pub, mouth open in laughter, eyes shining with drink, a cigarette in her hand. In this one, though, she was sitting on a bench rather than a stool, and, instead of having Jackson next to her, she had her arm round her mother, whose laughter was not quite so ready as that of Margy's. There were no other photographs in the room, nothing that suggested other children or grandchildren, or a husband. There was another crucifix, but this one was on a stand rather than on the wall, and was next to a chipped statue of Our Lady, her arms outstretched and her bare feet crushing serpents beneath her.

"Your tea alright?" Rachel asked Mrs Girvan. She was holding the mug, resting it on the arm of her chair, but she hadn't touched it, and looked at it now as if she'd forgotten it was there.

"Fine, thanks, love," she said, before tasting it. Her accent was Scottish, Glasgow filtered through years down South, beaten and curdled by drink and cigarettes.

Rachel stood up and went towards the TV set. She indicated the photograph and said, "May I?" before picking it up and looking at it. Mrs Girvan seemed to have no interest in the two women beyond the odd effort to be polite. Rachel wondered if she just didn't have the energy or if she felt that by not asking she'd never find out.

Rachel felt she was watching a woman who had recognised her fate and who knew that the end wouldn't be sudden, but would stretch out and need to be endured.

Slowly, Mrs Girvan took a sip of her tea. "Just right," she said. "Not too hot." She touched her hair with her free hand, patting her palm against her head, like she was feeling around in the dark for something. "She used to do it," she said. "Margy. Every fortnight or so. Make it look nice." It was grey and lank, sitting on top of her head and creeping down to her shoulders. Her face was thin and lined and her body frail, wrapped in a stained pink dressing gown that had grubby rabbits dancing on its pockets. Her blotched and veined legs could be seen through her thin tights, stick thin and jammed into tatty slippers. Rachel inched back towards the couch, reluctant to make a sound, eyes never leaving the woman who was softly shattering into pieces in front of her.

Mrs Girvan carried on. "She said she'd do it next time she came. Said she was in a rush."

"When was that, Mrs Girvan?" asked Rachel. "When did you last see Margy?"

From the door Susan spoke, her voice as soft as Rachel's. "Was it yesterday, Mrs Girvan?" The old woman didn't answer. "It's Sunday today," Susan said. "Did you see her yesterday?"

"Does she ever bring you anything?" asked Rachel. "Do any shopping for you?"

"She's very good. Looks after me. Makes sure I've got everything." She said it like her catechism.

Susan understood Rachel's brief glance and slipped quietly out of the room and back into the kitchen. She took the milk out of the fridge and checked the sell-by date. She hadn't thought to look before. Use by December 6 2007 the carton said. Last Monday, Susan worked out. She sniffed the open carton and sharply pulled her head back at the sour-sick smell. She thought of the old lady in the front room calmly sipping the tea she'd made for her and declaring it lovely and realised how a sense of numbness must have occupied her body, gradually shutting down all her senses, but leaving her mercilessly still able to breathe and walk and see and remember. For some reason she put the rancid milk back in the fridge, saw the black dots of mould on a lump of cheese and the dry crust covering the surface of the opened tin of beans.

She went back into the front room. Rachel looked up and Susan pulled her face into a grimace, trying to make her

understand that what she'd found didn't offer much hope.
Rachel nodded. She was holding a mobile phone that she'd seen beneath Mrs Girvan's chair. The old lady hadn't objected – hadn't reacted at all – when Rachel asked if she could take a look at it.
"Margy got it for me," Mrs Girvan said. "Told me to keep it switched on all the time. She rings me. Always have it with me."
"The battery's gone," said Rachel. "Do you have a recharger for it?"
For the first time Mrs Girvan turned to look at Rachel. "What, love?" she asked.
"A recharger," repeated Rachel. "You know, for when the phone goes dead?"
"Is it broken?" asked Mrs Girvan. She was becoming animated suddenly. "What if Margy's been trying to ring me?"
Rachel knelt next to Mrs Girvan, patting her arm and trying to soothe her sudden panic. Close up, her face looked stricken. "It's not broken, Mrs Girvan," she said. "Don't worry."
The old woman had twisted in her chair and taken a fierce grip on Rachel's hand. "You sure?" she asked, pleading, then repeated, "What if Margy's been trying to ring me? She'll be cross. She's shown me again and again how to use the phone. I keep forgetting." She tightened her grip on Rachel's hand, forcing the younger woman to mask a wince of pain, then just as suddenly released it and slumped back into the chair. And then she crumpled before Rachel's eyes, her face and features collapsing in on themselves, her head lolling as her tears and sobs burst through every defence she'd laid against them.
Rachel stroked the woman's lifeless hair and whispered a useless "Never mind" over and over again.
Susan, still at the door, watched awkward and useless. "I'll go and look for the recharger," she said, although Rachel didn't

hear her. Then she went out into the hallway and up the stairs, swallowing hard and wiping her own tears away.

There was no carpet on the landing. There, and in the bathroom and the two bedrooms, the wallpaper clung only in patches to the cold, damp walls. Susan had half-expected to find the spare bedroom a sort of shrine to the daughter who hadn't visited in well over a week, full of dolls and schoolbooks and baby pictures. But it wasn't. It was just like the spare room in her own flat, with a bed and bare mattress on which some boxes had been dumped. Quickly she turned and left the room and went into the front bedroom. A high, old-fashioned single bed sat in the middle of one wall, piled high with blankets, so well-made that Susan wondered how long ago it was since Mrs Girvan had slept in it. The wardrobe was too big for the room.

The phone recharger was plugged into a wall socket behind the bed, its cord lying twisted on the floor. Susan took it downstairs. Mrs Girvan had stopped crying, but her head remained rested against the back of the chair. Her eyes were open and staring, wet still with tears, and mucus seeped from her nose. Rachel hadn't moved either.

Susan tapped her on the shoulder and motioned her away. They both went back to the door, wanting to be as far as they could from Mrs Girvan without leaving the room. There was a socket just inside the door. Susan plugged in the recharger then connected it to the phone which Rachel still held. They both stared at the tiny screen, waiting for a sign of life. They shared a quick glance as each sensed in the other the same feeling: their thoughts were leaving Mrs Girvan and going back to Rachel's story. There'd surely be something here to help them reach Margy – a message maybe, saying she was heading off with some new man, saying how she could be reached, or maybe Billy was right and she had changed her mobile and this would give them the new number. Whatever it was, they'd be able to take a step forward, which would allow them to go back to Strangeways and show Billy they'd fulfilled their part of the bargain so he'd have to start talking about Crowley.

For a short while it seemed that the phone would remain dead, then, to each woman's relief, a battery icon appeared to the right of the screen, bars scrolling up inside it to show that recharging had begun.

"It's coming back to life, Mrs Girvan," Rachel called from the door, briefly taking her eyes away from the phone screen. The old lady ignored her, or didn't hear her at all.

Susan and Rachel looked at the Received Calls listings first, but found only one, from Thursday November 29th, made at 17.33, a call from another mobile, 07832 980 188. Susan noted the number down. In the Missed Calls list there were 18. The 14 most recent were from the same number – 0161 185 5000 – the calls made at various times over the period of the past week.

"Billy Jackson, you reckon?" asked Rachel.

"Got to be, I guess," Susan replied. "We can check anyway." She made a note of the number along with the times of the calls.

Three of the last four were more interesting. The last number in the list was Rachel's own, from earlier in the day. Then there were three others, all from Friday 7th. At 2.30 on that Friday afternoon there'd been a call from the same phone that had rung on Thursday 29th November. Then came two more, hours later, made in quick succession, at 23.51 and 23.56. The first was from a mobile, 0771 657 1001, the second from a landline, a Liverpool number, 0151 982 4994.

Again, Susan copied the numbers and times into her notebook. "That's a city centre number, isn't it?" she asked, half to herself.

"Hm?" Rachel replied. "Sorry, yes. I think so, at any rate." She was looking back at Mrs Girvan, still sitting in her chair, taking occasional sips of her tea, cold by now surely, sweet from the sugar and sour from the milk.

"Do you want to call these now?" Susan asked. Rachel didn't answer. "Rachel? These numbers. Are you going to give them a ring? It's your story, remember?"

Rachel stood up and moved over to the window, where the tatty curtain hid the world from Mrs Girvan's eyes. She pulled the curtain aside slightly, revealing grimy glass and a smeared view of the darkening day.

"I'm tired," she said, turning round. "And worried about her." She nodded across at Mrs Girvan. "Is there anyone we could call, do you think?"

"Only Margy," Susan replied. "And it's not our problem." Rachel looked sharply at Susan. "I know how that sounds," she said. "But it's true. We can't get involved with every dreadful situation we come across."

"I'm going to knock next door," Rachel said, suddenly moving quickly across the room. "Ask the neighbours. Maybe they can help."

"Ask them about Margy," Susan said, but she wasn't sure Rachel heard her. She was out of the room and the front door before Susan could get all the words out.

Susan stood up and pulled the sofa back round to its original position. She lingered alongside Mrs Girvan's chair, and gently stroked the old lady's hair. She murmured, "You poor, poor thing," and Mrs Girvan nuzzled against her touch, comforted by the soft voice, reminded of something long lost. She whispered in reply, "Margy," but Susan could tell she understood it wasn't Margy, only a memory of her.

She left the room and went into the kitchen, where she searched for a bin liner or carrier bags. Finding a bag to do the job, she began clearing away the rubbish, the stale bread, the opened tins, the grey cheese, the carton of sour milk. As she was doing so, she heard the front door close. Rachel came into the kitchen. Susan, a bin bag in one hand and a packet soup long past its sell-by date in the other, turned to look at her.

"Don't say anything," Susan told her, and Rachel smiled, a beaming grin. "Now, tell me what the neighbours said. I hope you asked them about Margy."

"No answer from one side," Rachel said. "It's boarded up. Talked to the woman on the left."

"And?" Susan asked. She scanned the room for anything she'd missed then tied the top of the bin bag up and put it down next to the back door.

"She knows Margy. Has seen her at least," Rachel said. "Although not for a while, last time maybe a fortnight ago, she couldn't be sure. Anyway, even when she came, it was only sporadically." Susan looked up. "My word," said Rachel. "Not hers. She tries to look in on her, and she's got a daughter of about 14 who knocks now and then. But Mrs Girvan doesn't always reply. Doesn't see much of her. Certainly hasn't seen her outside the house in a while. I gave the girl £30, asked her to get some shopping in. Only other visitor is a man. Here this morning, she said. Comes every Sunday. She always lets him in. A black man, she said, smartly dressed."

"A priest," said Susan.

"What?"

"He'll be the parish priest, I bet," she said. "Bringing communion to the housebound, the sick and the infirm."

"How can you be so sure?" asked Rachel.

"Every Sunday, for a start," Susan told her. "And the crucifix, the statue of Mary in the front room. And her name. Girvan. She'll be a good Scots-Irish Catholic, right at home here in this city. I said you can always tell, didn't I?" She smiled.

"What are you grinning at?" asked Rachel. "I thought you hated that about Liverpool."

"Oh, I do," said Susan. "I'm smiling because the priest is black. Eugene wouldn't like that. Just hope Father gets a transfer to his parish, that's all."

Susan and Rachel said their goodbyes to Mrs Girvan. The old woman replied – "Okay, now. See you love." – but neither Rachel nor Susan believed she really registered what was happening. Walking back to the car, Susan suddenly stopped. "Don't say I've got a parking ticket," she said, and pointed to the windscreen. "Not here, surely."

Rachel strode down the path and took an envelope from under the wiper blade.

"It's not a ticket," she said. "It's addressed to me."

Nervously, standing in the road by the driver's door, she opened the letter. "'Why are you wasting your time here?'" she read aloud. "Sweeney." She crumpled the note in her hand. A black car going too fast down the road beeped its horn loudly as Rachel swayed further into the road. That and the note tipped Rachel over the edge. "What's your problem!" she yelled after the car. Then she slumped against Susan's Rover and began to cry.

"Hey," Susan said softly. "Come on, don't."

"What the fuck do you expect?" Rachel shouted. "It's not you getting these notes, is it? These messages. It's not you he's watching!"

Susan guided Rachel into the car. Rachel said nothing for the entire journey. Her hands trembled and she couldn't stop it. By the time they reached Hope Street it was just gone four and already dark. Susan wanted Rachel to come in, but she refused, saying she just wanted to get back home, have a bath, try to forget everything. Before they parted, Rachel copied the times and numbers of the calls they'd taken from Mrs Girvan's phone.

"I'll try these tomorrow," she said flatly. "Maybe Margy will answer. And if she doesn't, I'll still have something to make Billy Jackson talk."

"Don't worry," said Susan. "Sweeney will have got to him. He'll talk, Margy or no Margy. When are we seeing him next?"

"Depends how soon Sweeney sorts the Visiting Orders," Rachel replied. "I hope to God it's soon. I can't stand this much longer."

"Be patient," Susan told her. "Billy will talk this week." Rachel nodded and turned to get into her car. She opened the door and got in behind the wheel. Susan rested her hand on the edge of the door.

"That was him, wasn't it?" said Rachel, looking up at Susan. "Outside Mrs Girvan's house, that car that nearly hit me. It was Sweeney, or one of his men. Like the man who barged into me in Manchester."

"Coincidence," Susan said, but she knew Rachel didn't believe it and she didn't believe it herself. "Sure you don't want to come up?" She repeated her offer. She desperately wanted Rachel to say yes, and not just for her colleague's sake. Suddenly she didn't want to climb the stairs and get through another evening alone. Especially not a Sunday evening, when loneliness and responsibility and worry crowded the mind.

But Rachel again said no. "I'm shattered," she said. "I'd be no company for you."

"Okay," Susan told her, although it was anything but. She watched Rachel drive away then let herself into her building. The hall and staircase still retained elements of the original building – the width and sense of space, the tiled floor, the elegant banister curved and worn with time – but Susan noticed none of this as she trudged her way to the top of the house. From inside each flat she passed she could detect the sounds of ordinary life - music, television, muffled conversations. Her own flat was silent, dark and cold. She turned the central heating on and went round switching on the lights. She looked through her collection of CDs, picking out *Revolver* by The Beatles. She wanted melody and pace and noise and life, not introspective jazz or the mournful romance her classical selection offered. She put the television on as

well, although she took no notice of what the programme was. All she wanted was light and sound and
movement and warmth, anything but the cold silence her life was usually surrounded by.

She made a cup of coffee – she smelled the milk before she put it in the mug and was thankful to find it still fresh – and took it to the couch where she'd slept the night before. The blanket was still there and she slipped off her shoes and curled her legs beneath herself and pulled the blanket around her. She sipped her coffee and watched unseeing the TV screen and pushed away the thought that her pose somehow aped Mrs Girvan's. She felt her mind go blank.

Chapter Twenty

Sunday Evening 16 December
Susan had no idea how long the telephone had been ringing when she finally woke up. She had incorporated the noise into her dreams before opening her eyes slowly. The phone was on the table next to the sofa. She picked it up immediately, no idea if it was Sunday still or if Monday had come and gone. She said her name down the phone and noted that The Beatles had finished and the sky was darker than before and that a slow comedy was ambling towards its conclusion on the television. She reached for the remote and turned the volume off.

"I didn't think you were in," the voice said. "I was just about to give up and call you again tomorrow."

Susan mumbled something in reply.

"Don't tell me I've got you out of bed, Sue. It's only just gone 7." Sue, she registered. Sue. Who is this, she asked herself.

The man on the other end of the line guessed her uncertainty. "It's Brian here," he said. Brian? He was a mind-reader. "Brian Nulty," he explained further. "You said you'd call me. Remember?"

"Brian," Susan said and repeated, "Brian. Sorry, Brian. Completely forgot. Been out with Rachel all day. Yesterday too." She yawned.

Brian laughed. "Well, while you two have been out gallivanting, I've been doing the rounds of Liverpool's massage parlours. Even did a couple in Birkenhead, for added glamour."

Susan yawned again and pressed her palm against her forehead, rubbing into her eyes. She went to move the blanket to one side so she could sit up, and noticed that it was damp. She must have fallen asleep without finishing her coffee, and it had tipped up and spilt over the blanket.

"Anything?" she managed to ask. A full sentence was beyond her just yet.

"Nott'n definite," Brian told her. "I was askin' if any of the girls 'adn't been around at all lately. Well, it's the nature of the business. They aren't the most reliable of people, and, of course, they don't sign contracts." He paused. Susan blearily sensed him flicking through his notes. Meticulous, Brian was. Always had been. She smiled vaguely at the thought of Brian telling his wife he was going to spend his Sunday in assorted massage parlours, and how she'd say 'have a nice time, dear' and tell him when dinner would be ready.

Nulty waited for some response from Susan, but none came, so he just continued. "A couple of names cropped up more than once, so I'll need to follow those up, or pass them on to Nolan. 'e's in charge of the investigation."

Susan had let Brian's voice drift away. It lulled her, and her mind moved far from his words.

"Margy Girvan," she suddenly said. She was fully awake instantly. It was as if she'd heard someone else say the two words; she certainly wasn't aware of saying them, had had no reason to say them.

"What was tha'?" asked Nulty.

Susan repeated herself: "Margy Girvan." When she heard the words again it was suddenly obvious. She leant forward on the sofa, her hand gripping the receiver tightly. "Brian," she said. "Have you got a Margy Girvan on that list of yours?"

"'ang on," Brian said. He caught the urgency in her tone. "Margy," he said. "No Girvan, but I've got a Margy. Twice. A parlour in Wavertree. And another one in Norris Green. Why?" he asked.

"I know who it is, Brian," Susan told him. "Her surname's Girvan. Margy Girvan. She lives in Belle Vale. Lived in Belle Vale."

On the television, the comedy had ended. The credits scrolled up over a landscape of green rolling hills, the figures of three old men looking bemused and scratching their heads as a younger man climbed from some sort of contraption that had crashed into a dry stone wall.

Susan and Nulty talked for a few minutes more then said their goodbyes. When she put the phone down, Susan stood and shivered. She pulled the blanket around her shoulders and walked over to the kitchen where she poured herself a glass of white wine. The wine was crisp and cold in her throat; she sipped her way through the glass then poured herself another and lit a cigarette to go with it. She stood at the window, staring with glazed eyes over the lights of the city stretching down towards the river. It had started snowing again. She could pick out big flakes drifting through the blazing orange lights, muffling and stilling the houses and roads and pavements. She found herself thinking about Michael, wondering if he was still young enough to be excited by the magic that a heavy snowfall brings.

For the second time that night, she was roused by the phone ringing, and took a while to register the sound. Eventually she picked it up, returning to the window before answering it. She thought it might be Brian Nulty calling back with a list of questions, so was surprised to hear Rachel's voice.

"Not disturbing you, am I?" Rachel asked.

"No, no," Susan lied.

"I've felt a bit better since I got back," Rachel told her. "Mum kept dinner for me, then I had a long soak in the bath. How about you?" She didn't wait for an answer. "I was thinking something about Billy Jackson. What do you think if I…"

Susan interrupted her. "I've just had Brian Nulty on the phone," she said.

Rachel was momentarily confused. "Brian Nulty? Who…Oh, of course, sorry. What did he have to say for himself?"

Rachel was in a good mood, excited by the weekend's events, refreshed by consideration of all that had happened.

"It was me doing the saying," said Susan. "I think I know

who the murdered prostitute was." She explained her thoughts and told Rachel all about the conversation with Nulty. The whole story left Rachel subdued, her good spirits dissipated.
"So what's he going to do, then?" Rachel asked. "Does he think it's her?"
"Thinks it could be. You know Brian," Susan said, then corrected herself. "Sorry, you don't, do you? He's not one to get carried away."
"I think I would have guessed that," Rachel said.
"But it's given him something to work on. Said he'd pass the information on, let the investigating officer know Mrs Girvan's address. They can do blood tests, DNA, you know."
"What did he say about the mobile phone and all the numbers?" asked Rachel. Susan was silent. "Susan," Rachel said, her tone stern. "You did tell him, didn't you?"
"No," Susan eventually said. "I didn't. Look, I know I should've…" She let the sentence trail, then tried to rationalise. "It's just a guess on my part, really. Probably rubbish. Just because we spent the day looking for Margy."
"But you said Nulty told you he had a couple of mentions of a Margy missing," Rachel said. Then her tone shifted. "Besides, you know, don't you? You know it's her."
"I think I do," Susan said. "Don't ask me how or why. And don't, for God's sake, call it woman's intuition. But, yeah, I think I do. It just feels right. Sounds stupid, doesn't it?"
Rachel ignored the question. "What am I going to tell Billy?" she asked. "We're seeing him Tuesday, if what Sweeney told you is right."
"It will be, don't worry about that. Anyway, don't tell him anything," Susan said. "What can you tell him? Just say you think you've found her new number. It's the truth, after all."

Chapter Twenty-one

Monday 17 December
BREAKTHROUGH IN POLICE BID TO IDENTIFY MURDERED WOMAN
Police feel they might have made some progress in their attempt to put a name to the woman found murdered at the Northern Warehouse just over a week ago..
After intensive inquiries throughout Liverpool's red light districts and known massage parlours, police say they are closer to identifying the victim.
"The same name kept cropping up in our search," said Inspector Brian Nulty. "Just the first name, but it's more than we had before."
Police will not release the name for the time being, but are concentrating their searches now in the Lee Park, Belle Vale and Netherley areas of the city.
By Susan Clarke. Story spiked.

He answered the call on the second ring.
"It's your turn now," the voice said.
"I've already started," the man replied, and ended the call.

Susan faced her reflection in the mirror of the ladies' toilets in the *Mail* building. The grey in her hair matched the grey of her skin, and both felt brittle and dry to the touch. She rested her hands on the edge of the basin, pushing the collar of her new coat up towards her ears. Behind her came the familiar sound of retching from one of the cubicles, followed by the toilet flushing and the bolt being drawn back on the door. Rachel emerged. As she approached the basin next to Susan's, the two women's eyes met in their reflections.
"Don't say a word," said Susan.

Rachel smiled and said nothing. She reached into her bag and took out a small bottle of mouthwash. She rinsed her mouth and gargled before spitting the green liquid into the sink.

"Not planning on doing any kissing are you?" Susan asked. "Is this going to be Bassett's lucky day?"

"You trying to make me be sick again?" Rachel said. "Anyway, I'm sure Bassett's used to the taste of vomit on a girl's mouth." She passed a packet of paracetamol to Susan. "Hangover, is it?"

"Yes," Susan admitted. She looked down, embarrassed, concentrating too hard on squeezing the tablets out of the foil packet. "It was a bad night last night," she said, her eyes still downcast, rolling the pills between her fingers. "Sometimes," she began. "Well, just sometimes…that's all."

Rachel made her way to the door. "No need to explain," she said. She gripped the handle but hesitated before pulling at the door. "Listen," she said. "The visiting orders have come in, one for each of us. They're for tomorrow." Susan nodded. "I'm frightened, Sue," Rachel said. "The notes, the texts, that man knocking me over in Manchester, the car yesterday. I don't mind being punched by him, but this sense that he's watching me and I don't know what he's going to do next..."

"I've got to be honest, Rachel. I can't say anything that'll help," Susan said. "We can't go any faster. We have to keep plodding on, and hope things break soon. In the meantime…" She let the sentence drift.

Tears ran down Rachel's face. She made no sound, seemed almost not to know she was crying. "I'm cracking up," she said.

"No you're not," Susan replied. "I'm not going to let you." Rachel breathed deeply and wiped the tears away. Finally she pulled the door open but let it swing shut again, as if she needed a little more time, but also needed a pretext to keep her

with Susan. She took a couple of steps back into the room.
"How about you?" she asked.
"How do you mean?" Susan replied.
"Busy day ahead?"
"The usual, I guess," said Susan. "I need to see what Bassett has in store for me." She turned and looked at Rachel. "Are you trying to ask if I'm planning on telling Brian Nulty about Mrs Girvan's mobile?"
"Yes," Rachel said.
"Well," said Susan. "I'm going to speak to him, certainly. If they've got a new lead to follow, then that means a fresh story, especially if they reckon they can put a name to the body."
"But that's not answering the question, is it?"
"I'll see how the conversation goes," Susan said. "If the police are going round to Mrs Girvan's house, then they'll get the phone for themselves, won't they?" Rachel looked dissatisfied. "Look, Rachel, I don't want to sound like some hack in the films. I'm not going to yell hold the front page. But this could be a good story. It's a long time since I've had one. It feels nice. Anyway," she went on. "You know about the phone too. Why don't you tell Nulty?"
"Because you're right," Rachel admitted after a while.
"Despite everything, it does feel nice, doesn't it?"
They agreed to meet up later that day for coffee then left the toilets together. As they headed up the corridor towards the office, they met Trevor Bassett going in the opposite direction. Bassett reached out an arm to stop Rachel.
"Not still knocking around with the washed-up old bike, are you?" he asked.
"Piss off, you little prick," Rachel told him, before hurrying to catch Susan up.
In the office they went their separate ways, Rachel making a point of calling across to Susan to remind her they were meeting for coffee later. Susan smiled at Rachel's display and then headed for her desk in the corner. She put her new coat

on a hanger she'd brought from home and hung it on the window latch. Then she sat down and called Brian Nulty. The phone rang twice after reception put her through.

"Nulty."

"Brian?" she said. "It's Susan Clarke."

"Alright there, Sue," Nulty said. "How you doin'? We're talkin' a lot, aren't we, eh? I hear nothing for years, then it's twice in two days."

"Not complaining, are you, Brian?" Susan asked. She felt a small glow inside, enjoying the teasing, pleased with the arrangement she and Rachel had made for coffee. Small things, she knew, but it felt like she was stumbling out of her exile.

"Not me, love, not me," Brian said. "I'd better make the most of it, though."

"How do you mean?" she asked.

"I've passed on that information you gave me," he told her. "DI Nolan's the only man to speak to from now on. Orders from above. Assistant Chief Constable Crowley."

"Oh," Susan said. "You've not upset one of the bigwigs, have you?"

"I 'ope no'," Brian told her. "If I rock the boat, it's me who gets seasick. No, it's fair enough, I guess. I only stuck me nose in because it looked like the case involved a prostitute."

"One of your girls, eh, Brian?"

Nulty laughed. "The wife calls them tha' an' all," he said. "No, it was Nolan's case from the start. I just lent a hand where it wasn't wanted. If there's another murder, then the situation might change, but, until then…" He let the sentence trail.

"So, what's the thinking?" asked Susan.

"ACC Crowley is convinced she was a prostitute. Nolan agrees, of course. Those two go way back." Nulty paused. "To be honest, I agree too. That area, that time of night, the clothes she was wearing. She 'ad to be, really. No, what I don't like is the attitude that comes with i'. If she'd been a schoolgirl, or a housewife, or a secretary, we'd see more action. Because she's a prostitute, though, it doesn't matter like. Until another one is killed, of course. Then it's a big deal. A serial killer. Then they'll all be fighting to get in front of the cameras. And your editor might move it nearer the front page."

"Don't bet on it," Susan told him. "Jack the Ripper couldn't shift the capital of bloody culture from our front page. Well," she said, "I'd better have a word with this DI Nolan. Should be able to get something for tomorrow's paper. Could even call it progress."

"Let's 'ope so," Nulty said. "Well, I'll say goodbye, Sue. Keep in touch. Don't leave it another 5 years."

"I won't, I promise," said Susan. "Bye, Brian. And thanks." Nulty couldn't connect her, so Susan rang the switchboard again and asked to be put through to DI Nolan. She lost count of the number of rings before someone finally picked up the phone.

"DI Nolan?" Susan asked. Whoever had picked up the phone didn't answer her. Instead, Susan heard the receiver being dropped onto a desk and a voice shouting, "Eddie? Phone!" She waited another age, almost giving up, before the phone was picked up.

"Yeah? Nolan here." Susan couldn't place the accent. Northern, yes, but not from Liverpool.

"Hi, DI Nolan," she began. "This is Susan Clarke here, from the *Morning Mail*. We spoke last week."

"Did we?" Nolan asked. "Well, I'll take your word for it."

"It was about the murder at the Northern Warehouse," Susan told him. "I understand you're back on the case now."

"Never off it, love," he said. "Who told you I was?"

"Well, I understand Brian Nulty has been working on it."

"Yeah," Nolan said. "Only 'cos I told him, mind. I'll let him do the legwork for me, but he doesn't take over my cases."

"I see," said Susan. "I understand you're working on a fresh lead. You think you might be able to identify the body at last." She slipped the final two words in, her voice sweet and innocent, but hoping he'd notice the dig. If he did, he didn't show it, but Susan didn't reckon she was talking to the sensitive type.

"I've nothing to say," Nolan told her.

Susan persisted. "I believe you're hoping to take a blood sample, or a DNA sample, from someone you think might be a relative of the dead woman."

"Listen, love," Nolan said, his voice sneering and sarcastic. "It sounds like you've got all the facts anyway. Why don't you just go ahead and write your story."

"Can you tell me when you expect to have the results?"

"Like I said," Nolan told her. "You write what you want. I'm not saying anything until there's something to say." He put the phone down hard.

Susan looked at the notes she'd made and reckoned there was enough there to make something for tomorrow's paper: Police following a fresh lead...Hoping to be able to identify the body...Waiting for DNA testing to confirm the name of the brutally murdered woman. She wrote up what she had and passed it onto the subs' desk.

She worked through her lunch, making phone calls, writing filler stories, occasionally wondering if she should have mentioned Mrs Girvan's mobile phone to Brian. She wished in a way that she had: she would have enjoyed trying out theories regarding the significance of the numbers it contained. In the end, though, she was glad she'd kept it to herself. She wasn't going to do anything to help Nolan. At around half two, engrossed in writing a story about a children's choir performing on the steps of St George's Hall, she felt a tap on her shoulder. It was Rachel.

"You eaten?" Rachel asked her. Susan shook her head. "Come on, then," Rachel said. "Coffee and a sandwich. But we're not going to the Mercantile. Not unless they've started serving ciabattas."

"I think they'll serve anyone," Susan said. "Doesn't matter what their star sign is." She got her coat, pretending to take umbrage at Rachel making fun of her use of the hanger, and the two women left the office.

They turned up Old Hall Street and headed for Dale Street. Thick cloud filled the sky and a cold wind was feeding from the river and hurrying them along the pavement. Shop and office windows showed attempts at festive decorations, chains of tinsel and spray snow drifting against the corners of the panes. The pavements were busy with people taking advantage of the season to enjoy late, boozy lunches or make quick shopping trips which took them over their allotted hour. Approaching a Caffe Nero, Rachel slowed. She touched Susan's arm and said, "Come on, this'll do." They went in and took two stools at the end of the bar stretching inside the window.

Rachel ordered their food. When she got back to Susan, she asked, "How's your morning been? Speak to Nulty?"

"Yes," said Susan. "And DI Nolan."

"Who's he?" asked Rachel.

"He's in charge of the Margy case," said Susan. "And a real prick too. Barking down the phone, calling me love, sneering at the press."

"I think I know the type," Rachel said. "Tell him about the phone?"

"No, I didn't. And I don't feel guilty about it either. I wouldn't give him the froth on this coffee." She sipped her drink, enjoying the view of the street from her spot at the window. "I feel sorry for Mrs Girvan, mind," she said. "If he's going round to try and confirm the identity of the body."

"You're sure it's Margy?" asked Rachel.

"I'd say so. Wouldn't you?"

"Yeah," agreed Rachel. "Just thinking about seeing Billy

tomorrow, that's all."

"Well, worry about that tomorrow," Susan said. She reached into her handbag and pulled out her phone. She rolled it round in the palm of her hand. "Let's call them now," she said. "See if anyone answers."

Rachel raised her eyebrows and got her notepad from her coat. She opened it at the page where she'd written the numbers and times of the calls. "Let's think first," she said. "You do know, don't you, that if the body is Margy Girvan, chances are one of these numbers will be the killer's?"

Susan nodded. "Oh, don't worry," she said. "I'm very clear on that."

"Okay," said Rachel, moving aside the plates and cups and putting the pad between them. "Let's have a look. Let's go through this first, see if we can narrow things down." She looked at Susan, who was staring at her quizzically. "I know what you're thinking," Rachel said. "But I'm not trying to put this off. I just need to go through things slowly, say things aloud, make sure I've got things right." She pointed with the nib of her pen at the 0161 number. "This'll be Jackson, calling from Strangeways, right?"

"Right," Susan agreed.

"This one," Rachel said, putting an asterix next to 07832 980 188. "Called Friday 7th at half two in the afternoon. And before that, on Thursday 29th, just gone 5.30. Margy? Do you think?"

"I'd say so, yes," Susan said. "Although calling once every nine days doesn't make her the best daughter in the world. But, if you're asking me to guess, I'd say Margy." She sipped her coffee. "Certainly more likely that her punters would be calling late at night rather than in the afternoon."

"It doesn't much matter, though, to be honest, does it?" Rachel said. "I mean, I'm just trying to get things clear in my mind. Any of these numbers could be her. But if she's dead she won't be answering, no matter which one it is."

"But," said Susan. "Like you said before, her murderer might be. Which may make you a little more careful about what you say if someone picks up."

Susan watched as Rachel reached into her bag and took out her mobile. She was gripping fiercely and her face was set grim and tight. Susan felt she was watching a child struggling to turn will into action. She reached across and gently took Rachel's hand in her own. "Here," she said softly. "Let me do the first call, okay?"

Rachel nodded. "Yeah," she said. "Thanks." Then she added, "Sorry."

"Don't be silly," Susan chided. "It's no bother. Besides, I'm ringing Margy's phone. You're the one calling the killer."

Rachel's smile showed more relief than humour. "I don't know what's the matter with me," she said. "I'm being stupid."

"You're being nervous," Susan told her. "It's natural. Don't be so hard on yourself."

"I shouldn't be like this, though," Rachel said.

Susan was still holding her hand. She squeezed it and Rachel looked up at her and Susan held her gaze. "Look," Susan said. "We both know you're good. We both know you're heading for the nationals some day soon. But this isn't easy. You can't expect just to breeze through it. We're trying to find a murderer, someone who beat a woman's face to pulp with a brick, then set her alight. This is real."

Rachel felt her eyes begin to water with tears, but she breathed in deeply and held her tears in check. "Yes," she said. "It's real."

Susan winked at her. "Exciting though, eh?" she said and this time there was more humour than relief in Rachel's smile.

"Now," said Susan. "Enough of this girly stuff. Let's have a look at this number." She turned Rachel's pad so it was angled more towards her and leaned over it so she could see the number better. Rachel's sudden attack of nerves had given her the chance to play the role of carer and protector, reassuring the younger woman that everything was going to be alright. Doing so had boosted her own confidence but, still, saying the numbers aloud as she keyed them into her own phone, she knew she was speaking with a jauntiness she didn't quite feel. She pressed call and held the phone to her ear. "Well," she told Rachel. "It's ringing." They both waited, then Susan covered the mouth piece with her hand and said to Rachel, "Voicemail." Rachel was about to reply but Susan raised her hand for her to be quiet.

"Oh hi," Susan said into the phone. "I'm trying to track down Margy Girvan. I'm not even sure this is her phone, but I hope it is. If someone gets this message, could they call me back, please? Thanks." Then she added her own number and ended the call. "That was stupid," she said.

"How do you mean?" asked Rachel. She was now eager to make the next call herself, feeling a little embarrassed now at her earlier reluctance.

"I shouldn't have left my number. At least, I should have given the office number." She banged her fist on the counter, shaking the empty cups and plates. "I should have thought about it before calling. Showing off, I suppose."

"But we can still do the other calls, can't we?" Rachel asked. She wanted to do it now, but hesitated seeing Susan's sudden change of mood.

"What?" Susan replied. "Oh, yeah. Course." But when she saw Rachel about to press call on her own phone she quickly reached to stop her. "Wait," she said sharply. "Let's think." Rachel was suddenly irritated. "What about?" she snapped. "Why can't I just call? You did."

"Yes," Susan said. "And I shouldn't have. I said you were right to be nervous and I should have been more careful myself. We can't just leave a message for a killer saying we're Susan and Rachel, let's meet for a coffee and discuss your crime."

"So what then?"

Susan thought for a moment, wishing she'd taken the time to do so before her own call. "Okay," she said. "We'll do the landline next. If it goes to an answer machine, don't leave a message. If anyone picks up, tell them your name's Julie and you're calling from..." She paused. "Calling from Radio Merseyside. Their number's been picked at random and they've won £100 worth of shopping vouchers for a range of city centre shops. All they need to do is give you their name and address."

"You've done this before," said Rachel. She keyed in the landline number and waited. After several rings, someone answered. "Hello," Rachel said as breezily as she could manage. "My name's Ju..." She stopped mid-sentence. "I'm sorry," she said. "Could you repeat that for me, please? And you work there? Thanks. No, no, that's all. Thanks." She ended the call.

"What was all that about?" Susan asked. Rachel was scribbling something in her notebook. When she finished writing she held it up for Susan. "The Warwick Royal Hotel?" she read out loud.

"That was the bar," Rachel added. "It was one of the staff who answered. That call was from a pay phone in the bar of the Warwick Hotel."

"Okay," said Susan. "Let's try the final number then. You okay to do it?" Rachel nodded, and Susan said, "Remember. You're Julie, calling from Radio Merseyside."

But there was no reply, and Rachel followed Susan's instructions not to leave a message on the voicemail. The two women sat silently for a while, both suddenly tired and aware of how keyed up they'd been for the past half hour.

"Can you smoke in these places?" Susan asked after a while. Rachel shook her head. "No," she said. "This is the future, remember?"

"You can smoke in the Mercantile." Susan smiled weakly.

"Come on. They still let you smoke on the street."

They put their coats on and went outside, where Susan immediately lit a cigarette, struggling to shield the flame from the cold wind which still bit up from the river. She inhaled and held the smoke in her lungs. "Well?" she said. "Shall we go?"

Rachel nodded and began to head back down the road. Susan stayed still.

"Where are you going?" Susan asked.

"The office," said Rachel.

"You don't fancy a walk down to the Warwick then?"

"Shouldn't we be getting back?" asked Rachel. "We've been gone ages."

"We're working on a story, Rachel," Susan said, exasperated. "This is the type of thing we're meant to do."

"But I'm supposed to be subbing for the late edition," Rachel said.

"Call in and tell them," Susan told her. "Ask Bassett to cover for you."

"Oh, yeah," said Rachel. "After I called him a prick this morning. He's hardly likely to do me any favours, is he?"

"Come off it, Rachel," Susan said. "Tell him you're sorry, that you'll make it up to him. Tell him he owes you one. Make it sound like you mean it."

"And then when he wants the favour returned?"

"Then tell him to piss off and call him a prick again. You're good-looking and young enough to get away with it."

Rachel smiled. "You've done this before too, haven't you?"

"A long time ago," said Susan. "When I was young enough and good-looking enough to get away with it. Mind you," she added. "I was also stupid enough to let the likes of Bassett sleep with me too."

"I'll learn from your mistakes, then," said Rachel.

"Make sure you do." Susan took a last drag from her cigarette and threw the stub into the road.

Chapter Twenty-two

The walk down to the hotel took Susan and Rachel through the growing evidence of Liverpool's supposed resurgence. Dozens of huge cranes bested the lead grey sky as contractors rushed to throw up new shopping units, car parks and entertainment complexes. The pavements had been ripped up and pedestrians were directed along pathways guarded by flimsy-looking barriers, while cars struggled through narrowed lanes where lines of traffic cones showed the way to contraflow systems and temporary diversions.

The Warwick Royal Hotel predated the very latest building work by about five years. It stood on the river side of the dock road, separated from the Albert Dock by the Kings Dock, where a mixed development of shops, apartments, concert arena and conference centre was rising gradually from the rubble. As recent as the Warwick was, it was already looking dated. It had been built quickly and on the cheap, at a time when the local council had grabbed at any sign of inward investment, regardless of architectural quality. Not far away, new four and five star hotels were going up in slivers of steel and gleaming glass, taking advantage of the recent relaxation in rules regarding the heights of new buildings. The Warwick was only three storeys high, a simple, squat, unimaginative red brick building whose grimy windows allowed a grainy view of the brown river currently churned by the cold winds coming straight in from the Irish Sea.

Inside, the hotel was bland, functional and impersonal, with nothing to distinguish it from countless other places up and down the country. The colour scheme was maroon and gold – the carpets, chair covers and staff uniforms all striped in the two colours. On the walls, in cheap pine frames, hung prints of hazy watercolours depicting the usual Mersey river front scenes, the ferries, the Liver Building, the two cathedrals.

Susan thought she recognised the style from her visit to the Adelphi Hotel just a few days earlier, the same attempt to create character on the cheap.

They went straight into the bar, stuffy and oppressive and overwarm. There were no other customers. Behind the bar, a fat girl squeezed into a black skirt and maroon and gold waistcoat was wiping ashtrays and rearranging bottles in the low fridge and trying to pin up a strand of tinsel which had fallen limp over the optics. She'd made the Christmas effort too, with a red Santa hat and a plastic box pinned to her waistcoat with a string hanging from it. If you pulled the string a Santa slid down the chimney and then popped back up again. Susan approached the bar wondering just how many customers leaned across and pulled the string and thought they were the first ones to do so. At the table they'd chosen right by the window, in the furthest corner of the room, Rachel had taken off her thick coat and heavy sweater and was making the call to Bassett while Susan got the drinks. She was just finishing when Susan returned.

"Oh thanks, Trev, you're a love," she said. "And sorry again about this morning." She ended the call, surprised how easy it had been to sound coy and flirtatious and sincere.

"Very impressive," Susan said, putting down the drinks. "We'll make a woman of you yet." Rachel smiled and Susan went on. "They all fancy you, you know."

"I know," said Rachel, then laughed. "Oh God, sorry. That sounds really big-headed, doesn't it?"

"It's true, though," said Susan.

"What's true is that I'm a woman under 30 and I've got a pulse," Rachel said. "Of course they fancy me. Some of them would even compromise on the pulse."

Susan laughed. "Ah, I remember those heady days. Under 30! Seems like a lifetime ago. When you could smile and touch a man on the arm and he'd give you whatever you asked for."

"I can't do that," Rachel said.

"You should try it," Susan told her. "Hard work, brains, flirting, they're all useful tools. Just don't do what I did. My trouble was I didn't stop at their arms."

"Do you regret it?" Rachel asked suddenly.

"Regret what?" Susan replied.

"You know," said Rachel. "The way it's all turned out. Could have been different."

"Yes," Susan said. "It's funny, they say you should only regret the things you didn't do. But that's just crap. I regret so much of it. Look at me. Look at where I live. How couldn't I?"

"Peter too?" asked Rachel. "Do you wish you and he were still together?"

"Yes. Yes I do, to be honest." She clapped her hands against her thighs as if to shake herself away from the slump she was heading for. She was recognising the signs. The wine was sour but still tasted good enough to finish and then order another glass and then stop on the way home for another bottle. "Anyway. Let's forget it. Get your pad out and let's see what we've got."

Rachel did as she was told. She took a sip of her mineral water and moved round so she and Susan were sitting next to each other, their chairs pressed together. Her notebook was open on a fresh page.

"Okay," she said. "Friday 7th December." She wrote the date neatly at the top of the page and underlined it. She continued to write as she spoke. "One. At 2.30 in the afternoon Margy's mother gets a call from…" She flicked back to the previous page to make sure she got the number right. "…07832 980 188."

"Right," said Susan. She'd got her own notes out and spoke as Rachel wrote. "Then, two, at nine minutes to midnight, someone calls Margy's mum from 0771 657 1001. Followed five minutes later by three, a call from here. 0151 282 4994."

"Okay," said Rachel. She lifted the pad and held it between them. "Let's carry on assuming that call number one is from Margy."

"On her new mobile phone," Susan said. "Just ringing to see if her mum's alright. And I think we can safely say that the other two calls weren't to Mrs Girvan." She looked up at Rachel, who seemed unsure. "Yes," she said. "I know they could be. It might have been Margy, ringing from here, needing to speak to her mother. It might have been the parish priest, making a midnight check on his flock. But…"

"Yes, I know, I know," said Rachel. "Chances are, it was a punter – or punters – calling for Margy. Someone who didn't know she'd changed her phone." She paused. "Do you think it was the same man? That both calls came from the same punter?"

"Yes," said Susan. "I'd say so. The two calls were made close together, only a few minutes apart. And we've got to deal in likelihoods, for the moment at least, else we'd just twist ourselves into knots."

Rachel took another drink. Susan continued to ignore her own, and lit another cigarette instead. She tried to waft away the smoke from Rachel's face.

"Why should the same man call from both his mobile and from the landline here?" asked Rachel.

Susan shrugged. "Could be any number of reasons. Too noisy, poor reception, privacy."

Rachel looked around the empty bar. "Don't think you could get more private than this," she said.

"Now, maybe, yes," said Susan. "But Friday night, nearly midnight. I bet even this place gets packed. Especially on a Friday night, everyone coming back to the hotel bar, looking to carry the evening on."

"Well, then," said Rachel. "Let's ask, shall we? See if the girl at the bar was serving that night."

They made their way over to the bar. The fat girl had given up trying to look busy and was now just leaning back against the till, arms folded, eyes glazing over. She took a moment to notice Susan and Rachel standing in front of her but, when she did, she clicked into life, gave them a festive smile and asked them if they wanted the same again.

"Fine for drinks," said Rachel. "Wouldn't mind a packet of crisps though. Cheese and onion?"

The girl reached down into a shelf below the bar and brought out Rachel's crisps. As Rachel was giving her the money, Susan said, "Not exactly rushed off your feet here, are you?"

The fat girl smiled. "No, thank God," she said. "Gorra splittin' 'eadache." Her accent was thick Scouse, the words scraping out of her mouth.

"Late night last night?" Rachel asked, smiling.

The fat girl nodded and smiled back, full of mock regret. "I know my limit," she said. "But I just ignored it. Still. Christmas, isn' i' eh?"

"You on till late tonight?" Susan asked.

"Oh, yeah," the girl replied. "I get a break from four till eight, then work through till closing."

"When's that?" said Rachel.

"You tell me," she said. "Like I said, it's Christmas, isn' i'? We keep servin' till they don't want no more. Any more, I mean," she corrected herself. "Management's said we've got to improve the way we speak. Someone said we'd be doin' language courses, learning French and tha', you know, for this Capital of Culture thing."

"You work here full-time?" Susan asked. She finished her drink. "I'll have another, thanks." She saw Rachel staring straight ahead, but knew she wanted to look at her.

"Actually," she said. "I'll just have a diet Coke."

"Ice?" the girl asked. Susan nodded. The girl went on. "Full-time, yeah. When I started I was only doin' a couple of shifts

a week. While I was at college, like. Then I dropped out –
too thick – been full-time ever since."

"Like it?" said Susan.

"Oh aye, it's okay," the girl said. "Don't like the uniform
much, mind, but it's alright."

"Meet plenty of people," Rachel stated.

"You meet all sorts," the girl confirmed with feeling.

"I bet you do," said Susan.

"I hear it was packed out last Friday," Rachel said.

The girl looked thoughtful as she handed Susan her change.
"Last Friday?" she said. "This one just gone? No, normal,
like, really."

"The Friday before, maybe," Rachel said.

"The Friday before?" Once again the girl thought hard. Then
she remembered and giggled. "God, didn't think they'd ever
leave! Some big do, it was. Left 'ere at four in the mornin'.
Can you believe that? Four o'clock in the mornin'. On again
at twelve and all!"

"Wedding, was it?" asked Susan.

"No, it wasn't," the girl said. "Wouldn't have minded if it
was. Something to celebrate, isn't it, a weddin'? No, this was
some big council thing, I think."

"The council?"

"Something like that," said the girl. "Some bloke told me he
was the mayor, anyway. Said he wanted me to help re-elect
him." She giggled. "Only got the joke the next day. Cheeky
bastard. Good tips though." She thought again for a moment.
"What was i'? Must have been somethin' big. They 'ad a
meal in the restaurant – booked the whole place – then came
in here. Someone took loads of photos. 'ere, wait there a sec.'
The fat girl left the bar and went into a back room. She came
out holding a printed sheet of thick paper. "The mayor left me
his number. Mobile, of course. Wouldn't want his wife to
pick up the phone if I called the 'ouse." She handed the paper
to Susan, who turned it over and read it, holding it so Rachel

could read it at the same time. It was a menu for a five-course meal to mark the launch of the latest development intended to enhance the river front and bring world class hotel, conference and leisure facilities to the city of Liverpool. All the distinguished guests present were welcomed by the company in charge of the development, O'Hare Design and Construction.

Susan read the words and felt her mind lurch. She gripped the brass rail round the edge of the bar and hoped she was hiding her reaction.

"So?" the fat girl said to Susan. "What do you reckon?"

Susan stumbled for words. She felt herself redden. "What?" she said. Suddenly she had no idea what the girl was talking about.

"Should I call 'im?" the barmaid asked.

"Who?" said Susan.

Rachel came to her rescue. "She means the mayor," she said. "The man who gave her his number that night."

Susan said, "Oh" forcing herself away from the name on the menu. Rachel took over. "You know he's probably not the mayor, don't you?" she said. The girl nodded. "And that he's bound to be married?"

"Oh, I know tha'," the girl said. "I might be fat but I'm not soft." She considered for a while. "I think I'll call 'im. He was a laugh."

Susan and Rachel left the girl to her empty bar and made their way back outside. They walked in silence, past the boards encircling the construction work going on at the King's Dock, bearing computer generated images of how the finished product would look, with virtual couples strolling through the central plaza while virtual business people dashed up the steps to the conference centre and virtual women studied their laptops on the conveniently located sun terraces.

They ended up at a bench overlooking the Mersey, just far enough in front of the Albert Dock to mean that the wind buffeted them as they sat down, lashing strands of hair across both their faces. Rachel, in a futile gesture, pushed her hair back out of her eyes, only for it to be blown straight back again.

"It means nothing," she said to Susan. "You know that, don't you?"

"Yes," Susan replied. "It was just seeing the name. It shocked me. I didn't even connect it with the story. It was just a reminder of them. That's all. Every now and then I remember there's no safety net."

"What do you mean?" Rachel asked.

"These past few days have been good," she said. She laughed half-heartedly. "This sounds stupid. But it's like being alive again, after so many years just feeling numb. I've enjoyed being good at the job again. But then I see that name or hear Bassett saying what he does about me. I remember the flat where I live and my hair going grey and the lines on my face. I don't know." She sighed. "It's funny. People always say everything'll be alright. And I think, how do you know? What if it isn't? Not everyone will be alright."

"Now I don't know what to say," said Rachel. "I was going to tell you everything would be alright."

Susan looked at Rachel and laughed. "And it probably will be," she said.

"So, what do you want to do now?" asked Rachel.

"About the hotel, you mean?" Rachel nodded. Susan carried on. "I'll ring Peter. Talk to him. Maybe get to see him and Michael. You? You sorted out the next visit to see Billy Jackson at Strangeways?"

"It's tomorrow," Rachel said. "The visiting orders arrived at the office this morning. Sweeney's doing again. There seems to be nothing he can't swing. He's got me where he wants me, that's for sure."

"Don't forget you're getting a story out of this," said Susan. "It's not all one-way traffic. Just try to forget how scared he makes you feel."

Rachel nodded. "You with your dead prostitute, me with Sweeney and Billy Jackson," she said. "Have you any idea which story is whose any more?"

"I've wondered that too," Susan said. "I reckon they're both ours. That okay with you?"

"That's okay with me," Rachel told her.

Later that evening, alone in her flat, Susan checked her phone for messages. There were seven, with not a single word spoken on any of them. When she dialled to find the last number to call, a recorded voice simply told her the number was withheld. She told herself it meant nothing and called Peter.

Chapter Twenty-three

Tuesday 18 December
LIVERPOOL MORNING MAIL
POLICE HOPE FOR DNA LINK
Police are hoping that they'll soon be able to put a name to the woman found murdered at Liverpool's Northern Warehouse over a week ago.
After extensive inquiries, DI Nolan, the officer in charge of the case, is hopeful that DNA evidence will provide the answer to the mystery of the woman's identity. A woman who is believed to be the mother of the dead prostitute, who was bludgeoned to death with a brick and then set alight, will provide a DNA sample today. Police are hoping for conclusive results, which will fill in the gaps in their enquiry.
A note of caution was sounded, however. Speaking yesterday, DI Nolan said, "I'm not prepared to speculate on findings. Let's just wait and see what the results are and then take it from there."
By Susan Clarke. Story spiked.

Susan was early. It was just after eight the next day when she pulled up outside Rachel's house in Childwall. The plan was to get there at about a quarter to nine, leave her car there and then make the journey to Strangeways in Rachel's. But she'd woken up at five and been unable to get back to sleep, her mind full of the phone call she'd made to her ex-husband the night before, how pleased he'd sounded to hear from her and how eagerly he'd agreed to meet up with her later that day. He said he'd bring Michael too. Nerves filled her stomach at the prospect of seeing her son and at the image of the three of them sitting together in a McDonald's, shopping bags at their feet maybe, the air full of laughter and chatting and Christmas songs, just like a normal family. There was unease too. The blank messages left on her machine troubled her. She tried to tell herself the same platitudes she'd have given Rachel – it's probably nothing…just a coincidence – but she they were no help. So Sweeney was inching his claws into her now, as well as Rachel, she thought. She'd got the message, without a word being spoken. He was ratcheting up the pressure, yet she knew they could only go as fast as the story allowed them to. That wouldn't wash with him, though.

She looked at her watch, toying with the idea of waiting in the car for another forty or fifty minutes, or slowly walking back to the newsagent's she'd just driven past so she could kill time pretending to read a paper. She jumped at the knock on the car window. She hadn't noticed Rachel's father coming out of the house and walking up to the car.

"Sorry," he said, leaning down to the window as Susan opened it. "Didn't mean to give you a fright." He smiled. "You must be Susan. I'm Rachel's dad." He reached his hand in through the window and Susan awkwardly shook it. "Rachel says you won't have had breakfast and your car doesn't have any heating, so she ordered me out here to bring you in."

Susan smiled back at him and said she'd love to as long as it was okay and he assured her it was. She got out of the car and he ushered her up the path. She liked his manners and the fact that he introduced himself as Rachel's dad rather than telling her his name. She sensed his pride and knew that the house would be warm and welcoming and full of family pictures and souvenirs and that Rachel and her mother would tease him and he would pretend not to love it.

"I thought that was you skulking outside," said Rachel. She was sitting at the kitchen table eating breakfast. "You do know we don't normally allow cars as old as yours in Childwall, don't you?"

"Won't happen again," Susan said. "Promise. Maybe I could leave it out of sight while we're out today."

Rachel's mother took out a cup and saucer from one of the

cupboards. "Would you prefer tea or coffee, Susan?" she asked. "Rachel said you wouldn't have had any breakfast, so I've made some more toast. You sit down."

Susan did as she was told. "Gosh," she said. "Thank you. Coffee, please, if it's no trouble. This is really nice of you."

"Nonsense," said Rachel's father, taking his place back at the table.

"Besides," said Rachel. "We're only putting on a show. If you weren't here we'd be in front of the television eating pop tarts and smoking."

"Take no notice of her," said Rachel's mother. "For someone supposedly so intelligent, she talks an awful lot of nonsense."

Susan smiled. She took the coffee and settled at the table. For a fraction of a second her mind flashed to an image of Peter, Michael and her at their own kitchen table, in their own home, but she forced the thought away before it could affect her.

"Hear you're taking Rachel to Strangeways, Susan," said Mr Jack. "It was only a matter of time."

"He's been dying to make that joke ever since I told him you were coming here," Rachel said. She took a last gulp of tea and stood up. "I'll just go and brush my teeth and then we can be off. You don't mind me leaving you with these two, do you?"

"I'll manage," Susan told her. Fifteen minutes later, they were on their way.

This visit was a lot different from their first. There were no queues of women and children waiting to go in with them, no waiting in a crowded anteroom, no sharing of communal space with guards lining the walls. Within minutes of their arrival at Strangeways, Rachel and Susan were shown into a private interview room, where Jackson was sitting at a metal table, already waiting for them.

"You two must have some pull," Jackson said as they came in. They had to ask him to repeat himself. His face was puffed and swollen and both his eyes were black. Blood had dried on a scab at one corner of his mouth and he could only speak out of the other.

"What happened, Billy?" asked Rachel. It was a genuine question but she regretted saying it before the words were out. She knew what had happened.

"Guess," Jackson said. "Your mate put the word out, didn't he? And I walked into a door."

"Sweeney," Rachel said. She went to pull out one of the chairs opposite Jackson, but it was screwed into the floor and didn't move, so awkwardly she manoeuvred into it instead. Susan sat next to her. Rachel noticed how she hadn't made the same mistake with the chair, and that she sat down with much greater ease.

"If it's any consolation, Billy," Susan said, "Rachel herself got a going over from Sweeney on Saturday."

"It aint," Jackson said. He was trying to sound gruff and unfeeling, but lacked the conviction, and Susan heard the tone of the decent, shy man they'd met the previous week. From her bag she took five packets of cigarettes and three large bars of milk chocolate and pushed them across the table to Jackson.

"So," Susan said. "Not much point us asking how your weekend was."

Jackson smiled and winced with pain as he did so. "No," he said. He looked down at the cigarettes and chocolate in front of him. He took a deep breath, as if preparing himself for something he didn't want to hear. Eyes still downcast, he asked, "Anything from Margy? See her?"

Susan started to answer, but Rachel got in first. "She was out when we got to her flat," she said. "Nice place too. You were right. We saw her mum, though. Had a good long chat with her. Margy had been on the phone to her. You were right about the mobile too. She has changed it, got a fancy new one you can take pictures with. We got her new number from her mother." Susan wrote down the number on a scrap of paper she'd taken from her bag and handed it to Billy. He took it from her and stared at it, caressing it gently between his thumb and fingers. Immediately he brightened and looked up at Rachel and Susan. He had forgotten all about the beating he'd got from Sweeney's men.

"I knew it," he said excitedly. "I told you, didn't I? I knew she'd have got herself a new mobile. One with a camera! She were always going on about getting one with a camera. God knows why, mind. A phone's for calling I told her, not taking pictures. You want a proper camera for that. Old-fashioned she said I were. Right too. I am. But nowt wrong with that, is there?"

The two women shook their heads. "No, Billy," Susan said. "There's nowt wrong with that."

Billy was a different man suddenly. He opened one of the chocolate bars. Susan and Rachel both refused his offer of a piece, so he broke off a chunk for himself and bit into it cheerfully. "No point saving this, eh?" he said. "Might as well make a start now. Christmas after all." He savoured the taste. "I'll give her a call later," he said, smiling at the prospect. He pointed a finger at Rachel. "Now then, lass," he said. "I've got a question for you." He paused, relishing the moment. "Know what TIC means?"

"Tick?" Rachel said. She looked confused and spoke without confidence, wondering why Billy looked so pleased with himself. "Do you mean, like credit?"

Billy laughed out loud.

"Taken into Consideration," said Susan. "T-I-C."

Billy banged the table with his hand, his eyes lit with delight. "I knew she'd know," he said, now pointing at Susan. "I said to meself, that one'll know, not the young'un. Not that you're old like, love," he added to Susan. He chuckled to himself. The walls, bars, warders and locks surrounding him no longer mattered; nor did the beating he'd received. The pain that came when he talked didn't hurt any more. All that mattered was the number for Margy's new phone, the scrap of paper on which it was written neatly folded in his pocket. He'd tell these nice young girls everything they wanted to know, didn't care why they wanted to know it. And he'd treat himself to a few more pieces of chocolate while he was telling them. Billy looked at Susan and Rachel and guessed the reason for their confused expressions.

"You've not asked me a question yet, have you?" he said. "That's why you're looking like that. What's he on about, you're asking yourselves. Well," he went on. "I'll tell you. Sweeney's lads gave me a good going over. You can see that for yourselves." He waved a hand in front of his face. "But they're polite boys, thoughtful. They were kind enough to tell me why. Tell them what you know, they said. Tell them why you're here."

"So?" said Rachel. "Why are you here?"

"I were caught," Billy replied, pleased with himself.

Susan sensed Rachel's impatience and frustration with the way things were going. Rachel wanted to be in control of things, but Billy was in charge. Susan reached her hand under the table and patted Rachel's thigh. Let him have his fun, the touch said. Let's just listen and see where he takes us.

Billy Jackson was warming to his tale. "Stupid, really," he said. "I'm normally more careful, do a bit more research, like. But this time I got a word that this big house would be empty. Owners away for the night or something." He helped himself to more chocolate. "Any road, they weren't. Came home while I were upstairs. Could have kicked myself. Felt like one of them druggies I did. You know, no thought, no consideration of the job. Tried to jump out of a window. Broke me ankle. That's how I got here." He sat silent, waiting for a response from the two women sitting opposite.

"Not much of a story, Billy," Susan said. "We were kind of expecting more."

"Oh," said Billy. "Were you now?" Rachel's impatience bubbled to the surface. She found herself about to snap at Jackson, but, once again, Susan just touched her leg gently and she got the message.

"Fancy a cup of tea, Billy?" Susan asked. "Or coffee, maybe? We can stay a while, have a nice long chat. No rush."

"Canteen won't be open, will it?" Billy replied.

"Oh, I'm sure we can sort something out for you," said Susan. "Tea, is it?" Billy nodded and Susan went to the door and opened it. The warder outside wasn't too happy with the request, but he agreed in the end and soon Billy had a mug of tea in front of him.

"Can't have all that chocolate without something to wash it down, eh?" Susan said when the warder had left the room.

"Aye," Billy said. "And nice to be waited on too."

"So," said Rachel. She still felt anxious inside, keen to get on, but tried to mask it with a soft tone. "I don't think Franny Sweeney would have sent me out here if that was all you had to tell us. Do you?" The mention of Sweeney's name acted as a reminder to Billy and he reached up and cautiously touched his cheek. The bone felt soft beneath his skin.

"No," he replied. "I don't reckon he would." He sighed heavily, feeling his fun was over. "Alright then, lass. I'll get on with it."

"Thanks, Billy," Susan said. She smiled.

Billy sipped his tea, wincing slightly as he swallowed.

"Last time we were here," Susan said, "We asked you about a copper called Crowley. Used to work in Keighley. Where the house was that you broke into. You said you knew him."

"I said I knew of him," Billy corrected her. "Only met him a couple of times. Hear he's over in Liverpool now. Nearly at top of tree. Well, he weren't so high when I knew of him, but he was still too mighty to talk to the likes of me."

"So how come you met him?" asked Rachel.

"Saw him," said Billy. "That's more the truth of it. I were interviewed a couple of times. Over in a Keighley nick. He were hanging around when I went in. Stared at me, he did, smiled a bit. Did a bit of chatting with the copper who interviewed me. Laughed at me."

"Laughed at you?" asked Rachel. "How do you mean?"

"You know," Billy said. "Sneering, like. Like I were nothing."

"So he never talked to you?" Rachel asked. "You were never introduced?"

Susan and Billy both started to laugh. "It weren't a cocktail party, love," Billy told her. I weren't walking round place mingling, with a little sausage on a stick." He looked at Susan and nodded his head towards Rachel. "She's a good'un, your mate, in't she?"

Susan shared Billy's smile while Rachel blushed. Still smiling, Susan said, "At the start, when we were first in, you asked us if we knew what TIC meant."

Billy nodded. "Aye," he said. "That's right."

"Why?" Susan asked.

"Ask me when I last had a McDonald's," Billy told her.

"Well?" Susan said.

"Five week ago," Billy replied. He turned to Rachel. "Ask me when I last went to cinema." Rachel raised her eyebrows. "Same," Billy said. "Five week ago. Ask me if me and Margy have ever had the chance of a bit of a cuddle since I came in. Or if I can ever get hold of any stuff to keep other lads in here sweet with me."

Susan and Rachel said nothing.

"TICs!" Billy said, triumphantly. "Taken into consideration. Couple of dozen other burglaries that I had nowt to do with. I put me name to them, didn't I?"

"You admitted to crimes you didn't commit?" asked Rachel. "Why? You just volunteered?"

"Volunteered!" Billy scoffed. "You are green, aren't you, love? Course I didn't volunteer." He drank some more of his tea. "It were suggested to me," he said. "And I went along with it. Makes the coppers look good, doesn't it? They can tell everyone how many cases they've sorted. In return, I get looked after. Bit more time inside for me, maybe, but a nicer time while I'm in here. Few trips out, chance to get a bit of time alone with Margy. No harm done. Both sides happy."

"It was suggested to you," Rachel repeated. "By whom? Not Crowley."

"No," said Billy. "Told you, didn't I, he were too grand for the likes of me. It were his mate."

"His mate?" Rachel said. "Come on, Billy, tell us straight. Don't keep us guessing."

"His mate," Billy said. "The one who interviewed me. The one Mr Crowley had a quiet word with before he talked to me."

"What was his name Billy?" Susan asked. Like Rachel before her, her patience was now exhausted. "Tell us his name."

"Nolan," said Billy. "DC Nolan. Nasty bastard."

For a moment, neither woman spoke. Then Susan said, "And you're sure about that? That name?"

"Course I'm sure," said Billy. "I know I'm getting on but I'm not daft." He took some more chocolate as if to mark the end of his story with a little treat.

Susan and Rachel got up to leave. As she put on her coat, Rachel said, "We'll be in touch, Billy, to get details. And have a think of any other cons you know who might have been used like this."

"Well," Billy replied, "You know where to find me." He took the note with Margy's phone number out of his pocket and held it up to show her. "And thanks for this."

Neither woman said anything.

Outside, Susan and Rachel walked to the car in silence. Neither noticed the few flakes of snow drifting out of the grey sky. Despite the cold, they didn't get straight into the car. Susan lit a cigarette and leaned back against the passenger door.

"The same Nolan?" Rachel asked her.

"Must be," said Susan. "Has to be. Crowley comes up with the idea for fiddling the figures. Nolan's the one who gets his hands dirty. Then, when Crowley gets the big promotion he's been looking for, he brings Nolan with him. Easy enough to check, anyway."

"And now he's organising tests with Mrs Girvan, to confirm it really is Margy who's dead," said Rachel. "And Billy's back in there looking forward to giving her a call on her brand new mobile phone."

Susan sucked on the cigarette. "We couldn't have told him," she said. "Who knows how he would have reacted. And besides, we don't know, do we? Not until the tests confirm it."

"I know," said Rachel. She got her car keys out of her handbag. "Come on. Let's go."

Chapter Twenty-four

On the way back, Susan called Brian Nulty. He confirmed that Nolan had come to the Merseyside force from Keighley, joining not long after Crowley had arrived. They were close, he said, but wouldn't be drawn further. He did tell her though that Nolan had started the testing process to check for matches between Mrs Girvan and Margy.

"So what do we do now?" asked Rachel when Susan had finished the call.

"Talk to Allen," she said. "This could be a really nice, big story. We need his go-ahead."

"Won't be easy," said Rachel. "He and Crowley seem pretty tight."

"Oh," said Susan. "That reminds me." She took a folded sheet of newspaper from her bag. "When I got home last night, after we'd been to the hotel, I dug this out." She unfolded the paper – the front page of a copy of the *Mail* – and angled it so Rachel could see it without taking her eyes off the road for too long. "It's from the other Saturday. I had it with me when we went to Peter Kavanagh's, remember?"

Rachel nodded. "Taken at the Warwick Royal Hotel. The launch of your ex's new venture."

"My ex-father-in-law's new venture, to be specific," Susan said. "I don't think Peter's got it in him." She put the paper back in her bag. "I rang him last night, you know. Peter," she added. "Not Eugene. I'm meeting him and Michael this afternoon. We're having a late lunch. I thought I'd have a chat with him about that night. Find out who was there. I need to give Michael his present anyway. Need to buy Michael his present first."

"You won't be seeing him on Christmas Day?" Rachel asked.

"No chance," Susan said. "Eugene and Imelda wouldn't stand for it. No, I'll see him today, and then maybe again some time over the holidays. If he wants."

"I'm sure he will," Rachel said.

They spent the rest of the journey in silence, both too preoccupied with their thoughts to speak. Susan noticed that Rachel was checking the mirrors more than usual, but she made no comment. She toyed with the idea of telling Rachel about the blank messages left the night before. She didn't know whether it would make Rachel feel better that she wasn't the only one targeted, or just remind her that Sweeney was watching. In the end she decided against it. Back at Rachel's house, Susan told Rachel she'd call her later and asked her to say thanks for breakfast to her parents. Then she got straight into her car and drove back to her flat.

Susan walked down the hill from her flat and into town. It was her day off. Up until this past week or so, she had hated every moment of any time away from work, unless she had a bottle of wine open, when, after her first glass, she could allow the alcohol to give her false hope or simply enjoy the way it masked the pain. She would certainly never have ventured out into town, to push through the crowds of people milling around the shops. And especially not approaching Christmas, when every string of tinsel and every note of every carol would serve as a reminder to the emptiness and desolation of her life.

Today though, it didn't feel too bad. She'd be seeing her son, for a start, even though it would be all too brief a meeting. And she'd be seeing Peter, too, a decent man she'd treated badly but who'd never blamed her, no matter how dreadful he must have felt coming home and finding her in bed with Gerry Dalton. That might have been part of the problem, his meekness. Certainly, there'd been a time when that was how she'd rationalised it. Now, though, someone gentle and caring and kind…She stopped herself before she thought too much, reminded herself it would never happen, that she'd seen to that. No, she told herself, be content with the lift provided by the last couple of weeks of working with Rachel; be grateful for that and don't get greedy.

The snow that had fallen in Manchester had not touched Liverpool, but the sky was still a solid grey and the air still cold. Although it was only lunchtime, the light was weak and dusk seemed ready to draw in at any moment. Christmas decorations filled the windows of the city centre shops. In the streets, fairy lights had been hung between lampposts and wrapped around the massive tree the council had put up at the bottom of Bold Street. They hadn't yet been switched on, however, and so seemed pointless and depressing. The crowds of people made their way in and out of the shops with a gritty and joyless determination.

There was plenty of time before Susan was due to meet Peter and Michael, and she found herself savouring the opportunity to wander round the shops, feeling a growing lightness in complete contrast to the grim faces around her. She headed down Church Street, aiming for a sports shop which she was sure was there. She intended buying a present for Michael only, but she suddenly decided she would get a gift for Peter too, and Rachel, and her parents. She laughed at herself, at her spontaneous embracing of the Christmas spirit, feeling like Scrooge waking up on Christmas morning. She turned round and made for Waterstone's where she bought books and cards for Rachel and Peter, taking advantage of the free gift-wrapping service on offer. Then she went to a record shop and picked out a CD she thought Rachel's father might like, a remastering of an early Stan Getz album. Rachel's mother got a scarf from John Lewis. Finally, she found the sports shop she knew was around there somewhere and bought Michael's present, taking an especial pleasure from this purchase.

By the time she'd finished, she realised she was late for Peter and Michael, so dashed out of the shop and hurried to McDonald's, the bags of shopping banging against her legs. She arrived slightly breathless and was instantly overheated by the warmth of the café. But her smile was broad and genuine, and became brighter when she scanned the seats and spotted her son and her ex-husband standing up and waving to catch her attention, laughing at this deranged-looking woman madly pulling off her scarf and unbuttoning her coat, her hands full of shopping.

"Alright, you two," she said, arriving at the table. "I don't look that funny, do I?"

"Yes," Michael said. "You do."

"He's right, I'm afraid," confirmed Peter. "Like some mad bag lady." Michael laughed at the description.

"Okay, then," Susan said. "That's it. No presents. I'm going to give these away to the first person I see when I leave here." She made as if to turn and go, delighted when Michael grabbed her arm and pulled her back.

"No, Mum, don't go," he said. "Wait until you've given me my present. Then you can go." She leaned down towards him and he stood up to her and they hugged and kissed each other. More awkwardly, Peter and Susan kissed each other on the cheek.

Susan sat down. The three of them squashed together on the seat of the semi-circular booth.

"So," Susan said to Michael. "How are you? You're looking well."

"Fine," Michael said.

"And how's school?" she asked.

"Okay," he replied.

"He's turning into a teenager, I'm afraid," Peter said. "A couple of years too early. Everything's fine and okay. You won't get much more out of him." He ruffled his son's hair. "Will she, eh?" Michael squirmed away, pushing closer to his mother as he did so. Susan held her ground, letting her son press into her.

"Right," Peter said. "Let's get something to eat, shall we? You having the usual, Mike?" Susan fought back the pang of regret that she didn't know what her son's usual was, as well as the urge to tell Peter that his name was Michael, not Mike. Michael nodded and Peter turned to Susan. "How about you?" he asked. "What do you fancy?"

"I don't know," Susan said. "You know, I've never had a McDonald's before." Peter and Michael looked at her in amazement. "Is that so awful?" she asked them.

"Yes!" they replied in unison. She laughed at their response, but was also painfully and suddenly aware that the reason she'd never had a McDonald's before was because she had spent so little time with her son. Once again, she fought back the desire to wallow in more regret, became determined that this would be a good day, untainted by any negative feelings. "So, Michael," she said. "What do you recommend? Why don't you choose for me?"

"Okay," he replied. "Do you want me to pick the wine as well?" He grinned.

"Oh," said Susan. "I see you're a bit of a smart alec, aren't you? Maybe I won't give you this present after all."

Peter slid round the booth seat and stood up. "I'll go and get us the food," he said. "Don't worry," he told Susan. "I'll pick carefully for you." He walked over and joined the end of one of the queues for the counter, all the customers with their necks craned to see the menu above them, and their arms dragged down by shopping bags.

Susan squeezed Michael's hand. "It's nice to see you," she said, feeling tears sting her eyes. He smiled back at her, and she was thrilled to see he was still young enough to enjoy a show of simple affection from her.

"You see me every week," he said. She looked at him and he went on, "When I'm playing rugby. I've noticed you. I look out for you."

"You're a good little player," she said. "A good scrum half." She waited for his reaction and wasn't disappointed. "Oh yes," said Susan. "Your mother knows what a scrum half is. Impressed?"

"Yeah," Michael replied, nodding vigorously. "But I'm not that good," he added. "Grandad Eugene keeps telling me I need to be tougher. He says I look scared when I play. I am scared too."

Susan patted his hand. "It's rugby, Michael," she told him. "You'd have to be stupid not to be scared. And you're certainly not stupid. Besides," she went on, "your grandfather never played rugby in his life, so what would he know?" She looked around to see Peter the counter, giving his order to a flustered boy in the red uniform. "No," she said. "If you ask me, the only thing you need to be worried about when it comes to rugby, is when you pass to the right. Your pass to the left is fine. But the other way…"

Once again she was delighted to see the look of wonder and surprise in Michael's eyes. "Mr Gibbons says that!" he exclaimed. "He says that too! He takes us for rugby."

"It'll be because you're right-handed," she said, blithely. "Your right-hand controls the spin of the ball when you're throwing left. Going the other way, off your weaker left hand, well, there's not so much control. You just need to work on it." She played her trump card. "Maybe what you could do is turn it to your advantage. Go to pass to your left, but dummy it. Spin round completely and give it right, but facing behind you. See what I mean?"

His mouth was gaping open as he nodded. "I've seen what's his name do it," Susan continued. "The England player. Matt Dawson."

Peter had returned to the table. As he struggled to put down the cardboard trays laden with burgers and fries and drinks, Michael gushed at him. "Dad!" he said. "Mum knows who Matt Dawson is!"

"Who?" said Peter.

Michael wailed. "Dad! Matt Dawson! He used to play for

England."

"Oh," remembered Peter. "The one who's on TV a lot. On *Question of Sport*."

"That's right!" Michael said. "She knows who he is!"

Peter smiled at Susan and she preened in return. He distributed the food for them, a plain burger and coffee for himself, chicken nuggets and dipping sauce with a strawberry milkshake for Michael. To Susan he passed a Big Mac, large fries and a Coke. Michael showed her how to open the burger box and put the fries into it, so they were on one side and the Big Mac was on the other. She took a bite of the burger.

"Oh my God," she said.

"Don't you like it?" Michael asked.

"I love it!" said Susan. "I'm never going to eat anything else!"

After they'd finished eating, while Michael was taking the trays of rubbish to the bin, Susan handed over the presents to Peter.

"This one," she said, indicating the bag from the sports shop. "That's Michael's. I bought it just now. You don't mind wrapping it for me, do you? Only, I probably won't see him before Christmas Day."

"No problem," said Peter. He looked inside the bag and started laughing. "You're still causing trouble, I see."

"I don't know what you mean." Her voice was all innocence.

"An Everton kit?" he said. "Of course, it will have completely slipped your mind that Dad's got season tickets for Liverpool."

"Has he? Really?" said Susan. "I could have sworn it was the other way round. I always get the two teams confused. Comes of being from Hampshire." She tapped Peter's present. "This one's for you," she said. "It's nothing much. A book."

"You shouldn't have," Peter told her. "But thanks." He looked embarrassed. "I haven't got you anything," he said.

"Don't worry," she replied. "I've probably taken enough from you already."

Michael returned to their table. "Mike," Peter said to him. "What do you say we take your Mum round the shops, buy her something for Christmas?" He turned to Susan. "That okay with you? You don't have to get back to work or anything, do you?"

"No," Susan said. "It's my day off. I'd love to. If you're sure."

"That's settled, then," Peter said. "They can do without me for a few hours yet."

They left McDonald's and began wandering from shop to shop, Michael insisting that Susan try various perfumes and calling her over to look at jewellery and watches he thought she might like. In the fifth shop they went into, Susan said he should choose something while she waited by the door; that way it would be a surprise. Peter gave Michael some money and went to wait with Susan.

"He's having a great time," Peter said. "He likes being with you. I'm sorry you don't get more of a chance to be together. Maybe…"

Susan interrupted him. "Look, Peter," she said. "I've got to be honest. I was really looking forward to seeing him today. You too," she added. "And Michael's not the only one to be having a great time. But there was something I wanted to ask you, to talk to you about."

"Go on," Peter said, suddenly a little guarded.

"That woman who died, the one murdered on your site," Susan said. "Remember?"

"I'm hardly likely to forget, Sue, am I?" he answered. "I found her body."

"Yes," said Susan. "Of course you did." She pulled him by the arm, against the wall, and lowered her tone. "You know I got the story. Well, it looks like someone got in touch with her that night."

"Yes?" Peter said. "What's that got to do with me?"

"She was called from the Warwick Hotel, just before midnight. Where you were having your dinner, to launch the new project. We found her phone."

"You don't think I've got anything to do with it, do you?" Peter was indignant. He pulled away from her.

"No," said Susan. "Of course not. You wouldn't harm a fly. I'm not even saying it was anyone to do with your party. But…You couldn't let me have a guest list, could you? So I can do some checking."

"You haven't just arranged this whole afternoon so you can ask me that, have you?" Peter asked.

"Of course not," Susan said. She was aware that Peter's voice was raised and that some of the people around them were looking. She pulled him close again. "I could have just asked you, when I called last night. I wanted to see Michael. My son. You said yourself I hardly get to see him."

Peter calmed down instantly. "I know," he said. "I know. If it was just down to me I'd…" The sentence trailed away. "It's complicated. You know that." He sighed and smiled at her. "I'll get the guest list for you," he said. "It's not a problem, though I don't know what good it'll do."

"Neither do I," Susan replied. "But you never know."

Peter saw that Michael had made his purchase and was on his way back to them. He was beaming with satisfaction, delighted with his choice.

"Look," Peter began to say to Susan. His phone rang. He looked at the screen to see who was calling him and grimaced when he saw it was his father. "I'm sorry," he told Susan and answered the call. Susan guessed who it was from as she listened to Peter begin sentence after sentence only to be interrupted and bullied. Finally she heard him say, "Okay, I'll be right there." He ended the call and turned to Susan and Michael. "I've got to go. I'm needed back at the Northern Warehouse site," he said. "Sorry. But why don't you two stick around for a while? There's no need for Michael to come with me. You could drop him at the site whenever it suits."

Both Susan and Michael grinned and jumped at the chance to spend more time together and Michael immediately suggested a few shops they could go to.

"Mum's already bought you an expensive present, you," he said to his son.

"Don't worry," Susan said. "I'm sure we can find some stocking-fillers. You do still have a stocking, don't you?"

They left the shop. Darkness had settled and the Christmas lights had come on. Suddenly the scene was a great deal cheerier than it had been before. As Peter was about to take his leave, he turned to Susan and said, "That list you wanted. Maybe I could bring it round."

Susan nodded. "Yes," she said. "I'd like that."

Chapter Twenty-five

It was completely dark when Susan took Michael to the site to meet his father. They'd taken a taxi, having called Peter first to let him know they were coming. He met them at the turn-off from the main road, ostensibly so the taxi wouldn't have to turn into the building site itself, but really so there'd be no chance of Susan and Eugene meeting.

Peter was standing waiting for them when the taxi pulled up at the corner. Susan paid the driver off and let the cab go without thinking of how she was going to get back to her flat. Also, she didn't want just to open the taxi door and let Michael jump out. She wanted a proper goodbye, not just with him, but with Peter too.

The three of them stood there together. When Susan looked down the narrow side road leading to the site of Liverpool's latest hotel and the scene of Margy's murder, all she could make out were the lights shining weakly in the site hut. The rest was blackness.

"How's the story coming?" Peter asked. "About the murder, I mean. I've not seen much in the paper about it."

"There's not much to tell," Susan told him. "And I don't think anyone's too interested to be honest." She lowered her voice, even though Michael had wandered a few yards away from them and was showing no interest anyway. "You know, just a prostitute. No-one will miss her." She thought of Billy.

"It's funny," Peter said. "Maybe I've watched too much television, but I was expecting chalk outlines and arc lights, police in those funny suits checking everything. There's been nothing really."

"They talked to you, though?" asked Susan.

"Not really," Peter replied. "It was strange. I mean, I'm not complaining. But I was expecting to be questioned. I found her, after all." He thought for a while. "No, someone came down on the Monday after it had happened, had a quick chat with me, and Dad, and one or two of the others who were here. Not many, though. We haven't really got going yet."

"Not having problems, are you?" Susan asked. She pulled her scarf tighter around her neck, then dug her hands deep into her pockets. The cold air was damp too, and starting to seep into her.

"No," said Peter. "Not really. The usual with a job like this. And nothing Dad can't sort with a couple of calls. We thought we might have a bit of trouble the other day. A planning officer said we'd exceeded the boundary stated in the original application. But he spoke to someone. He seems to know everyone in this city." He took a sheet of folded paper from his coat pocket. "I found a copy of the guest list," he said. He held it out for her and she took it from him. She noticed that he held the sheet so there'd be no danger of their fingers coming into contact. It only took a split second for her to wonder whether this was because, even after they'd been divorced for so long, he couldn't bear to touch her or couldn't bear not to touch her. He was different now from the way he'd been during the afternoon. Not distant, but just a little tense, a little too aware, and she knew it was because Eugene was close by.

"Thanks," she said. "I don't know what good it'll do. I'm not expecting the name of a well-known prostitute killer to leap out at me." She put the folded sheet into her bag. "What was the party like?" she asked. "Enjoy it?"

"Hated every minute of it," he replied. A sudden, latent bitterness had infected his voice, threatening for a moment his usual mildness, which just as quickly came back to the fore. He smiled. "You know me," he said. "I don't really like these things. Never know what to say to people, can't join in with the way the others behave. Fat, bald, wheezing men calling the waitresses darling and grabbing at them. You'd have liked it though." He realised what he'd said. "Sue, I'm sorry. That came out wrong. I just meant…"

Susan smiled tenderly at him. She laughed a little. "Don't worry. Even if you did mean it, I'd have deserved it. But I know you didn't. Anyway, I wouldn't have enjoyed it. Not these days." She felt awkward, too conscious of what was being said. "I'd better go," she told him. "I'm off now, Michael," she called. He came over and kissed her. "You have a good Christmas and I'll see you soon. Have another McDonald's, maybe, or show you how to throw a spin pass off your left hand." Michael laughed in response.

"Look, Sue," Peter said. "Do you want a lift back home? You've let the taxi go."

She turned to see that Peter was right. The taxi had gone, but she saw a black saloon car idling at the kerb, a little way down the road. Suddenly she desperately wanted a lift, but knew it might make things a little difficult for Peter with Eugene. She told him, "No, it's okay thanks. Thought I might pop into the office before I get back." She half-turned and waved her arm vaguely in the direction of Old Hall Street and the *Morning Mail* building.

"Oh, right," Peter said. "Hold the front page, eh?"

"Something like that," said Susan. She thought for a moment about moving towards him to kiss him goodbye, but decided against it. Instead, awkwardly shifting again, she just said, "Well, bye then." Then she added, "I know you've given me this guest list." She patted her bag. "But you could still pop round. You know. If you're passing."

"Right," Peter said. "I will. Thanks."

Susan said goodbye to Michael again and then turned and headed back down the main road towards the city centre. She found herself walking more quickly than normal, with her chin tucked into her scarf and her hands pushed down deep into her pockets, adopting the pose of someone moving purposefully, with a place to go, intent on getting home and out of the cold. In truth, though, it was nothing like she felt. Despite the freezing air, an uncomfortable heat pinned the surface of her skin and she felt her forehead start to bead with sweat. She waited for the black car to pass her, and soon it did. The driver gunned the engine and roared by her, too fast for Susan to catch the number plate in the darkness of the early evening. She realised she'd been holding her breath. She stopped and tried to take deep, calming breaths. Gradually she relaxed, but not enough to make the tightness in her stomach disappear. The little lie she'd told to Peter came back to her and she decided she'd go to the office after all, walk to her desk, pretend she was looking for something, maybe call Nolan and ask him about the progress of the tests to determine once and for all if the body found on Peter's building site was Margy Girvan. And she hoped that Rachel would still be there, and would maybe fancy a drink or something to eat with her.

Chapter Twenty-six

The harsh strip lights of the editorial office glared over the partitioned desks, sending their reflections out beyond the windows and into the blackness outside. Susan looked at her watch and saw that it was well after six. She glanced over to where Rachel normally sat, but couldn't see her, and for some reason didn't want to go over there, didn't want it to look like she'd come in especially to see her. She went to her own desk instead, where she called the police station and asked for DI Nolan but was told he'd already gone home. She put the phone down and sat in her chair for a while. She realised she was still wrapped in her coat, and still uncomfortably warm, even more so now she was inside. She stood up and undid some buttons, before making her way over to where Rachel normally sat. There were a number of people milling around, waiting for late stories to come in to be subbed for the next day's edition. Distracted herself, Susan didn't notice the strange atmosphere of the office, the unusual tension that made people speak in whispers even when saying the most ordinary things.

Rachel was at her desk, hunched over her keyboard even though she didn't appear to be doing anything.

"Hi," Susan said, standing behind her.

The sound surprised her, and Rachel spun round quickly in her chair, before breathing a heavy sigh of relief when she saw who it was. "Oh, Susan," she said. "Thank God you're here."

Susan was bemused. "Why?" she asked. "What's the matter? I just came in to see if you fancied a drink. I'm surprised you're still here, to be honest."

"I'd love one," Rachel told her. "It's been awful here. But I can't go yet. I've got to wait. Allen told me wants to see me before he leaves."

Susan pulled a chair from the empty cubicle across the way. She moved it next to Rachel, who shifted up so there was room for them both.

"What's Allen still doing here?" Susan asked. "He's normally long gone by now, off to some golf club dinner or something."

"He's shut up in his office with Gerry Dalton," Rachel said. "They've had the most furious row. Still having it for all I know. Just can't hear them anymore. But before, they were screaming at each other, yelling all sorts of stuff."

"Gerry?" Susan said. She was amazed. "Gerry hasn't raised his voice in years. Certainly not to Allen. The most he ever says to him is yes."

"Not tonight," said Rachel. "I thought they were going to start hitting each other."

"Well what's it all about?" Susan asked.

"Us," said Rachel. "Well, maybe just me."

"You!" Susan laughed. "But you're the golden girl! What are they doing? Fighting over your hand in marriage?"

"It's not funny, Susan," said Rachel. Nervously she lifted herself up out of her chair, peeking over the top of the partition to make sure Allen's door was still closed. "As soon as I got in this morning, he shouted at me to get into his office. Wanted to know what I thought I was up to, why I've been in and out of here for the past week or so, getting Bassett to do my work for me."

"What did you tell him?" Susan asked.

"Well, I told him the truth." She leaned back in her chair, her face open, as if to look at Susan more carefully. "Why not?"

"No, no," Susan said. "You're right. Why not?"

Rachel leaned towards Susan again, and again she dropped her voice. "I told him about Sweeney, the calls and the messages and so on, and how I'd been out to see Billy Jackson. How we'd been out to see Billy," she added. "And I told him what Billy said to us this morning. About Nolan."

"Did you mention Crowley?" Susan asked anxiously.

"Well…yes, I did," Rachel replied. "I mean, he was why Franny Sweeney called in the first place, wasn't he? Was that alright? There's no reason why I shouldn't have, is there? I mean, Crowley and Allen know each other, but..." Her shoulders slumped. "I didn't think. I couldn't think. He's never talked to me like that before."

Susan patted her hand. "No," she said. "There's no reason why you shouldn't have told him. No reason at all. What about Margy?" she asked. "Did you mention her?"

"I tried to," said Rachel. "But he wasn't listening by then. He'd called Gerry Dalton in and was ranting to him about me. Demanding to know why he couldn't keep his staff in check." She lowered her head, embarrassed. "He said Dalton was like everyone else in here, blinded by my...by the sight of my tits."

Susan smiled. "Well," she said. "They are very nice." She saw Rachel wasn't in the mood for jokes just yet, and added, "He's a bastard, Rachel. A stupid, ignorant bastard. Anyone could have told you that. You've just seen it for yourself now, that's all."

"Yeah, I know," said Rachel. "You're right. It's just..." She stopped as she became aware that a strange hush had descended on the office. It wasn't uncommon for there to be rows, but this one had been different. As Susan had said, Dalton never disagreed with Allen, so everyone present had become highly sensitive to the slightest movement or change. Gerry Dalton had come out of Allen's office and headed for Rachel's cubicle. He was about to say something when he saw Susan was with her, so he changed and simply said, "You'd better come too." The two women got up and followed Dalton back into the editor's office. Dalton was too pale, Susan noticed, and his skin looked dry as well. His eyes looked smaller in his head, but Susan saw that was simply because of the dark rings around them. There was something shabby and downtrodden about him, his slumped shoulders and his cheap clothes giving the impression of a man who for too long hadn't been bothered. Susan had sometimes wondered if he was her male counterpart. But when he turned round, standing with his back to the filing cabinet to the right of Allen's desk, she saw there was something else there too. His eyes were red, as if he'd been crying, but there was a set look about them, a determination not to give in. It wasn't a look she'd seen in Dalton before. He looked like a schoolboy who wasn't going to give in to the class bully. He would fight him, and carry on fighting him even though he knew he'd lose. Allen was the bully, of course. He was sitting behind his desk, his back to the window with its view over the city skyline. Unlike Dalton, his clothes were expensive, but he lacked taste. His grey suit had a sheen to it. The jacket hung on the back of his chair. His shirt was pink, with white collars and cuffs. He'd rolled his sleeves up, revealing thick forearms. On one wrist was a heavy gold watch, while on the other was a gold bracelet, and he wore a ring on each hand. For the second time in a matter of days, Susan realised how like Eugene he was, not in the way he was dressed, but in his shape and presence. He was a touch taller than Eugene, and not so fat, but like her former father-in-law, the fat was solid, not soft and flabby.

He barely acknowledged Susan and Rachel as they came in behind Dalton. Only when Susan went to take one of the two chairs on her side of the desk did he speak. It was a snarl, full of contempt and designed to threaten.

"Who said you could sit down?"

Susan ignored him and sat down anyway. She snorted with mild derision. "Come off it, Hugh," she said. "Who are you meant to be? The headmaster or the gangland boss?"

He leant forward across the table at her. "How dare you speak to me like that!" he said.

She looked him directly in the eye. She felt calm and relaxed, aware she wasn't putting on an act. She simply wasn't going to let this man intimidate her. In fact, she found him a little bit amusing, so the smile was genuine when she lightly told him, "Stop being such a prick. Why do you want to see us? Why have you been ranting at Rachel when she's working on a bloody good story?"

"Stay in the chair," he said. "I wouldn't be surprised if you couldn't stand up straight anyway."

Susan saw this for what it was, a weak insult made too late in the exchange, so she ignored it. Allen knew it too, so turned to Rachel and snarled at her instead, although with less conviction than before. "You might as well sit down too then." This wasn't going the way he'd intended it to. Susan had thrown him.

He swept his hand across the desk as if indicating work they'd brought in to show him. "This story of yours is a load of shit," he said. "There's nothing there." Neither Rachel nor Susan responded. "All you've got is the word of some old con who's having a go at the man who arrested him."

"Sweeney too," said Rachel. Susan's presence had given her confidence.

"A thug and a killer," Allen said. "Another one with a grudge."

"If there's nothing there, then we won't find anything," Susan said. "But we won't know until we start looking, will we? If Billy Jackson's lying, then it'll fizzle out."

"It'll fizzle out anyway," Allen snapped. "There's no way either of those two police officers would put a foot out of line."

"I didn't realise you knew them, Hugh," said Susan blithely. Allen looked up sharply at Susan. He knew perfectly well she was lying. "I know Assistant Chief Constable Crowley," he said. "I've met him at a number of functions. He and I sit on a number of the same committees. That's what happens. I don't know this other one."

"DI Nolan," said Dalton, speaking for the first time. His gaze was on the window. He seemed to be trying to look through the blackness.

"Why are we taking sides on this?" asked Susan. She lit a

cigarette, knowing how Allen had struggled to give up smoking. "You don't mind, do you Hugh?" Allen shook his head. "Will you not even let us look into it?"

"Not a chance," Allen said.

"We should," Dalton said. The three others in the room looked at him. Like his gaze, his voice seemed far away. "We can't just ignore it."

Allen shifted in his chair. "No," he said and repeated, "No." He looked at Susan. "And stop sending in those stories about that whore who died. I told you before. You're wasting everybody's time. Now you can go. I'm late." Rachel and Susan got up and made for the door. Dalton started to follow them. "Not you, Gerry," Allen sneered. "You're giving me a lift, remember?"

Dalton sighed. "Yes," he said. "I remember." He closed the door behind Rachel and Susan.

Having left Allen's office, Rachel and Susan found themselves the focus of attention for all the reporters still working in the main room. Hearing the door open, they'd risked a glance up from their work to see who had come out. It was safe to stare at the two women, so stare they did. Frank Hayes, one of the older men who worked there, doing freelance subbing shifts, hummed the funeral march as Susan and Rachel trudged back to Rachel's cubicle.

"Piss off, Frank," Rachel said wearily as she passed him.

"Don't be like that, Rachel, love," he replied. "You're one of us now you've had a bollocking off the great man."

She smiled at him wearily. "That's some consolation," she said as she put her coat on.

Frank came over to her. "I mean it," he said. "Remember, whatever he said, he doesn't know what he's talking about. If he's having a go at you, you must be doing something right." He gave her the tabloid size sheet he was holding.

"Tomorrow's front page," he said. He read out the headline. "'City Action Group Demands Government Funding For

Trams.' Of course, Hughie boy just happens to belong to this city action group. Thinks he's a mover and shaker and wants everyone to know it. I don't know how many times we've featured this story in one way or another over the past year. Nothing ever happens, except Allen and his pals get another name check."

Susan took the page from Rachel, who was too wrapped up in her own thoughts to notice anything other than Frank's soothing tone of voice. "Okay for me to take this, Frank?" Susan asked.

"Sure," he replied. "I won't even charge you for it."

They watched Frank return to his seat. Rachel looked at Susan. "Drink?" she said.

"Drink," Susan replied.

Chapter Twenty-seven

They took the lift down to the underground car park, where their heels echoed on the bare concrete as they walked to Rachel's Mini. Rachel unlocked it a few yards away but, when she was about to open her door, she looked across to Susan on the passenger side.
"Is it okay to get drunk on a Tuesday night?" she asked.
Susan smiled back at her. "In some cultures it's compulsory," she replied.
"Then let's do it," Rachel said. She locked the car and they headed out onto Old Hall Street, where they soon found a taxi.
"Where to love?" the driver asked Rachel.
"Oh," she said. "I don't know. Susan?"
The driver sighed, feeling it was going to be a long night with his fares getting more and more drunk as the evening wore on. It was only seven-ish and already these two didn't have a clue.
"The Albert Dock," Susan told him. "Pan-American Bar, please." She settled back in her seat and Rachel turned to look at her in surprise.
"The Pan-American Bar," she said. "Bit swish, isn't it? Not Peter Kavanagh's or some other old pub round your way?"
"Just feel like a change," said Susan. "Maybe we can pick up a couple of footballers."
The taxi took them along Wapping and dropped them outside the entrance to the bar, on the south side of the dock. They were back to near where they'd gone the previous day when they'd visited the Warwick. Instead of going straight into the bar, Susan walked the few yards to the waterfront. Rachel followed her. Leaning on the rail, they looked down at the murky river below them, listening to the water slapping hard against the stone sides of the river wall. Beyond the river was the Wirral, lights burning from the shadowy buildings of Wallasey, Birkenhead and Ellesmere Port.
Susan lit a cigarette, struggling to shield the flame of her

lighter from the cold wind. "Do you realise," she asked, "that it's all happening here?"

"How do you mean?" Rachel replied.

"Along the river," Susan said. "The Warwick's a few hundred yards down there." She gestured to the left. "Up that way," she went on, pointing right, "maybe a mile or so away, if that, is where Margy's body was found. Even Franny Sweeney; carry on north along the coast and you'll come to him. It's like everything's clinging to the water." She flicked her cigarette out into the Mersey. The burning tip arced downwards and then disappeared.

The two bouncers on the door of the Pan-American Bar took little notice of Rachel and Susan as they walked past them and through the doors. The place was busy, full of couples and groups enjoying the lead-up to Christmas, but, despite the number of people there, the atmosphere was one of measured enjoyment, nothing too loud or raucous, no festive pop songs blaring from the sound system. All the seats were taken, apart from two stools at a narrow wooden bar to the right of the entrance opposite where Rachel and Susan had come in. They grabbed those. Cut into the wall beside them was a narrow strip of glass, horizontal to the floor, through which they could peer out and see the water of the dock itself, which the vast building enclosed on four sides, apart from a gap on the east side, with access to more water and a sight of the city further inland. Through this gap, the shapes of cranes at rest could be made out dimly gleaming against the night sky, towering over the Three Graces – the Liver Building, the Cunard Building and the Port of Liverpool Building. All three had been constructed in the early 20th Century, to announce the city as a port of international prestige. At the top of the Liver Building, the twin guardian birds of the city were illuminated an eerie metallic green

"It's a good-looking place, Sue," said Rachel. "I know you. say you hate the city, but you've got to give it that."

"Alright," she said. "I'll grant you that. Mind you, it's the people I can't stand, not the buildings."

A waitress – slim and attractive and dark, nothing like the pudgy girl squeezed into the Warwick's maroon and gold – came and took their drinks order, a double vodka and tonic for Rachel and a large red wine for Susan. She returned shortly, leaving the bill with them on a sleek silver tray. Susan and Rachel turned away from the crowded room and sat facing the window.

"A double, eh?" said Susan. "You mean business."

Rachel jerked her thumb over her shoulder at the people behind them. "I'm not going to let these Christians have all the fun," she said. Her glass was full to the brim and she bent her head down to it and slurped from the surface of her drink, to avoid risking spilling any by picking it up.

"Cheers," said Susan, and raised her glass and took a sip of her wine. She noticed Rachel had taken the straw from her glass and was tapping it anxiously against the side of the ashtray. "Thinking about Allen?" she asked.

The question pulled Rachel out of her thoughts. "He called me a stupid little bitch," she said. "Made it sound like I just flutter my eyelashes and all the men eat out of my hand. Doesn't think of me as a reporter at all. Just a pretty face and a nice voice who'll end up reading the regional news night after night."

"There are worse things," Susan said. Then she went on, "Anyway, you know that's not true. What Frank Hayes said was right. Allen is an idiot who's forgotten he works for a newspaper, if he ever even knew. All he's interested in is his position, thinking he's a big fish in whatever size pond Liverpool is now." She took from her bag the copy of the guest list Peter had given her earlier that day and spread it out flat between them on the table. "Look at this," she told Rachel. "It's the list from the Warwick that night Margy was killed. Allen's on it. Crowley. Councillors, businessmen, committee chairmen, some of those instant has-been comedians this place throws up. They'll all have been sitting round that night, fat and drunk and sweating, telling each other how great they are, patting each other on the back, feeling up the waitresses as they brought round the prawn cocktail."

"Gerry Dalton's on that list," Rachel said. "And Peter would have been there too. Are they like that?"

Susan's tone changed, became quieter, sadder. "Not Peter," she said. "And Dalton? I don't know. Once maybe, but not now. Not now Allen's castrated him."

"He stood up to him today," Rachel said. "You weren't there, remember? Yelling at him, out of control."

Susan swivelled on her seat and looked at Rachel. "You're not going to listen to Allen, are you?" she demanded. "You are going to follow this through? This story from Billy Jackson?"

"Yes," she replied.

"You'd be an idiot if you didn't," Susan said sternly.

"I said yes, didn't I?" Rachel replied. "You still going to help me?"

"Of course I am," Susan said. She thought for a moment. "You'll need to get hold of Billy's charge sheet. And write up what he said today. Better still, go back and interview him properly, get everything he says on tape." She felt herself getting excited. "And talk to Brian Nulty about Nolan. Tell him what Jackson told us. He's straight, Brian. He'll help put us on the right track." She sipped her drink and added, "I've got to talk to Nolan anyway, mind. Find out how he's going on with those tests on Margy's mother."

"And tell him about Mrs Girvan's phone?" Rachel asked.

"No chance," said Susan. "Not after what Billy said today about him. Anyway, he should have found it himself when he went to see her. If he bothered looking, of course," she added. "Just a dead whore to him." She nodded at Rachel's glass. "Fancy another?" she asked.

Rachel hesitated. "I'll just have a diet Coke," she said. "I feel better now, not so desperate to get drunk. How about you?"

"I'll have the same," Susan said. "I'm not that desperate to get drunk either. Which makes a change." She looked around to see if she could catch the waitress's eye. "Or we could just go," she said to Rachel. "You know, if you'd rather."

"No chance," Rachel replied. "We've not picked up any footballers yet, have we?" Susan smiled, and again decided not to tell Rachel that Sweeney was on her trail too.

Chapter Twenty-eight

The buzzing began in her dream, a long, loud, insistent monotone followed by short bursts of irregular lengths, followed by a long drone again. It was all perfectly normal, the sounds fitting in naturally with the events occurring in Susan's subconscious as she slept. Rachel's father was there, Michael too, both sitting with Susan drinking and smoking listening to some jazz quartet at the Pan-American. Rachel was their waitress; she looked good in her maroon and gold uniform. Then gradually Susan's mind clawed her awake. The dream characters disappeared, Susan instantly unable to remember anything that had happened after it had all been so clear and logical. Only the buzzing remained.

At first, she reached for the alarm clock. Then she realised that it was someone at the door downstairs and she let herself fall back against her pillow. She still had the clock in her hand. Holding it over her, she squinted at the luminous dial and saw it was just after two and sighed angrily. That was one of the problems of living in a building that opened straight onto the road, especially at this time of year. Drunks stumbling their way along Hope Street in search of taxis or women or men or more drink sometimes thought it hilarious to start pressing at the doorbells of the houses. There were times when the city's much heralded cultural quarter lacked a little culture. Probably all the flats in her building were getting the same treatment. It was like a kids' game. What had she heard it called? Knock down Ginger? That was it, where a gang of children rang a doorbell and then ran away. Except whoever was pressing at her buzzer wasn't running away, just leaning on the button, over and over again.

Annoyed, Susan tore back the duvet and pushed herself out of bed. She shivered, wearing only a T-shirt, and made her way barefoot out of the bedroom and down the hall to the internal door of the flat, next to which was the intercom. She shut her eyes against the glare of the hall light as she switched it on, then pressed the button on the intercom box to answer the door downstairs.

She snapped, "Who is it?" She didn't get the reply she was expecting. When this had happened before, she'd heard laughter, or a voice asking if she was a taxi, or, once, a man wanting to know if she was Tracy, the girl he'd met earlier that night in some club.

This time though, the voice downstairs said her name. Slurred, and breathy, and drunk, and desperate, but it definitely said "Susan." And repeated it. It was a man's voice, she recognised that at least, and it sounded like whoever it was was sliding down the door as he was speaking.

"Who is it?" she repeated, but the voice simply answered with her name again, and then ordered her to let him in. A plea more than an order, the desperation that she'd heard before now showing itself in sobs.

"Stay there," Susan said. "I'm coming down." She hurried back to her bedroom and pulled on jeans, a jumper and a pair of shoes. Her mind searched to think who it could be and came up with just the one answer: Peter, her ex-husband. Not that she'd recognised his voice, and certainly not that she'd ever known him to be so drunk, but that was the only name that presented itself in the weird logic of what was happening.

The lights in the communal stairwell were old and on timer switches. You pressed a round plastic button in the wall and then made your way down or up to the next one on the next floor, hoping to reach it before the first switch turned itself off, sending you fumbling in the pitch black, spreading your fingers along the wall as your eyes fought to accustom themselves to the darkness. Susan dashed down the stairs, punching each switch with the side of her fist as she went, rushing to open the front door and bring Peter inside.

The buzzing had stopped by the time she opened the door. Whoever it was was now slumped down on the steps leading up to it, his back against the railings that ran alongside them, head lolling forward. It wasn't Peter, though. Susan saw that straight away. The man looked up at her.

"Gerry?" Susan said. "Gerry, is that you?" The hall light switched itself off as she spoke. Making her way back down the hall to turn it on again, Susan realised that what she was feeling was a crushing disappointment. She didn't know why, but she'd wanted it to be her ex-husband. Regardless of the state he was in, no matter how drunk, no matter why he was there, she'd wanted it to be Peter. She'd wanted to take him upstairs, help him undress, put him in her bed and then go and sleep on the couch. She'd make him a cup of tea in the morning, weak and milky the way he liked it. She was suddenly lonely, and yearned to have someone to look after. But she didn't want to look after Gerry Dalton.

She went back to the front door. Dalton was struggling to stand up and Susan let him struggle.

"What the hell do you think you're playing at?" she hissed at him. "What are you doing here?" She watched as he stood as upright as he could manage, gripping the railing with his right hand for support. To her eyes he cut a pathetic figure. A dribble of sick oozed from his mouth. His thinning hair needed cutting. His clothes were just a little too small, the waistband of his trousers pushed down by a slight paunch, the hems of the trouser legs not quite long enough to rest on his shoes. He looked cheap, but he wasn't. He'd just stopped caring.

"Can I come in?" He was trying to sound coherent, but his words skewed out of his mouth and his head sagged forward, eyelids drooping.

"No," Susan whispered firmly. "No you fucking well can't." She was raging inside but spoke with control. She was angry with Gerry and knew that the reason she was so angry was because he wasn't Peter. If he'd been Peter, she'd be giggling as she helped him in, loving the role reversal; during their time together, it had always been him helping her. "Go home Gerry," Susan said. "I don't know what you thought you were going to get from me turning up like this. Some old time's sake screw maybe? Allen put you up to this?"

Dalton shook his head and muttered, "Not Allen. Not Allen." His head carried on moving from side to side of its own accord. "Hate Allen." He fell to his knees, which cracked against the hard edge of the stone step. He crumpled to the step below, unaware of the pain he was causing himself. "Can't go…always driving him…same voice calling." He tried to look up at Susan but couldn't hold the position. "Your voice…hate your voice…three bags full Mr Allen…" he said as his head sagged back down to his chest.

Susan had no idea what he was talking about, could barely make out the words coming out of his mouth along with the saliva and the traces of vomit.

"You can't stay there, Gerry," Susan said. She looked up and down the street. Outside the Carriage Works Hotel, opposite the Philharmonic, taxis were coming and going, picking up the late-night party-goers coming out of the hotel bar. They were a little raucous, but controlled, their shouts of goodbye to each other echoing softly back towards Susan. Smart and happy and merry, they were oblivious to Susan standing there above Dalton, still on his knees but now slumped forward, his arms locked in front of him, trying to support himself. Susan bent down slightly. She still didn't want him there, but she had lost her anger. She spoke softly. "Go home, Gerry," she said.

"Not home," she heard him reply. "Here…your voice…"

"No, Gerry," said Susan. "You can't stay here." She searched her memory for his wife's name. "Shall I ring your wife?" she asked. The name came back to her. "Do you want me to phone Maureen?" That was it. Maureen. She'd been unfaithful to Peter and Gerry had cheated on Maureen. They'd stayed together though, had another child to add to the two they'd had already. Susan remembered Allen smirking at her when he personally asked her if she wanted to sign the card congratulating the Daltons on the birth. Maureen had never known about them.

Dalton seemed to find an anger of his own. He jerked his head up at Susan, who stepped back automatically. "Not the phone," he said. He spoke with a sudden fury, which then died immediately as he said, "Not Maureen. Can I come in?" But Susan was determined. She wasn't going to let him into the flat, couldn't face trying to drag him upstairs, then pushing him away as he groped at her, shoving his face towards hers with the conviction that only a drunken man can have of how attractive alcohol makes him and how desperate the woman in question is to have him. She wasn't going to let him sleep on her couch with a bucket next to him to catch the sick, wasn't going to see him in the morning and watch his shamefaced realisations and listen to his hungover apologies.

She told him firmly. "You're not coming in, Gerry." She looked back down the street and wondered if she could go and get him a taxi, but decided it wasn't on. Even if there was a cab free, there was no way any driver would take him in his condition. Gingerly she bent down towards him. She tried to feel in his jacket pockets for a phone, to see if she could ring his house and ask Maureen to come and get him. She had a horrible feeling that the conversation would end up with her agreeing to drive him home herself. Maureen most likely wouldn't want to leave the children alone in the house while she drove out for him. And the conversation with her would be so awkward, Susan trying to tell Maureen that her drunken husband had turned up on her doorstep at two in the morning and now needed a lift home.

In the end it didn't matter. As she tried to reach into one of his pockets, Gerry lunged at her in fury. He screamed, "Get away from me!" He touched his hand to his coat, patting the pockets, feeling for whatever was there. Then he said "Get away from me" again, but this time without conviction, mumbling the words.

"I was only looking for your phone, Gerry," Susan explained. "So I could ring Maureen."

Gerry pushed himself to his feet and lurched down the steps to the pavement. "No phone," he said, partly to Susan, partly to himself. "No Maureen." He found what he was looking for in his pocket and pulled out his car keys. He began to weave along the pavement.

Susan rushed down after him. "No, Gerry," she said. "You're not going to drive in your state." She wondered how he'd ever managed to get to her in the first place. She tried to pull him back, grabbing at the hand holding the keys, but he pushed her away, sending her down to the pavement. As she stood up she heard the click of a car unlocking, the sidelights flashing twice on a grey Volvo a few yards away. Gerry pawed at the rear nearside door and pulled it open. He leaned on the door and tried to focus on Susan. He yelled for one last time. "No more stories" came slurring out of his mouth. And again, "No more stories," as he crawled inside and lay down on the back seat, leaving the door wide open. Susan followed him and looked inside. He was already asleep. She shut the door and thought to herself that he could rot in there for all she cared. She began to walk back to her building, but suddenly stopped and turned to look more closely at the car. It was parked between two others, she noticed, neatly tucked in against the kerb. There was no way he could have parked it like that, not with the amount he'd obviously drunk. Briefly she wondered where he'd been that night but she pushed the thought away. There were plenty of places round here, she thought, pubs, restaurants, bars. He could have been in any one of them. She wondered if there'd been something special on at the Hope Street Hotel, then wondered why Dalton had been drinking at all. He was always the designated driver, the chauffeur whose presence allowed Allen to have a skinful so often.

Leave it, she told herself. Not my problem. She went back inside and headed up the stairs, pressing each landing light to guide her way as she did so. She was nearly back at her door when the buzzer sounded again. She cursed Dalton and hesitated before wearily turning and making her way back downstairs.

She opened the door ready to say Dalton's name and tell him to leave her in peace. A single blow caught her on the nose. It was only a light tap, a left arm jab, but it was enough to knock her off balance and made her stagger back. The man followed swiftly behind his punch, kicking the door shut with his foot. He took Susan's chin in his right hand and tipped her head back, supporting her as she tilted to the floor with his left hand on the back of her head. Once she was on the floor he pinched her nostrils shut with one hand and covered her mouth with the other. He was wearing black leather gloves and a balaclava. He knelt beside her and pushed downwards. Susan couldn't breathe. Panic filled her and she squirmed and kicked and struggled but the man was almost nonchalant as he ignored her writhing and simply continued to suffocate her. Susan's vision swam. The light in the hall clicked off. Just as she was about to pass out, the man released his grip, as if he knew to the second how long Susan's lungs would hold out. He left just as quickly as he came in, closing the door softly behind him. Susan lay on the floor, trembling. Eventually, she struggled to her hands and knees and crawled up the stairs to her flat. She lay in bed and cried until, finally, she slept.

Chapter Twenty-nine

Wednesday 19 December
EXTRACT FROM THE LIVERPOOL MORNING MAIL
WEBSITE, GUIDE TO THE REGION
No visitor coming to Liverpool in its year as European
Capital of Culture will want to miss Crosby.
A small town lying on the coast just a couple of miles north
of Liverpool, Crosby can be reached from the city along
the A565, via Seaforth, Litherland, Bootle and Waterloo,
and is also easily accessible via public transport.
Proud of its separate status, Crosby has nevertheless
become more or less a suburb of Liverpool, affluent and
elegant, possessing imposing houses, tree-lined roads,
excellent schools, thriving shops, and an independent
cinema whose quirky shows reflect the community of the
area.
In recent years, its fame has spread around the country
and beyond as visitors have poured in, all heading for the
Crosby shore to see an installation by the artist Antony
Gormley, the same man responsible for Gateshead's Angel
of the North.
Officially entitled Another Place, it is known locally as the
Cast-Iron Men. Stretched along the sand, at various
intervals and distances from the water, the installation
consists of 100 identical cast-iron figures, all about 6' tall,
faces blank, legs together, arms at their sides, rigidly
standing to attention, staring out into the Irish Sea.
They can appear mystical and mythical, looking out
westwards in an evocation of adventure and exploration
and the need for knowledge. From a distance they can
appear alien, invaders emerging from the water like
creatures from old science fiction films. And they can
summon a chill fear in people watching from the

promenade as the tide comes in, unflinching as the water reaches up their bodies and finally swallows them.
But your visit should not begin and end at the sea shore. Crosby contains a wealth of cafés and independent shops full of delights and curiosities...

It was to Crosby's shore and the cast-iron men that Gerry Dalton came in the early hours of Wednesday morning. He had never intended to get so drunk, had had no plans to see Susan and harangue her. The only thing he'd had in mind for sure when he left his wife and children and house on Tuesday morning was coming to Crosby and never leaving. It was luck that he woke up. A tramp had been banging on the car window and Dalton had eventually come round. At first he didn't know where he was and clawed his hands against the back seat of his car as if searching for something familiar, something to jog his memory. As his eyes struggled to focus on the tramp at the car window, he became aware of the banging in his head. He'd only been asleep a couple of hours, and was still drunk, but the hangover was there too, raging and dominant. He was cold and his mouth was dry and he was desperate for water. He ignored the tramp and clambered over into the driver's seat. He found his car keys in his jacket pocket. Before he started the engine, he held his hands up in front of his face. They were shaking, each finger trembling, but only with cold and all the drink he'd had. Not with anything else. He said the words aloud. "It's just the drink and the cold," he said, hearing his voice as if it were someone else's, his mother's maybe, from years ago, reassuring him, telling him he was alright really. He heard the words and realised they were true. It was just the drink and the cold. Nothing else.
He started the car, put the headlights on, switched on the heater. The clock on the dashboard told him it was just after 4.15. He had a few hours of darkness yet. Carefully checking

his wing mirror, not wanting anything to prevent him reaching his destination, he slowly eased the car away from the kerb and headed down Hope Street towards the Anglican Cathedral. He thought for a moment of taking a different route, through the city centre so he could go down Old Hall Street, past the entrance to the offices of the *Liverpool Morning Mail*. But that would be a little sentimental, and no-one would know he'd done it anyway; it would be a little play for his own amusement only. Besides, heading down Upper Parliament Street and then right onto Wapping – the dock road – he'd still pass by the bottom of Old Hall Street, would still be able to take a glance up at the building where he'd worked for the past 15 years. And he could still imagine someone in there, looking out of one of the windows in the editorial office, seeing the deputy editor waiting at the lights before turning left and taking the road to Crosby.

The streets were largely empty and the lights were with him, so it wasn't long before he was heading north on the A565, the Mersey on his left, the road black and slick with rain in front of him. When he got into Crosby, he actually missed the sign that would have taken him to the shore, but he just took the next left and worked his way down the roads, always with a sense of the direction he needed in order to emerge at the sea front. He even smiled to himself once or twice, amused at the fact that he was going to such great pains in order to kill himself in exactly the way he wanted. And he wasn't even sure why he'd chosen that way. There were simpler methods, surely, more certain ones too. But no. He liked the method he'd chosen and he didn't see why he should change his mind. And as he let the words sound inside his head, he found himself at the promenade. He guided the car into the car park and parked facing out to sea, just in front of the coast guard station, where he'd parked the last time he was here, with Maureen and the three girls. No, he corrected himself, not the three girls. Laura hadn't been with them. Where had Laura been? he asked himself. He turned the engine off and leant back in his seat. For some reason, he needed to remember where Laura was that day, why she hadn't been with them. That's right! She'd gone camping with that girl from school, Joanna, and her mum and dad. He smiled to himself, pleased he'd remembered, then unbuckled his seat belt and got out of the car, almost with a spring in his step.

He closed the driver's door and then stood for a moment or two, his arms resting on the roof of the car. His was the only vehicle in the car park and not a single light shone in any of the houses that lined the other side of the promenade road. He felt alone, but didn't mind that. If anything, he felt invigorated, purposeful. Having other people around would only hinder him, might even prevent him from carrying out what he had in mind. And he didn't want that. He was all set, had thought everything through. He'd always been careful with money and had invested cautiously but wisely. He was a thorough man too, and liked to keep everything in order. Not for him simply throwing every letter that arrived in a drawer and hoping it would somehow take care of itself. No, the house was paid for, there was plenty of money in the bank. Maureen and the girls would be fine. They'd have no reason to miss him, and no reason to fault him for how he'd left things. The letter he'd sent to his solicitor would arrive that morning, or should do, at least, even allowing for the Christmas post. He'd explained everything in that, all the arrangements. That would tell Maureen everything except why, and he was sure she could find an answer to that question, even though it wouldn't be the truth.

He shook himself from his thoughts. This won't get the baby bathed, he chastised himself. He made his way to the back of the car where he opened the boot and fumbled around inside for the torch he always kept there. That found, he switched it on and took out the plastic carrier bag, heavy with the chains and locks he needed. He felt himself uncertain for a moment.

He didn't want to take the carrier bag with him, because he worried that it might blow away, and he didn't like that idea of littering the beach. There was no way round it, though. He wouldn't be able to carry the chains without it. He just hoped that when the time came, he'd have the chance to put it in his pocket.

He shut the boot and locked the car, then left the keys resting on the top of the back offside tyre, hidden from view by the overhang of the bodywork. Someone should find them there, he reasoned. A policeman should have sense enough to look, surely.

Satisfied that he had everything he needed and that he'd left all in order, Gerry made his way down the steps and onto the sand. He held the torch steady in front of him, the beam pushing and then disappearing into the void ahead, and walked towards the sea. The tide was out – that was the whole point – but he wasn't sure how far he needed to walk. When he'd rehearsed the whole business in his mind, it had been straightforward, almost literally. Walk over the beach to the cast-iron statue furthest from the road. That was all, no problem. Now though, actually doing it wasn't proving so simple. Finding the statues in the dark wasn't easy. Although there were a hundred of them, they were spaced far apart up and across the beach. And how would he know which one was furthest from the road? He didn't want to chain himself to one and wait for the tide to come in, only to find that the water didn't reach higher than his knees. He'd look stupid, like some failed escapologist, standing there like an idiot for the amusement of early morning dog walkers.

He trudged on, pushing the thoughts of failure from his mind. Just walk straight ahead, he told himself. You're bound to find a statue soon, and once you've found one, it should be easy enough to find another. It was like that when he'd first come to see the cast-iron men. At first, even in daylight, it had been tricky to spot them, even though they were six feet tall. Once he'd found one, though, he couldn't stop seeing them, still and rigid and staring, some completely clear of the sea, others seemingly straining to keep their heads above water.

And so it proved. He found one statue, stopping for a moment to cast the torch over its gnarled, encrusted, rusting form. And then he marched onwards to another and then another and another, until he was sure that there were no more left to find, that this one was his, closest to the sea, furthest from the shore.

Gerry Dalton put the carrier bag on the ground and tucked the torch under his arm, each movement sending the beam across the area in front of him, at times letting him look at what he wanted, at others leaving him just staring into darkness. Despite the fact that he'd been out here for some time, his eyes still hadn't adjusted to the pitch black of the winter night. Still, he worked quickly and well, and soon found the best way to do things. He positioned himself directly in front of the statue, pushing his back against the iron man's front, his heels hard against the iron man's toes. Then he bent down and passed the first chain round and round his legs and ankles and the legs and ankles of the cast-iron man behind him. He nearly tumbled forward into the hard ridged sand as he secured the heavy padlock to the chain, but he just about managed to keep his balance. Grabbing the bag and lifting it up, he took out the second chain which he wrapped around both his and the iron man's waist, again fastening it tight with a padlock. He took the last chain out and awkwardly slung it round behind him, bringing it in a loop encircling the two necks. Once that was fixed snugly, he took the last item from the bag, which he tucked into his jacket, happy he was leaving no litter. This last thing was a pair of handcuffs, a joke gift from a policeman he'd known a lifetime ago. Gerry just about managed to put his hands behind the iron man's back and slipped one of the cuffs under a loop of the chain. He cuffed each wrist and pushed the clasps down tight. Then he could relax, exhausted by the unexpected strain demanded by his chosen method of suicide. He steadied his breath and settled to wait, chained to the cast-iron man behind him, the tide approaching from the darkness ahead, at ease and peaceful like a child tucked up cosy in bed.

The exertions had caused him to break out in a sweat. His skin had become clammy and his shirt had stuck to his chest and back and stomach. Now, though, having finished, he enjoyed the wind coming off the sea to cool him. He felt comfortable, not just physically, but mentally too. His emotions, so turbulent in the last couple of weeks, were calm and at ease. He noticed with a smile that he no longer had a hangover. He even felt relaxed enough to doze a little, although the chain around his neck dug into his skin and made it a little difficult to swallow.

He wondered what time it was. He'd forgotten to check and now, of course, it was too late. Still, I don't suppose it matters, he acknowledged to himself. Just the tide matters, that's all. And he settled to wait for it, patient and content.

As he waited, Gerry thought of his wife, Maureen. Theirs had been a decent marriage, he felt. He'd been unfaithful just the once, or, at least, with just the one woman. Susan Clarke. She had seduced him. Well, not seduced exactly. That wasn't the right word for the likes of me, Gerry thought. They'd been out one night, a group of them from the office. Susan was, as usual, the life and soul, keen to keep the night going, chastising those who wanted to get home as being unable to stand the pace, wimps too keen to get to their beds. They'd ended up at some club, he and Susan dancing together, and she'd just moved in and kissed him and kept on kissing him, her arms around him, pressing him close. He'd not resisted. Why not, he wondered. Politeness? Maybe, but no. He was flattered and, besides, he lacked the strength of character to resist. So he kissed her back, even though he was sure it

wasn't him she wanted. He was just there. They had sex in
the alley round the back of the club. It was awkward and
uncomfortable and unsatisfactory for both of them. He hadn't
said so, naturally. That wouldn't do. That would almost be
like having a backbone, or at least an opinion. He
remembered he was surprised when, the following day, she
made it clear she wanted to do it again. And so they did, twice
or three times more, until that last time when her husband had
come home and found them in bed together. They hardly
spoke after that. Funnily enough, he thought, he'd become
deputy editor in much the same way. Allen had picked him
because he was there, weak and nodding, happy to oblige,
even though he didn't really want to do it.

The cold surprised him. He wasn't expecting it. He didn't
know why not. After all, it was December, and this was the
Irish Sea. Nevertheless, it was a shock, washing icily over his
shoes, soaking into his socks and the bottom of his trousers. I
grow old, I grow old, I shall wear the bottoms of my trousers
rolled. Where did that come from? He asked himself. I've not
said that line for years. Eliot, isn't it? That's right. He heard
his voice speaking aloud to himself, shouting above the wind
that was now a roar, but keeping the intonation of a chatty
reminiscence. I am not Prince Hamlet nor was meant to be.
Am an attendant lord, one who will do…

He struggled to remember how it went after that, and then
stopped struggling. That was enough, really: one who will do.
That said it all. That's what I've always been, Gerry said.
One who will do.

At his knees now. He couldn't really feel his feet. Too cold.
His teeth started to chatter. Uncontrollably, like joke shop
teeth scuttling pink and white over the Christmas table,
children laughing and then reaching to wind them up again
when they stopped. The water bit cold and burning into his
thighs. I don't want this comic death, Gerry thought, my teeth
chattering like this, like some joke ending, no dignity, no

sense of calm. He forced his body to calm itself, and his teeth stopped chattering. He breathed deeply, in and out, fighting the cold that was eating into his body. I want to know what's happening. I want to feel the water hitting my face like so many slaps, slapping and slurping into my mouth and down into my lungs.

Dawn seeped into the sky, fighting the mist. Gerry turned his head to his left and could just about make out the emerging outlines of the docks down the coast towards the edge of Liverpool. Hulking buildings, thin, fragile, towering cranes, the giant propellers of the turbines catching the wind, generating heat and light and power.

His chest, his neck. Losing consciousness, the cold lulling him to an early, undeserved sleep. His daughters wouldn't mind. He loved them and they loved him, but he was a peripheral figure in the lives of all the people he loved. He would offer and they would take. Not nastily, no unpleasantness, not selfishly. It was just the natural order of things. They'd be alright, though. There was the pension plan he'd sorted out, the life insurance policy payout, the death in service benefit. Plenty for Maureen and the girls to be more than comfortable. The girls would go to university. There'd be no problem financially anyway.

His chin, his mouth. Salty and foul it tasted. Again, what did he expect?

He and his cast-iron companion, chained together, letting the tide come over them both, chest to back like lovers.

Gerry smiled in relief as the water came over his head. This was the end he wanted. This made everything alright. When the tide came back over him, returning to the sea, he and his iron mate would still be locked together, each as lifeless as the other.

Chapter Thirty

By 9.30 that morning, Susan had already been in work for an hour and a quarter. She'd woken early and hurried out of the flat, desperate to get into the light and noise. She wanted to work, to keep her mind occupied and away from the nightmare of that hand pressing down over her mouth. Now she was huddled into her corner of the office, her back towards anyone coming in. She had called the police station looking for DI Nolan seven times. She tried again an eighth time.
"Well," she said, "Have you any idea when he will be available?"
The voice on the other end of the line was male and belligerent and now became suspicious. "Who is this?" he asked. When Susan told him, he turned aggressive. "What do you want him for?" he demanded, the emphasis on the "you", as if he recognised her name and held her responsible for something. Another real charmer, Susan thought. Where the fuck do they get them from?
"I'm ringing about the murder of the prostitute on Little Porter Street," she said. "I want to know if there's been any progress in identifying the body. DI Nolan said he was sorting out blood and maybe DNA tests."
"And?" the voice said.
Susan lost patience. "And what do you think?" she snapped. "Has there been a positive identification or not?"
"You need to talk to DI Jefferies," the man said. "He's in charge of that one."
Susan scribbled the name in her notebook. "Jefferies?" she asked. "Not Nolan?"
"Are you deaf?" the man said. "Or are you just stupid?"
"If I was stupid I'd have joined the police. What's your name?" Susan asked. But the man simply hung up the phone without answering. She put her own phone down and stared at the name on her pad. For the ninth time that morning, she

rang the station, this time asking to be put through to DI Jefferies.

"Jefferies here." Another man's voice, this time not aggressive, but harassed and preoccupied, a man with too much to do. Susan told Jefferies why she was calling and heard him shifting papers on his desk, searching for the right sheet amid so much else. Eventually he found what he was looking for and told her that, yes, a positive identification had been made, after tests had been carried out on a Belle Vale woman. The body found on Little Porter Street was that of Margaret Mary Girvan. He added her age and full address and told Susan that the funeral was due to be held later that day at Our Lady of the Assumption parish church.

"Bit quick, isn't it?" Susan asked.

"Not my decision," Jefferies told her, voice neutral, too busy to give it much thought.

"Whose then?" Susan asked. "DI Nolan's?"

"Look," said Jefferies. "I'm sorry, but I'm up to my eyes in things right now."

"How come you've taken over the case?" Susan asked. "Is Nolan on leave?"

"God knows where Nolan is," Jefferies told her. "All I know is that I came in this morning with five more jobs on my desk." He seemed to regret letting his emotions show. When he spoke again, his voice had regained its neutral note.

"Listen, Miss Clarke," he said. "I've got to go."

"Will you be at the funeral?" she asked. But he'd already put the phone down.

Susan swivelled her chair and stared unseeing out of the window to her left. Instead of the rooftops and roads, all she could see was the image that had drifted into her mind of Mrs Girvan sitting in her chair in the front room of her decaying little house, the walls wet with damp, what little food there was rotting slowly in the kitchen. Susan recalled how Mrs Girvan meandered in and out of lucidity, how she registered only superficially the presence of the two reporters and their questions. And yet Susan knew that the poor old woman reserved a part of her mind for her Margy, and how that part of her mind would always be sharp and aware and aching for the phone to ring and for Margy's voice to say hello. Susan hoped that Nolan had been tender with her, but doubted that had been the case. The needle would have dug like a knife into her thin arm, maybe again and again, searching for a vein from which to take the blood that would match Margy's own. Susan pictured Mrs Girvan clutching the mobile phone that Margy had given her, willing it to ring, sure that it would. Gingerly Susan touched her bruised face and instantly her body ached for a drink. A vodka and tonic, lots of vodka, lots of ice, a splash of tonic, a clean, searing drink that would spread cold and numbing through her whole body, erasing present and past and making the future easy to cope with. Think of something else, she told herself. Think of the story. And she pulled herself away from the idea as the thought of the mobile phone dragged Susan back to the conversation she'd just had with the new man, Jefferies. What had happened to Nolan, she wondered. How come he'd suddenly disappeared from the map? And what about Mrs Girvan's phone? She wished desperately that she'd taken it from Mrs Girvan's house, instead of simply noting down the numbers and keeping quiet about it.

Susan picked up her phone and dialled the three digits of Rachel's internal number. She hadn't seen her that morning, had perhaps been avoiding her, and wasn't sure if she was in. The call was answered almost straight away, although it was a moment or two before Rachel spoke, and then it was a cursory, "Yes?"

"It's me," she said.

"Susan," Rachel repeated, and then pulled herself together. "Susan, sorry. I'm miles away."

"What's up?" asked Susan.

"Oh, nothing, really," Rachel said. "Allen's stalking round the place asking if anyone's seen Gerry Dalton. Apparently he didn't pick him up last night and now hasn't shown up for work this morning. It's like he suspects us of something."

"He'll be sleeping it off," Susan said.

"How do you mean?" Rachel asked. "Who'll be sleeping what off?"

"Gerry," said Susan. "He was round at my flat last night. Well, this morning. Never seen him so drunk. Never seen anyone so drunk. He wasn't the only visitor either."

"Doesn't sound like Gerry," she said. "What do you mean, not the only visitor?"

Susan ignored the question, although she also desperately wanted to answer it. "The police have just confirmed the body's Margy," she said. "Funeral at 4.30 this afternoon. Fancy it?"

"Yes," Rachel told her. "You got hold of Nolan then?"

"That's the funny thing," Susan said. "A new man's in charge of the case. Someone called Jefferies. Nolan's not at the station."

"Couldn't be anything to do with what Billy Jackson told us, could it?" Rachel asked.

"Not sure how it could," said Susan. "But the timing's a bit strange, isn't it? I'm going to give Brian Nulty a call. See what he can tell us."

She rang off and called Nulty immediately but he, like Jefferies, was either unable or unwilling to talk. He did, however, tell Susan that he'd be going to Margy Girvan's funeral and might get the chance to speak to her then.

Susan tried to force all thoughts of Margy and her mother and the attack out of her mind, determined simply to get her head down and work. As well as the story regarding the identification of the murdered body to write, there was the usual pile of banal press releases to sort through, write up and then send on to the subs for them to reject or cut down depending on how much space there was in tomorrow's paper to fill. She was glad there was enough mindless material to keep her off the events of the night before until it was time to leave for Margy's funeral.

Chapter Thirty-one

The foul atmosphere at the paper that morning was still concentrated in and around Allen's office. He'd shut himself in there after finding no-one able to tell him where Gerry was, slamming the door and pulling down the blinds on the windows looking out over the editorial room. Intermittently he'd violently haul up the blinds and cast his glare around the room, looking for a victim to confront and bully. Anyone would do, no reason was too petty – Christmas tinsel around a work station, slovenly dress, talking too much when there was a paper to put out. Eventually, instead of making single raids before returning to his office, he came out and stalked through the entire floor, quizzing everyone about what they were doing, taking his dark cloud with him, until tension and doubt and worry had seeped into every corner. Finally, he reached Susan.

"Where is he?" he hissed at her. She turned round in her chair. Allen was breathing heavily and the slab of fat around his stomach pressed hard against his shirt, straining the buttons. The closeness of another man leaning over her so soon after the attack swept panic through her but she forced herself to stay calm. Allen ignored the bruising on her face.

"Hugh," Susan said. She breathed slowly and deeply. "Didn't hear you coming."

"Where is he?" Allen repeated.

"If you mean Gerry, I don't know," she told him. She didn't want a confrontation, didn't want to be drawn into a row with him. "I saw him late last night. He came round to my flat, dead drunk. But he didn't come in and I've not seen him since."

Allen leaned in close to her, sweat and aftershave filling the air around her desk. She tried to inch the chair away from him, but Allen just pressed closer. "You lying bitch," he said. "Fucking him again, were you? Bastard left me waiting like a twat last night, and now he's not shown up this morning. Still in your bed, is he?"

Susan stood up, holding her hands out in front of her, trying to placate Allen. "Hugh," she said, softly, trying to keep the fear out of her voice. "Calm down. I promise you, he didn't come in. I saw him for a few minutes only."

Allen changed tack suddenly. He pushed into her space and yanked at the computer screen, turning it so he could see what she was working on. It was the story about Margy's body being identified.

"What did I tell you?" he screamed. The entire office stopped, everyone risking quick glances to see Allen pushing his face against Susan's, almost touching her forehead with his. "What the fuck did I say to you yesterday? Won't you learn? Tell me."

Susan backed off as far as she could, but found herself pressing only against the window behind her. "Hugh, what's got into you?" she said. She felt her heart start to race. It seemed like panic was infecting her lungs and affecting her ability to breathe.

He was yelling and spittle from his mouth spattered Susan's face. "Drop this! Nobody gives a shit about this dead whore. Got that?" He stepped back, then grasped the back of Susan's chair and sent it spinning across the floor, slamming it into the wall a yard or so from where Susan was standing. He left her there, shaking, and strode back to his office, where he once more pulled down the blinds, cutting himself off from everything.

Rachel was the first over to Susan, who was recovering her breath and trying to stop herself shaking, fighting back the tears. Rachel said nothing but held Susan's hand, while Frank Hayes recovered her chair. It was Frank who spoke.

"Jesus, Sue," he said. "Did he not like your Christmas card or something?"

Susan felt for the arms of her chair and eased herself down.

Instinctively, she covered her face with her trembling hand and bowed her head.

Rachel knelt by the side of Susan's chair. "What was all that about?" she asked.

"God knows," Susan said. "Dalton, I think. Maybe. I don't know. I've never seen him like that before."

"Why don't you go home?" Frank suggested. "Allen's not going to say anything after that display. You could have the union onto him."

"No," Susan said. "I'll stay. I've got plenty to finish off here." She looked up at Frank. "Thanks," she told him.

"I take the hint," Frank said. "I'll leave you with Rachel here. You two go off to the ladies', eh? Everything gets sorted in there." He reached down and patted Susan's arm, making her flinch, then left them alone.

"Do you want to?" asked Rachel. Rachel gently reached up to Susan's hand and eased it from her face. She saw the bruising for the first time, the discoloration around her eyes, the impress of the attacker's hands over her mouth. "Sue, Christ…" she began. Susan nodded. She took her cigarettes and lighter from her handbag, then she and Rachel went to the ladies' toilets.

With the door closed behind them, Susan lit a cigarette, inhaling the smoke as deep into her lungs as she could. Then she began to sob.

Rachel let her cry. Eventually, Susan spoke. Her voice was thick with tears and mucus. She gave a dry laugh. "I've never been much for this, you know?" she said. Rachel looked puzzled. "An en masse visit to the loo, I mean."

"Oh," Rachel said, smiling. "A gang of women all huddled round the mirror, putting their lippy on and saying who fancies who. Me neither."

"Get you," Susan said. She sniffed. "'Lippy'. You are a Scouser, aren't you?" She turned and looked at her face in the mirror. It looked pale and lined. "I'm old," Susan said. She dabbed at her mascara before trying to repair the damage her tears had done.

"No you're not," Rachel told her. "You just look it, that's all."

Susan laughed, then stopped. "It's a strange day," she said. "You ever been to a funeral before?"

"This'll be my first," Rachel replied. "You?"

"A couple," Susan said. "My grandfather's. My mother's."

Rachel was quiet for a moment. "How do you think Mrs Girvan will be? Think she'll know what's going on?"

"Oh yes," Susan said. "I've a horrible feeling it's the only thing in her life that she'll know for sure."

Chapter Thirty-two

The funeral service wasn't due to start until 4.30 that afternoon, but Susan and Rachel arrived half an hour early. They wanted to see people turning up, and wondered if either Nolan or Billy Jackson might be there.

The Roman Catholic Church of Our Lady of the Assumption had been built in the 1960s, alongside the new communities it was meant to serve – Lee Park, Belle Vale and Netherley, just a few of the estates created to house the inner city poor swept out to the fringes of Liverpool by the post-war planning ideas. Like the houses surrounding it, it felt like a quick and cost-effective solution rather than a place of worship. It was squat and circular, with triangular shapes reaching out of it to make points at regular intervals round its circumference. It was supposed to suggest a crown, but the best it managed was a shoddy, tawdry one.

Susan and Rachel parked in the car park. Theirs was the only car there. Despite the cold, they waited outside next to the car rather than going into the church. Night was beginning to thicken and the sky above them was a slab of heavy concrete grey. Susan lit a cigarette. Rachel gave her a strange look.

"What?" asked Susan.

"The cigarette," Rachel said. "I don't know. Is it okay to smoke at a funeral?"

"It is if it's a cremation," Susan replied. She walked across the car park. Rachel followed.

"We did a story on this place, you know?" Susan said. "A couple of months or so ago. A robbery."

"It was the parish club wasn't it?" said Rachel. "The attackers waited outside until the staff started to come out," Rachel said. "Then they jumped them and tried to drag them back in. A shot was fired."

Susan nodded towards the pane in the door. "And there's the bullet hole," she said.

They both turned at the same time at the sound of a car pulling into the car park. Its headlights swept the cracked concrete as it turned and then stopped close to the steps leading up to the entrance of the church. Susan and Rachel watched as a teenage girl got out of the front passenger seat, while a woman got out of the driver's side. The girl was in school uniform, a blue plaid skirt and blue blazer. The woman was in black trousers and jacket.

"That'll be the girl and her Mum who live next door to Mrs Girvan," Susan said.

"Kirsty," Rachel said. "I don't know what the mother's name is." They watched Kirsty open the rear door of the car. Eventually, Mrs Girvan edged out. She was as spare and thin as before, but now she looked shrivelled, her cheap coat swamping her crumbling frame. Susan and Rachel walked over to them. Kirsty's mother recognised them and smiled.

"How is she?" asked Rachel. She was looking in concern at Mrs Girvan.

"I don't know," the woman replied. "Kirsty's been great with her, going in nearly every night, haven't you love? But she never says much, does she? She doesn't know what's going on if you ask me."

The cold air seemed to be cracking the skin drawn across Mrs Girvan's face.

"We'd better get her inside," Susan said. Kirsty drew Mrs Girvan towards the steps. Mrs Girvan followed Kirsty's lead, her shoes dragging on the concrete. She seemed unable to do more than inch her way over. Rachel, Susan and Kirsty's mother followed. Eventually they entered the church. Kirsty kept hold of Mrs Girvan with her left hand, so she could momentarily dip the fingers of her right into the stoop of holy water in the porch. Mrs Girvan watched Kirsty bless herself. The gesture triggered some sort of recognition and she dipped her crooked fingers into the holy water. She slowly raised her hand to her forehead, dabbing the water against the dry skin.

Then the gesture deserted her, and she let her arm fall useless to her side. Kirsty took it again and guided Mrs Girvan towards the door into the church proper. Kirsty's mother hung back with Rachel and Susan.

"This isn't our church," she said. "We go to St Mary's in Woolton Village. This is nearer, but…" She could finish the explanation. "I'll go and help Kirsty."

"Where's the priest?" Susan asked.

"I don't know," Mrs Hogan said. "I don't know anything about the arrangements. Just that the service was today. A police officer called round to tell us, after he'd finished at Mrs Girvan's house. Late yesterday it was." She left Susan and Rachel in the porch.

"They've really rushed this, haven't they?" Rachel said.
Susan nodded. "Nolan has, anyway."

The porch was large, with pews laid out for latecomers to sit. It was separated from the body of the church by a large sheet of glass. Susan walked over and looked through it into the church. The few lights that were on distorted her view, but she was able to see through her own reflection that Kirsty had guided Mrs Girvan to the front pew, right in front of the altar. To their left and right the rest of the long benches curved with the structure of the church, rippling out from the altar like waves from a stone thrown into a still pond. The pews didn't completely encircle the altar, though. To the right was a grey brick wall, with a door to the sacristy and tired posters advertising God's goodness. On the left was a recess, in which Susan could just about make out a nativity scene, plastic shepherds and wise men and Mary and Joseph figures round a plastic Jesus. In front of the altar, between it and the front pew, Margy Girvan's coffin rested on two trestle stands. It had been delivered early, but there was no sign of by whom. There had been no hearse in the car park when Susan and Rachel had arrived

Susan looked at her watch. Only ten minutes to go before the.

service was due to start and no sign of life on the altar. She had been to a few services a long time back and remembered bustle around the altar, people lighting candles and arranging the missal just so for the priest. She heard the door of the church open behind her. She and Rachel turned to see Brian Nulty coming in. Like Rachel and Susan, he ignored the stoop of holy water. He nodded a hello as he made his way towards them. When he saw Susan's face, Brian began to speak, but a shake of Susan's head told him not to.

Susan inclined her head towards the font. "I think we might end up outnumbering them," she said.

"Who d'you mean?" Brian asked.

"The Catholics," Susan said.

"Oh, right," Brian replied. He seemed to feel uncomfortable and awkward.

"What's up Brian?" Rachel said. She spoke at her normal volume, then heard how loud her voice sounded and dropped it to something near a whisper, feeling the crushing effect of a silent church on her usual behaviour. "Susan was only joking. You know that."

"Oh, yeah," Brian said. "I know tha'. It's just, well, I'm surprised to see you here, that's all. In the circumstances, like. You especially, Susan."

"Circumstances?" Susan repeated. "What do you mean? We just came to pay our respects to Margy."

"I meant...I meant what with Gerry Dalton," said Brian. "I just didn't expect to see you. That's all."

"What are you talking about?" Rachel asked. "What about Gerry Dalton? What's happened?"

"He's dead," Brian said. "Didn't you know?"

Susan felt behind her for the pew. She suddenly felt weak and clammy and cold. She sat down heavily, her head swimming with an instant lightness. She clamped her knees together, head bent forward, like she'd adopted the crash position for an emergency landing. Rachel took the pew in front of her and Brian the one behind.

"I'm so sorry, Sue," Brian said softly. "I just assumed you both knew. He was found sometime around lunch time today."

"I saw him last night," Susan said. "He wanted to come in but I wouldn't let him. I watched him get into his car. Into the back though. I'd never have let him drive, not with the amount he'd drunk." She looked up pleadingly at Brian first and then Rachel, seemingly desperate for their understanding.

"How did he die?" Rachel asked. "Was it driving?"

Brian shook his head. "Suicide," he said, still softly. "He chained 'imself to one of those figures on Crosby beach – you know, the cast-iron men? – then just waited for the tide to come in." He instinctively knew that Susan was still looking to blame herself. "'e'd planned it, Sue. Left letters for his wife and girls, strict instructions for the solicitor. Didn't tell 'im what 'e was planning. Just said go round the house this afternoon and then open the letters."

"Did he leave a note?" asked Rachel. "Does anyone know why he did it?"

"Not so far as I know," Brian said. "I asked around when I 'eard the name." He hesitated. "You know, because…As far as I can gather, a note was the only thing he didn't leave."

"No wonder Allen was in such a filthy mood this morning then," Rachel said. "He must have known."

Brian looked up. "'e couldn't 'ave," he said. "The body wasn't found until 1-ish."

"He'll just have been pissed off that Gerry wasn't there to chauffeur him around last night," Susan said. Her voice sounded mechanical, toneless. She touched her face. There were no tears.

The priest entered the church from the sacristy. He was alone. This was to be a service cut to the bone. No altar boys, no choirs. At the same time as the priest arrived on the altar, the church door opened. Brian, Susan and Rachel looked over to see Billy Jackson enter, preceded by one prison officer and followed by another. He was handcuffed to the one ahead of him. He face was set like stone, but it was clear to the three watching him that he'd been crying. He ignored them, didn't even see them, and allowed himself to be led into the church. The warders with him didn't care about the noise they made. It was obvious a trip to Liverpool had been the last thing on their minds when they'd arrived at work that morning.

Brian stood up and touched Susan lightly on the shoulder. "Come on," he said. He went into the church and Susan and Rachel followed, taking their seat on the last bench on the far left of the church, close to the plastic baby Jesus in his tatty crib.

The priest was circling the coffin, swinging the censer in long arcs over the closed lid. As it swung, the links of the censer chinked together, the tinny sound soon dying in the still and near-empty church. As far back as she was, the scent of the incense hit Susan's nostrils, sweet and smoky, rushing her back to the times she had been to church before, following in the wake of the O'Hares.

Father Ndlovu's words echoed off the unplastered brick. He was tired and lonely, far from his Lagos home. He had reluctantly agreed to do the service at the last minute, something to do with his desire to cooperate with the police, but he was busy with preparations for Christmas, too busy really to give any time to this meagre service. His heavy Nigerian accent slowed the pace, but he wanted it over with. The only thing the priest knew was that in the coffin was the body of a prostitute, murdered a couple of weeks ago but only identified in the past couple of days. The mother was the only relative. Father Ndlovu made a mental note to try to visit her again soon. No time before Christmas, but he knew that wouldn't matter much. If she was aware enough to feel any grief at the death of her daughter, at the vicious switch in the natural order of life and death, there would be no better or worse time to visit. He forced himself to concentrate on the words of the service, to give the words the meaning he was sure they held.

Susan didn't notice the speed of the service. She was vaguely aware of Rachel next to her, preoccupied by Brian Nulty's news but nevertheless turning round to stare at Billy Jackson. Susan herself was occupied by her own thoughts. She was calmly examining her reaction to news of Gerry's death. Maybe it was shock, but the initial response, staggering back onto the pew behind her in the porch, had given way to a sort of numbness. But that wasn't quite it. She wasn't holding any feelings at bay. She simply wasn't feeling anything more than surprise and sadness at the death of a colleague. Brian's particular concern for her had been wasted. She knew that once she'd had a little time to assimilate the news, she would simply get on with her life. There'd be no gaping hole. And yet this was a man she had taken to her bed more than once, albeit some years ago. This was a man she had held and pulled inside her and moved beneath in some approximation of pleasure. She wondered what that said about her, but couldn't think of an answer.

The service finished in a rush of activity. Four men in black suits and white shirts, two without ties, simply moved quickly up to the front of the church, picked up the coffin and took it out through the porch and into the car park, like furniture removers keen to get the van loaded. It was only as they made their way into the porch that Mrs Girvan seemed to recognise something of what was happening, like she'd slowly been fitting together pieces of a jigsaw puzzle in her mind. At first, she turned and tentatively called out, "Margy?" calling the name with a question, as if she'd heard the back door of her house open and close and was checking it was her little girl coming in from school. Then fear took her throat and the cry became one of anguish and pain. "Margy!" This was a yell torn from her body. She struggled to her feet and knocked a missal that slammed against the cold tiles of the church floor. She shuffled awkwardly to the end of her pew, but couldn't move quickly enough to stop the coffin. She cried her dead daughter's name once more, and everyone in the church who heard the single screeched word knew at once that Mrs Girvan suddenly understood everything that had been going on. Susan had been right. Mrs Girvan would never grasp anything fully again, but the fact of her daughter's death would remain with her clear and crystal and cold.

Everyone in the church was taken by surprise at the speed at which the coffin had been removed, then transfixed by Mrs Girvan's reaction. Father Ndlovu had made to follow it, then given up, bemused. He stood now, just outside the rail which encircled the altar, at which people came and knelt to receive communion. Brian went to speak to him, while Rachel made to follow Billy and try to catch a few words with him. He too was being rushed out, by the warders accompanying him. They wanted to be in the van and back on the motorway as soon as possible. Susan hesitated, not knowing whether to go with Nulty or Rachel, and so was rooted to the spot by her uncertainty.

Eventually, she went outside, following Rachel. On the road beyond the wall of the car park she saw the hearse leaving with Margy's body. It drove past a black van, next to which, on the pavement, Susan made out five figures. She could see Rachel, and Billy, flanked by the two prison wardens. Billy was shouting, yelling at Rachel, trying to break free of the wardens' grip to get at her. As Susan drew closer, she tried to make out the fifth figure, but couldn't. It was a man, she was sure of that at least.

Susan called Rachel's name, at which the man behind the others lifted his head, exposing his face to the weak light of the street lamp across the road from them. Something about Susan seemed to put him on guard. He reached for Billy, pulling him away from the prison officers and back towards him. He put his face close to Billy's then just as quickly turned away from the group, breaking into a trot then jumping into his car and speeding away. He'd left the engine running, obviously not intending to stick around for very long.

If the man who'd just left the scene had said anything to Billy, he didn't seem to have heard. He was yelling at Rachel still. "You bitch!" he shouted. "You fucking bitch! You must have known! You couldn't tell me, could you? You had to keep it from me." He saw Susan. "You and her too," he said. "You and her and fucking Sweeney and Nolan!" He was overtaken by his own sobs.

Susan instantly sharpened on hearing Billy's words. She ignored his accusations. She wasn't going to waste time reasoning with him. "Did you say Nolan?" she demanded. Billy in turn ignored her. "Billy," Susan went on. "Did you just say Nolan? Was that DI Nolan? Billy!"

Finally Billy took notice of Susan's questions. She was close to him now, her face leaning in to his. He had stopped struggling, and the wardens had eased their grip on him slightly. Billy looked Susan in the eye, then spat in her face. "Fuck you!" he hissed. The prison officers dragged him away, stuffing him into the back of the van.

Rachel and Susan watched the van leave. Susan took Rachel's offer of a tissue and wiped the spit off her forehead and nose and cheeks. "That must have been Nolan," she said quietly. She seemed unaffected by Jackson spitting at her, her mind trying to put some order into the events of the day.

Slowly, the two women walked back to the church, just as Brian Nulty was coming out.

"What's going on Brian?" Susan asked loudly. "What's happening here?"

Brian didn't answer straight away. He looked at Susan sadly as he walked towards her and Rachel.

"Stop yelling at me Susan," he said quietly.

"What's all the rush about, Brian?" Susan asked. "Where're they taking the body at this time of night? And what was Nolan doing here?"

At this last question, Brian immediately changed demeanour, his face becoming interested and watchful, aware of one wrong thing too many in a whole catalogue of things that sat uneasily with him.

"Nolan?" he said. "You sure?"

Susan wasn't, but didn't let on. "Just a minute or two ago," she said. "Talking to Billy Jackson."

"Why the interest in DI Nolan, Brian?" Rachel asked quietly. Her voice was flat and still, in contrast to Susan's. She felt shaken up inside, Billy's words just the latest in a series of blows she'd taken, fast reminders from Sweeney and Allen and now Jackson that the shield she'd put up between her working self and her real self was crumbling bit by bit, but she certainly wasn't going to walk away from the job.

"Something's going on," he replied. "I don't know wha', but it is." He turned and gestured with a sweep of his arm which took in the church, the three women struggling into the car, and Father Ndlovu, standing bemused and uncertain at the top of the steps. "This wasn't right," he continued. "Not morally and certainly not in terms of procedure. The body's being taken to the crematorium. Father Ndlovu told me. A police officer whose name he didn't catch sorted it all out, badgered him into that bloody awful service. It's all 'appened too fast. Not even a post-mortem."

"And Nolan?" Rachel asked again. "Why the sudden change when you heard his name?"

Again, Brian paused before answering. "Nolan went on sick leave this morning. Long term, or so the rumour 'as it. Suddenly 'e's off. Can't take it any more. Talk is that Crowley's pushing him for early retirement on full pay. 'e'll get it too, with Crowley behind him. Those two go back a long way, pretty much arrived together." He smiled without humour. "Thick as thieves," he added.

"So what's happening?" Susan asked. "What do you think's going on, Brian?"

"I honestly don't know," he replied.

"Do you think Nolan had something to do with Margy's death?" Rachel asked.

Brian looked shocked. "No!" he said definitely. "God, no. 'e's a lot of things, but not a murderer. And he's never done a thing off his own bat in his life either."

"Brian," Susan said. "Rachel and I have been speaking to Billy Jackson. At Strangeways. It's Rachel's story really." She looked at the younger woman, who nodded to her to go on. "Billy Jackson was arrested by Nolan in Keighley, before Nolan came over here. Jackson said Nolan got him to admit to a number of offences he'd not committed, to falsify the clean-up rate. Billy agreed to it so he'd get an easier time of it inside, get to see Margy."

Brian nodded sadly. "Been talk of tha'."

"So this long-term leave is too neat," said Rachel. "Going now, just as Billy Jackson starts talking. It's not coincidence."

Brian tried to take it in. "But 'e couldn't have sorted it all by 'imself," he said.

"Crowley could have helped him. Thick as thieves, you said. And Billy mentioned Crowley too," Rachel said.

"Maybe, but if 'e was involved with Jackson," Brian replied, "We won't find out. Crowley's too clever."

"But you wouldn't be surprised?" Susan asked. Brian shook his head.

All three of them suddenly felt tired. "Look," said Brian. "Call me tomorrow. We can meet up, maybe, 'ave a look through the notes you made when you talked to Billy." He went to his car and drove away, heading to Margy's mother and a sleepless night with a woman whose sole reason to live had been bludgeoned to death.

"Don't worry," Susan said to Rachel. "Not all funerals are like this."

Rachel laughed briefly. Then she smiled tenderly. She nodded at Susan's face. "Are you going to tell me what happened?"

"Yes," Susan said. "But not here."

"A drink then?" Rachel asked.

"Stupid question. Somewhere nice and normal," Susan replied.

"We'll drop the car off at my place," Rachel said, "then walk up the road to The Neighbourhood."

They didn't notice the parish priest still standing at the top of the steps to his cheap church. With the car park empty, Father Ndlovu turned and went back inside. There were still four more days to Christmas, and too much still to do.

Chapter Thirty-three

The Neighbourhood was crowded, but they found a table, and one that suited their mood and purpose, at the back, in the corner, under but behind a speaker which crooned out Christmas songs from Sinatra and Crosby and Peggy Lee, the music directed away from Susan and Rachel and into the centre of the room. They were in complete contrast to the other customers. Susan and Rachel were silent, pale and tired, while crowded round the other tables were mixed groups of chattering 30-somethings, all possessed of good incomes, good looks, happy children and nice houses in a desirable catchment area.
Susan had wanted a vodka and tonic followed by another vodka and tonic, but agreed to share a bottle of red from the specials board, so long as that was quickly followed by another one. This wasn't the evening for moderation. Neither of them had been keen to eat, but their waitress was insistent, so they'd asked for a basket of pitta bread and a selection of dips. In the event, when it arrived, they wolfed the food down and ordered the same again, suddenly realising how hungry they actually were. It was the same with the wine. The first glasses went down quickly and easily and were soon refilled. Only then, when the food and alcohol had worked their way into their systems, did Susan and Rachel feel like they could talk.
"How do you feel?" Rachel asked. Susan raised her eyebrows. Rachel would have to be more specific. "I mean about Gerry Dalton," she clarified.
Susan played with a piece of pitta bread. "Sorry he's dead, sorry it was suicide. Sorry to have lost a colleague, sorry for his family. But that's it. Maybe I should feel more."
Rachel shrugged. "I don't know," she said. "I'm not being judgemental."

Susan leaned forward, toward Rachel. "I tell you what else, though." There was an urgency in her voice. She went on. "I want to know why. It's not just Brian who feels something's not right."

"I know what you mean," Rachel said. "I feel the same. And I tell you who else feels something's wrong."

Susan spoke in the pause Rachel left for her. "Allen?" she said.

"Exactly," replied Rachel. "He can't have been in such a foul mood simply because Gerry left him to make his own way home last night. But if he knew Gerry was dead, how did he find out so soon? The police didn't know about it until after lunch."

"Maybe he didn't know," Susan said. "Maybe they'd just had words the night before."

"And I'd like to know more about this Nolan business," Rachel said. "Funny coincidence, isn't it? He takes early retirement on health grounds the day after Billy Jackson tells us what he did." She paused. "If you're not going to tell me of your own accord, I need to ask. What happened to your face?"

Susan told her. She kept her voice calm and level, but felt if she looked at Rachel while she spoke then she would start crying. When she finished, Rachel asked, "Who did it, do you reckon? Sweeney?"

Susan nodded. "If not him in person then one of his boys."

"But why you?" asked Rachel. "Mistaken identity?"

"I don't think it matters to him," said Susan. "Sweeney knows we're working together, so which of us he gets is immaterial. He just wants Crowley, and this is his way of getting it done. The notes, the texts, the car following us. Now this."

"What next?" asked Rachel.

Susan shrugged. "Whatever we do, we have to do it quickly. Sweeney's not going to give us Christmas off."

"We need to blitz it," said Rachel. "Both stories.

Everything's too tangled to let us just focus on the one."
Susan nodded, then she drained her glass and filled it.
"You're right. I can't think straight as it is. We need to talk to Billy again," she said. "And Allen too, maybe. Certainly we need to find out exactly what's happened with Nolan."
"And Gerry's wife," said Rachel, then corrected herself. "Widow, I mean. We need to have a talk with Gerry's widow. Find out if he left a note."
Rachel and Susan let the words hang there, frightened of the possible implications. They needed to calm down and tried for a while to talk about other things – plans for Christmas, how good the wine tasted, the dress a woman a couple of tables away was wearing – but it was no use. Either they could sit in silence or talk about the stories they were working on, and the directions their thoughts were taking them. It was Susan who asked the question they'd been trying to avoid answering.
"The Jackson business seems clear enough," she said. "We just need proof. But the other thing. What do you reckon?"
Rachel knew exactly what she was asking. "Really?" she replied reluctantly. Susan nodded. Rachel breathed in deeply. "Gerry," she said. "Gerry Dalton murdered Margy Girvan."
"Looks like it, doesn't it?" Susan said. "He was at the party at the Warwick, no distance at all from where she was killed."
"He was in his car," Rachel continued. "No need for a taxi to take him there. He wasn't drinking, so he could just drive himself, be back at the Warwick easily in time to pick up Allen. And, let's face it, nobody was going to miss Gerry, were they? Not until they needed a lift home. He wouldn't even need to sneak out."
"Yes. But," Susan said, "why did he kill her? You're right, he wouldn't have been drunk. He'd have been in control."
"But it wasn't a frenzied attack, Sue." Rachel leaned forward and put her hand on Susan's. Susan smiled at the gesture.
"Look," Susan said, moving her hand and picking up her

glass. "There's no need to pussyfoot around about this. Not for my sake. I'm not trying to defend him for any other reason than to work out what happened and why he did it."

"I know," said Rachel. "Sorry. So why would he have done it? Does…Did Gerry seem the type to kill? He didn't even seem the type to sleep with prostitutes."

"I don't think many men do seem the type to sleep with prostitutes, to be honest," Susan said. "But they do, all the same."

"Okay," said Rachel. "Let's forget about the why. We'll probably never know anyway, even if he did leave a note. What about the sequence of events? The phone calls from the Warwick to Margy's old phone."

"Right," said Susan. She shifted the empty pitta bread basket from between them, thean cast her eye around the room. "Can you smoke in here?" she asked. "It seems the type of place that's banned it."

She lit her cigarette anyway and took a long drag. "It's nearly midnight at the Warwick," she went on. "Gerry's been sitting there, stone cold sober, sipping at a Coke, pretending to laugh at Allen's jokes. Or maybe just wandering around, drifting out to reception, tired of being ignored. He fancies a shag."

"This doesn't sound right," Rachel interrupted. "It doesn't sound like Gerry. Fancying a shag!"

"Okay, so whatever was going through his mind, however you'd like to put it," Susan said. "He rings Margy."

"He would have been in the main room," Rachel said. "He first phoned on his mobile, remember? Let's say it was too noisy, so he went out into reception to use the phone there. There's no reply from Margy, because it's not her phone any more. Mrs Girvan's got it, and the batteries are dead."

"He must have been a regular with Margy, you know?" Susan said. "He doesn't just pluck her number out of thin air. He's got it in his phone."

"She didn't have his number, though, did she?" said Rachel.

"How do you mean?" Susan asked.

Rachel leaned in again, ignoring the cigarette smoke. "When we looked at Margy's phone, it just gave the number. The number wasn't listed under a name. You know, like I've got yours in my phone as Susan. If you call me, that's what's displayed on my phone. Susan, your name, not your number."

"But there's no reason why she should, is there?" Susan replied. "She's not going to call him, is she? It's the punters who need the number of the prostitute. Not the other way round."

"Okay, okay," Rachel conceded. "You're right. Go on."

"When he rings the second time, and finds the phone dead," Susan said, "he realises he's calling the old number. So, he rings the new one instead, and meets up with Margy."

"She didn't have the phone for long," said Rachel. "He must have seen her quite soon before the night she died, so she could pass on the new number. Billy didn't have it, remember?"

"Well, anyway. That's what must have happened." Susan drank some more wine and topped up both their glasses. "We need to find Gerry Dalton's phone."

"Where does Nolan fit into all this?" Rachel asked.

"Why should he?" Susan replied. "It's just coincidence, isn't it? Nolan being involved with Margy's boyfriend."

"So why should he put so much effort into rushing Margy's funeral, having her cremated?" Rachel asked.

Susan thought for a while. "He only rushed it once the body was identified," she said. "Maybe he thought it would tip Billy over the edge, make him say something about the false records?"

"But what difference would it make to anything if the body was cremated or in the ground or in the morgue?" Rachel said. "Once she's dead, and Billy knows about it, that's what'll tip him over the edge. And how did Billy even hear about the death?"

"I don't know," Susan admitted. The memories and the pain from the night before were still with her. Both bottles in front of her were empty. She couldn't suggest another to Rachel. She could wait, though. She had plenty to drink back at the flat. It was the only thing that would get her back there. She said again, "I don't know." She thought for a while. "I've got the guest list for the Warwick party back at home. I can't remember Nolan's name being on it, but I'll check."

"Are you saying he and Dalton were mixed up together in it all?" asked Rachel.

"We're just playing with ideas here, Rachel," said Susan. "We need to talk to all those people we mentioned before to try and get some facts. And we need to have a look for Gerry's phone too."

They left the bar and caught a taxi. The driver dropped Rachel at her house before making the journey to Hope Street. Susan looked up and down the road as she got out of the cab, but she didn't know what she was looking for and saw nothing unusual. She asked the driver to wait until she got inside. Once there, Susan climbed the stairs to her flat slowly and tentatively, punching each landing light switch as she reached it, sometimes just too late, leaving her panicky as she groped around in the dark. It was still early, only just after half past nine, and she was too drained to sleep. In her kitchen, Susan took a bottle of vodka out of the fridge. She unscrewed the top slowly, then let it drop on the work surface with a soft clatter. She poured herself a drink and took it into the bathroom, where she began to run a bath. Then she poured the drink away, down the basin. She sat on the toilet seat and cried, softly, soundlessly. It was as if the tears belonged to someone else. She felt no sadness inside, only a resigned acceptance of the way her life was. Empty, apart now from the ache of fear that the attack had brought on.

They weren't tears for Gerry Dalton, although she thought of him. She was crying because Gerry Dalton was the last man who'd held her, and now she was alone and scared. It didn't even matter to Susan at this moment that theirs had been sham intimacy. All she could think of was the arms around her, and the fact that that was over 5 years ago now. At first, after the separation from Peter, she had still had offers, but she'd turned them down, knowing that the married men who made the offers saw her as easy pickings. Soon, though, the offers dried up. "The truth is," she said aloud, "no-one is interested." The words clicked off the tiles of the bathroom. Still crying, Susan stood up, avoided the mirror, and went to the living room. She selected a CD from the rack, *Mahler's 5th Symphony*. She turned the volume up high and returned to her bath. The water was too hot, but she forced herself in, and lay there listening to the music coming in from the other room, the clear trumpet heralding the start of the symphony's journey from darkness to light.

She stayed in the bath until the music finished, then got out, dried herself and went to bed, where she lay awake for an hour, listening to the happy Christmas shouts of people down on the street outside, coming in through the open window along with the chill night air.

Thirty-four

Thursday 20 December
LIVERPOOL MORNING MAIL
MURDERED PROSTITUTE NAMED
After extensive enquiries, Police have finally identified the body of the woman murdered at the Northern Warehouse earlier this month.
The body is that of Margaret Mary Girvan, of Belle Vale. Police discovered the name after blood tests conducted on the woman's mother. They confirmed that Margaret Girvan was a prostitute who worked mainly in two of Liverpool's massage parlours. Her funeral was held yesterday at Our Lady of the Assumption RC Church in Belle Vale.
Police said that they are no nearer finding a motive for the murder, in which Miss Girvan was beaten and then set alight.
However, in a further development, the officer in charge of the case, DI Nolan, has gone on immediate and long-term sick leave, to be replaced by DI Jefferies. DI Jefferies was unable to say when he hoped to conclude his investigation.
By Susan Clarke. Story spiked.

Rachel came into the office slightly later than usual. She slipped in and joined the back of the group of reporters and secretaries and managers that Allen had gathered together just outside his office. She looked around the faces until she saw Susan. They nodded to each other, then turned to listen to what the editor was saying.

All the staff that had gathered at Allen's behest knew he was going to talk to them about Gerry Dalton. Some were in combative mood, angry that they were only being told now, when the story was already a day old. Allen himself, without a by-line, had written the piece about the death that had gone in that morning's paper, a brief column, containing no more than the perfunctory facts, hidden away on the inside pages. Susan had seen it and been struck by the similarity with the way Margy Girvan's death had been reported. Then again, she'd thought, the statues were an important part of Liverpool's status as Capital of Culture, and Allen had been on the committee set up to raise the money to keep them on Crosby beach, rather than have them transported to New York, as had been the original plan.

"Gerry Dalton was found dead on Crosby beach yesterday," Allen began. "It looks like he killed himself. The funeral's on Saturday morning, at 11.30, at All Hallows Church in Allerton. Anyone can go, unless you're down to work then. I won't be reducing the staff to a skeleton and the rotas remain unchanged. No swapping simply to go." He turned to go back into his office, but was called back assorted shouts of disapproval.

"Why can't we all go?" someone had asked. Allen had made himself unapproachable in the time he'd been editor, but people's feelings were so strong they were overcoming their timidity.

"Why didn't we have it on the front page?" another demanded. Allen paused to cast his stare across the faces in front of him. "First," he said, "We can't all go because we have a paper to run. Nothing stops that. Second, it wasn't newsworthy enough. It was the suicide of a local man, nothing more. To put it on the front page would have been self-indulgent."

"He was one of us." It was Gerry's secretary, Monica, who'd said the words. "We could have been self-indulgent." She began to weep.

"Save your tears for Saturday," Allen said. Again, he turned to go.

"What did his note say?" This was Rachel's question, which she asked having summoned all her nerve. Susan took a sharp intake of breath when she heard it. She found herself admiring Rachel's courage, especially after Allen had torn into her just the other day. She also appreciated the cleverness of the question: not 'Did he leave a note?' but 'What did the note say?' She saw Allen was rattled. His look of stern contempt for both Dalton and the staff left him briefly, momentarily replaced by doubt, consternation. He recovered himself quickly, but his voice still showed uncertainty when he answered Rachel.

"No note," he said. Then he coughed and cleared his throat. "There wasn't a note."

"How do you know?" Rachel hadn't gained any more courage, but still she pursued the question.

Allen had recovered his tone of contempt. "Dalton's widow told me. Don't question me."

Allen glared at Rachel, even as Monica screamed at him, "Call him Gerry! Don't call him Dalton! He did everything for you!" She ran at Allen and began to slap at his face and chest. Still staring at Rachel, Allen pushed the woman away.

"Somebody take her home," he ordered, and went back into his office, closing the door and drawing the blinds so no-one could see in.

The staff group maintained its shape for a few seconds, horseshoed around the editor's door, then seemed to make a collective decision to break into its individual parts and disperse. Some of the women regrouped around Monica, stroking at her and making soothing noises before leading her away. Rachel stayed fixed to the spot. Frank Hayes stopped on the way back to his desk and placed a hand on her shoulder. "Well, Gunga Din," he said. "You're a better man than I am." Rachel only managed a brief smile once he'd moved away. Then the space in front of her was filled by Susan.

"Hell of a question, Rachel," Susan said. "Where did that come from?"

"I don't know." Her reply seemed to come from far away

. She forced her focus to Susan. "I really don't know," she repeated, this time more in her normal voice.

"Well," said Susan. "It certainly got him rattled."

"It did, didn't it?" Rachel said. "He didn't seem bothered by anything else, though, did he? It was like he hated Gerry, and was only making the announcement for form's sake." The two women moved away at last, heading for Susan's corner desk. "Why do you think that was?" Rachel asked.

"I'll tell you why." Unnoticed by either woman, Bassett had caught up with the pair and listened in on their conversation. "No-one asked you, Trevor," said Susan. "Just leave us alone, eh?"

Bassett ignored her. "It was because Dalton was weak. The boss despised him for it. All the lifts he gave him, all the 'yes sir' answers, the lack of ideas. Hugh just used him, but couldn't stand him."

"Hugh, is it?" said Susan. "Since when have you and Allen been on first name terms?" Bassett blushed. "Fancy Gerry's job, do you? I'll get you a chauffeur's cap for Christmas. You'll look great."

They left Bassett standing trying to think of a reply, and continued back to Susan's corner. Rachel pulled over an empty chair. "What's the plan for today?" she asked.

"I'm going to try and find out what's happened with Nolan," Susan replied. "We need to get a few things sorted. Try and get some definites. For all our theories, we're short of facts."

"Do you think we got a bit carried away last night?" said Rachel. "About Gerry?"

Susan leaned in closer. "To be honest," she said, "I just don't know." She picked up a pen and started doodling in her open notebook. "So many things make perfect sense after a bottle of wine."

"And we had two," said Rachel. "We could have sorted out the Arab-Israeli conflict."

"And still had time for Northern Ireland," added Susan.

"Seriously, though," she went on, "it still sort of makes sense now, but…"

"But we've got to back it up with facts." Rachel finished the sentence for Susan, then added, "And fast."

Susan had stopped doodling and began writing names instead. She wrote them and then went over them again, pressing the pen down onto the paper: Allen, Nolan, Billy Jackson, Maureen Dalton. Rachel looked down at the list Susan had written.

"I'll talk to Allen, try and find out what happened the night Gerry killed himself," Rachel said.

Susan looked surprised. "You sure?" she asked.

Rachel nodded. "Positive. I'll play the little girl with him, apologise for upsetting him. He says I do it, so why not? I might even cry a little."

"What about Billy?" Susan asked. "Are you going to arrange another visit? We need to get more details about this arrangement he came to with Nolan over in Keighley."

"I'll call Franny Sweeney," Rachel said. "He seems the man to speak to if you want to get into Strangeways in a hurry."

Susan whistled. "Sweeney and Allen," she said, admiringly. "You're getting a taste for this lark, aren't you?"

Rachel smiled. "Yes," she said. "We've got to meet them head-on."

"I've already started," Susan said, touching her face.

Chapter Thirty-five

Back at her desk, Rachel called Sweeney and left a message saying she wanted more visiting orders. There was no nervousness, no subservience in her voice. She knew Sweeney wanted Crowley, and she felt the pressure he was exerting, but she was doing this for herself, not for him. Without giving herself time to think, Rachel stood up and marched to Allen's door.

"You've just missed him," someone called from a desk close by. Rachel turned and saw it was Jake Burgin who'd shouted to her.

"Thanks," she replied. She walked quickly out of the office, grabbing her coat on the way. She didn't want to be hanging around waiting for Sweeney to call back and Allen to return. Now that she'd summoned up the courage to talk to him, she wanted to get it over with. She hoped that, wherever he was going, it was by car. Reaching the lift, she got in and pressed the button for the basement car park.

The lift doors opened onto the concrete space, crowded with cars, strip lights burning and flickering overhead. Rachel had no idea what car Allen drove or where he normally parked. Then she remembered: he never normally parked anywhere. That was Dalton's job. She stepped out of the lift, anxiously looking around her. From over her left shoulder she heard the noise of gears being mangled, and a car stop-starting to get out of a tight space. When she turned and looked, she saw a dark blue Mercedes half-in, half-out of its bay, and, at the wheel, Allen sweating and struggling. She walked over and stood next to the car, awkwardly waiting until Allen noticed her. She watched him fumbling to locate the button to wind the window down. He did and pushed his red face out at her.

"What the fuck do you want, princess?" he asked. "Got more insolent questions for me, have you? You'll be lucky to still be in a job by Christmas if you have." He pulled furiously at the wheel and the Mercedes lurched backwards. He'd forgotten he was still in reverse. Angry now, Allen got out of the car, banging the door against the side of the Citroen next to him. "Fuck!" he said, and slammed his door shut.

His shirt was clinging to his chest and stomach with sweat. How could he have got like this so quickly? Rachel wondered. He stepped towards her, and Rachel suddenly felt vulnerable, suddenly felt aware of the fact that she was alone in a basement car park with an angry, aggressive man she'd only recently annoyed upstairs. Involuntarily, she took a step backwards.

"Well?" Allen demanded. He half-smiled, half-sneered. Rachel held herself straight. "I've come to apologise," she said. "To say I'm sorry for the way I spoke to you upstairs. You know," she added, "when I asked you what the note said."

"What made you think there was a note?" Allen asked. His pose was aggressive: hands on hips, feet wide apart. Rachel felt he was bearing down on her.

"No reason," said Rachel. "Only there normally is one, isn't there? People who commit suicide usually leave a note, to explain why they've done it."

"And what makes you think Dalton would have left me the note?" Allen asked.

"Well, you were friends, weren't you?"

Allen snorted. "Friends! Hardly! Why would I want to mix with the likes of that spineless idiot?"

"He drove you around, though, didn't he?" Rachel said. "He was driving you the night he killed himself."

Allen suddenly looked wary. He stepped back towards his car and leaned against the door, his arms folded. "You know that for sure, do you?"

Rachel didn't, but said she did.

"Alright," said Allen. "Yes, he was driving me that night. There was some function on at the Hope Street Hotel. A

Christmas party for a committee I'm on. Dalton dropped me there and was due to pick me up at around half past midnight. Only when he turned up, late, leaving me standing like a prick out on the pavement, he was pissed. I sent him packing. No idea what happened to him next."

Rachel was starting to feel more confident. She wasn't sure how or why, but Allen seemed on the back foot. "He went to see Susan Clarke," she said. "She lives on Hope Street, not far from the hotel."

"So? What's that to me? I thought they'd stopped shagging each other years ago." The last sentence was bravado, Rachel was sure of it. He was trying to be cocky, but it wasn't quite coming off. She felt she was getting to something, without knowing exactly what it was.

"They did," Rachel said. "Gerry just wanted to talk to her." "What about?" The edge had gone from Allen's voice. He wanted to know, Rachel saw that, and couldn't hide it. Rachel ignored the question. "Did you know Gerry was going to kill himself?" she asked. Allen was silent. "Only, you were in a foul mood yesterday morning, the worst anyone's ever seen you. Gerry Dalton's body wasn't found until lunchtime." "Then I couldn't have known, could I?" Allen was trying to recover his anger and superiority. "And if you want to see a foul mood, just carry on asking these questions." He turned to get back into his car. Again, he hit his door against the car next to his, this time almost deliberately. His window was still down. Rachel stepped towards the window to say something else, but Allen already had the car in first gear. He screeched out of the space, scraping the rear bumper down the length of the car to his left. Rachel had to jump to get out of his way. She watched the car speed towards the exit. She was pleased with herself. She ran back to the lift, anxious to tell Susan what had happened. She'd annoyed Allen, really annoyed him, but she'd maybe scared him too. Now they just needed to work out how.

Chapter Thirty-six

Susan had left the office however by the time Rachel got back. Like Rachel, she'd hurried out, on her way to the Roman Catholic cathedral at the top of Brownlow Hill, which was where Brian Nulty had told her she'd find Assistant Chief Constable Crowley when she'd rang to speak to him about DI Nolan.
"What's he doing there of all places?" she'd asked. Then she continued, before Nulty had had a chance to reply. "Don't tell me. Some sanctimonious gathering of all the bigwig Mick bastards who like to think they run this city."
Brian had laughed. "Very ecumenical of you, Sue," he'd said. "But if you mean a mass to celebrate the efforts of the Knights of St Columba, then you're right."
"So he's one too," she'd said, half to herself.
"Eh? As well as who?"
"Never mind," Susan had said, but she'd meant Eugene O'Hare. Brian was unable to tell her any more about what was happening regarding Nolan. It had all gone very quiet, he'd said, so she'd thanked him again, promised him another drink and dashed out.
Now she was standing on the newly paved square at the bottom of the steps that led up to the Cathedral entrance. Cathedral Plaza it was called now. Everything had to have some fashionable new name, she thought as she stared up at the building looming over her. She wrapped her new coat tightly around her, fighting against the cold and wishing she had drunk less the night before. She wondered how Rachel was feeling. Fine, probably, she thought. Young enough to fight hangovers with ease. Besides, of the two bottles they'd finished off, Susan had had more than her fair share.
A few tourists were scattered around her. Even at this time of year, Liverpool attracted visitors from overseas. They mainly came for the Beatles, but some wanted to see more. Susan

watched people taking group photographs, straining to squeeze both people and building into the single shot. She wondered if any of them would be heading out to Crosby beach afterwards, to see the cast-iron men. She pictured them in her mind, motionless figures bound together by police tape, sightless, mute witnesses to Gerry Dalton's last breath.

She began the climb up to the entrance. She hated the building, thought it was a monstrosity, grey and stained concrete wrapped in a circle, like an upturned funnel, tapering to a drum topped with spikes that stabbed into the bleak winter sky. Eugene had proudly told her how quickly it had been built, with money raised by the poor Catholics of the archdiocese who wanted their own temple in a city where Protestants had lauded it over them for too long. But Susan just saw it as built on the cheap, thrown up in the 1960s when the original design, by Edward Lutyens, had proved too expensive. All that was left of Lutyens' work was the crypt, brown and dark and buried deep into the top of Brownlow Hill where a workhouse had once stood.

Reluctantly, Susan went inside. She ignored the holy water and went straight through the porch and into the cathedral. She found herself thinking of Our Lady's, where Margy's mortal soul had been tossed into eternity. There were echoes of the cathedral in the smaller church, certainly. Only here, the benches curved all the way round, with the altar in the dead centre. When it was sunny, the altar was bathed in a spectrum of colours cast by the light through the stained glass windows of the drum directly above. Only a little light came through today, and the electric lights they'd been forced to turn on left the building stark and cold.

Susan stood just inside the doors. She looked for Crowley but couldn't see him. There were too many people, or, rather, too many men. The Knights of St Columba rarely let their womenfolk intrude on any of their gatherings. Susan had no idea how much was left of the service, but was glad to leave anyway. She decided to wait for Crowley outside. She stood with her back to the concrete wall to the side of the main entrance, lit a cigarette and waited for the service to end. She was on her third when she saw the worshippers begin to file out. She had the feeling that Crowley would be one of the last to leave, but started to look out for him straight away nevertheless. She'd remembered earlier that she'd never actually seen him in the flesh, but felt she could recall enough about him from the many times his picture had been in the paper. A tall, spare man who looked as if he was always calculating three moves ahead, he had towered over Eugene and Allen on the front page photograph the *Mail* had used a couple of weeks ago, from the launch party at the Warwick, the night Margy had died. Still, his body was narrow so, despite his height, he didn't have the power or energy or force that Eugene had – or Allen for that matter. He might beat them for intelligence, but for brute strength and decision, her editor and her ex-father-in-law would have him beat.

The crowd of men coming out of the porch doors were milling around at the top of the steps. No-one was in a hurry to leave, and a logjam was building up. Susan had to stand on tiptoes to try and catch sight of Crowley, but, finally, she saw him. He was there in his full dress uniform, immaculately pressed, silver buttons gleaming, his cap on his head, pushing his way through the crowd in her direction. It seemed that he had something to say to every person he pushed past – a greeting and a smile and then he'd move on. One man grasped his arm and pulled him conspiratorially close. The man whispered something in Crowley's ear and then they both burst out laughing, although Susan got the impression that Crowley didn't find the remark entirely to his taste. Then he left the man and continued through the crowd. He was wearing one leather glove and carrying the other in the same hand, along with a silver-topped officer's cane. Susan saw him raise this hand in greeting and thought for a moment he was gesturing towards her, but then Crowley stopped and stood with a group of soberly dressed men with whom he began talking. They looked serious, earnest. Susan scornfully imagined how easily they might kid themselves into thinking they were deciding fates and affairs of state. She waited for them to finish, watching Crowley carefully and planning the best way to approach him.

After a few more minutes Susan saw the priest who'd conducted the service arrive, still dressed in his full robes. This seemed to be the signal for the crowd of men to disperse. Susan watched as they all took their turns shaking hands or waving goodbye to the priest before setting off down the steps to the plaza below, laughing and joking, all ready for the next stage of their celebrations, the important one, where they could eat and drink and grope the waitresses in the sanctimonious afterglow of their recent communion.

She waited for Crowley to leave his group and say his farewells to the priest. As he took the first step down, gloved hand on the railing, she overtook him and blocked his path. She looked up at him, the extra steps adding to his height. Like the spiked crown to the cathedral, he seemed to loom over her.

She smiled brightly and held out her press card for him to see. "Assistant Chief Constable Crowley?" she said. She beamed at him. "I'm from the *Morning Mail*." She deliberately didn't say her name, in case he'd connect it with Margy Girvan. He looked cautiously at her, but didn't show any sign of recognition. Susan gratefully ploughed on. "I was wondering if I could have a quick word with you," she said. "We're doing some festive pieces and we thought a story on all the good work the Knights of St Columba do would be really nice for this time of year." Again she was grateful as she saw Crowley relax a little. He even appeared to smile slightly. "Well, yes, of course," he said. "What can I tell you?" Susan decided to keep this up for one question at least.

"Which city group will be receiving your special charitable gift this year?" she asked. The question sounded dreadful to Susan, but Crowley seemed happy enough with it.

"Well," he began. "As you no doubt know, we like to spread our charity around, but every Christmas we select one group of underprivileged people in the community for particular attention." He paused, while Susan pretended to take careful note of his words. "This year, that attention is going to helping disabled children participate in a wide variety of sports. We intend…"

Susan interrupted him. "So there won't be any special donation made to DI Nolan's retirement fund?" she asked. At first, he didn't seem to catch her words. Then his face turned to stone and he tried to go round her. Susan stepped to bar his descent. "Why has DI Nolan retired so suddenly?" she asked.

Crowley ignored her question. "Let me pass," he ordered, but Susan shifted across with each step sideways that he took, leaving them dancing awkwardly. Later, Susan would laugh at the picture of them in her head, like some amateur Fred and Ginger trying to make it to the bottom of a grand staircase. Crowley's patience was quickly exhausted and he pushed her aside, which Susan took as a desperate measure for so careful and senior a figure to do in public.

She stayed on her feet but couldn't stop him passing. She shouted down after him. "Has DI Nolan's sudden retirement got anything to do with the accusations of a Strangeways prisoner that Nolan doctored arrest figures while he was working with you in Keighley?" It was a long question, but Crowley heard all of it, even as he was attempting to hurry down the steps. Susan saw him come to a sudden halt. She waited for him to turn round. He did so, but Susan was surprised by his expression. She'd been expected shock and anger but the look on his face was closer to that of smug victory.

He took his time responding. "You're Susan Clarke, aren't you?" He didn't wait for an answer. "The bruises suit you. I would be very careful if I were you, Miss Clarke," he said. It wasn't a threat. He spoke sarcastically, as if he was genuinely concerned for her reputation. "I think you could end up looking very foolish even taking such a story to your editor. You have to have proof, you know."

Susan tried to bluster it out, but she was worried by his smugness. "We've got a prisoner ready to swear it's true. And give us evidence."

He smiled up at her. "Have you now?" he said. He tipped his cane to the peak of his cap and turned and sauntered down the steps. Susan just stood watching him go, arms limply hanging by her sides.

She stayed there staring after him, until he reached the bottom of the steps and climbed into a black car that was waiting for him, double parked. It took a few moments before she realised it was her mobile phone she could hear ringing. Still preoccupied, she found the phone in her bag and read Rachel's name displayed on the tiny screen.

Chapter Thirty-seven

When Susan answered, Rachel immediately caught the sense of being elsewhere in her voice. "You sound miles away," Rachel said. "In all senses. Where are you?"

The question jolted Susan into an awareness of the fact she'd been standing in the same spot for quite a while, staring into space while tourists and private worshippers passed her on their way up or down. "I'm just outside the Catholic cathedral," she said, finally starting to move, picking her way down the steep steps.

"Oh, yes," Rachel said. "Got religion, have you?"

"It wouldn't be this one if I had," Susan told her. "You sound very chipper. What's up?"

"I'm not sure, to be honest," Rachel admitted. "I've just had a long chat with Allen, down in the basement car park."

"A nice, romantic spot," Susan said. "Don't think I'd like the idea of talking to Allen in a place like that."

"I know what you mean," said Rachel. "I felt a bit vulnerable at one point. Funny thing was, though, so did he. And not just vulnerable. A bit scared maybe."

"Scared?" repeated Susan. "How do you mean?"

"I'm not sure. One minute he was all aggressive and bullying…"

"That sounds like our Hugh," Susan interrupted.

"Then next thing he was on the back foot. Maybe not scared exactly, but…worried."

"What was it you said that got him rattled?" asked Susan.

Rachel paused. She wasn't sure that she should have told Allen about Dalton going to Susan's flat that night. "Look, Sue," she said. "I wasn't planning on saying it, but it just came out. I told him about you seeing Gerry, the night before he killed himself. Is that okay?"

Susan answered straight away. "Yes," she said. "Of course it is. Why wouldn't it be?" She thought for a moment. "I told him myself, actually. Yesterday, when Gerry didn't turn up in the morning. Allen said he didn't know we were still shagging. Charming, eh? Don't worry about it."

Rachel still felt uneasy. "It was just his reaction. I just told him, you see. I was trying to find out what had gone on between them that night. You know, because he seemed to know something was up before the body had been found."

"Maybe he was just pissed off because Gerry had left him standing on the pavement to make his own way home. And because he hadn't turned up for work either." Susan had reached the bottom of the steps and was back in Cathedral Plaza.

"Maybe," Rachel said. "It's just that when I said to Allen that you and Gerry had talked, he suddenly changed. Listen, fancy meeting for lunch?"

"Another ciabatta?" Susan replied.

"I was thinking of something even more upmarket," Rachel said. "Ever eaten at the Hope Street Hotel?"

Susan laughed. "We're getting a long way from the Mercantile, aren't we? Any particular reason you want to go there?"

"No," said Rachel. "I just remember what you said the other day. We spend plenty of time with the flotsam. And we need to talk things through. Might as well do it in luxury. I'll see you there in about fifteen minutes."

In the end it took Rachel half an hour to make the short journey from Old Hall Street to the hotel, her taxi crawling through the latest roadworks snarling up the city centre. Susan was sitting in the lounge, sunk deep into a leather armchair, her coffee cooling on the low table in front of her.

The Hope Street Hotel had started life in the 1800s as the London Carriage Works Company. Its latest incarnation had seen developers, like so many others, taking advantage of Liverpool's resurgence to move in and renovate the building. The distinctive yellow London brick exterior had been kept, but inside it was now an elegant, understated, expensive hotel, its restaurant praised by food critics from London, amazed to find Liverpool offering more than fish and chips and kebabs. Rachel ordered a water and sat down on the leather sofa to Susan's right. "I forgot to ask you what you were doing up here," she said, then added, "You didn't sound yourself on the phone at all, by the way. Anything happened?"

"I spoke to Crowley," Susan told her. She explained about the mass for the Knights of St Columba and everything that had passed between her and the assistant chief constable.

"Just the opposite of me and Allen," Rachel said when Susan had finished.

"How do you mean?" Susan asked.

"Well," Rachel began. "You had Crowley spooked when you sprang the Nolan question on him, then he turned calm and confident. Practically skipped down the steps, you said. With Allen it was the other way round. He was fine until I said you'd spoken to Gerry, then he got rattled. Any idea what it all means?"

Susan was tired and confused. "Fuck knows," she said.

"We've spoken to two of the four we wanted and got nowhere," said Susan.

"I wouldn't say nowhere," Rachel protested.

"No?" Susan spoke sharply and immediately apologised. "It's not you. It's just we still can't pin anything down. You're right. We are getting somewhere, judging from the way things went with Allen and Crowley, but we've no idea where that is."

"Maybe Jackson can help us," said Rachel. "I'm hoping we'll get another visiting order soon."

"Maybe." Susan went quiet. For a while Rachel wondered if she'd forgotten she was there. At last she spoke. "Still reckon Gerry for the Margy murder?"

"Don't you?"

"He was in the area the night she died," Susan said. "He was at the hotel where she was called from. He'd been acting strangely. He's committed suicide. Yes. It still looks like him. Whether we'll be able to prove it or not is anyone's guess. We need his mobile."

"The funeral's Saturday," Rachel said. "We can ask the widow."

"Yep," Susan said. "That's a conversation I can't wait to have."

Rachel finished her coffee. "What are the chances of finding someone here who was on the night Allen was waiting for Gerry?"

"The way things are going," Susan said, "I'd say slim to non-existent."

She was wrong. One of the porters had been on that night. He'd heard the row, but not what was said. The drunken man was incoherent. He was lurching around the pavement, saying he didn't care any more, over and over again. He'd even grabbed the bigger man by his lapels, but the man had just swatted him away. He was sorry he couldn't help more. Rachel and Susan thanked him and went into the restaurant for lunch.

"I don't suppose any of this means poached egg on toast," Susan said, studying the menu.

Rachel grinned, then the smile left her and she looked thoughtful. "You know," she said, putting her own menu down. "I don't think you've told me exactly what it was Gerry said to you that night."

Susan shrugged and turned down the corners of her mouth. "He was drunk," she said. "Rambling. I could barely understand him and what I could catch didn't make much sense. I'm not even sure he knew it was me he was talking to."

Rachel shook her head. "He knew alright," she said. "He came to you for a reason."

"Do you think so?" Susan asked. "I just assumed it was luck.

You know, a merging of events and places. He was due here, at the hotel, to pick Allen up. Allen got shot of him and he stumbled down to my place. At first, when I saw it was him, I thought Allen had put him up to it. You know, some sort of lad's joke. Go and give her another one. An anniversary shag."

"How do you mean?" asked Rachel.

"It's 5 years since Gerry and I had our affair." Susan heard her own words. "Affair," she repeated. "What a stupid word."

The waiter came and they ordered without enthusiasm. Around them the place was filling up with elegant couples and groups of business people, all studiedly casual and all looking much more at home than either of the two women.

Susan stared at the menu again when the waiter had left them. "I'm not even sure what I've just ordered," she said.

Rachel ignored her and went back to the subject of Gerry's late night visit. "This was the first time, wasn't it?" she said. "Since the two of you had had your affair. The first time he'd come to the flat?"

"Yes," said Susan. She thought carefully. "The first time he'd spoken to me outside work since it happened, come to mention it. Even in the office, he usually did his best to avoid me."

"So what was different about that night?" asked Rachel. "And don't just tell me it was because he was drunk. What did he say?"

The waiter returned to the table, carrying two enormous white plates. Susan stared at her meal: a tower was stacked in the centre of her plate, circled by a trail of what looked to her like blackcurrant sauce. "I still don't know." Rachel tutted. "I mean what I ordered," she said. "Not what Gerry said to me." Rachel cut into the food stacked on her plate and collapsed her own carefully constructed tower. "So?" she said impatiently. Susan thought for a while. Eventually, she said, "Allen."

"What about him?"

Susan explained. "I asked him if Allen had put him up to this and he said 'Not Allen. Hate Allen'." She forced her mind back to the scene on the steps of her building, seeing herself standing there, the drunken man at her feet, the hall light behind her switching itself off. "He said he hated driving him. It was like he'd just had enough. 'Same voice calling' he said. Then later, he said 'hate your voice'."

Rachel interrupted her. "Wait a minute. I don't understand. He said those exact words? 'Your voice'?"

"Yes," said Susan.

"Why should he hate your voice?"

"My voice?" Susan said. "I didn't think he meant my voice. Like I said, I'm not even sure he knew I was there. It was like he was talking to someone else. Like it was something he'd rehearsed saying to Allen but never got round to."

"Maybe," Rachel said. "But surely you don't kill yourself just because you're tired of driving the boss around? Do you? What else did he say?"

"That was it really," Susan said. "Oh, I remember now. God, how could I forget this?"

"What?"

"Well, it was strange," Susan said. "I offered to call his wife for him. Maureen. And he reacted really badly. He looked angry, mad. Like he would have lashed out at me if he could. 'Not Maureen' he said." She stopped and thought some more. "No," she said. "That wasn't it. 'Not the phone'. That was it. Then he said 'Not Maureen'. But it's funny, all the anger had gone by then. When he said his wife's name it was like he'd lost his strength. Said it like a little boy. Then, the last thing – 'no more stories'." She took a sip of water. "Does that help?" she asked.

"I've no idea," Rachel replied. "Maybe Maureen will be able to tell us."

Neither woman wanted a dessert, and each felt the room was

becoming too stuffy to stay in for much longer. They paid the bill and went outside. The sky had cleared to a brilliant blue and Hope Street was lit by cold sun. They walked for a while, then stopped and stood against the railings encircling the grounds of the Anglican Cathedral.

"Have you ever been down there?" Susan asked. She nodded below them, to a small park cut out of the rock on which the cathedral had been built, like an open basement to the building above.

"No. What is it?" said Rachel.

"St James's Cemetery," Susan told her. "Built before the cathedral, out of an old quarry. There's a path that leads down to it, wide enough to take funeral carriages. I go down there sometimes. A necropolis. A city of the dead."

"Nice," said Rachel.

Susan pointed to a structure like a Greek temple, just inside the cathedral gates, at ground level. "That's the mortuary chapel. I think there's a Tracy Emin statue outside there now, a tiny iron bird on top of a pole."

"Not an iron man, then," said Rachel.

Susan half smiled. "No, not an iron man." They turned and started walking back towards the Hope Street Hotel. "You going back to the office?" Susan asked.

Rachel looked at her watch. Half past two. "Yes," she said. "I've a couple of hours before my shift finishes. You?"

Susan shook her head. "I'm on a half day today."

"What'll you do?"

"Brian Nulty gave me Nolan's address," said Susan. "I'll go and see if anyone's in. I won't be holding my breath though."

"He'll have done a runner, won't he?"

"If he's got any sense he will have," Susan said. "There'd be no point him hanging round here, would there? Not if Billy Jackson's starting to talk."

"Still, though," said Rachel. "It won't do him any good. Wherever he's gone, they'll find him. They'll just bring him back and prosecute him."

"He might feel he's got a better chance of cutting a deal this way," Susan said. "Crowley will have things arranged so nothing sticks to him. All the blame will fall on Nolan. If he's holed up somewhere abroad, he might have more control when they do track him down than if the coppers just turned up on his doorstep early one morning. He could even get in touch with them. Tell them what he knows and what he wants in return. Crowley would be a bigger catch than Nolan, that's for sure."

"Whatever reason he's done it for, that just leaves us Maureen Dalton and Billy to talk to," said Rachel. A taxi was nosing its way into Hope Street from Blackburne Place. Rachel hailed it. Before she got in, she said to Susan, "Call me after you've been to Nolan's. Let me have the bad news."

"I will," Susan replied, and shut the door after Rachel.

Back at the office, Rachel subbed as many stories as she could with the minimum amount of attention. With half an hour to go before her shift ended, she went through what she and Susan had achieved in their short time working together. In terms of stories that actually went into the paper, there was very little, just a few short fillers by Susan, about Margy's murder, her identification, her funeral, and the complete lack of progress made by the police in their attempts to find the killer. Rachel herself had contributed nothing that had made it into print. All she had was conjecture and – as yet – unsubstantiated accusations. For days now, her head had been buzzing with ideas and possibilities, but they'd simply been swirling round, with neither a starting point nor a conclusion.

Chapter Thirty-eight

She switched her computer off and left the office. Instead of going straight home, Rachel made her way through the complicated cone system laning the Strand and drove all the way along the river road out to Speke. She needed time at the health club, if only to clear her mind and replace the suggestion of a headache with a proper, physical tiredness. Once there, she was delighted to find the pool more or less empty, and she swam length after length for nearly 40 minutes, before treating herself to a quarter of an hour in the steam room. When she came out of the changing rooms, her black hair still wet from the shower, she felt relaxed and ready for a quiet evening at home watching the television or maybe having a game of chess with her father.

It was nearly seven by the time she got back to the house. As she pulled her car behind her father's Mondeo, her mobile phone bleeped: a text message from Susan, saying, as they'd both expected, that there was no sign of Nolan at his flat and the neighbours hadn't seen him for a week or so. She sent a brief reply then went to the front door, hoping there was something stodgy and substantial for dinner.

Rachel was surprised to find both her father and mother standing in the hall waiting for her.

"Rachel," her father said. "Where on earth have you been?" He spoke with an edge of anger, and as if he was trying to keep his voice down. Rachel felt her hackles rise. In her head certain phrases were beginning to assemble, ready to tell her father how old she was and how she shouldn't have to report in and anyway why couldn't they simply call her on her mobile? Mercifully, it wasn't a conversation they had often, just every now and then, almost to clear the air.

Before she could reply, Rachel saw the distress in her mother's eyes. There was a touch of fear there too, and a sense of something out of the ordinary, something that had upset her parents' ordered world. Her father spoke again. "You've a visitor," he said. "He's been here for over an hour. Really, I wish you'd tell us when you've invited someone." He nodded towards the first door off the hall, the one that led to the front room.

Rachel looked baffled. "I've not invited anyone," she said. She opened the door and went in, her gym bag still over her shoulder, and saw Franny Sweeney sitting in her father's armchair. He was smiling broadly. The bag slipped off Rachel's shoulder, catching in the crook of her arm. Nervously, hoping she wasn't making it obvious to either Sweeney or her parents that she was scared, she turned and told her mother and father she was sorry she was so late and she'd forgotten she'd invited someone. Out of years of habit, her mother asked if they wanted tea or coffee, but Rachel said no thanks and shut the door. She just about managed to reach the sofa before her legs gave way. It wasn't just the shock. It was the sense of invasion and violation, and the physical memory of the time Sweeney had punched her viciously in the stomach. Bile rose in her throat at the thought of the punch, but she swallowed it down. She looked at Sweeney, who had stopped smiling.

"Lovely house," he said. "Lovely area. Lot of yids, of course, but then you can't have everything, can you?" His voice was soft, and his accent subtle, as if he'd deliberately tried to lose it. Only traces of Liverpool remained.

"Why are you here?" Rachel asked. She forced herself to breathe calmly, in, out, in, out.

"Guess," Sweeney replied.

Rachel shook her head, confused. "Something to do with Crowley? Billy Jackson?" she said. "Just tell me." There, the panic was obvious.

Sweeney stood up and walked across the room to stand directly in front of Rachel. He spoke calmly, matter-of-factly. "Yes," he said. "Something to do with Crowley and Billy

Jackson. Did you think I'd drive twenty miles just to have a nice chat over coffee and a mince pie?"

Rachel stared down at her knees. "What?" she demanded. "Just tell me." She had the feeling she'd said something similar to Sweeney before, fear and resentment and anger forcing the words out of her mouth.

Sweeney reached down towards Rachel. Even though she wasn't looking at him, she sensed the movement and flinched, tensing herself against the anticipated pain. Sweeney, however, simply stroked her hair, tenderly and gently. "Billy Jackson's dead," he said. His tone, like his touch, was soothing. "He killed himself in his cell last night. An overdose, apparently, although no-one knows how he got the drugs."

Rachel forgot about the fact that Sweeney was stroking her hair with a lover's care and looked up at him, aghast. "What?" she said. "I only saw him last night."

Sweeney stopped touching Rachel's hair. He took a handkerchief from his pocket and wiped his palm on it before putting both his hands in his pockets. "I don't care, you know." His voice remained tender.

Rachel struggled to match the meaning of the words to the tone Sweeney had used. "What? What do you mean, you don't care?" she asked.

"I mean I don't care that he's dead," said Sweeney. "You've still got to get Crowley, like I told you." Rachel stared at him, puzzled by his words. Sweeney went on. "Remember that first time we met?" he said. "When I told you about Crowley and said I didn't want anything in return?" He paused. "That was a lie."

"How, though?" Rachel said. "If Jackson's dead, who else do I talk to?"

"Oh, come on, Rachel," Sweeney said. "You've got to do some of the work yourself. You don't want to be too much in debt to me." He smiled and added, "Believe me. I'm thinking of you, you know."

"Is he the only one you knew of?" asked Rachel. "Jackson, I mean."

Sweeney stopped smiling. "Don't push it, Rachel."

But she did. "And don't come the heavy with me or Susan," she told him, amazed to hear herself saying the words.

Sweeney stared blankly at her. "You, or one of your bully boys," she went on. "You can leave her out of it. If you have to hit someone, hit me."

"What are you talking about?" he asked, genuinely interested.

"Don't play the innocent," Rachel said. "You nearly killed her."

"Who?" said Sweeney. "Susan Clarke? Not me." Rachel could see straight away that he wasn't lying. There was no reason for him to. He'd revealed how many men he'd killed. He wouldn't hide it if he'd attacked Susan. She tried to work out the implications.

Suddenly, Sweeney clapped his hands together, and rubbed them vigorously. "Cold outside, eh? Well, I'll be off." He moved away from Rachel, opened the door and stepped out into the hall. "No need to see me out," he told Rachel, then he called out, "Nice to meet you Mr and Mrs Jack! Merry Christmas!" He opened the front door and walked down the path to the road. As he reached the pavement, a car pulled alongside him. Sweeney opened the rear door, climbed inside and the car pulled away.

Rachel heard the door close behind Sweeney. She was stunned both by the intrusion and what he had to say. She wanted nothing more than to remain on the sofa and let the numbness she felt slide out of her body. But she knew she couldn't. She had to call Susan straight away, but she knew her parents would shortly come into the room, rightly demanding to know who that man was and what he wanted. She forced herself on to her feet and made herself smile. She opened the door, wanting to meet her parents as they came in, wanting to make everything seem as normal as possible. As she pulled the door towards her, her father pushed it open from the other side.

"Rachel," he said. "Who was that man? What did he want? He'd been here for over half an hour before you came home."

"I'm sorry Dad," Rachel began.

"He just pushed his way into the house, told us he'd wait. It was just as well your mother wasn't here alone," he said. Rachel nodded and began to make her way upstairs. "And where do you think you're going?" her father added.

"Just leave it, Dad," Rachel replied, continuing on up.

"What did you say?"

Rachel turned sharply. "I said leave it!" she shouted. She went to her room, leaving her father speechless at the bottom of the stairs.

Susan was just about to get into the bath when Rachel rang. "It wasn't Sweeney," Rachel said as soon as Susan answered. "What are you talking about?" Susan asked, and listened with growing alarm as Rachel told her everything that had just happened.

"As if it wasn't bad enough being shoved by Sweeney," Susan said when Rachel finished. "Now we're being pushed the other way, only this time we've no idea who's doing the pushing."

"Crowley, you reckon?" Rachel asked. "Nolan too?"

Susan nodded and said, "Stands to reason, I guess. They're the ones with it all to lose when Billy's story comes out."

"So what do we do?" said Rachel. "Who are you more scared of, Sweeney or Crowley?"

"If you'd asked me before the other night, I'd have said Sweeney, no contest," said Susan. "Now I'm not so sure. But it doesn't matter."

"How do you mean?"

"I mean it doesn't matter because we stick to the story," Susan told her. "That's our job, remember? But let's be careful, eh? And quick, too."

"But with Billy dead?" Rachel asked. "Where does that leave us?"

"Don't worry, Rachel," Susan said. "If Crowley was mixed up in this business with Billy Jackson, then he'll have done the same with other cons. We'll just have to track them down, that's all. Nolan too. He can't have just disappeared, can he? Someone'll know a forwarding address, or a bank account for his pension to be paid into."

By the end of the call, Rachel felt better, although only marginally. Sweeney wasn't a patient man. If he said he wanted something to happen to Crowley, then he would expect it done. Susan's suggestions were right, but they'd take a long time to bear fruit and Rachel didn't know how much longer she could endure the thought of Franny Sweeney breaking into her life whenever he chose. And then on top of that, it now looked like Crowley and Nolan were ready to go to any lengths to stop them doing exactly what it was Sweeney wanted.

There was nothing she could do about it tonight, though, except pretend everything was alright. She changed into a pair of tracksuit bottoms and a hooded sweatshirt and went back downstairs. Her father was sitting his usual armchair, the chess board set up on a table to his right, next to the chair Rachel always took. Her mother was on the sofa, glasses perched on her nose, the paper folded at the crossword, her mouth moving slightly as she suggested possible answers to herself. To mark the approach of Christmas, Mr Jack had selected a festive CD compilation, and Bing Crosby and Frank Sinatra crooned softly from the stereo. Rachel told herself everything would be alright and sat down to play chess with her father. Nothing was said about the earlier row, but Rachel made up her mind to move out as soon as possible. She couldn't have teenage rows at her age, and she couldn't have killers barging their way into her parents' home either.

Chapter Thirty-nine

Saturday 22 December
LIVERPOOL MORNING MAIL
SHOPS BRACED FOR FINAL MAD DASH
Liverpool's retailers are expecting a busy Christmas Eve. Shoppers looking for last-minute presents will flood the city centre, according to retail analysts.
"All the signs are good," said Leslie Gray, Head of Liverpool Chamber of Commerce. "Not only will people be looking for presents and food for the festive period, but we expect plenty of bargain hunters too, as many shops are beginning their sales early."
By a Liverpool Morning Mail Staff Reporter.

He assumed it was a coincidence, seeing him here like this. He would have had no idea he'd be here, that was for sure. He held out his hand and the other man took it. The other man didn't let go, just squeezed it tighter and tighter. His arm began to buckle and his body twisted to the right. The other man smiled and said, "What did you think you were doing? I'll sort it."
The man managed to say, "Sure you can?" and the other man tightened his grip, as if to punish him.
"I fixed the other thing, didn't I?" He smiled, released his grip, and walked away.

All Hallows Church stands on an island surrounded by three quiet roads, close to but hidden from the bustle of the shops on Allerton Road and the traffic on Mather Avenue. It serves a wealthy, comfortable parish of large houses and settled families in a part of Allerton full of parks and playing fields and trees, the bare branches of which stretched against the brilliant blue sky on the morning of Gerry Dalton's funeral. Under the tolling bell, the mourners quietly filed into the church and began filling the pews, some taking the time to admire the stained glass windows designed by Burne-Jones, fired into sparkling light by the low Christmas sun.

Susan and Rachel waited outside. Susan was smoking, and in her mind she placed the rich brown brick of this church next to the crumbling fabric of Our Lady's, where Margy had been rushed through only days before. Neither woman felt much like talking. Susan had spent the day before working quietly in the office, trying to chase down Nolan, while Rachel had had the Friday off, spending it shopping with her parents, looking at flats for sale, trying to forget about Franny Sweeney and Crowley, and talking to Strangeways about Billy Jackson's death. They were both tense. They knew that the plans they had for today were crucial to their chances of making progress on their story. But their feelings were mixed. They were about to say goodbye to an old colleague – in Susan's case an old lover – who they'd liked and who they now suspected of a brutal murder.

Susan flicked her cigarette into the road. "Better go in," she said to Rachel, who nodded in reply. "You look nice," Susan said as they walked up to the heavy wooden door of the church. Rachel was all in black – dress, coat, gloves. "Thanks," she replied. "I bought the dress yesterday. Seems like I've got a rash of funerals to go to."

"They're like buses," Susan said humourlessly. "You go your whole life without one and then three come at once. Did you find out when Billy's is?"

"They wouldn't tell me." She lowered her voice to a whisper as they entered the church. "Just said cause of death. Overdose. Don't know how he got the pills."

"They should ask Nolan, if they can find him," Susan said. They stopped talking and walked a few rows up the aisle, squeezing onto the end of one of the pews to the left.

A few minutes later the congregation rose. A shaft of sunlight beamed through a pane of the stained glass, slicing through a section of mourners, leaving their heads gashed in pale scarlet. The organist began playing *Jesu Joy of Man's Desiring* and the coffin was carried up the aisle by six of the *Mail*'s staff: two reporters, including Frank Hayes; one man from accounts; one from sales; one of the paper's drivers; and Allen, looking uncomfortable and reluctant to take his share of the load. The coffin was followed by Dalton's immediate family – his plain, pinched wife and three plain and dumpy daughters, the eldest of whom looked to Susan like she was enjoying the grief just a little too much. Maureen struck Susan as looking serene, as if she had accepted that Gerry's death was inevitable and, perhaps, the best thing all round. Susan wondered what Maureen knew, if anything, and then wondered how on earth she might get around to asking her.

The service was slow, measured and respectful. The vicar spoke of Gerry's dedication to his family, his quiet humility, his gentle manner. He sounded like he knew him, maybe knew a side to him that was never seen at the office. He spoke with real feeling of his regret that Dalton couldn't share the pain that drove him to such a desperate, wasteful act. Frank Hayes gave both readings. The congregation joined with the choir to sing *Jerusalem* and, at the close of the service, *Abide With Me*. Both Susan and Rachel were struck by the contrast with Margy Girvan's funeral, but neither mentioned it to the other, and each felt like a slight imposter, unable to join in fully with the expressions of sadness, loss and sorrow.

At the close of the service, the congregation slowly and respectfully followed the coffin, which was to be taken to Allerton Cemetery for a private burial, family only. People shuffled about on the pavement, squinting in the bright sunshine and forcing hands into gloves and pockets against the cold.

Susan and Rachel stood slightly apart. Frank Hayes approached them.

"Going back to the house?" he asked. The two women

nodded. "I never know what to call these things," he added. Rachel looked bemused. "Call what things?" she asked. Frank replied, "These things after funerals. They're receptions, I suppose. Only you can't really call them that, can you? You say that for weddings."

Susan touched Frank on the arm gently. "Call them things, Frank. That's as good a name as any."

Frank smiled at Susan, silently thanking her for her tenderness. "I should know," he said. "I've been to enough of them lately. You do, though. At my age."

Rachel tried to change the subject. "You read beautifully, Frank."

"Thank you," he replied. "You know, the funny thing is, I didn't like the man much. Didn't dislike him either, mind. I was neutral about him. That's maybe why I feel a bit upset. You shouldn't work in the same office as someone for so many years and then feel neither one way or another about them, should you?"

"I don't know, Frank," Rachel said. "You feel what you feel I guess."

"I suppose so," said Frank. "Right, I'll get off. You two okay for getting to the house?" They said yes. "I'll see you up there, then." He moved away, then stopped and turned round and said, "Allen wouldn't do it. The readings, I mean. Refused point-blank. That's the only reason I did it."

Gerry Dalton's house was about five minutes' drive away from All Hallows, on an estate just off Gypsy Lane. The development was about thirty years old, but local people still referred to it as new. The houses were well-built but squeezed together to maximise the builder's profits. The gardens were small and ran straight onto the pavements without any boundary walls to give a sense of enclosure. The Dalton family house was identical to most of the others on the estate, a characterless red brick box, nice enough, but with no distinguishing features. Just like Gerry, Rachel thought. The garden was neat and dull. Even at this time of year, the lawn looked immaculate, and box shrubs, shaped into spheres, were spaced at regular intervals down the side border, next to the driveway, along the front and up the other border back towards the house. Their shiny green leaves gleamed.

Not everyone who'd attended the funeral service had come back to the house. Allen had driven away from All Hallows in the direction of his golf club with no more than a cursory explanation and farewell to Dalton's widow. Still, the area around the house looked like it had been invaded. Cars were left on pavements and verges as close to the house as possible, their occupants reluctant to walk a step further than they had to. Rachel and Susan parked a little way away, round the corner, on Gladstone Drive, rather than Palmerston Way, which was where the Daltons lived.

Susan walked slowly from the car, ostensibly so she could have a cigarette. Rachel saw it wasn't that simple. She watched as Susan repeatedly flicked the lighter before finally it held its flame.

"Nervous?" she asked.

"Yes," Susan replied. "We're going in there to sneak around and try to find his phone. Of course I'm nervous. Aren't you?"

Rachel nodded and smiled. "Yes," she said. "Me too. But I was hoping you'd have done this before so you could guide me through it."

"I have," said Susan. "A long time ago, though, and never just after the man's funeral."

As slowly as Susan walked, they were soon there.

They walked up the path and stepped through the porch and into the house. The hall way, like every other room, was decorated tastefully but blandly and without personality or life. The carpet was beige, the skirting boards were white and the walls were magnolia, and the colour scheme stayed the same in every room. Susan and Rachel walked through the hall and out into the kitchen, beyond which a conservatory had been added. There, a table had been laid with finger food. Frank Hayes and the driver who'd helped carry Gerry Dalton's coffin had volunteered to serve the drinks, because nobody else would. Susan took a glass of lukewarm white wine. Rachel had a diet Coke. For form's sake, they went into the front room. In there was a cream three-piece suite, two glass-fronted bookcases, a coffee table and a television. There were no books. Over the white wooden mantelpiece, above the fire with the living gas flame, was a huge photo portrait of Dalton's wife and three daughters, ranged by the photographer from biggest to smallest, which meant that the eldest daughter came before her mother. The picture had been softened round the edges, but not enough to take the bluntness out of the eldest's eyes.

The room was by no means full. Rachel was surprised. The church had been packed. It was as if people had felt they'd fulfilled their duties by attending the service but decided that coming back to the house was asking too much. She looked out of the window and saw that already the cars parked on the pavements were starting to disperse. A quick drink and we'll go: Rachel wondered how many people had said those words as they'd entered the house that day.

Susan also saw that attendance was thinning. She steered Rachel away from the window and towards the door out into the hall. "We'd better do it now," she said. "Leave it any longer and there'll just be us here." She moved to the bottom of the stairs. "Toilet up there, is it?" she said to a woman she didn't recognise, who smiled and nodded in reply. She hurried up the stairs, followed by Rachel, who realised she was still holding her glass of Coke and didn't know what to do with it.

On the landing, they waited until the man leaving the toilet headed downstairs before trying each door. After finding two bedrooms, they came across a box room containing a desk, a chair, a filing cabinet and three shelves. It was the closest Gerry Dalton had ever come to having a room he could call his study. Rachel and Susan slipped in. The window overlooked the back garden, just as neat and mundane as the front. On the desk was a pair of binoculars, which Rachel guessed Dalton used to look out at the birds using the feeder hanging from the far washing line post. There was just the one photograph, on the lowest shelf, featuring a young and beaming Gerry Dalton flanked by two other young men standing outside a building, each holding a copy of a broadsheet newspaper.

"Bit pathetic, isn't it?" said Rachel. She ran her hand over the empty surface of the desk. "This tiny room with its cheap self-assembly desk. His sanctuary, you reckon?"

"Maybe," Susan replied. "He'd have needed one, if those daughters are as hard-faced and demanding as they look. Mind out of the way." Rachel stepped back towards the wall, to allow Susan to sit down in the swivel chair and start looking through the drawers down the right side of the desk. The contents of each were neatly arranged, and it took Susan no time to see there was nothing of interest in them – certainly not the mobile phone they were hoping to find. "Try the filing cabinet," she told Rachel. She pulled the chair in towards the desk to let Rachel pass behind her. Rachel pulled open the top drawer, just as the door opened and Dalton's widow came in. Maureen's expression didn't change. She simply looked from Susan to Rachel and then back to Susan and asked, mildly, "What are you doing?"

Chapter Forty

Susan and Rachel both froze the moment Maureen spoke. Susan felt her face flush and her stomach rolled in shock at the sight of the pale, frail woman with weak eyes standing in the doorway. Maureen repeated her question, looking directly at Susan. This time her tone was sterner, but it seemed like an effort to make it so. She appeared to be a woman to whom meekness and acceptance came naturally, so, even though anger was now fully justified, she wasn't quite sure how to display it.

Susan tried to speak but couldn't. She felt caught, utterly without excuses. Rachel's reaction was completely the opposite. She saw Susan's helplessness and this seemed to direct her to take control. Her initial reaction had been a split-second of fear, when she'd looked to Susan for her lead, but now she felt the responsibility was hers, and she welcomed it. "Why did Gerry kill himself, Maureen?" she demanded.

Maureen had seen Rachel in the corner by the filing cabinet, but only now did she really register her presence. She turned to look at the pretty, dark-haired young woman who'd so boldly demanded information from her. The sense of authority which she forced herself to feel began to ebb away. It was her turn to stumble for a reply. "What…why do you want…I don't know," she managed.

"That's why we're here," Rachel told her. "That's what we're looking for. A reason." She pulled open the top drawer of the filing cabinet, quickly looked inside, then shut it and opened the second drawer down. "Do you know why he did it?"

"No," Maureen said. She leant against the wall, suddenly incredibly weary. Quietly, Susan, thankful that Rachel had grabbed the initiative, stood and guided Maureen into the chair by the desk.

Rachel flicked through the files hanging in the drawer. "Sure?" she asked. "He didn't leave a note?"

"No note," said Maureen.

Susan had recovered sufficiently to ask her own question. She spoke soothingly, crouched down by the side of Maureen's chair, gently invading her space. She felt embarrassed to play her part in a good cop/bad cop routine with Rachel. Maureen probably didn't deserve this.

"Did you know he was going to kill himself, Maureen?" she asked. "Were you surprised?"

"Yes," Maureen said. She frowned and stared down at her hands lying useless in her lap. "I mean, I knew he was going to. Afterwards, I mean, when I heard. I wasn't surprised." She began to pick at the material of her black skirt. "He'd been…it sort of made sense."

"What do you mean?" Susan probed. "How had he been?" Maureen started to speak as if she was in the room by herself. She was responding to the questions, but she wasn't talking to anybody. "Angry. No," she corrected herself. She searched her mind for the right word. "Agitated. Couldn't settle. Couldn't sleep. That wasn't like him. He forgot things. Forgot to put the old papers out for recycling. That wasn't like him either. Then, the night before he…He did everything. Went through the house taking all the plugs out, checking the windows were shut and the doors were locked. I didn't think anything of it, just Gerry back to normal. Now, though…I don't know. He slept well. Nearly overslept. He was really cheerful when he set off for work." She stopped for a moment as she thought. "Maybe these things only become significant afterwards. Maybe it means nothing."

"Why was he agitated?" Susan asked. Maureen shrugged her shoulders.

Rachel had stopped rifling through the drawer and was standing looking down at Maureen. "When did he become agitated? When did he start acting differently?" she asked. Maureen seemed visibly to deflate. It wasn't Rachel's question particularly, it was just tiredness and disappointment and the realisation that life wasn't supposed to be like this but it was. Her shoulders slumped. It was like she was contracting, her brittle skin shrink-wrapping against her flimsy bones.

"A couple of weeks ago," she said. Rachel and Susan strained to hear her. She wasn't whispering; it was as if her voice was fading along with her body and spirit. "For years he'd been quiet and steady. He never brought work home, never talked about his day. He was kind and thoughtful and he provided for us but even when he was as close as he could get to me he always seemed far away. Then, suddenly, he became jumpy, agitated, like I said." She looked up at Susan. "I liked it. Even though I could tell something was bothering him, he became more alive. He snapped at me a few times, but I didn't mind that. I liked the life of those few days."

Rachel had been looking in the bottom drawer, listening to Maureen's answer. Now she took something from inside it, stood up, and held it towards Maureen. "Did Gerry always keep his mobile phone in the bottom drawer of the filing cabinet, Maureen?"

Maureen looked at the phone. She showed no further curiosity about it. She simply said, "That's not Gerry's phone." She reached into her handbag and took out another, chunkier, older phone. "This is Gerry's," she said.

"Are you sure, Maureen?" Susan asked. "You couldn't be confused, could you?"

"No," said Maureen. "I've kept this one with me since Gerry died. He left it here the last night he went out. It hasn't rung, but I needed it to contact Gerry's friends about the funeral." She corrected herself. "People Gerry knew, I mean."

"Switch it on," Rachel told her and Maureen did as she was told. When it came to life, Susan rang the mystery number that they'd collected at Margy's mother's house. She and Rachel stared at the phone Maureen was holding and watched it stay mute.

"So whose is this?" Rachel asked. She held up the phone that she'd taken from the drawer.

"I don't know," Maureen replied.

"Have you ever seen it before?" asked Susan. "It's not one of the girls', is it?"

Maureen chuckled. "Oh no," she said. "You don't think they'd let their phones out of their sight, do you? They are teenagers, you know."

Susan stood up straight and looked over at Rachel. For a moment they stared blankly at each other, both wanting to be away from Gerry's widow so they could talk openly. Susan nodded towards the door and began to edge over to it.

Maureen, head still bowed looking down at her lap, sensed the two women moving out. "I knew," she said.

Susan was eager to find out what it was Maureen knew, but she managed to keep her voice soft and gentle. "Knew what, Maureen?"

"Know, I should say," Maureen said. "I know. About you and Gerry. He told me, as soon as it happened."

Susan flushed. She suddenly became aware of just how small the room was. The walls seemed to close in on her, and she felt like Rachel and Maureen were about to press against her. "I'm sorry," she said.

"It doesn't matter," Maureen replied. "I found out your marriage ended. I'm sorry about that."

Susan swallowed hard. She pulled the door towards her. It seemed to put up a fight and she felt she had to struggle with it to get out. Without waiting for Rachel, she rushed down the stairs and out of the front door. She didn't stop until she reached Rachel's car, where she leaned on the roof and gasped air into her lungs. She'd never had any idea that Maureen had known, never had any reason to think she did, and couldn't figure out why now she cared so much that tears were stinging down her cheeks. Rachel caught up with her but stopped a couple of yards short, sensing that Susan wanted no contact or kind words. She just wanted to cry and smoke the cigarette which she put in her mouth and lit with shaking fingers. Susan rested her forearms on the roof of the Mini. She cried only briefly, but didn't wipe away her few tears, leaving them to dry on her cheeks in the cold air. She sniffed and swallowed and allowed her breathing to settle and her thoughts to come to rest. She had no idea why she'd reacted that way. It might have been the surprise, she thought. Or shame, or regret, or simply the acknowledgement that mistakes had consequences, that they couldn't simply be consigned to a past that wasn't part of your proper life, that they weren't things that could be wiped clear.

She became aware of Rachel hovering a few steps away and turned to her. She smiled weakly and ruefully at her and told her she was sorry.

They got in the car and drove in silence the short distance to Allerton Road, where Rachel squeezed the Mini into a space close to Allerton library. They both felt the need to put some distance between them and the house. Rachel looked at Susan and said, "Shall we?" Susan nodded and Rachel took out of her pocket the mobile phone she'd taken from the bottom drawer of Gerry Dalton's filing cabinet. It was nearly new, with photo and recording features, its casing bright orange.

"Margy's," said Rachel. It wasn't a question.

"Must be," Susan replied. "But let's check. Have a look in the number file and see if her Mum's number is there."

Rachel switched the phone on and found the file. She took the cursor down to 'Mum' and then read out the number to Susan. Susan nodded and read back to Rachel the number they'd got for Mrs Girvan's phone, the one Billy Jackson had given them on their first visit to Strangeways.

"One last check," said Susan. She found on her phone the number they'd long thought was Margy's new one, and pressed dial. It took a moment to connect, then the mobile phone in Rachel's hand buzzed against her grip and rang with the theme tune of a TV comedy show that hadn't been popular for a year or two. Neither woman said anything; neither felt any sense of elation or even relief. A question had been answered, that was all. A question that simply led them to another one and then another one. They both let the phone ring, until Susan's own phone ended the connection.

"So," Rachel said. "What was Gerry Dalton doing with Margy Girvan's brand new phone?"

"And who made the call to it from the Warwick at nearly midnight on Friday December 9th?"

"Allen," Rachel answered. "It must be, surely? You rang the number at Dalton's house. The phone Maureen had didn't ring. Gerry couldn't have called Margy. It must have been Allen."

"Let's have a walk," she said. She got out of the car and put her coat on. Rachel did likewise. The sun was still bright and the air was still cold. Susan lit a cigarette. "I just thought it might be nice to be outside," she explained. "Among normal people doing normal things. Buying Christmas presents and food and wrapping paper and cards." She began to walk along the road, heading away from where they left the car, past cafés and restaurants and estate agents and jewellers.

"Why Allen?" Susan asked.

"Because who else could it be?" replied Rachel. She stopped and faced Susan and the two women let the other pedestrians walk round them. "Look," Rachel continued. "I don't know why. I just know that it can't be anyone else. Not from what we know anyway. Gerry drove Allen the night Margy died. He took him to the Warwick and took him from the Warwick. Allen must have called Margy. And killed her too," she added. "Or maybe they both did. Either way, we know they were together and we know Gerry finished the night with Margy's phone."

"So now all we have to do is prove it?" Susan said

Rachel took hold of Susan's arm. She was smiling. "No. We

don't, Sue," she said. "The police need to prove it. We've got to tell them."

"No chance," Susan said. "This is our story, Rachel. It's a terrific story. We can solve a murder. We'll tell them once we're sure it's him. Not before." She continued to walk, crossing the road where Queen's Drive cut across Allerton Road.

"What about Brian Nulty?" Rachel asked, following her. "We can tell him, surely?"

Susan stopped and turned to look Rachel. "No," she said. "We're not telling a soul until we know. This'll be a front page splash, Rachel. I've not had one of those in years. I don't know if you've ever had one." Rachel's look towards the pavement told Susan she was right. "And it'll make the nationals. The editor of a major provincial newspaper guilty of the murder of a prostitute. This is a fantastic story. Promise me. No-one."

Rachel nodded. "Promise," she said. And she was happy to. Telling the police might be the right thing to do but a front page splash to her name would be a better thing to have. "There's no point, really, is there? Until we're sure."

Susan grinned. "That's my girl," she said. "You'll never make a proper reporter until you can rationalise your actions."

"And besides," added Rachel. "It'll be good to have one big splash before Sweeney or Crowley gets us." Susan looked at her and saw she wasn't joking.

Chapter Forty-one

Tuesday 25 December
Susan and Rachel had both volunteered for double shifts on Christmas Day, Susan because she was single and Rachel because she was Jewish. And they enjoyed it. The office was lightly staffed so it was busy, but everyone who was there had volunteered for it and was in good spirits. Allen had taken the day off. To Susan and Rachel it felt like a spell in a phony war. Hostilities had been declared but there was no sign of the enemy, so all there was to do was enjoy the sense of excitement that the prospect of his appearance brought.
As their shifts ended on Christmas Day, the two women met up and left the office together.
"He's not in tomorrow, either," Rachel told Susan. "I've just checked with one of the other subs. The day after at the earliest."
"It can wait," said Susan. They waited for the lift to take them to the basement car park. "What are you doing tomorrow?" she asked. "You in?"
Rachel shook her head. "No," she said. "Thought I might have a lie-in and then go to the gym maybe. Then eat too much of my mum's cooking. Fancy coming over?"
"Not for the gym," Susan said. The lift arrived and they stepped into it. "After though, maybe." She thought for a moment. With a slight hesitancy, she said, "Actually, I was going to ask if you fancied meeting up in the morning. I'm taking Michael out. You could come too, if you like. Though I've no idea what we're doing."
"Why?" Rachel asked. "I mean yes, but surely you want time with Michael, just the two of you."
Susan hesitated. "I have to get him back for three-ish," she said. "Imelda and Eugene are having their annual Boxing Day party. I think Allen will be there."

Rachel smiled. "I'd love to," she said. The lift doors opened. Susan made to step out and then hesitated. Rachel looked at her, puzzled.

"I suddenly realised there could be someone waiting here for us," she explained. "It's easy to forget when we're together, or with the others upstairs."

Their cars were parked at opposite ends of the car park. They went to Susan's first, then she drove to Rachel's and dropped her there.

"What time tomorrow?" Rachel asked.

"I'll pick you up at 11," Susan said. For a reason she couldn't explain, she felt both relieved and happy. "I'll have Michael with me."

Rachel smiled and nodded. "11 it is," she said. She made to move away. "And Happy Christmas."

"Thanks," Susan said. "Happy Christmas to you too." She waited until Rachel was in her car and they left the car park one after the other.

The relief and happiness Susan had felt slipped away as quickly as it had come. She didn't mind Christmas night alone – she was used to it – it was the prospect of getting from the car and into the flat that worried her. The fear that she had managed to keep at bay during the day was clawing back at her. She just prayed it would go forever soon.

Chapter Forty-two

Wednesday 26 December
LIVERPOOL MORNING MAIL
COUNTDOWN STARTS IN EARNEST
With Christmas out of the way, all eyes in the city are now focused on the countdown to the start of Liverpool's reign as European Capital City of Culture.
Local councillors and Culture bosses have stressed that everything is place to make 2008 a fantastic year for the city. The opening ceremony is to be held at St George's Hall, beginning at 8pm on New Year's Eve. As well as the largest fireworks display the city has ever seen, there will be performances from local dance troupes and music by some of Liverpool's best known bands.
"I can't tell you how excited I am," said Council Leader Connor O'Brien. "Nothing can stop this from being a wonderful year in Liverpool's history."
By a Liverpool Morning Mail Staff Reporter.

Michael lived with his father only a few minutes' drive from where Rachel lived with her parents. The house was just off Woolton Road, in Cabot Green, a cul-de-sac shaped like a horse shoe on the edge of Gateacre, opposite the Black Woods and fringed by Childwall Woods. There were no more than five other houses in the green, all detached, each in a different design, but all built at the same time in a chalet style. Eugene and Imelda lived next door. They'd been there from the late 1970s; Peter and Michael had moved in not long after the divorce from Susan. Susan had always sensed that Peter had moved there against his better judgement, but he'd done it at a time when he was vulnerable and needed support, and he'd always struggled to stand up to his father anyway.
Preparations for the party next door were already well under way when Susan pulled into Peter's drive. Caterers' vans

packed the space around Eugene and Imelda's house. There was a man on the balcony overlooking the front, checking the outdoor Christmas lights. Michael was waiting in the porch, eagerly anticipating his mother's arrival. Rachel waited in the car while Susan walked to the door. Again she was flooded with warmth at the sight of the son she saw irregularly. He was at that stage where he flitted between childhood and adolescence, when he could gleefully clutch the stunt kite his father had given him for Christmas and at the same time try to let his hair grow into some fashionable style. Susan looked at him and wondered if she'd done the right thing in staying away so often as he grew up. She'd thought it was best and, of course, Eugene and Imelda had placed obstacles in her path. And for so long she'd felt she hadn't deserved to see him. Now, though, that wasn't a consideration. She needed to see her son, to spend time with him, and he, thankfully, bore no resentment towards her and put no distance between them. Peter came to the porch when he heard Michael shouting that his mum had arrived. He was wearing jeans and slippers and a hooded sweatshirt that zipped up the front. "He's been waiting here for an hour at least," Peter said, opening the door and letting Susan step in. When he saw a look of pain and concern flash across Susan's face, he quickly went on. "You're not late. I mean, he's excited to see you."
Susan smiled in relief. "What's that you've got there?" she asked Michael.
"A stunt kite," Michael told her. "Dad gave it to me." Peter gave Michael a little dig in his back. "And thanks for the Everton kit," he said to his mother. He smiled. "Grandad didn't like it much, mind." He turned and looked at his father. "Can I take the kite?" he asked.
Peter looked out at the still, grey day, cold and drizzling steadily. "I don't think it's the weather for it," he said. He ruffled Michael's hair. "Besides, I want to be with you the first time you fly it. You need an expert with you."

"Yeah, right," Michael said. He gave the kite to his father, then sat down on the chair in the porch and put his shoes on. "We won't be too long," Susan said to Peter. "I'll have him back in time for the party."

Peter rolled his eyes. "Don't worry," he said. "There's no rush. He doesn't have to be here for the start. It's mainly Dad's friends. There'll be no-one of his age there." He paused and winked at Susan. "Not even Katie Richards." Michael glared up at his dad.

"Ooh," Susan said. "Katie Richards, eh? You can tell me all about her, Michael."

Peter gave Michael a hug which Michael pretended not to respond to, then Susan and her son left the house and walked down to the car, where Rachel was waiting.

They went to Border's, where Susan and Michael scoured the children's section. Michael wanted to look for Alex Ryder books, as his English teacher had recommended them. Susan bought all the ones they could find for him, and managed to get some Biggles and Jennings books too. She remembered they'd been among her brother's favourites when he was around Michael's age. Rachel left them to it. She stayed among the CDs and DVDs until they found her and announced they were off upstairs to Starbuck's. Rachel went with them. They ate toasted paninis and drank hot chocolate.

It was gone half past two by the time they got back to Cabot Green. The caterers' vans were now on Peter's driveway. On Eugene's drive and squeezed into every available space the green offered were the cars of the O'Hares' guests. Judging by the makes, Rachel guessed no-one who was there was short of money: BMWs, Lexuses, Mercedes, Porsches. Instead of the workman who was there before, Peter was now on the balcony. He was leaning on the rail, a glass of champagne in his hand, though it looked like a prop rather than something he was actually drinking. His face brightened when he saw Susan's car pull up. When only Michael got out, Peter called down and told him to invite his mother in. He saw Rachel in the car and told Michael to invite her too. He watched Michael leaning in through the driver's window. Eventually, Susan got out, as did Rachel a few moments later. Peter went back inside the house and soon appeared at the front door. Rachel liked the fact that Peter came down the drive beaming with pleasure at seeing Michael again. They were a team and the father ruffled his son's hair and showed real interest in the books he'd been bought. Rachel had heard a woman say once that one of the things that she found most attractive in her husband was that he was a good father. She appreciated this now on seeing Peter with Michael. He greeted Susan warmly too, but Rachel sensed that, on both their parts, the attraction was long gone. He was glad to see her, certainly, but there was just as much relief there, and he met Rachel in much the same way. These were people with whom he could be himself and feel easy.

When Rachel entered the house, having, like Susan, insisted she'd have just the one drink and then go, she understood why Peter had been so eager for them to come in. The house was crowded with smug fat men and bony women wearing too much make-up and too few clothes. The women gave the new arrivals a quick glance. They weren't interested in Michael. Susan they could dismiss because of what she was wearing; Rachel was too young for them to consider acknowledging. These were people Peter had to kowtow to and handle and court. The man swilled their drinks and ate without tasting. The women simply drank and smoked. A thin blue haze was beginning to buckle against the ceilings.

Peter guided Susan and Rachel to a corner of the open plan living room while he took Michael to help him carry their drinks. They'd both asked for diet Cokes. Susan, on edge because she didn't want Imelda or Eugene to see her, at least until Peter returned, wished she'd asked him to put a vodka in hers. They almost cowered into the corner, ill at ease and nervous of attention, eager to scan the room for any sign of Allen. In the end, he saw them first.

"Well, well, well," Allen said. "What in God's name are you two doing here? Come to serve the drinks?" He was wearing a roll neck jumper that stretched across his stomach and added extra chins. His face was florid with drink. He had a glass of red wine in one hand and a bottle of red wine in the other. He leant in close, pushing his head between the two women.

"What's the matter?" he asked. "Cat got your tongue? Not going to talk to me?" He pretended to cry.

Susan kept her eyes on Rachel as she answered him. "We're just here for a quick drink, Hugh," she said. "Peter's getting us one now."

"Oh, Peter, yes," Allen said. "Your ex. One of them anyway. The one you married."

Susan turned to her editor. "Look, Hugh," she said. "Just leave us alone, okay? We'll be gone soon. You can pick on us again when we're back in the office."

"Oh, don't worry about that," Allen said. "I won't be back in the office. At least, not the office of the *Liverpool Morning Mail*. That esteemed organ." He seemed very pleased with himself.

Both Susan and Rachel looked at him, puzzled. "What do you mean?" Rachel asked.

"Haven't you heard?" Allen replied. "Well, I don't suppose there's any reason why the likes of you should have." He gestured expansively with his right arm, sending red wine splashing onto the cream carpet. "As of January 1st I will no longer be editor of the *Morning Mail*. Instead, I'll be managing editor of the *Belfast Herald*. Promotion," he added. "And a hefty rise in salary. I'm having a leaving party on New Year's Eve. Don't tell me you haven't received your invitations yet?" He laughed humourlessly and turned away from them and made his way over to a group on the far side of the room by the buffet table.

Rachel watched him all the way. She saw him reach for a samosa and force it into his mouth. She was suddenly boiling with anger and injustice. She turned to speak to Susan but stopped as she saw she had already got her mobile out of her bag and was scrolling through the numbers.

Susan found what she was looking for and looked up at Rachel. "Let's get the bastard now, shall we?" she said. Rachel nodded and Susan pressed dial and held the phone to her ear. After a moment she said, "It's ringing."

They stared at Allen, willing him to hear the ring tone over the noise of the party, willing him to squeeze a hand into the pocket of his trousers and take his phone out.

And then a different voice answered, one that Susan knew immediately. "Hello," the voice said. A man's voice, one still with a thick Irish accent despite the number of years he'd spent in England. Eugene O'Hare.

Before she could stop herself, Susan began to reply, saying "Hello" in return before choking her voice to silence.

"Ah, now," Eugene said. "I'd know that voice anywhere. It's the lovely Susan, isn't it? Now what can I do for you?" he asked. "And more to the point, how on earth did you get this number?" His voice was light with laughter and menace.

Ignoring Rachel's questions, Susan's eyes searched frantically round the room. She found Eugene. He was standing by the patio doors, casually leaning against the glass, smiling broadly. Holding the phone to his left ear, he was looking right back at Susan. His smile grew even wider as he saw her looking at him. He waved cheerily at her, and then stopped smiling.

As she saw him, Susan realised she was still holding the phone to her own ear. She took it away and pressed to end the call.

"What's going on?" Rachel demanded. Susan ignored her. "Susan," she insisted. "Did someone answer?"

"No," Susan managed to reply. She put her phone back into her bag and began to push her way out.

Rachel followed her. "But you said hello," she said.
Susan didn't break step, not even as Peter and Michael came towards her with their drinks. She reached the front door and then stopped and went back to Michael. She hugged her son as tightly as she could and told him goodbye, then went straight back to the front door and out to the car.
Rachel grabbed hold of her arm as Susan went to open the car door. She swung her round to face her. "Susan!" she said. "What's got into you?"
"Nothing!" Susan snarled. "I got the answer machine, that's all. Now get in!"
Rachel refused. "Not until you give me the truth," she said. She was breathing heavily, her stomach nervous with the impending row.
But Susan wasn't going to argue back. "Then walk home," she told Rachel. She got in the car and slammed the door. She reversed out of her space, churning up the grass on one of the verges as she did so. She drove recklessly. She made one stop, at a Bargain Booze where she bought forty cigarettes and a bottle of vodka. Then she drove straight to the Warwick Hotel where she booked a room for the night.
She sat on the bed and chain smoked and waited. When the call came she listened to what Eugene had to say. When he finished, she said "Yes" and then switched her phone off. Then she opened the vodka.

Chapter Forty-Three

Thursday 27 December
LIVERPOOL MORNING MAIL
SHARP UPTURN PREDICTED FOR CITY ECONOMY
Liverpool can expect 2008 to be a boom year financially, business analysts yesterday predicted.
"There is so much optimism around the city, and with good reason too," said Steven Barry, of the City of London firm Corbright and Cooper. "It is largely due to Liverpool being Capital of Culture for 2008, but there are other factors too."
Retailers have reported record profits for the Christmas period and are confident the spending will continue. Restaurant bookings are up and bar and café owners say their takings have soared compared to previous years.
City hoteliers have also reported record bookings for the year ahead, with no rooms available at all during certain particularly busy periods.
Long-term investment forecasts are strong. The Liverpool One retail development in the city centre will open some time next summer, creating up to 400 jobs. There is also massive reinvestment in the city's docks and airport.
"I think investors will be delighted with the results of their speculation," added Steven Barry. "Those that have taken chances will see a pleasing return on their risk."
By a Liverpool Morning Mail Business Staff reporter.

Otterspool Prom is a park towards the south of the city. It sits behind Aigburth and stretches along the banks of the Mersey towards the private Victorian housing estates of Cressington, Fulwood and Grassendale Parks and Garston Docks beyond them. It is a popular spot with kite fliers and families and skate boarders and joggers who can run all the way along the river to the Albert Dock. This was where Eugene had told Susan he would meet her.

He'd been matter-of-fact on the phone, told her that he and Peter were taking Michael to fly his new kite at the prom and asked Susan if she'd care to join them. Susan had woken early and had stalked around her room restlessly. She got there at 10.30, half an hour before they were due to meet.

There were plenty of people around near the main entrance. The grassy areas were filling with children with their new presents – kites, bikes, footballs, footballs kits – all braced against the cold but glad that yesterday's rain had gone and been replaced by another day of bright, freezing sunshine. Susan felt safe enough initially, but Eugene had specified the car park at the far southern edge of the promenade, and this was empty. No other cars, and no-one playing on the grass in front of her. The only sign of life were the two or three kites she could see flying over the tops of the trees and bushes to her right.

She turned off her engine and waited. The sunshine glared through the windscreen and Susan had to squint to see the banks of the Wirral opposite and the Welsh hills in the distance beyond. Tiredness crept up on her despite her nerves. She was nearing the end and felt she might have to drag herself over the line.

The black car was next to her before she realised it, swung in fast and hard, tight to her car door so she was unable to open it more than an inch. She fumbled to take her seat belt off but fear was making her clumsy. When she finally managed to undo it and scramble across to the passenger door, it was too late. He was already climbing in and reaching over to her, ignoring her scratches, her feeble punches, her attempts to draw up her legs and kick out at him. He was reaching for her throat, his hands gripping her neck and then squeezing, firmly, steadily, relentlessly. His thumbs pressed in on her and she began to choke. Time slowed, her resistance ebbed away. In a flash of clarity she looked at him and calmly registered that it wasn't Eugene. She knew the face though. Who was it now? Her eyelids widened, pushed open by her eyes bulging out of her sockets as if the man's grip was tight enough to squeeze them from her head. She put a name to the face. That was it. Crowley. Assistant Chief Constable Crowley.

And then suddenly the man's hands were no longer around her neck. He had been wrenched out of the car by another man reaching in from the passenger door.

Susan flopped onto the empty seat next to her, desperately raking the air back into her lungs. She coughed and retched and spat and clawed at the open door until she was out of the car and on all fours, sharp stones digging into the flesh on her palms and knees. She collapsed and rolled over onto her back, still choking and rasping the air into her, her chest and stomach rising and falling as the breaths came in and out.

And above her, she saw Eugene and Crowley. Eugene had pushed him against the side of her car, his left hand gripping the policeman's shirt front.

"I told you before," Susan heard him say. And then she saw him draw back his right hand and Crowley cowered in anticipation of the blow. Eugene laughed and simply slapped him across the cheek. He let him go and Crowley slid along Susan's car and back to his own. She heard his door slam, the engine start, and metal on metal as Crowley's car scraped against her own as he reversed back and out of the car park.

"Peter drove," said Eugene. "He's parked a little way away, back down there. Michael's with him." He reached down and helped Susan up. "You get yourself right. I'll walk back to the boys and you can join us when you're ready."

Susan did as she was told. She cried, then dried her eyes and checked her face in the driver's mirror. Then she lit a cigarette, smoked it down to the filter and told herself she was fine. She got out and walked back down the road, stopping at the edge of the grass when she saw Michael, Peter and Eugene standing together about 25 yards away.

Michael, despite the cold, wasn't wearing a coat. He was dressed in the new, full Everton kit that Susan had given him. She smiled, and winced at the pain the smile gave her. She watched the three of them. Eugene seemed relaxed and happy. He smiled and joked with Michael, and almost tenderly helped him take the kite out of its plastic cover and attach the streamers to its base. She gave them enough time to get the kite ready and up in the air, then walked towards the little group, huddled in the centre of the grass, necks craned upwards to watch the kite's progress.

The wind blew in off the river in gusts. It struck against the kite one moment, nearly dragging it out of the boy's hands, then the next it died and let the kite drop towards the ground. He handled it well, though, using the two strings to twist it up and away from the grass and back into the air. As she walked towards them, Susan let herself forget why she was there and what had just happened and watched her son with simple, burning, untainted pride. The closer she got, the more apparent it became to her that Eugene was watching him also, with exactly the same emotions evident on his face.

Peter and Michael had their backs to her. The kite looked ready to rip out of the boy's hands and swirl its way over the river to the Wirral, but Michael was refusing to lose control. Susan checked her collar was up and her coat buttoned right to the neck. She didn't want Michael to see any marks. Nor Peter, for that matter. She called out. "Hi, there, you three!" They turned to see who it was. Michael's face showed delight and surprise, and pride that his mother was there to watch him master the sports kite.

"Well, what do you know?" said Eugene. "Come to see the lad conquer the air, have we Sue? Or did you just want to make sure he was wearing this dreadful Hallowe'en costume you got him for Christmas? You're a naughty girl, Susan

Clarke. You know I was dead set on him being a Liverpool fan."

Peter looked uncertain. He was shocked to see his ex-wife there, and even more shocked to hear his father bantering with her like they were old friends.

Eugene didn't give Peter a chance to say anything more than a quick hello to her. He put his arm on her shoulder, sensing her flinch, and guided her past Michael and down towards the path that lined the river. "We'll leave you two youngsters to it," Eugene said. "Sue and I will have a little stroll and a chat."

At the railing, Susan stepped away from Eugene's touch. She leaned on the iron rails and looked down into the mud of low tide. Eugene had his back to the river. He was leaning back, his elbows resting on the top rail behind him, pushing his chest out powerfully.

"You want to walk a little further?" Eugene asked.

Susan looked over to Michael and Peter, clearly in view. "Here's fine," she said.

"Suit yourself," said Eugene, and smiled.

Without looking at him, she said, "Thanks." Saying it hurt in more ways than one. Eugene simply shrugged.

"You didn't seem surprised yesterday," Susan said. "When you heard it was me on the phone. Did you know I'd call?"

"I wasn't surprised," Eugene replied. "I'd done my best to make sure no-one would find out, but then these things have a habit of getting out. Something always crops up that you haven't considered. And I like to take things in my stride."

Susan offered him a cigarette which he refused. "Have you given up?" she asked.

"No, no," he replied. "But I don't like the boy knowing I smoke. Bad example." Susan put the packet back in her handbag without taking one for herself.

She brushed the hair from her eyes and tried to collect herself. She couldn't pin her feelings down to just one emotion. Fear was leaving her, being replaced by amazement and confusion and relief and, although she couldn't quite believe it, amusement. Eugene was so calm and unthreatening, and it seemed genuine.

"You're going to tell me, aren't you?" she asked, a smile appearing despite herself. "I mean, you're actually going to tell me what happened. Without me having to question or try to threaten you."

It was Eugene's turn to sound amazed. "And why wouldn't I?" he asked. "You're an intelligent woman. You've probably worked most of it out for yourself. It wouldn't be fair to leave you with half the picture. Especially with you being a journalist and all."

"But aren't you worried that I'll write the story, go to the police?" she asked.

Eugene smiled. "Now that's the last thing I'm worried about," he said. "You wouldn't put young Michael through that, now, would you? The shame of his old granddad going to prison. And for a prossie's murder at that!"

Susan shook her head. She wouldn't. She'd known that from the moment Eugene had answered the call. And it wasn't just the shame. She might not have liked Eugene, but Michael loved him and he loved Michael. He might bully and tease him, might seem hard on him, but there was nothing Eugene wouldn't do for her son, and there was no way Susan could ever do something to hurt her boy.

"And what about me?" Susan asked. "If you tell me everything, then how do I know I'll be safe? You've killed one woman after all."

Eugene spread his arms wide. "Now, Sue," he said. "If I was thinking like that, why didn't I just let Crowley get on with it back there? There's a world of difference between killing a whore and killing the mother of my grandson. And I've always liked you, anyway." He leant towards her, making her flinch, but he just winked and lowered his voice to a conspiratorial whisper. "Just don't tell Imelda, eh?" He stood up straight again. "Besides, you're not soft, are you? I bet you've made sure already that I'll get it in the neck if anything happens to you."

Susan nodded slowly. "I sent a package to my solicitor today. Copies of all the notes I've made, Margy's phone, everything I could think of. If anything happens to me, Michael, Peter and the police will get those copies. It might not be proof. It might not all stand up in court, but it'll be enough to get the police asking questions and turn them against you forever." She pointed at Peter and Michael, still flying the kite, laughing and joking together, to make sure Eugene knew who she meant.

Eugene chuckled. "Sent a package to your solicitor, did you?" he said. "And there was me thinking people only did that in films. You'll be gunning for the DA next. Now, tell me what you know already."

"You killed Margy Girvan," Susan said. "You and Gerry Dalton and Allen maybe. You met her for sex and then killed her, then set her alight."

"You've got the gist of it, anyway," Eugene said. "Well, then," he went on. "I'd better tell you exactly what happened so you can write those letters again with all the facts." And he settled himself comfortably to tell the story, leaning against the railing like it was the bar of his golf club. According to Eugene it was a jaunt that had gone a little wrong, something that was awkward at the time but that would soon turn in to an anecdote that would amuse his table at some Knights of St Columba dinner. He even warmed to the story, his accent thickening as he got further into it.

"You know when it happened," he began. "We were all at that Warwick place, for the launch of work on this new venture of ours. I'd had a few, I can tell you, and this idea struck me. Give old Margy a ring, I thought. I mentioned it to one or two of the lads, and they were keen. Nothing like seeing to the same whore to bring men together. Allen was one of them, you're right about that. And Dalton too, though that milksop wasn't so keen. Didn't want to dip his wick, but Allen had a word and we'd got ourselves a driver. Save on the taxi fares." He shivered and put his coat collar up against the wind. "Getting old," he said. "The cold never used to bother me. Let's walk a bit, eh? What do you say?" Susan said she was fine where she was, with plenty of people around them. "Fair enoughski," Eugene said, and he continued with his story. "Where was I? Oh, yes, I know what I was going to tell you. You got it right with Dalton and Allen. But I'm surprised you left one man out." He paused, unable to understand the look of confusion on Susan's face. "Assistant Chief Constable Vincent Crowley!" he announced. "Why do you think he was trying to kill you today? And who do you think it was attacked you at your flat? It was Crowley! He and Allen reckoned they could get you to back off."

Susan was amazed, her head spinning with this latest revelation. "I thought it was all to do with Billy Jackson," she said. "I never for a moment thought…"

"Billy Jackson?" asked Eugene. "Who the fuck's Billy Jackson?"

"He's nobody now," Susan said. "Go on with your story."

He shivered again and rubbed his hands together. "I gave Margy a ring on my mobile. I'd used her plenty of times in the past. Met her at a massage place over in Norris Green. She didn't give out her number to anyone, mind, just a few special customers. Good tippers, like me. Well, I told you I'd had a bit to drink, didn't I? Only went and rang the wrong number to start with. Finally it dawned on me and I got the new number. Nipped out so I could hear myself think. Reckon I might have tried the phone in the hotel. Some things go a bit hazy after a few." He smiled broadly. "Now look at who I'm telling that to. Anyway, Margy was in town, not far from where we were. Told me she was having a night out with friends, but I think she was looking for punters. Getting on a bit, was Margy. She knew she'd soon be too old for the parlours. I didn't say anything, mind. No point hurting her feelings.

"We arranged to meet and Dalton drove us there. She squeezed in the back with Allen and Copper Crowley." He looked ruefully at Susan. "Now, I wasn't the only one to have had a few, but the difference is, I can hold it. Crowley can't. Started shooting his mouth off, telling Margy our names, fucking introducing us to her! Can you believe it?" He shook his head, perplexed. "I won't apologise for the language, by the way. I know you've used worse yourself. Do you know what, he even told her he was a copper? Thinks he's God's gift that one. Reckons nothing can touch him. Backfired on him, though, that did. I told Dalton to take us down to the site, so we could have a bit of privacy while we took our turns. He parks round the corner and I take Margy down the alley. I get first go on her, naturally.

"When it comes to Crowley's turn, big Vincent couldn't get little Vincent to stand to attention, if you know what I mean. Now, from what I could gather afterwards, Margy couldn't stop herself from laughing. I mean, no-one likes a copper, do they, and this fellow had been playing the big 'I am' since she first gets in the car. Crowley can't keep his temper. Belts her one. When he comes to get me, I find her spark out on the ground, bit of blood coming from the back of the noggin." Eugene stepped out to face Susan. He held his hands out in front of him, palms facing each other. "Now, Sue, this is the part I don't like. I'm not proud of myself, but it had to be done. I don't know if she was dead, but I did know I couldn't leave things like that. I told you, didn't I, Margy was getting on. Time's not kind on women, especially women on the game. And I knew Margy. A lovely girl, don't get me wrong, but she had a temper and an eye for the main chance. If she was only unconscious, then the first chance she'd get she'd come looking for cash, from each of us, and lots of it.

Crowley had told her his name, rank and number for fuck's sake!"

"Why would that bother you?" Susan asked. "You wouldn't be dragged into it, and even if you were, you don't exactly have a reputation to preserve, do you?"

Eugene nodded. "Okay, okay, I admit it. I deserve that. But you never know how these things end, do you? I'd just made a speech that night launching the biggest, most important project of my life. And, besides," he said. "And I'm not ashamed to admit it, I saw another angle. I could do a favour for a top copper, and the editor of the local rag, 'cause he'd have been on Margy's list for a call. Sort it out, Eugene, I told myself, and these bozos will be falling over themselves to do you favours." He stopped and took a deep breath. Susan wondered if there was any remorse there. Eugene looked down at the river and said, "So I did. I sorted it out. And I made sure each of us played some part in it. Like the four musketeers. All for one and all that. No-one could say he didn't do his bit. To bind us together. Even Dalton. I wish I hadn't, mind. Told that soft beggar to get rid of Margy's mobile."

Susan suddenly couldn't care whether Michael saw her smoking or not. She took a cigarette from her bag and lit it, telling herself that her hands were shaking because of the cold. "You sorted it out," she hissed. "You fucking beat her till her face was mush and then set her on fire!"

She'd expected Eugene to react angrily and he did. "I know what I did," he said. "You don't need to tell me! But I'm not going to tell you I'm sorry. I didn't want the body to be recognised, so that's what I did. I beat her and beat her and then we poured petrol on her and burned the poor fucking cow. And I'd do it again if it meant getting on. I didn't enjoy it. I'm not some fucking psychopath you know. But I'm not going to step aside if something gets in the way of me and my family and my business. Especially not some whore."

"Some woman, Eugene!" Susan was shouting. "Some fucking woman!"

Eugene snorted with anger and threw his arms into the air. Then he turned and gripped the railing in both fists, as if he was ready to rip it from the concrete. Susan turned her back to him. To anyone observing from a distance, they looked for all the world like some comic caricature of a couple for whom the stresses and strains of Christmas had just erupted into a row which they'd make up later on.

Eventually, Susan turned back to look at Eugene. She was calmer now, and so was he. He pointed to her face, where the bruising still showed.

"None of that was me, you know," he said. "It's important you know that."

Susan touched her cheek. "I never…" she began. "I mean I thought it was all to do with…something else." She laughed.

"It was their idea," said Eugene. "I put a stop to it. Tried to anyways."

Susan shook her head. Once again they settled into silence. This time, it was Susan who broke it.

"I want something," she said.

Eugene snorted again. "Everything's a negotiation, isn't it?"

"Three things," Susan corrected herself. "Michael. I want to see him regularly. I want him to stay with me. You can sort it with Imelda."

"And?" Eugene asked.

"I want Crowley," Susan said.

"And how am I supposed to do that?" Eugene asked. "Get him to admit to the murder and ask him nicely not to mention me?"

Susan ignored the sarcasm. "Not for the murder," she said. Again she tried to brush her hair back, but the wind was doing what it liked with it. "Do you know a DI Nolan?"

Eugene laughed. "Do I know DI Nolan?" he echoed. "That little wanker. Crowley's fixer. Leave it to me, the Assistant

Chief Constable said. I'll put my man on the case, make sure we only get dead ends. It's ended up with me forking out good money to get him out of the country sharpish and set him up with a little nest egg!"

"So you know where he is?" Susan asked quickly.

"I do that," Eugene answered. "I should do. I put him there."

"He can give me Crowley," Susan said. "Tell me how I can get in touch with him."

Eugene took his mobile out of his pocket. He pressed a few buttons and then said, "Got a pen?"

Susan hurriedly got her notebook and pen out of her bag. Eugene read out a long number which Susan copied down.

"It's my pleasure," Eugene said. "I won't be sorry to bring bad luck to either of them."

"Ring Nolan today and tell him someone will be in touch," Susan told him. "And make sure he'll talk."

"And how do I do that?" Eugene asked.

"Pay him," said Susan. "Give him enough money to get him talking and promise him more when he's finished. Tell him I want names and dates and Crowley properly stitched up. If he tells us enough, then he won't be named in the paper."

"Yes ma'am," Eugene said. "Anything else? You said three things."

"Allen," Susan said. "I want him too."

Eugene shook his head. "No," he said. "I can't help you there. What do you think I could do? Have a word with a few of the boyos back home and get him kneecapped?"

Susan shrugged. Eugene smiled at her. "Face it, Susan, dear," he said. "Some people just get away scot free."

They'd reached a truce. Susan looked across to Michael and Peter. Peter was holding the kite. Michael was having a kickabout with some boys who'd also turned up in their new Christmas football kits. Susan slowly began to walk over to them. Eugene followed her

Peter saw them approaching and called Michael over. He was.

flushed with exercise and fun. Eugene saw Michael's shoelace was undone.

"Here, Mikie," he said. "Let me do that for you." Slowly he began to kneel down.

"Don't Grandad," Michael protested. "I can do it myself."

"Ah be quiet," Eugene fondly told him. "You'll soon be big enough to do everything for yourself. Let me do it while I still can." He rested one knee on the ground and pulled Michael's foot towards him and tied up the lace.

Susan still had the pen and notebook in her hand. She passed them towards Peter. "Eugene's said it's okay for me to see a bit more of Michael," she said. "He reckons it'd be a good idea for me to have his mobile number. So I can get in touch in case I need to find Michael quickly. He can't remember it himself." Even to her ears, it sounded weak.

Peter hesitated before taking the pen and pad from her. He looked over to his father, who nodded back at him.

"And make sure you write the words Dad's mobile next to it," Susan said. "I have to write down so many numbers I need a reminder."

Eugene smiled up at Michael. He tapped his foot to show him it was done. "Your mother's a shrewd woman, Michael O'Hare," he said, admiring the smooth way Susan had just got herself an extra piece of protection. It wouldn't matter if he changed his phone now. The number was there on a piece of paper in his son's writing and the same number would remain in the calls log of Margy's phone. Maybe not enough for the police, but, along with everything else she had, enough to turn Peter and Michael from Eugene forever.

As soon as she was back in the car, Susan rang Rachel. They'd not spoken since Susan had driven off the day before. When Susan began to explain, Rachel cut her short. "Don't say any more about it," Rachel told her. "I should have realised how hard it must have been for you in that house. I don't blame you for getting upset."

Susan thanked her. Then she told her how she could get in touch with Nolan, but told her to wait until later that night before making the call. When Rachel asked how she'd found out, Susan told her it was a tip off from Brian Nulty.
When she got home, Susan rang the office. She was sick, she said, and didn't know when she'd be back in. She'd sort out a doctor's note. She didn't even get the name of the man who'd taken the call.

Chapter Forty-four

Tuesday 1 January 2008

It was lunchtime. Susan was sitting in the bar of Peter Kavanagh's, a pint of Guinness in front of her, her cigarette burning in the ashtray. She was struggling to do the *Telegraph* crossword and didn't notice Rachel come in until she sat down opposite her.

Rachel couldn't stop grinning. "As soon as you've finished that," Rachel said, "I'm going to buy you another. I can't thank you enough."

Susan put the paper down and smiled back. "So you got hold of Nolan then?" she asked.

"Got hold of him, met him, got the whole story," Rachel replied. "He couldn't wait to tell me, like he was in a rush to move on. Names, dates, the lot. I've written it up. The lawyers are looking at it now. There shouldn't be any problem with it, though. I'll need to add more, of course, but there's plenty for the moment. He was in Geneva, of all places. Holed up in some poky hotel drinking himself stupid."

"I could think of worse things to do," Susan said. "He'll have implicated himself, though, surely?"

"Yes," said Rachel. "But he reckons he can swing a deal. He gets a minimum sentence in some nice open prison while they throw the book at Crowley."

"Has the new editor seen it yet?"

Rachel nodded. "The new temporary editor, you mean. Someone from upstairs. Just until they appoint a permanent replacement. Showed it him last night."

"And?"

"And he loved it. Said it was just the thing we should be doing. No-one wants to read about the city of culture all the time, he said."

"He's right there," said Susan. "Have you got a reaction from Crowley?"

"He wouldn't speak to me," Rachel said. "But I told him what I had. What we had. He's got to resign, surely?"

"I'd have thought so," Susan said. "If he hasn't done already. Not that it'll help him escape prosecution, and a lengthy spell inside." She lifted her glass to her mouth. "Something to drink to, I'd say."

"Just a shame we couldn't bring the Margy murder to a satisfactory conclusion," said Rachel.

"No," replied Susan. "We just hit a dead end. Still, can't have everything." She gulped at her drink.

Rachel stood up. "Let me get myself one and I'll catch you up."

Trade in the pub was slow. Only a few regulars were tempted in to try to cure their hangovers with a few more drinks.

Susan and Rachel stayed for an hour, before leaving the pub. The new year had begun in a bright, brittle sunshine that was too weak to melt the ice which had settled overnight. Outside the pub, Rachel stopped. She passed Susan her phone, flipped open ready for Susan to read the screen.

"From Franny Sweeney," Rachel said. "It came this morning. God knows how he finds out about things so fast."

Susan read the message aloud. " '*Good girl. I'll be in touch soon. Happy New Year. FSX*'." She handed the phone back to Rachel, still flipped up.

Rachel took it from Susan and hurled it at the wall just a short distance across the narrow alleyway. It crunched against the brick and fell broken and twisted to the cobbles. They left it lying there and walked away, back to Hope Street.

Made in the USA
Charleston, SC
01 November 2016